UNEXPECTED
BLESSINGS

BOOKS BY BARBARA TAYLOR BRADFORD

❧

SERIES

THE EMMA HARTE SAGA

A Woman of Substance
Hold the Dream
To Be the Best
Emma's Secret
Unexpected Blessings

OTHERS

Voice of the Heart
Act of Will
The Women in His Life
Remember
Angel
Everything to Gain
Dangerous to Know
Love in Another Town
Her Own Rules
A Secret Affair
Power of a Woman
A Sudden Change of Heart
Where You Belong
The Triumph of Katie Byrne
Three Weeks in Paris

BARBARA TAYLOR BRADFORD

❧

UNEXPECTED BLESSINGS

St. Martin's Paperbacks

UNEXPECTED BLESSINGS

Copyright © 2005 by Beaji Enterprises, Inc.
Excerpt from *Just Rewards* copyright © 2005 by Beaji Enterprises, Inc.

Cover credits: Wedding gown "Spellbound" created and designed by Suzanne Neville, Suzanne Neville Ltd., Knightsbridge, London, www.suzanneneville.com. Photography and art direction by Generator, creative consultants to Suzanne Neville, www.generator-creative.com.

Library of Congress Catalog Card Number: 2004051202

ISBN: 0-312-98574-6
EAN: 9780312-98574-5

Printed in the United States of America

St. Martin's Press hardcover edition / January 2005
St. Martin's Paperbacks edition / October 2005

10 9 8 7 6 5 4 3 2 1

For my husband, Robert Bradford,
to whom I owe so much,
with all my love

CONTENTS

~

THE THREE CLANS

✃

THE HARTES

(Shown in line of descent)

EMMA HARTE. Matriarch. Founder of the dynasty and business empire.

HER CHILDREN

EDWINA, DOWAGER COUNTESS OF DUNVALE. Emma's daughter by Edwin Fairley. (Illegitimate.) First born.

CHRISTOPHER "KIT" LOWTHER. Emma's son by her first husband, Joe Lowther. Second born.

ROBIN AINSLEY. Emma's son by her second husband, Arthur Ainsley. Twin of Elizabeth. Third born.

ELIZABETH AINSLEY DEBOYNE. Emma's daughter by her second husband, Arthur Ainsley. Twin of Robin. Third born:

DAISY AINSLEY AMORY. Emma's daughter by Paul McGill. (Illegitimate.) Fourth born.

HER GRANDCHILDREN

ANTHONY STANDISH, EARL OF DUNVALE. Son of Edwina and Jeremy Standish, Earl and Countess of Dunvale.

SARAH LOWTHER PASCAL. Daughter of Kit and June Lowther.

JONATHAN AINSLEY. Son of Robin and Valerie Ainsley.

PAULA McGILL HARTE AMORY FAIRLEY O'NEILL. Daughter of Daisy and David Amory. Sister of Philip.

PHILIP McGILL HARTE AMORY. Son of Daisy and David Amory. Brother of Paula.

EMILY BARKSTONE HARTE. Daughter of Elizabeth and Tony Barkstone. Half sister of Amanda and Francesca.

AMANDA LINDE. Daughter of Elizabeth and her second husband, Derek Linde. Twin of Francesca, half sister of Emily.

FRANCESCA LINDE WESTON. Daughter of Elizabeth and Derek Linde. Twin of Amanda, half sister of Emily.

OWEN HUGHES. Son of Robin Ainsley and Glynnis Hughes. (Illegitimate.)

HER GREAT-GRANDCHILDREN

TESSA FAIRLEY LONGDEN. Daughter of Paula and her first husband, Jim Fairley. Twin of Lorne. Half sister of Linnet, Emsie, and Desmond.

LORNE FAIRLEY. Son of Paula and her first husband, Jim Fairley. Twin of Tessa. Half brother of Linnet, Emsie, and Desmond.

LORD JEREMY STANDISH. Son of Anthony and Sally Standish, Earl and Countess of Dunvale. Brother of Giles and India.

Toby Harte. Son of Emily and Winston Harte II. Brother of Gideon and Natalie.

Gideon Harte. Son of Emily and Winston Harte II. Brother of Toby and Natalie.

Natalie Harte. Daughter of Emily and Winston Harte II. Sister of Toby and Gideon.

Hon. Giles Standish. Son of Anthony and Sally Standish, Earl and Countess of Dunvale. Brother of Jeremy and India.

Lady India Standish. Daughter of Anthony and Sally Standish, Earl and Countess of Dunvale. Sister of Jeremy and Giles.

Patrick O'Neill. Son of Paula and her second husband, Shane O'Neill. Brother of Linnet, Emsie, and Desmond. (Deceased.)

Linnet O'Neill. Daughter of Paula and her second husband, Shane O'Neill. Half sister of Tessa and Lorne. Sister of Emsie and Desmond.

Chloe Pascal. Daughter of Sarah Lowther Pascal and Yves Pascal.

Fiona McGill Amory. Daughter of Philip McGill Amory and Madelana O'Shea Amory (deceased).

Emma "Emsie" O'Neill. Daughter of Paula and her second husband, Shane O'Neill. Half sister of Tessa and Lorne. Sister of Linnet and Desmond.

Desmond O'Neill. Son of Paula and her second husband, Shane O'Neill. Half brother of Tessa and Lorne. Brother of Linnet and Emsie.

Evan Hughes. Daughter of Owen and Marietta Hughes.

Winston Harte. Emma's older brother and business partner.

Randolph Harte. Son of Winston and Charlotte Harte.

Winston Harte II. Son of Randolph and Georgina Harte. Brother of Sally and Vivienne.

SALLY HARTE STANDISH, Countess of Dunvale. Daughter of Randolph and Georgina Harte. Sister of Winston II and Vivienne.

VIVIENNE HARTE LESLIE. Daughter of Randolph and Georgina Harte. Sister of Winston II and Sally.

TOBY HARTE. Son of Winston II and Emily Harte. Brother of Gideon and Natalie.

GIDEON HARTE. Son of Winston II and Emily Harte. Brother of Toby and Natalie.

NATALIE HARTE. Daughter of Winston II and Emily Harte. Sister of Toby and Gideon.

FRANK HARTE. Emma's younger brother.

ROSAMUND HARTE. Daughter of Frank and Natalie Harte. Sister of Simon.

SIMON HARTE. Son of Frank and Natalie Harte. Brother of Rosamund.

THE O'NEILLS

SHANE PATRICK DESMOND "BLACKIE" O'NEILL. Founding father of the dynasty and business empire.

BRYAN O'NEILL. Son of Blackie and Laura Spencer O'Neill.

SHANE O'NEILL. Son of Bryan and Geraldine O'Neill. Brother of Miranda and Laura.

MIRANDA O'NEILL JAMES. Daughter of Bryan and Geraldine O'Neill. Sister of Shane and Laura.

LAURA O'NEILL NETTLETON. Daughter of Bryan and Geraldine O'Neill. Sister of Shane and Miranda.

PATRICK O'NEILL. Son of Shane and Paula O'Neill. Brother of Linnet, Emsie, and Desmond.

LINNET O'NEILL. Daughter of Shane and Paula O'Neill. Sister of Emsie and Desmond.

EMMA "EMSIE" O'NEILL. Daughter of Shane and Paula O'Neill. Sister of Desmond and Linnet.

DESMOND O'NEILL. Son of Shane and Paula O'Neill. Brother of Linnet and Emsie.

THE KALLINSKIS

DAVID KALLINSKI. Founding father of the dynasty and business empire.

SIR RONALD KALLINSKI. Son of David and Rebecca Kallinski.

MICHAEL KALLINSKI. Son of Ronald and Helen "Posy" Kallinski. Brother of Mark.

MARK KALLINSKI. Son of Ronald and Helen "Posy" Kallinski. Brother of Michael.

JULIAN KALLINSKI. Son of Michael Kallinski and his former wife, Valentine Kallinski. Brother of Arielle and Jessica.

ARIELLE KALLINSKI. Daughter of Michael Kallinski and his former wife, Valentine Kallinski. Sister of Julian and Jessica.

JESSICA KALLINSKI. Daughter of Michael Kallinski and his former wife, Valentine Kallinski. Sister of Julian and Arielle.

Part One

~

THE STORMY PETRELS

Summer 2001

The name "petrel" is said to be a diminutive of Peter: when feeding the bird flits and hovers just above the water, often with feet pattering on the surface, appearing to "walk on water" as St. Peter did in the Bible story.

—FIELD GUIDE TO THE BIRDS OF BRITAIN

I

Evan Hughes stood in the middle of the fashion floor of Harte's department store in London's Knightsbridge. It was seven o'clock in the morning, and nothing stirred. By eight the cleaners would be moving around this vast space, and by nine a few of the dedicated sales staff would be arriving to prepare for the store doors opening at ten. Now, though, she was totally alone.

She loved this store and this floor in particular. It was her domain. And hers alone. Last week she had been made head of fashion, a big promotion which had thrilled her. But in her personal life, Evan had big decisions to make.

As she moved slowly across the floor, making for the new haute couture fashion displays, she couldn't help thinking about the first day she had walked into Harte's. January 2001. Eight months ago now. She had been very lucky that day. Quite by chance she had met the man of her dreams and found the job of her dreams. She had certainly never thought her dreams would come true that day. But in some ways, they did.

Pausing for a moment, Evan glanced around, her intelligent, light gray-blue eyes devouring everything: the fashion displays under bright lights, the elegance of the whole floor, such an important one in this prestigious department store, considered the greatest in the world.

Harte's of Knightsbridge had been founded by one of the most famous merchant princes ever known: *Emma Harte*. She had been dead now for thirty years, and the store was run by Emma's granddaughter Paula O'Neill. Paula, an elegant woman in her mid-fifties, had inherited her grandmother's skills and brilliance as a retailer, and her daughters Tessa and Linnet were following in her footsteps. Both of them worked at the store; Tessa was in charge of the first three floors, which sold cosmetics, perfumes, leisure wear, lingerie, and active sports clothes. Linnet, Tessa's half sister, was in charge of the fashion floors and worked with Paula on public relations.

It was Linnet O'Neill who had hired Evan to be one of her assistants, and for the first few months Evan had helped Linnet put together a retrospective of fashion, which had been a huge success and pulled many new customers into the store.

Linnet. Tessa. Ambitious and complicated, they were now part of Evan's life.

As a reward for all her hard work and dedication, Linnet had given her this promotion . . . and Evan was in her element.

Evan stood in front of the couture fashion displays which had been finished late last night. They were great, she decided. The display staff had done a good job with the clothes she had selected.

Turning away, she walked down the floor, making for

her office. Tall, slender, and dark haired, she was good-looking, elegant. Back at her desk she glanced at the photograph of Gideon Harte. She had fallen in love with him, and he with her, that first day when he had bumped into her in the corridor. She had been looking for the management offices, and he had led her there, all the while firing questions at her. And it was Gideon who had told his cousin Linnet about her; Linnet had subsequently interviewed her and given her a job.

Sitting back in her chair, Evan thought about the past eight months and all that had happened.

She had never expected to find a second family in England. Only a year ago the only family she knew were her mother and father, and her two adopted sisters, who lived in Connecticut. But all that had changed because of her grandmother Glynnis Hughes. On her deathbed her grandmother had told Evan to go to England to find Emma Harte, adding that Emma was the key to her future. And Evan had done exactly that, only to discover Emma was dead. But she had fallen in love with the store and decided to get a job there.

And now here she was, working at Harte's, planning a future with Gideon, and struggling to adapt herself to a whole new family . . . because she herself was actually a Harte. It was Paula who had discovered through Emma's diaries that Evan was another great-granddaughter of Emma Harte's, because Evan's grandmother Glynnis had given birth to a son fathered by one of Emma's sons. And that child was Evan's father.

They had welcomed her, treated her kindly and with enormous understanding, but at times things had been difficult for Evan. So many things to unravel, so much to accept, so many people to get to know. Sometimes it seemed endless to her.

Most troubling of all was the knowledge she had

about her father's biological father . . . which she had been afraid to relay to him. Would her father, Owen Hughes, welcome the information? Would he really want to know that the man who had brought him up was not his father after all? She didn't know, and she continued to wrestle with these questions.

Evan knew she had to come to a decision. Her mother and father were coming to London in a week or so, to spend time with her and have a vacation. Could she look her father in the eye and *not* tell him the truth? Could she keep it a secret? And should she? Nobody could advise her really. Gideon had told her to do what she thought best, and everyone else had been noncommittal.

The ball was back in her court.

Then there was Robin Ainsley, her new grandfather, the man who had been her grandmother's lover during the Second World War. He had been a pilot in the Royal Air Force, a Battle of Britain pilot, and her grandmother, Glynnis Jenkins then, had been a young woman from Wales who worked as Emma Harte's secretary, in this very store.

Evan liked Robin; her feelings were even stronger than that. And she knew only too well that he longed to meet his son Owen Hughes. But would her father want to meet this *stranger* . . . a stranger who was his real father? His mother's lover. *Oh God.*

Evan turned on her computer and after a few moments started to work on it, but within an hour the troubling thoughts about Robin, Glynnis, and her father's imminent arrival began to intrude. Turning the computer off, she made her decision. She would take Linnet's advice and go to Yorkshire after all for a week's rest. And she would go to see Robin Ainsley, still needing to know about his relationship with her grandmother, and most of all to truly understand why Robin and Glynnis had never married.

"She was beautiful and glamorous, and the most sexually potent woman I've ever known, but I realized we would be disastrous together in the long run. We would've ended up killing each other," Robin finished with a small sigh. He sat back in the wing chair, his eyes on Evan.

She was silent for a moment, digesting his words, and then she said slowly, "Because you were so volatile together, is that what you mean?"

"Exactly. We never had a peaceful moment."

"You weren't compatible?"

"Not in any way, except in bed. But one cannot build a lasting, lifetime relationship on sex alone."

Evan nodded and eyed him carefully, then confided, "Gran was always pounding it into me that compatibility between a man and a woman was the most important thing of all. And I know that she was compatible with my grandfather, I mean Richard Hughes."

"Please don't correct yourself, Evan," Robin said in a quiet voice, shaking his head. "Richard Hughes *was* your grandfather, just as he *was* your father's father. Glynnis was a wonderful young woman when I knew her. But put very simply, she wasn't suitable for me, nor I for her, not on a normal, everyday level. We were far too explosive, and it was my fault as much as hers."

"Is that why you finally broke up with her?"

"It is. At that time our quarrels were increasing, and alarmingly so. Life with her was hell."

"But she was pregnant, Robin, and you did nothing. . . ." Evan's voice trailed off as she realized she might have sounded accusatory. She had not meant to place blame.

"We've already discussed this," Robin responded patiently. "But I shall explain one more time. . . . We broke up. I started seeing Valerie Ludden. She and I were compatible and became seriously involved. When Glynnis told me she was expecting my child, I had already made a commitment to Valerie. However, let me say this, so you truly understand. I would not have married your grandmother even if there had been no other woman in my life. We could not have led a worthwhile life, and she knew that, too."

"I'm sorry, Robin, I am being a bit of a pest, aren't I?"

"That's all right," he responded, a faint shadow touching his mouth. "I understand your need to know everything."

"I wonder why Glynnis wouldn't allow you to help her financially."

"Pride, for the most part, so *I* believe."

"She let Emma Harte come to her rescue, though."

"She did. My mother loved Glynnis like a daughter, and Glynnis knew this, and she knew how much my mother sympathized with her. When my mother was a girl, she had been in a similar predicament, pregnant by a man who wouldn't marry her, and obviously there was a great deal of empathy there."

"Thanks for talking about this, Robin. I really needed to know exactly what went on between you and my grandmother all those years ago."

"Passion. I was also in love with her; it just wasn't enough for a steady, stable life." He smiled at her then, his face softening with tenderness, his faded blue eyes benign, loving.

Evan smiled back at him, reached out and took hold of his long, slender hand, squeezed it in hers. The two of them were seated on the large sofa in the library at Lackland Priory, Robin's house in Yorkshire, meeting for the first time in several weeks, and they were glad to be together again, to have this chance to get to know each other better.

The old man and the young woman. Related by blood but total strangers until recently. The grandfather. The granddaughter. Two people who had only just discovered each other's existence, and wanted to be friends, to understand each other, to find closeness, even the intimacy of family, if that was possible. The younger striving to comprehend a disastrous long-ago relationship, the elder hoping that his past actions would not damage him too badly in her eyes in the present.

The silence was broken by the ringing of the telephone, startling them both. Almost instantly it stopped; the phone had been answered elsewhere in the house by a staff member.

A moment later the butler appeared in the doorway. "Excuse me, sir, Doctor Harvey's on the phone. He would like a word with you."

"Thank you, Bolton," Robin answered, and excusing himself to Evan, he rose, striding over to the desk. Sitting down, he picked up the receiver. "Good morning, James."

Evan also rose and walked across to the French doors which opened onto the terrace of the ancient manor house. She stepped outside, closing the doors behind her, and took several deep breaths. The air was always clean and fresh up here in the Dales; it was a glorious morning in early August, the sky azure blue and without a cloud. A sunny, golden day filled with pristine light, just as it had been yesterday and the day before. She had grown to love this crystalline light, which she had discovered was so prevalent in the north of England.

Now she sat down on the stone bench and stared across the wide, green lawns that splayed out from the house and were bordered by flower beds filled with colorful perennials. Her eyes came to rest on the copse of trees which stood slightly away from the house to the right of the lawns. Beyond their opulent, leafy bowers she could see the rim of the moors, a dark smudge against the pale, blue-tinted horizon.

It was such a beautiful spot, this long valley in the middle of the Dales where Lackland Priory had stood for centuries. Pennistone Royal, Paula's house, was not far away, and in the past few months Evan had spent a lot of time in this area of Yorkshire, which was softer and much more lush than the surrounding, higher land.

Up there, on the moors, it was bleak for most of the year, neither pretty nor welcoming. She knew Linnet would not agree; *she* thought the soaring fells were glorious in their stark and solitary splendor. "I love those moors the same way Emma Harte loved them," Linnet had once explained to her. "My great-grandmother was a child of the moors, and she could never stay away from them for very long. I *yearn* for them, just as she did."

Emma Harte.

Evan turned the name over in her mind. Dead though she had been for thirty years, Emma still lived on, her spirit and presence almost as potent as when she was alive. Emma Harte was *her* great-grandmother, too, although she had not known this when she came to England in January. How her life had changed since then. *She* was a Harte. And had been accepted by this unique family, made to feel one of them.

Almost immediately her thoughts swung to Robin Ainsley, favorite son of the legendary Emma. Her father's biological father, her biological grandfather. A man she had met only a few weeks ago but whom she had quickly grown to like and knew she could easily come to love. There was something endearing about

Robin, even vulnerable, and she wanted to nurture and protect him. At eighty he seemed so alone.

Robin Ainsley had abandoned her grandmother, but he had had his reasons, and it *was* over half a century ago now. And if she were honest with herself, she had to admit that her grandmother had probably had a much better and certainly a more tranquil life without Robin. After all, they had been forever at each other's throats, according to him. And Gran had a loving husband in Richard Hughes, who had married her some months before her baby, Owen, was born. Richard had brought up Owen as his son. He had been a good father; no man had ever had a better one, her father said that all the time.

Her father's face insinuated itself into her mind's eye, and she felt herself tensing. Yet again she wondered how to tell him what she had so recently found out. Owen had idolized Richard Hughes . . .

"I'm so sorry to have left you alone," Robin murmured from the doorway, interrupting her thoughts. "I'm afraid Doctor Harvey can go on a bit at times."

Evan jumped up and swung to face him. "You *are* all right, aren't you? You're not ill?" she asked. Her voice echoed with sudden concern, and her eyes were anxious.

"I'm perfectly fine, my dear. In very good health, I do assure you. Doctor Harvey was merely ringing up to confirm our dinner engagement tomorrow evening." As he finished speaking, Robin stepped onto the terrace. "Let's stay out here for a while, enjoy Mother Nature. It's such a grand morning."

"Yes, it is," Evan agreed.

They sat down on the bench, and Robin went on, after a moment, "You said earlier that you needed to talk to me about several things, but so far we've only discussed my relationship with your grandmother. What else do you have on your mind?"

"My father."

"Ah yes, Owen. Does he know anything about . . . Emma's well-kept secret?"

"No."

"Did you lose your nerve, Evan? Surely not. Not *you*."

"No, not really. But I did decide it might be better to wait until he arrives in London later this month."

"Don't you think you ought to give him an inkling about what's happened *before* he comes? About me, I mean? It would prepare him for what will no doubt be a bit of a shock."

"It did cross my mind," Evan responded, biting her lip. "But then I decided it would be smarter to tell him face-to-face."

Robin frowned, his light-colored eyes fixed on the distant horizon. After a moment, he began to speak slowly, thoughtfully. "He's not going to like what he hears. After all, some of his illusions are going to be shattered. He'll certainly be angry with me about the past."

"And maybe he'll also be angry with his mother for not being truthful," Evan suggested succinctly. "Gran lied to him."

"Oh, I don't know about that, my dear. Glynnis did the right thing. Richard was married to Glynnis for some months before Owen's birth, and whilst he may not have made her pregnant, he loved that child as his own. Richard's behavior was impeccable, and I think Glynnis did what she thought was best."

"That's true, but . . ."

"But what?"

"My father's not easy, Robin."

A look of sudden comprehension swept across his face and he exclaimed, "I remember something, Evan. When Paula brought you here for the first time, you told us you thought your father had come across some papers after Glynnis died."

"I did. But he never actually said he found anything. It was just a feeling *I* had, that sprang from his sudden, rather odd attitude toward the Harte family."

"*Oh.* What kind of attitude?" Robin asked.

"He became a bit . . . well, down on them. I guess that's the best way of describing it. He wasn't happy about my job at Harte's, and that was mystifying to me because he had agreed I should visit London to seek out Emma Harte . . . just as Gran had suggested on her deathbed."

Robin ventured, "I think he stumbled on a diary, or letters, or other items from long ago, which Glynnis had perhaps forgotten about."

"That could be so," she agreed. "And what he found might have turned him off the Hartes. Is that what you're suggesting?"

"Yes, it is." There was a pause. "I wonder if it might not be wiser to let sleeping dogs lie, my dear. Why tell your father anything at all? He doesn't need to know about his paternity. Perhaps it would be more prudent to let it remain the secret it's always been. Why not let him continue to think Richard Hughes was his biological father?"

"That makes sense," Evan exclaimed and instantly felt as though a great weight had been lifted from her chest.

Almost as if he knew what she was feeling, Robin put his arm around her. "*We* know the truth, and that's all that really matters, isn't it?"

"Yes" was all she said, and she leaned against his shoulder, closing her eyes.

They did not speak for a short while, lost as they were in their own thoughts. Evan was thinking about her boyfriend, Gideon Harte, wondering how she would explain her sudden change of heart yet knowing that whatever she decided to do he would back her to the hilt. Gideon had an understanding heart, and he was sensitive to her feelings about her father. In fact, he himself had suggested, only the other day, that she might be better off not telling her father he was a Harte. She had been ambivalent; Gideon had then said he trusted her judgment.

As for Robin, his thoughts were centered on Evan Hughes. How glad he was that this young woman had come into his life. Very late in his life, that was true, but at least he had become aware of her existence. He liked what he had learned about her over the past few weeks. Once before he had held her close like this, when she had comforted him, and he was glad to hold her again, to bond with her silently, and to comfort *her.*

The day she had arrived with Paula to meet him for the first time he had feasted his rheumy eyes on her lovely face. He had noticed that she looked like his twin sister, Elizabeth, when she had been twenty-seven, as Evan was now. *Evan.* His granddaughter. His only grandchild. His blood flowed through her veins, and one day, if she married and had children, it would flow in their veins . . . she ensured the continuation of his bloodline, his genes. It had always been important to him, the flowering of a family, but before the arrival of Evan this had not seemed probable.

Instantly, Jonathan sprang into his mind, and a chill settled over him. He could only pray that his son would never harm Evan. Certainly Robin had made sure Jonathan understood that his inheritance was not jeopardized by Evan's advent. In fact, Robin had gone to extraordinary lengths to prove this to his son, involving both their solicitors and the execution of various binding documents.

Nevertheless, Jonathan was unpredictable. For a long time now Robin had considered his only child a loose cannon and, even worse, a sociopath; there was no way of knowing what he might do. Or when.

"Are you all right?" Evan asked, feeling Robin's sudden tension.

"Yes, yes, I'm fine," the old man answered, forcing a smile. "But I must admit I feel the cold, even on a sunny day like this. Let's go inside, Evan. I have something I wish to show you."

Together they walked into the library, and Robin murmured, "Do sit down on the sofa, I won't be a moment."

She did as he said while he hurried to the desk. Her eyes followed him. What a fine-looking man he was, tall and erect in old age, and today he was full of vigor. This pleased her. She had only just found him, and he was already eighty. The thought of losing him dismayed her.

A moment later Robin was sitting down next to her and handing her a snapshot taken a long time ago. Staring at it, she exclaimed, "It's of you and my grandmother. My goodness, what a gorgeous couple you were!"

He laughed in delight at her compliments. "We did look wonderful together, you know, everyone remarked on that. As you can see, I'm wearing my RAF uniform, and your grandmother is the height of fashion for the times, very much the glamour girl, as always. Well, anyway, it's for you, Evan."

"Oh, Robin, how lovely of you. But are you sure you want to part with it? You've had it for such a long time."

"Who better to give it to than—*our* granddaughter? I want you to have this picture of the two of us when we were young and in love, before things had gone so horribly wrong between us."

She nodded, touched his arm affectionately. "I shall treasure it always."

His blue eyes lit up, and he smiled at her. "Now, will you take pity on an old man and stay for lunch?"

"I'd love to," she said. But as she walked to the dining room with Robin, Evan knew there was trouble in store. Her intuition told her that her father would be difficult, and that the situation would more than likely explode.

2

Tessa Fairley Longden stood on the terrace, watching her small daughter bustling around like the proverbial mother hen, placing Daisy, her porcelain baby doll; Teddy, the bear; and Reggi, the rag doll, in the chairs Tessa and Adele had just arranged around the small tea table.

Once the child was satisfied, she looked up at her mother and said, "Daisy is keeping Teddy company, and I'll sit next to my Reggi."

"That's a good idea, Adele, and I'm sure they'll be happy wherever you've put them," Tessa answered, smiling down at the three-year-old, who was looking up at her questioningly.

As she spoke Tessa made a mental note to wrest the rag doll out of her daughter's clutches as soon as possible. It was dirty and bedraggled, quite disgusting-looking really, but the child loved it so much, never let it out of her sight. Tessa had long realized it was like a security blanket to Adele, but it did need washing, by hand, of course, so that it would not fall apart. Tonight, she thought, I'll wash it tonight if I can get it away from her.

She was enjoying being here in Yorkshire with Adele, her first bit of peace since leaving her husband, Mark Longden. Bending down, Tessa smoothed her hand over her child's silky, silvery blond hair, and murmured, "I'll be in the library working, sweetheart, if you need me."

Adele nodded and said in a solemn voice, "At your computer, Mumma."

"That's right." Tessa's heart overflowed with love for this beautiful child, the person she loved the most in this world. And now the divorce was in the works, she would concentrate on her child. Leaning over, she kissed the top of her daughter's head, lingering on the terrace; but after a second or two she drew herself up, took a deep breath, and walked briskly into the library.

It was Elvira's day off, and the nanny had gone into Leeds, leaving Adele in her care. Tessa had toyed with the idea of taking Adele with her to the Harrogate store, but in the end she had decided not to go after all. It was such a beautiful morning, it seemed almost criminal to keep the child cooped up in an office; she could just as easily work here at Pennistone Royal, on the plans for remodeling the Harrogate store, while Adele enjoyed the sunshine and the fresh air on the long terrace at the back of the house.

Tessa had decided long ago that the library was the ideal place for her to work when she was here. It was a long, spacious, airy room with a high-flung ceiling and walls paneled in light-colored pine. A peaceful spot, it was well insulated with its many floor-to-ceiling shelves filled with leather-bound books.

Earlier this morning she had set herself up at the far end of the library, near the French doors. These opened onto the terrace, where Adele could play until lunchtime.

Tessa had pulled the library table over to the glass doors, creating a makeshift desk. Adele was now in her direct line of vision; she could even hear the child chattering away to the teddy bear. She was readily available if her daughter needed her for any reason.

Tessa worked steadily at her computer for the next twenty minutes, pulling up the sketches of the areas to be redone, glancing up from time to time, smiling to herself, thinking of how well Adele played alone, talking to her dolls and the bear in the most natural way, as if they were alive.

Adele was a clever, inventive, and imaginative little girl, and she could read simple books even though she was not quite four. She was in some ways rather precocious, but not in an irritating way, like some children were. Adele was sweet by nature, endearing with her fey and somewhat whimsical mannerisms.

Adele turned and saw Tessa staring at her through the open glass doors, and she laughed, waved to her mother. Tessa waved back before returning to her work. She concentrated hard, endeavoring to pull together all her ideas for the much-needed changes at the Harrogate store. This was her special project at the moment; her half sister Linnet and her cousin India, along with Evan Hughes, had been given the task of creating a new look for the Leeds store. Harte's was revamping everywhere.

The loud ringing of the phone brought Tessa's head up with a start. When it continued to shrill, she wondered why no one was picking it up, then remembered she was alone in the house. Elvira had already left for Leeds; Margaret had gone to do the marketing in Ripon, and she had seen Evan Hughes drive off well over an hour ago. As for Emsie and Desmond, her O'Neill sister and brother were off riding on the moors.

Tessa hurried across to the Georgian desk next to the

sofa and grabbed the phone. "Pennistone Royal. Hello?" There was a great deal of static, and far away she heard a man's voice saying, "Tessa—. Is Tess—" Then the voice faded out completely.

It's Toby, she thought, my cousin's calling me from L.A. Holding the receiver tighter, she exclaimed, "This is Tessa Longden! Who is it?" Much to her annoyance, the phone went completely dead. She listened for a moment, said hello several more times, then hung up in exasperation.

She had barely taken a few steps toward the makeshift desk when the phone began to ring once more. Snatching the receiver from the cradle, she said in a distinct tone, "This is Tessa Longden. Who's calling?" There was no response, only static and sounds like lapping waves. "*Hello? Hello?* I can't hear you! Who's calling?"

Her frustration echoed in her voice; her cousin had gone to Los Angeles to see his wife, and he had promised to be in touch. No doubt this *was* Toby. On his mobile. The connection suddenly cut off, and with an impatient shrug she banged down the phone and headed back to her computer. No sooner had she turned away from the phone than its insistent shrilling brought her back, and she answered for a third time. *"This is Tessa. Who is it?"*

"Tess—" The voice broke up before the completion of her name, and then she was hearing only static and half a word here and there. She said "Hello" several times, but whoever it was was not making himself understood.

She stood with the phone glued to her ear for a few more minutes, then with great irritation she hung up, mildly cursing Toby under her breath. Couldn't he have picked up a landline?

It suddenly occurred to her that perhaps Toby had endeavored to reach her at the London store first, so she dialed her new assistant's private line. It was answered immediately.

"It's me, Patsy," she said at once. "I think Toby Harte might be trying to get hold of me. From the States. Using his mobile. But it's not working, he keeps breaking up. Have you heard from him this morning? Has he been trying to get me?"

"No, he hasn't," Patsy answered. "In fact, you've had very few phone calls so far today. Only Jess Lister about a dress you ordered. It's ready. She's bringing it over. And Anita Moore. She called to say she wants to show you her new line of cosmetics and body products. I said you'd be in touch with her early next week."

"Good. Well, look, if Toby does ring me from the States, please ask him to phone me on a landline. I'll be here at Pennistone Royal all day, and this evening, too. That'll be much easier."

"I'll tell him. Talk to you later, Tessa."

Tessa walked back to the library table and automatically glanced out at the terrace before resuming her work. She caught her breath in surprise. Adele was no longer sitting at the tea table.

Oh God, where is she? Tessa rushed through the French doors, looking up and down. Her daughter was nowhere in sight. Yet she was not in the habit of wandering off. Adele was an obedient child.

Alarm shot through Tessa. She swung around, glanced down at the tea table as if seeking a clue, and immediately noticed that the rag doll was missing.

Where *had* Adele gone? Down to the old oak, perhaps? As this thought flew into her head, Tessa ran over to the stone balustrade and looked out toward the dell at the bottom of the sloping lawns. Here an ancient oak spread its wide branches over a garden seat where

Adele often went to play. But there was no sign of her there now.

How did she manage to get down the steps? Tessa asked herself, and her alarm intensified as she raced along the terrace to the flight of stairs. She dreaded what she might find, a three-year-old child crumpled in a heap at the bottom. But Adele was not there either.

Panic spiraled into genuine fear as Tessa struck out toward the front facade of the house. There wasn't a soul in sight, not even the gardeners or the stable boys. It was ominously quiet, as if she was the only person left there.

When she reached the front door of solid oak banded in iron, Tessa stood for a moment, frowning. The door was ajar, and this surprised her. It was always locked for security reasons. Puzzled, she pushed the door open and went inside.

"Adele! Adele!" she called in her loudest voice, walking forward quickly. "Are you here, sweetheart?"

No one answered.

No child came running to her on plump little legs.

There was only the sound of Tessa's voice echoing back to her through the great Stone Hall. It struck her then that Adele might have gone to the kitchen looking for Margaret, wanting her favorite Cadbury's chocolate fingers for the dolls' tea party. Tessa rushed down the corridor into the kitchen. It, too, was deserted. Her heart sank, and dismay lodged in the pit of her stomach. Tears filled her eyes, and she leaned against the doorjamb for a second, endeavoring to gather her swimming senses as she tried to imagine where the three-year-old could be. *Where?*

Taking a deep breath, Tessa made her way back to the front of the house and walked out onto the gravel driveway. She asked herself where she should begin to search for Adele. It now seemed obvious that her little girl had wandered off into the other garden. Tessa suddenly understood that she would need Wiggs and his two assistants to start looking. And possibly the stable lads as well. The outer grounds at Pennistone Royal were vast, and there were several dense woods beyond the fields and meadows.

"Miss Tessa! Miss Tessa!"

At the sound of the head gardener's voice, Tessa spun around. Wiggs was hurrying toward her, and she saw that he had the rag doll in his hands.

She ran to meet him, exclaiming, "Where did you find the doll?"

The gardener came to a standstill and handed it to her. "Just around the bend in the drive." He glanced over his shoulder. "Yer knows that bend, Miss Tessa, it's just afore the house comes in ter sight."

Clutching the rag doll to her, Tessa said shakily, "I can't find Adele, Wiggs. She's suddenly gone missing, and I don't understand what she was doing out here. We must start looking for her in the grounds."

Wiggs gaped at her. "I thought she must've dropped the doll before she got in ter the car," he said, his face puzzled.

"What car?" Tessa cried, her eyes flaring with apprehension. "There was a car *here*?" Her voice was unusually shrill, and she gripped the gardener's arm.

"Yes. I heard the screech of tires as it drove off. Almost run over one of the ponies, it did that, and two of the stable lads ran after it, shouting at the driver, telling him to stop. But he didn't."

All of the color had drained out of Tessa's face, and she thought her legs would buckle under her as ripples of shock ran through her body. *Mark.* It had to be Mark. Yes. *Oh God, yes.* He had snatched their child. She snapped her eyes shut and brought one hand to her face, overcome by rising panic.

"You'd best go inside, Miss Tessa, and sit down for a bit," Wiggs was saying. "You look right poorly."

And as Tessa opened her eyes and took a deep breath, she heard the clatter of horses' hooves in the distance and turned around swiftly.

Wiggs glanced behind him and muttered, "That must be Emsie and Desmond coming back from their ride."

"Yes, it must," she agreed, and she thought her voice sounded oddly strangled in her throat. Turning to Wiggs, blinking back more tears, she managed to ask, "That car, Wiggs. What was it like? Did you see the driver? Was it Mr. Longden, do you think?"

Wiggs shook his head. "Didn't see the driver's face. But it was a man. Aye, it was. Car was black. A Mercedes . . . I think." He nodded, and his expression was suddenly confident. "Aye, it *was* a Mercedes, Miss Tessa."

At this moment her half sister and half brother Emsie and Desmond came around the bend, their horses walking at a slow pace. Emsie waved and called out cheerily, "Tessa! Hello." Desmond also waved, his handsome young face full of smiles.

Tessa raised her arm, beckoned them to come over, then changed her mind and ran toward them, Wiggs following in her wake.

Desmond, mounted on a superb black stallion, looked down at his eldest sister. Staring at her face, which was as white as her cotton shirt, he asked, almost sharply, "What's the matter, Tess?"

"It's Adele," she began and shook her head. "She's vanished. Into thin air." Her voice was shaking, and she stopped abruptly, turned to look at Wiggs. "But she could have been taken from here."

The gardener had known Tessa since she was a child, and he understood immediately what she wanted him to do. He had to explain. "It's like this, Desmond," Wiggs said. "There was a car here. I don't know who was in it. But it drove off hell for leather, almost collided with a pony that'd strayed on ter the drive. Two of the stable lads ran after the car, shouting, but the driver paid them no mind, didn't stop. Just shot out of them there front gates like a bat out of hell. I was walking up the drive . . . when I spotted Adele's rag doll." He nodded and finished. "I thought Adele must've dropped it when she got in the car. Not that I'm sure she did that, yer knows. But it seems likely."

"But you didn't actually *see* Adele in the car?" Desmond asked, a dark brow rising.

Wiggs shook his head. "Still, what with the doll being there on the ground, well, I mean, I just thought she'd gone off in the car."

Tessa took a deep breath, said in a worried voice, "Wiggs, please arrange for the outer grounds to be searched, and talk to Joe. He might know who was in the car. Maybe they'd been to see him about something—to do with the estate."

"I'll get a search going, Miss Tessa, but there's no way I can talk ter Joe. He's gone ter East Witton. And I don't think he's coming back. Not just yet. But nobody coming ter see Joe would drive like that, not with all the notices we've got posted, warning everyone ter go slow because of the horses. No, whoever was in that black car, well, them there folk were not from these parts. Locals don't go speeding around in cars when there's horses all over the place."

"I agree," Desmond said. He immediately dismounted, went to Tessa, and put his arm around her shoulders, wanting to comfort her. He was as concerned about her as he was about the situation. And what ought they to do, aside from searching the grounds?

Emsie followed suit, expertly jumping down from her horse. Turning to Wiggs, she said, "Would you mind taking the horses to the stables? We'll be there in a few minutes, Wiggs, to rub them down."

"Acourse I'll tek 'em back, Emsie," he replied, accepting the reins from her and reaching for Desmond's horse. "But one of the stable lads'll look after 'em. You should both be with Tessa."

Emsie smiled at him, a faltering smile, and he noticed that her face was as white as her half sister's. She looked frightened as well. He patted the seventeen-year-old's shoulder. "Try not to worry, lass, if she's around here we'll find Adele."

"I hope she *is* just lost," Emsie murmured, biting her lip. "I hope that's all it is."

Wiggs hurried away with the horses, thinking that Mark Longden had most likely grabbed the child. The whole staff knew about the upcoming divorce; there was a good bit of gossip about Longden. None of them liked him. He was the child's father. Surely he wouldn't harm her. But Longden was a bit of a bugger, so he'd heard. A boozer. Also on drugs. And a wife beater. A man who struck a woman was a coward, a bully, and a thug in Wiggs's opinion. It was good that Miss Tessa had left him.

Desmond and his sisters went into the house, and as they hurried into the Stone Hall, he took hold of Tessa's arm and said, "Shall I get you a brandy? You look as if you're about to pass out."

"No, thanks, Des. A cup of tea and an aspirin is what I want. Let's go to the kitchen."

He nodded, and he and Emsie followed Tessa down the corridor. In the kitchen it was Emsie who filled the electric kettle with water, plugged it in, then found the brown teapot and three mugs in the cupboard.

Desmond and Tessa seated themselves at the round table in the bay window, and Desmond took hold of Tessa's hand, hoping to reassure her. At fifteen Desmond O'Neill was mature for his age, and he looked older than his years. He started to speak but stopped, noting the distraught look on Tessa's face. He had always been sensitive to her emotions, and he understood that at this moment she was trying to think things through.

Tessa's mind was racing, and she felt sick, anxiety-ridden. She did not know what to do. How could she just sit and wait until Wiggs and the others searched the estate? That could take ages. And wasn't time of the essence? If Adele *was* lost, she would soon become frightened, and she might have an accident. Tessa wondered if she should join in the hunt. Could Adele have been grabbed by Mark? Or was Jonathan Ainsley behind this? She instantly pushed that thought to one side. The idea of Jonathan Ainsley being involved frightened her. If Mark did have their daughter, wouldn't he call Pennistone Royal to speak to her? Certainly he would never hurt Adele, he adored the child. But he wasn't himself these days, was he? Tessa shivered involuntarily.

Desmond saw this and said, in his most reassuring tone, "I'm sure she was in that car, Tess. Wiggs might not have noticed. I don't think Adele is *here*, on the estate, lost somewhere. Because on our way back Emsie and I would have spotted her. The only way to get to the fields is down the lane, and we came up it."

Tessa did not respond.

Desmond remained silent himself. He loved Tessa, and she loved him, and they had always been good friends; she wasn't really the ogre some of the family made her out to be.

Rousing herself from her thoughts, Tessa suddenly said, "I can't help thinking as you do. She was in that car, Des. And she's so little, she couldn't have got very far if she's wandered off."

"Who would take her without telling you—" He cut himself off. His eyes met hers. "Mark Longden. *Of course!* You think he's got her, don't you?"

"Yes."

"So do I. That's the answer."

Emsie carried the tray of mugs and the teapot over to the table, and as she put it down she said, "There's no one else to point a finger at. It's a nasty divorce."

"Unless someone else has—" Desmond paused, took a deep breath, and finished, "*kidnapped her.* For a ransom. This family's always been the perfect target for something like that."

"I've considered the same thing." Tessa closed her eyes once more and tried to control her trembling. "That's why I've got to be here, near the phone."

She was so white and her tension was so marked, Desmond was convinced she was about to faint.

Emsie's eyes caught her brother's as she poured tea into his mug. These two had always been perfectly in tune with each other. She was two years older than Desmond, yet it was he who was protective of her; they were best friends.

Silently, she mouthed, "*Linnet.* We need Linnet."

Desmond nodded, looked across at Tessa, waiting.

Despite her delicate beauty, Tessa Fairley Longden had a great deal of inner strength and an enormous amount of resilience. As she often said, she was not Emma Harte's great-granddaughter for nothing; there was a certain toughness about her, and she had determination.

Pulling herself together finally, she opened her eyes

and sat up a little straighter in the chair. "Thanks for the tea, Emsie," she murmured and took a long swallow of the brew with the aspirin. After a moment's thought, she glanced at the wall clock and continued, "It's almost eleven here. Six o'clock in the morning in New York. No use phoning Mummy and Shane—"

Emsie cut in somewhat peremptorily: "They'll still be asleep. What about talking to your solicitor?"

"No, no!" Tessa exclaimed and gave Emsie a hard stare. "You know very well what the family rules are, Emma's rules, which we've always followed. We deal with everything ourselves, for as long as possible, and with the help of the other clans if necessary. But no outsiders can be involved. Unless we have no other choice."

"You ought to call Linnet immediately," Desmond suggested, glancing quickly at Emsie, hoping Tessa wouldn't bite his head off. The strained relationship between his sisters often presented problems. Both wanted to run Harte's one day. But Linnet was the smartest in the family, other than his parents; he believed she was the best person to take charge in the absence of their mother and father.

Surprisingly, Tessa was not upset by his suggestion. Jumping up, she hurried over to the phone on the counter. "I think I'd better do that, Desmond. Right away."

Tessa was aware that Linnet had planned to come up to Pennistone Royal either today or tomorrow, so instead of ringing Harte's in London she dialed her sister on her mobile; Linnet was probably on the road already. It was answered almost at once with a crisp "Linnet O'Neill."

"It's Tessa. I've got a problem here."

"At the Harrogate store?" Linnet sounded surprised.

"No. At home. At Pennistone Royal."

"A problem *there*! What's happened?"

"It's Adele. I can't find her, and I'm frantic. I think it could be Mark's doing." Tessa's voice trembled, and she swallowed hard.

"If you think it's Mark, then it is," Linnet exclaimed. "Stay calm, I'm about an hour away. Don't call the police yet. We can deal with this ourselves."

"I know. Listen, Desmond thinks it could be a genuine kidnapping. For a ransom."

"Oh my God! Let's hope not. Tell me exactly what happened."

Tessa did as her sister asked.

When Tessa finished, Linnet said, "The phone calls were to distract you. It's Mark who's behind this. I'm absolutely positive. Still, I'm glad Wiggs is searching the grounds. She *could* have strayed away from the house. But she couldn't have gone far. Who's there with you?"

"Just Desmond and Emsie. It's Elvira's day off, Margaret went out marketing. And Joe's gone to East Witton."

"Desmond's pretty reliable and responsible. So is Emsie. I'm glad they're there. Where's Evan?"

"I don't know. I saw her drive off several hours ago."

"I'm sure she'll soon return. Now, stay there to take phone calls, and if Mark calls tell him to bring Adele back immediately. Be firm with him but civil. Try not to have a row."

"What if he wants to bargain with me? What if he wants something?"

"Promise him anything. Just get that child back in your arms. Mark can be dealt with later."

"All right. But what if it's not Mark? What if it really is a kidnapping, and they call, making demands?"

"Listen to them. Agree to their demands, but explain it's going to take you a while to get money together. Because I'm sure they'll be asking for money . . . that's what most kidnappings are about."

"I understand."

"Tessa?"

"Yes?"

"Nothing's going to happen to Adele."

"But—"

"I promise," Linnet cut in. "Don't go into the grounds. You must be there to answer the phone and *deal*. See you soon." With that she clicked off her mobile.

As soon as she saw a lay-by Linnet O'Neill pulled over and parked. She sat for a moment thinking about her sister's phone call and Adele's disappearance. She was furious. I knew that bastard wouldn't go quietly, she thought, her mind zeroing in on Mark Longden. She had never liked him, had always believed him to be avaricious, ambitious, self-promoting, and insincere. Years ago she had determined he was after Tessa's money, not to mention her prestige as a Harte; Linnet had never quite understood why such a beautiful and clever young woman as her sister had married him. And he wasn't a very good architect, in her opinion.

Their mother had told her recently that Mark Longden had physically and mentally abused Tessa, and Linnet hadn't been the least bit surprised. She had always been aware that underneath his phony charm he was a nasty piece of work.

Linnet sat thinking about Adele's sudden disappearance, and she realized she did not believe for one moment that the child had been kidnapped by strangers for ransom. It was Mark Longden. Her gut instinct told her that he wanted something from the Hartes, and he was using his little daughter as a bargaining tool. The bastard, she muttered again and cursed him under her breath.

"'Everybody has a price, and it isn't always money,' that's what Emma used to say to me," her mother had once told her, and Linnet had never forgotten those words. When it came right down to it, everybody had some kind of vulnerability, something they wanted to protect at any price, and very often money didn't come into play at all. There were other currencies.

From remarks her mother had made, Linnet knew that Mark Longden was not only drinking very heavily these days but also on drugs. That fact had troubled her then; it was certainly more worrying now. A man under the influence of combined substances could easily become irresponsible, erratic, and violent. She was fairly certain that Mark wouldn't intentionally hurt his only child. But what if something went wrong with him, or others, and in the process Adele got hurt?

It suddenly struck Linnet that thoughts of a similar nature must have occurred to Tessa. Never before had she heard her sister sound so vulnerable, and at such a loss about what to do.

Normally Tessa wanted to run everything and boss everyone around. And very often, because of Tessa's ambition to be their mother's heir apparent, the Dauphine as she called herself, she and Linnet had locked horns. But there was a family rule that went all the way back to Emma Harte and her brothers, and it had never been broken. No matter what the circumstances, a Harte was always loyal to a Harte. They had been brought up to stand strong and steady together in a fight, to defend each other against the world. To kill for each other, to take the bullet for each other, if necessary. Linnet knew all the Harte rules by heart and lived by them.

Linnet was well aware of her sister's love for her child. The entire family loved Adele. The three-year-old was like a Botticelli angel, with her silver-gilt hair, silvery gray eyes, and exquisite little face. She had touched them all in different ways. Linnet thought of Adele as one of those rare golden children. God forbid anything should happen to her.

What to do? Linnet asked herself. And where to begin? Start driving for one thing, she decided, releasing the brake and slowly pulling out onto the motorway.

Linnet knew she had to handle this. The very fact that Tessa had turned to her told her that her sister accepted that she herself was far too emotional to cope properly with the situation. I've got to deal with it fast, Linnet thought. Very fast. I've got to find Mark. Find that child. Before anything goes wrong.

Her parents were in New York with Aunt Emily and Uncle Winston, which meant the four senior and most powerful members of the Harte family were out of action for the moment. And so she must do her best.

What about Gideon Harte? She focused on her cousin, her best friend, for a moment. He could be extremely helpful. He ran the Harte newspapers, was brilliant and street smart, and he had every kind of resource at his disposal. Owning and running an international newspaper chain spelled one thing. Power. *Immense power.* Yes, she might have to pull Gideon into this, but right now what she really needed was an expert. A genuine professional. A policeman who wasn't actually a policeman.

Jack Figg.

The name leapt into her mind. Harte's security adviser, he was considered a member of the family. She had known him since childhood, thought of him as a friend. And so the moment she saw another lay-by ahead, Linnet pulled in and parked. She groped around in her carryall for her address book and quickly found his name.

A few seconds later she was dialing Jack's mobile number.

"Figg here," he answered almost at once.

"It's Linnet, Jack."

"Hello, Beauty. What do you need?"

"You, Jack. Please."

"I'm yours"—he laughed—"anytime you want me."

"Remember what you said at Shane's birthday party in June—that I could count on you in an emergency?"

"I do. And you can."

"Thanks, Jack. There's an emergency."

"Tell me everything I need to know."

She did so and gave him her own thoughts about what had happened.

"The phone calls *were* meant to distract her. Where are you now, Linnet?"

"Parked at a lay-by, about an hour away from Pennistone Royal. Are you in Robin Hood's Bay?"

"No, I'm outside York Minster with a friend. If I leave York now I'll probably arrive at the house the same time as you. But please tell Tessa you've asked me to help. Just in case I arrive before you."

"I will. And thanks, Jack."

"Anything for you, Beauty."

He was gone, and she was back on the motorway, picking up speed. There was hardly any traffic at the moment, and that was something in her favor at least.

Linnet concentrated on driving for the next twenty minutes or so; then, slowing down, she phoned Tessa. Her sister said there was nothing new. Wiggs and his search party were still looking. Linnet told her about

Jack Figg and his imminent arrival, and fortunately met no resistance.

A few seconds later she punched in Evan's mobile number, but her phone was turned off. No doubt Evan was with Uncle Robin, with whom she had been wanting to talk for several weeks. Linnet thought suddenly of her cousin India Standish. India had gone up to Leeds from London early that morning to start working on plans for revamping the store. Linnet was close to her cousin. In fact, everyone in the family loved India. She had a kind and loving nature. Many thought she was delicate, even frail, but her elegant aristocratic looks, inherited from the Fairleys, belied her character.

Linnet knew she was practical, down to earth, strong physically, and like their great-grandmother Emma Harte she was absolutely fearless. India worked with her in the fashion department of Harte's in London, and they had been close friends since childhood. India had grown up on her father's estate, Clonloughlin in Ireland, but she had spent every summer at Pennistone Royal. And Linnet loved to boast of India's brave deeds as a child . . . like the time she rushed out into the backyard at Pennistone Royal, wearing huge over gloves in order to separate two dogs, Joe's Jack Russells, fighting over a dead rabbit. Or the day Linnet's little sister Emsie had climbed into the big oak and got stuck in the upper branches. Undeterred by Linnet's warning that they would both fall out of the tree. India had climbed up it, sat with Emsie, and held her tightly until Linnet came back with Joe, the estate manager, carrying a tall orchard ladder.

Yes, Linnet decided, India would be helpful in this situation, and she got on well with the sometimes difficult Tessa.

India would be staying at Pennistone Royal for the

next few days, as she usually did. I'd better warn her about the situation, Linnet thought, before she goes over there. She dialed her cousin and waited as the mobile rang and rang.

3

That's *your* phone ringing, not mine," Russell "Dusty" Rhodes said, looking across at India Standish, who stood next to the window.

She frowned, glancing around the bedroom, exclaiming, "Heavens, where's my bag?"

"Over there, on the chair. Under your dress."

"Oh gosh, yes, you're right." As she spoke she ran to the chair, clutching the towel around her body; with her other hand she grabbed the bag, groped inside for the mobile phone and held it to her ear. "Hello?"

"India?"

"Hi, Linnet."

"Where are you? At the Leeds store already?"

"No. I stopped in for a few minutes, then went to . . . lunch."

Dusty grinned at her from the other side of the room and began to laugh.

She glared at him and silently mouthed, "Be quiet."

Linnet said, "India, there's a problem. Adele's disappeared. Several hours ago. And Tessa's frantic."

"Oh my God!" India sat down heavily in the chair.

"She could be lost in the grounds, might have just wandered off," Linnet went on, "but somehow I doubt that. Personally, I think Mark Longden snatched her, and so does Tessa."

"Yes, I agree. But surely he wouldn't hurt her—"

"True," Linnet interrupted, "but things sometimes do go wrong, so we've got to find her before anything untoward does happen. I've brought Jack Figg in to help, and there's a search party looking for her at Pennistone Royal. I should be there myself in half an hour."

"Perhaps I'd better come too."

"You might as well finish lunch, India. There's not a lot you can do except be there for Tessa. Obviously, she's very upset."

"I can well imagine." There was a slight hesitation, then India asked, "You don't think Jonathan Ainsley has anything to do with this, do you?"

"I sincerely hope not, but if he does it really changes the picture."

"Yes, you're right. But what do you—"

"Let's not go *there,* India. At least not yet. I'll see you later."

"I'll leave shortly." India clicked off the phone and put it back in her bag. Her face was paler than ever, her eyes anxious.

"What's happened?" Dusty asked, sitting up straighter in the bed. "You sounded frightened. No, not frightened, you're not frightened of anything, are you? *Concerned* is possibly a better word. Or alarmed."

India stared back at him, nodding. "I am a bit

alarmed, yes. Adele, Tessa's little girl, has vanished, and Linnet says it could be Mark Longden's doing."

"That's bad. What do *you* think?"

"I tend to agree. Mark's not very nice, and it's more than likely he took her."

"She's not lost somewhere on that vast estate perhaps?" A brow lifted again.

"It's possible, I suppose. But I think she would've been found by now. She's still a toddler. How far could she get? Linnet says it's several hours since she went missing, and there's a search party out."

"Why would he take her? Stupid question, Rhodes," he answered himself, shaking his head. "As a weapon in the divorce . . . he's using her in order to manipulate Tessa." He ran a hand through his black, wavy hair, and a look of contempt crossed his face. "*People*. What shits they are. He's a real bastard if he's using his child in that way."

India sighed, stood up, reached for her clothes.

"You can be there in less than an hour, so come back to bed." Dusty's voice was lower, suddenly almost tender, and he smiled at her seductively. She noticed yet again how white his teeth were against the tan of his face. "Come back to bed with me, let's do it all again," he insisted.

India shook her head. "I do think I have to go, Dusty," she answered, but regret registered on her face.

He could not fail to miss that expression. He saw the desire in her eyes. He threw back the sheets and got out of bed, walked toward her purposefully, still smiling that beguiling smile of his.

India thought his blue eyes looked suddenly dangerous, almost predatory. Her stomach lurched, and she felt weak; he always managed to make her feel this way at some point when they were together . . . shaking inside . . . swooning. She was his willing partner in anything he wanted to do with her . . . sexually aroused by a mere glance, the touch of his hand.

As he drew close she thought how good-looking he was, almost absurdly handsome. It was as if a sculptor had spent endless hours shaping most of his face: straight, patrician nose, broad forehead, high cheekbones, perfectly rounded chin. And elegantly arched brows above those dazzlingly blue eyes, which became soulful with passion, could turn icy cold in anger. He did not have one of those pretty-boy, matinee-idol faces, though; it was ruggedly handsome, with sharp angles and planes, as if the sculptor had suddenly wanted to finish quickly and had become slapdash.

His face matched his body. He had a solid torso—broad chest, wide shoulders above slender hips. About five feet eleven, he gave the impression of greater height and strength because of his powerful build. From the moment she had met him, she had been aware of his potency. No other man had ever affected her the way he did.

Now he was standing in front of her, the smile still lingering on his mouth. He pulled her into his arms and held her close to his body; the towel and her clothes fell to the floor in a heap, and her arms went around his shoulders. And as he bent his head toward her, his mouth found hers. He kissed her deeply, and she felt his erection against her thigh. For a moment she thought she would succumb, become an all-too-willing partner in his bed for a second time that day.

But then the brainwashing of years kicked in. She remembered the Harte rules, and she knew she had to go to Pennistone Royal. No matter how much she wanted this man, her upbringing overrode everything else. A

Harte was in trouble, and every other Harte must stand alongside, to defend their rights.

India gently pushed Dusty away, her hands resting on his chest. For a moment he resisted, then quite suddenly he stepped back and looked into her face, his own questioning.

"You know the rules," she murmured. "I told you about them ages ago."

"A Harte always goes to the aid of a Harte in trouble!" he exclaimed. "You don't have to embellish. I got it then, I get it now."

"Please don't be angry."

"I'm not," he snapped, turning away, walking over to the window, where he stood looking out, his stance rigid, his face a mask of discontent.

Without another word she collected her clothes, went into the bathroom, tidied herself up, pulled a black linen dress over her head, then slid her feet into high-heeled, black leather mules. When she returned to the bedroom, he was still standing at the window, but he had dressed, was wearing his jeans and a white T-shirt.

At the sound of her heels clicking on the parquet floor, he swung to face her. "Sorry," he mumbled, and for once he looked shamefaced.

India walked over to him, touched his cheek gently. "I *want* to stay, to be with you, you know that, and you also know how I feel about you. This sense of duty to the family is something I can't help." She shrugged and finished. "I suppose it's just . . . ingrained in me."

He caught her hand in his, brought it to his mouth, kissed it. "I know. And I'm a belligerent sod at times." He laughed his deep-throated laugh. "*Most* of the time, wouldn't you say? Okay, I'll let you go." He led her toward the door. "On one condition."

She caught the lightness in his tone, saw the laughter in those amazing eyes. "I agree to any condition," she said, "as long as it's a condition involving you."

"You'll regret saying that when you know what it is." He hurried her out of the bedroom and down the grand staircase.

"Will I really?" she asked, squinting up at him, her expression suddenly flirtatious. "So, tell me what it is, then."

"You have to sit for me." He stopped on the stairs, turned to look at her.

India gaped at him, her jaw dropping. "You want me to sit for *you*? You want to paint me? *Me?*"

He saw that he had startled her and realized her amazement was genuine. For a moment he was baffled. They had paused in the middle of the staircase, just underneath the domed glass ceiling. Light was streaming in, turning her hair into a silver halo, and her silvery-gray eyes seemed to be lit from within. In contrast, her face was sensual, her mouth ripe—and bruised. He caught his breath, wishing he could start painting right away. His fingers tingled.

She said quickly, "You're staring at me, and you have the most peculiar look on your face." Her hand came up to smooth her hair; suddenly, she felt self-conscious. "I know I look a mess."

He took her face between his hands and gazed deeply into her beautiful, transparent eyes. "I wish I could start painting you right now, capture you the way you look at this moment. So vulnerable and open, the sensuality still lingering. You look like a woman who has just been well and truly bedded."

"I was."

"You'll do it then? You'll sit for me?"

"If you really want me to, Dusty."

He smiled and took hold of her fingers, and they went on down the stairs hand in hand. When they got to the bottom, Dusty paused, gave her a long, thoughtful look. "How will you explain it?"

India frowned in puzzlement, returned his gaze with one that was slightly surprised. "I'm not actually following you."

"How will you explain the painting to your father?"

"I don't know what you mean, Dusty."

He peered at her more closely, wondering if she was being dense or perhaps even kidding him. Then he understood she was neither. Very simply, she didn't get it. He shook his head and began to laugh softly. After a moment, he explained, "Every one of my paintings is exhibited, even the portraits for private clients, and they are always photographed. Your father is bound to see photos of the picture I paint of you when they appear in the newspapers and magazines. He'll know I've been screwing you."

She winced inside; sometimes his bluntness took her breath away, but she gave him a sweet smile and answered, "Don't be so ridiculous, he won't know any such thing."

"He will, because the painting I intend to paint of you will be very sensual—the way you look now, and it won't leave much to the imagination."

"Oh, Daddy won't care, he's . . . a man of the world."

"He's also the Earl of Dunvale, and believe me, he'll care. He won't want the world to know I'm . . . you know . . . having it off with his daughter. *Me?* The notorious, rabble-rousing, working-class lad from the back streets of Leeds. Not 'alf he won't."

"Now you *are* being silly. You're the greatest painter in the world today. Everyone knows that. Anyway, I actually don't care what my father or anyone else thinks.

I'm twenty-seven and I can do anything I want. And I want to be painted by you, in fact I'm flattered that you asked."

"It's a deal?"

"Of course." She thrust out her hand. "Let's shake."

His boisterous laughter filled the air as he shook her hand; then he pulled her into his arms and embraced her. Against her hair he said, "There's another condition. Before I paint you we'll have to be together, if you get my drift. You do understand that, Lady India?"

"Absolutely, Mr. Rhodes. I'm in total agreement."

He put his arm around her shoulder. "Come on, I'll walk you to your car," he murmured and turned the handle of the French doors. They opened onto the terrace of the south facade of the house, where there was a portico supported by four soaring columns, and the wide terrace stretched the length of the house and around the two end wings.

The heat of the August afternoon hit them as they stepped outside, and Dusty said, "It's muggy, and it looks like rain." He glanced up. "Thunderclouds, India, but you'll get to Pennistone Royal before the rain starts."

"I hope so," she murmured, also glancing up and instantly thinking of the search party out on the estate in rainy weather. But she hoped Adele had been found, or returned, by now. She shivered when she thought of the missing child.

Dusty noticed and took hold of her arm as they headed for the courtyard. After a short silence, he said, "Maybe I should go with you. You're just three women out there and—"

"Four with Evan," India cut in.

"All right, four women. But you might need a bloke around. A bloke like me, who knows what's what. Mark

Longden could show up making demands, you know. From what you've told me, he's nasty."

"Yes, he is, but we'll be all right, please don't worry. There's Wiggs, the head gardener, and Joe, who runs the estate."

"And then there's that other rule, isn't there, India? No outsiders allowed."

India glanced at him out of the corner of her eye, trying to ascertain his mood. He had sounded slightly annoyed; spotting the hint of mischief in his eyes, she laughed. "Well, I will say this, you do learn fast, Mr. Rhodes."

"So do you, Lady India," he shot back, leering at her.

When she made no response, he asked, "How long do you intend to stay up here?"

"I'd planned to stay for a week before this happened. But who knows, I could be here longer now, if I'm out at the house and not at the store in Leeds. I've a lot of work there, and I'll have to stay until it's finished."

"When can I start the painting?"

"Tomorrow. Hopefully. It all depends."

He picked up on the concern in her voice and said quietly, "I'm sure Adele will show up later today, India, I really mean that. And certainly I hope so."

"Thanks, Dusty . . ." Her voice trailed off, and she searched in her bag for her keys, found them, and headed toward her car parked next to the barns.

"I do envy you this," Dusty said when he drew to a standstill, patting the hood. "An Aston Martin DB2/4, a piece of vintage mechanical art if ever there was any."

She smiled up at him. "Wasn't it nice of Daddy to part with his favorite wheels?" She kissed him on the cheek. "But then I am his favorite, you know," she added, getting into the car.

"Don't rub it in," Dusty responded, his laughter rising. "Give me a shout later."

"I will." After blowing him a kiss through the open window, she turned on the ignition.

Once the Aston Martin had disappeared from sight, Dusty spun on his heels and crossed the cobbled yard, went down to the ornamental lake. When he drew to a stop, he stood looking into its depths, taking pleasure at what he was seeing—a perfect reflection of the Georgian house on the hill, a mirror image clearly visible in that placid body of water as smooth as glass. How clever they were, those architects of the seventeenth and eighteenth centuries, he thought, nodding. Whenever the topography allowed, they set the house on a hill and created a man-made lake at the bottom so that the house was reflected in all its glory. A double image. Very impressive indeed.

Dusty had studied architecture for a time; he considered it part of his training as an artist. He was particularly interested in the designs of Andrea Palladio. And he had always thought that a Palladian villa set in a verdant English park was a very beautiful sight. He saw it as the perfect marriage of a building with nature. Dusty loved the classicism of the designs, because he loved all things classical, and of the Renaissance. William Kent, a follower of Inigo Jones, the great seventeenth-century architect, had designed and built his house, Willows Hall, over two hundred and seventy-five years ago, and it was pure Palladian. Dusty had fallen in love with it the first time he had seen it, although he had become concerned when he began to understand how neglected it truly was. But the surveyors he brought in had told him that it was mostly surface damage, that everything could be restored to its original state with some good repair work by master craftsmen.

He began to walk toward the house now, climbing the

grassy hill, and his thoughts automatically swung to India Standish. If anyone looked as if she belonged in this house it was she; after all, she had grown up in Clonloughlin in Ireland, a renowned Georgian house of impressive proportions. And so of course she was at ease with the grand overtones of Willows Hall. He knew he looked right in it, too, even though he had been brought up in a back-to-back, a far cry from this place indeed.

Dusty had lavished a great deal of time, effort, care, love, and money on Willows Hall over the past eight and a half years, and he had made it his own; he couldn't imagine living anywhere else.

When he reached the top of the hill, he stood gazing at the front facade for a moment, and he couldn't help admiring the way the pale stone gleamed in the afternoon sunlight; it looked as if it had been polished.

As he lifted his eyes to the sky, Dusty was happy to see that the thunderclouds had blown away; it wasn't going to rain after all. Turning, he walked the length of the terrace, making for his studio. This stood a little away from the house on the left, and it was of his own design. From the outside it looked like a guest villa, and it echoed the main house in its Palladian style.

Inside, the studio was one vast, open space with a ceiling that seemed to soar endlessly upward, and many windows on both sides. A series of skylights was set in the ceiling, and the whole area was filled with glittering northern light. Blinking, Dusty touched several buttons, and electric window shades slid into place, dimming the daylight, cooling the room.

He crossed to a drawing board, picked up a charcoal crayon, and quickly made a series of vivid sketches of India's face. Suddenly, he stopped, threw the crayon down, stepped away from the drawing board, went and lowered himself into an armchair.

Why was he painting her? The idea was ridiculous. It was asking for trouble. In every way. Trouble for her. Trouble for him. Her father wouldn't like her association with him; whatever *she* believed, *he* knew he was right. They came from entirely different worlds. She was an aristocrat from very high altitudes; he was a working-class boy. Yes, he was famous. Very famous, in fact. And rich. All because of his talent, and doing something he couldn't live without doing. Painting. But the Earl of Dunvale wouldn't care about those things. Other considerations mattered to a man like her father. Propriety and background, and stupid things like where he had gone to school, and what his father did, and whether he had a posh accent.

No, it wasn't fair to her, or to himself, actually, since he had no intention of becoming serious with India. *He* was wasting his valuable time with her when he could be painting, and he was setting *her* up to get hurt when he said good-bye. Yes, she was trouble. For a variety of reasons.

The red phone on the countertop began to ring. He looked across at it balefully, reluctant to answer it. But it didn't stop after six rings, so he got up, strode to the counter, snatched at the receiver.

"Hello?"

"Russell?"

"Hello, Melinda."

"How did you know it was me?"

"Recognized your voice."

"I want out of this place, Russell," she said. "Get Doctor Jeffers to release me."

"You know I can't. You've got to stay there until he thinks you're properly detoxed. Then he'll sign your release. I don't have anything to do with it, you know that."

"Russell, please ask him."

"You know very well he won't listen."

"Please don't punish me this way."

"I'm not doing that, Melinda. You signed yourself into the clinic."

"I'll tell Atlanta what you're doing to me."

"I'm not doing anything. Anyway, she's too young to understand."

"Is she all right?"

"Yes, she's wonderful. I spoke to your mother yesterday, and she said she's as happy as a lark. Look, Melinda, I've got to go. I'm working."

"Will you talk to the doctor? *Please.*"

"Yes, I will. I'll give him a ring tomorrow. Now rest quietly, and get well. 'Bye." He hung up and stared at the phone. Now *that* was trouble if anything was. And then some.

He groaned. What was he going to do about Melinda and his child? He dreaded the thought of someone finding out about them. Yet he knew it would leak soon . . . he was far too famous for it not to. . . . He let this disturbing thought go, unable, suddenly, to cope with it.

And why had he ever said he wanted to paint India? Because she was beautiful and sensual, and he had had a sudden image of the finished portrait in his head, and he couldn't ignore that. It was a vision, and when that occurred he had to fulfill it.

Unexpectedly, his thoughts veered to Tessa Longden and Adele. He fully understood how she felt. After all, he had a three-year-old of his own, and he could well imagine how beside himself he would be in the same circumstances.

India drove along the motorway at a steady pace; she was soon leaving Harrogate behind and heading toward the village of Pennistone Royal. The thunderclouds had drifted out to the North Sea, and the sky was a lovely pale blue again. She was relieved. There was nothing worse than tramping over sodden fields and meadows looking for a lost child.

Was she lost on the estate? No. Mark Longden had taken her out of spite. As a bargaining chip, as Dusty had suggested. *Dusty.* He was such a difficult man in so many ways, and so full of contradictions. And he was loaded with baggage, most of it about *his* background and *their* class differences, all of which she found silly. He wouldn't listen to her. But no matter, she had fallen in love with him the night she first met him, and nothing was going to change that. He was the only man she wanted, and she was determined to get him. Permanently. Marriage. That was her goal. But it wasn't going to be easy.

Dusty loathed being pinned down. Nor did he like to make commitments. That was obviously why he had never married or had a long-term relationship. "Love 'em and leave 'em, that's always been my motto," he had said to her when they met, as if warning her. And then he had begun to laugh uproariously, seemingly highly amused by his own attitude.

He laughed a lot, and she liked that. She couldn't bear glum people. He was usually in top form, cheerful, optimistic, and ready to take a chance on life, except when it came to wedded bliss, of course. That was verboten as a subject, not even open for discussion.

Dusty liked being one of the boyos, as he called his male friends, who were numerous and varied: actors, writers, politicians, journalists, "and," as he often said, "nobodies who I absolutely adore." He fancied himself Jack the Lad—Jack the *Bad* Lad. He enjoyed carousing and creating a stir, constantly referred to himself as a rabble-rouser. However, she had come to understand in the three months she had known him that much of this was an act. In point of fact, he drank very little, mostly nursed a Stolichnaya over ice all night, simply made a big noise about his consumption of booze. The men in the Harte family drank much more than Dusty. But then *he* needed a steady hand the next morning in order to do his work.

His style of painting was classical realism, and notable art critics had hailed him from the beginning of his career as the new Pietro Annigoni, proclaiming that he had inherited the mantle of the famous Italian painter, who had died in 1988. They called Dusty a genius with the same awe and reverence they had called Annigoni a genius. Dusty's paintings were very much in the manner of the great artists of the Renaissance, with attention to detail in the subject matter and background, whether interiors or exteriors. His portraits of the famous and his landscapes and seascapes were so detailed, his use of color so beautiful, people simply gazed at them, unable to tear their eyes away.

Anybody who painted as precisely as he did could hardly afford to booze it up; she had said that to him once, and he had grinned and winked at her. She felt the same way about his so-called rabble-rousing; even this was merely jovial boisterousness, with much laughter, loud voices, arm punching, back slapping. Much ado about nothing, something totally innocuous which the press played up. As he hoped they would. He loved his reputation.

When she had first understood that that reputation was something of a myth, she had burst out laughing. She had been walking through Harte's with Linnet when the truth dawned on her. Her cousin had stared at her, shaken her head, and said pithily, "People who burst into gales of laughter for no apparent reason get taken away in straitjackets. Especially when they're in the middle of a very posh emporium. Drawing attention to themselves."

"I'm sorry, Linnet," she had spluttered, "but I can't help it. I've suddenly realized my boyfriend is a bit of a phony."

This comment had instantly gained Linnet's undivided attention, and she had cried, "Oh, get rid of *him*. Immediately. We don't need anybody who's not true blue around here. Anyway, he'd get clobbered by the lads."

"What lads?"

"Julian, Gideon, Toby, and even young Desmond. They'd gang up on him."

"That's true."

"By the way, when you say *boyfriend,* are you referring to the VFP?"

"VFP? What's that?"

"Very Famous Person. You told me you were seeing someone very famous, but you never confided who he is."

"Russell Rhodes."

"*Dusty* Rhodes? The painter?" Linnet's eyes had widened.

India had simply nodded in response but was pleased by Linnet's surprise.

"He looks rather dishy, India."

"He is, but complex."

"Aren't they all," Linnet had responded, grinning at her.

She had laughed and answered, "But at least he's never been married, so there's no ex or children to contend with. In fact, he'd been unattached for quite a while before he met me."

"You know, Dad loves his work, we all do. He's always wanted Dusty Rhodes to paint Paula, but Mummy says she's too busy to sit all those hours for an artist. I wish she would, though, and so does Daddy."

"I agree. Dusty's the perfect person to paint your mother. He could do a wonderful medieval portrait of her."

Linnet had then asked her a lot of questions about Dusty as they continued their walk through the store; she had answered some but remained silent about others. She had discovered she didn't want to reveal too much about him or their relationship, at least not just yet. The real problem with Dusty was his attitude about her family. Without having met any of them, he had categorized them as *aristos*. "Too posh. Snobs. Hoity-toity, idle rich folks" was the way he described them. None of it was true, and she had endeavored to explain this, explain about her great-grandmother's impoverished beginnings, but he had swept her words away and changed the subject.

At first she had thought he suffered from an inferiority complex about his own background growing up poor in the back streets of Leeds. Certainly he was always making reference to this. But she had quickly come to accept that he didn't have an inferiority complex at all, far from it. He was one of the most self-confident and self-possessed people she had ever met, in command of everything, exuding charm and displaying perfect manners when he wanted to.

Yet Dusty continued to believe her father would look down on him, would condemn their relationship out of hand. But she knew her father and mother would like him, quite aside from the fact that they both admired his paintings. I have to give him time, she told herself, and slowed down as she came to the village. Within minutes she was leaving the small main street and heading for the road which would take her to the front gates of Pennistone Royal.

Her mind focused on Tessa and the current situation. She had no idea what she would have to face. She prayed that she would find Adele with her mother and not still lost. Or abducted. Prayed that tragedy did not lurk in the shadows.

Jonathan Ainsley crept into her mind, and she grimaced. From what she had learned lately, it appeared that Mark Longden was under his influence. How terrible. Could Jonathan be pulling the strings, was he the mastermind behind Adele's abduction? If that was what it was. She had no answers.

4

~

Linnet sat with Tessa in the upstairs parlor at Pennistone Royal, endeavoring to reassure her that Adele was all right, that she would soon be home, silently praying that her assurances would not prove meaningless.

Evan was with them, seated near the lovely oriel window, but she was an observer rather than a participant at the moment, knowing it was best to let Linnet handle everything. Tessa could be touchy, even caustic, at the best of times, and today was the worst.

"Mark would never do anything to upset or hurt Adele," Linnet said, touching her sister's hand, then taking it in hers. "He does adore her, you know, that's always been most apparent."

"Yes," Tessa responded, "but what if it's not Mark who has her. Perhaps Desmond was right when he suggested it might be a kidnapping for ransom. She could be with strangers, and therefore in danger."

"I really do doubt that," Linnet answered in a

stronger tone, wishing her younger brother had kept this opinion to himself. "And you must *trust* Jack Figg. He's the best and the smartest private investigator there is. Mummy's said that for years, and she's always relied on him in a crisis. And don't forget, he was head of Harte's security for years."

"But he's been retired for some time now," Tessa pointed out, a sudden shrillness in her voice.

"Semiretired, to be exact. He still works full-time for those who need him, such as former clients he's remained close to, like us. Anyway, you know very well our mother put him on retainer and used him to do that in-depth check on Mark Longden several weeks ago. She filled us in before she went off to New York."

"Yes—" Tessa's voice broke, and tears welled in her eyes again. She wiped them quickly with a tissue and continued shakily, "I'm so worried about Adele I can hardly bear it. She's such a little girl, and she must be so scared, even if she is with her father. I mean, being snatched off the terrace will have frightened her. I feel so helpless, I don't know what to do."

"Listen to me," Linnet said in her firmest, most confident voice. "We don't know *how* she was taken, whether it was awful or not. Actually, I'm sure it wasn't." Hoping to calm Tessa, she went on. "I'm sure Mark made it seem like a game to Adele, you know, putting his finger to his lips so she would be quiet, smiling at her, beckoning. Yes, I'm quite certain that's what he did. It's obvious he wouldn't want to frighten her. She would've made quite a racket, I think, if he'd just rushed in and grabbed her."

"You seem so certain it *is* Mark, like me." Tessa gave Linnet a hard stare, and her eyes narrowed slightly. "I just hope to God we're right. What is Jack Figg actually *doing* right now?"

"He's in the library, on the phone a lot, talking to people who work for him. I never question his methods, and neither should you. Let it suffice for me to say that he has contacts everywhere in the world and in all walks of life. If anybody can find Adele, it's Jack, believe me."

Glancing across at Evan, Tessa said slowly, "*You* had lunch with Uncle Robin at Lackland Priory today. Did he mention Jonathan? Where he's living these days?"

Evan tensed. Tessa had sounded almost accusatory, but she kept her voice level as she answered, "No, he didn't mention Jonathan. I'm sorry, Tessa, I don't know anything about him. But he's more than likely out of the country. In Hong Kong. Robin would have told me if Jonathan were in England. . . . You see, he would have warned me. I know Robin worries a lot about Jonathan doing me harm out of spite."

"And all of *us*, too, for that matter!" Linnet exclaimed, her green eyes flashing. "He's had it in for Mummy and her offspring for ages. In fact, I think he has it in for every one of the Hartes. He'd like to mow us all down with a machine gun and be rid of us once and for all. And all because he feels cheated by Emma Harte. He's a nasty piece of work. But Mums says he always was when they were growing up."

"That's true," Tessa agreed. "And to think Mark let himself fall into his clutches." Tessa sat back on the sofa, twisting the tissue in her hands, her face ringed with misery. She fervently wished she had not married Mark Longden. All he had ever done was create misery for her, not to mention the verbal and physical abuse he had meted out lately. Now he had stolen their child. Bastard, she thought.

Suddenly the door flew open, and India came in, almost at a run. "Hi, everybody," she said then made a beeline for her cousin Tessa; she knelt down next to her and took hold of her hand. "I'm so sorry this happened," she murmured, looking at Tessa intently. Her face was full of compassion, her eyes warm and loving. "I'm here for you, whatever you need. You only have to ask."

Tessa nodded, attempted a smile. It faltered instantly, but she managed to say, "Thanks, India, I'm glad you're here."

Watching India commiserate with Tessa, Evan couldn't help thinking how much alike they looked, like sisters actually. It was very apparent they were closely related; both had silver-gilt hair and silvery gray, luminous eyes, pale complexions and delicately wrought faces. They were lovely looking in a soft, feminine way, and she knew their striking resemblance came from their shared Fairley bloodline.

Evan had also heard the family legend that their great-great-grandmother Adele Fairley had been a famous beauty—elegant, aristocratic, and possibly slightly mad. And that it was from her these two had inherited their silver-blond hair and extraordinary eyes, as well as their angelic faces. Little Adele had the same looks. She was part Fairley, and to Evan she did not appear at all like a Harte. The thought of the missing child made her shrivel inside. What if Adele were in some kind of danger? Everyone had mentioned Mark, or a kidnapper looking for money, but hadn't anyone thought of a pedophile?

Immediately Evan shoved that thought aside, it was too awful to contemplate. She glanced across at Linnet, who was a true Harte with her halo of red hair, green eyes, and dynamic personality. Gideon had the same coloring and upbeat attitude. Evan couldn't help but admire Linnet this afternoon. She had taken charge in a quiet but confident way and was handling everything with true diplomacy. Not only did she convey great pos-

itiveness, but she had managed to keep Tessa calm.
Evan knew how much Tessa was suffering; she had no
idea what to do, which was so unlike her.

Linnet's cell began to ring, and she got up, walked
over to one of the tall windows, stood talking for a moment. Evan knew it was Julian. Linnet had asked her to
be a bridesmaid at her marriage to Julian in the winter,
and she had been thrilled to accept. Gideon was to be
best man and India the other bridesmaid.

Evan's eyes wandered around the upstairs parlor.
Linnet had once explained to her that this had been
Emma Harte's favorite room, and she understood why.
It was gracious, charming, and spacious, with a high
ceiling and tall, leaded windows. There was a carved
mantel over the fireplace, and the walls were a sunny
daffodil color. Two large, comfortable sofas were covered in a floral chintz fabric vibrant with scarlet and
blues, greens, and pinks on a pale yellow background.
The Aubusson rug was obviously a valuable antique, as
were the pieces of furniture, made of mellow, ripe
woods. Linnet had also explained that the room had
never changed; it was simply refurbished with the
same fabrics and colors, a reflection of Emma's great
taste.

Evan loved art and was particularly interested in English landscapes. For a moment her gaze rested on the
museum-quality Turner hanging on a side wall; then it
swung to the oil painting above the mantelpiece. This
was of Paul McGill, the love of Emma's life; he was
wearing an army officer's uniform, and it had apparently been painted in the First World War. What a handsome man he was, she thought. No wonder Emma had
succumbed to his charms.

"Evan, let's go down to the kitchen and rustle up a
pot of tea," Linnet said. "And Margaret will make us

some smoked salmon sandwiches. I'm starved. I didn't have lunch."

Evan sat up with a start, brought out of her reverie by Linnet's voice. "Okay!" she answered at once, hating to be caught off guard.

"What about you, Tessa?" Linnet asked.

"I couldn't eat a thing! Food would choke me!" she cried, shaking her head almost violently.

"India? Do you want something, darling?" Linnet's auburn brow lifted questioningly.

Her cousin nodded. "Tea with lemon would be nice, and so would a smoked salmon sandwich. Thanks."

"I thought you'd had lunch," Linnet murmured, then stopped short. "Oh, but you never finished it, did you? Instead you drove here." Linnet stared hard at India, but her face remained quite expressionless.

"That's correct," India responded evenly, her own face as blank as her cousin's. But she couldn't help wondering if Linnet had guessed she had been with Dusty. No matter; Linnet was always on her side, whatever she did.

Jack Figg was seated at the large Georgian desk in the paneled library, his attention focused on the papers spread out in front of him.

After a moment he lifted his eyes and looked across at Linnet, who was seated on the sofa with Tessa. She was grim and intent, but holding her own as he knew she would. It was Tessa he was worried about.

Her face was stark, chalky, her eyes swollen and red rimmed from weeping. He understood how worried she was, and his heart went out to her. Aside from being a compassionate man, he had once lost a child in death, and his grief had been searing. Now he prayed that Adele was alive. Instinctively he felt that she was, and he wanted more than anything to trust those instincts. Goddamn it, she *has* to be alive, he thought, willing it to be so.

Seated on the other sofa near the fireplace were India Standish, whom he had known since she was a child, and Evan Hughes, the newcomer to the family, another great-granddaughter of Emma. He could see the concern on their faces as well, and he knew that all of these young women had been waiting for an update from him.

So had young Emsie and Desmond, who had rushed after him as he traversed the estate with Wiggs and Joe. They were now sitting on the upholstered library fender, obviously being extremely careful about opening their mouths. He had warned them that if they wanted to stay in the library they had to remain quiet.

Without preamble he began to speak to Linnet and Tessa. "It's turning four-thirty, and it's just over five and a half hours since Adele disappeared." He paused, his eyes sweeping over them, then he went on: "I'm afraid I don't know where she is. But I do know where she *isn't*, and that's here at Pennistone Royal. She's not in the fields, the meadows, the woods, or the gardens, which have all been thoroughly scoured. *Twice.* I've even had Wiggs drag the pond. Fortunately, all he found were weeds. Nor has Adele been seen in Pennistone Royal village, although two or three people did notice a black Mercedes driving through at high speed around lunchtime. That's obviously the same car which was seen here in the drive by Wiggs and the stable lads."

"What about Mark? What about Mark?" Tessa cried, clutching the rag doll to her as she had done on and off during the day. "Have you tried to find *him*?"

"I have indeed," Jack responded softly. "I spoke to his secretary, who told me he had taken a few days off—"

"He came up here to grab Adele!" Tessa interrupted,

her voice rising. "I bet anything he's in Yorkshire. With Jonathan Ainsley. They're in this together." She looked unusually agitated, and her eyes flashed.

"He could be up here, of course," Jack said, "but he's certainly *not* with Jonathan Ainsley. I've had one of my people check Jonathan's whereabouts, and he's in Hong Kong at this very moment. He's been there for several weeks."

"Perhaps Mark took Adele back to London with him, *if* he grabbed her," Linnet ventured, giving Jack a long, hard stare.

"He's not in his apartment, nor is he at the house in Hampstead. Both places have been checked out."

"But the house is locked up—" Tessa began; then her voice faltered when she saw the irritated expression flashing across Jack's face.

"Yes, the house *is* locked up, Tessa, and so is Mark's apartment. But we do have our ways of checking things out."

"I understand," she said meekly, leaning back against the sofa, ignoring Linnet, who had poked her in the ribs, warning her to shut up, she had no doubt.

"I've phoned Mark's mother in Gloucestershire," Jack continued. "She was not at home but was expected early this evening, according to someone called Dory."

"Dory's the housekeeper," Tessa volunteered. She cleared her throat and went on somewhat tentatively, "Mrs. Longden's a bit of a doting mother, but she's a decent woman. If Mark took Adele to her home, she would insist he bring her back to me at once."

"*If* his mother knew he had Adele without your permission," Jack pointed out. "Mark might not tell her. Anyway, I think that in all probability he's somewhere in Yorkshire. We must find him."

"But how?" India asked, frowning. "It's like looking for a needle in a haystack, isn't it?"

"Only too true," Jack agreed. "It's not going to be easy, even if we go to the police. We may have to do that, and soon. I've spoken at length to Gideon. I told him we might need to blast the news of Adele's abduction all over the media, starting with the Harte television network and newspapers. Gideon agrees. But we're not going to do that just yet. Before we go to those lengths, or go to the police, I want to give Mark a chance to bring Adele home to you, Tessa. Tonight, if that's at all possible."

"But what if it's not Mark who grabbed her?" Tessa asked, sounding tremulous again. "What if it's a kidnapping?"

"We'd have had a ransom note or some kind of communication from the kidnappers before now," Jack explained. "By the way, Tessa, at my request Gideon spoke to Toby in Los Angeles this afternoon. Toby hasn't been trying to get hold of you today. So I'm positive it was Mark calling you this morning in an effort to distract you while he took Adele. Or it was someone who was working with him."

"I didn't really recognize the voice," Tessa replied. "Although it did sound familiar, I suppose that's why I thought it must be Toby."

Leaning forward, his arms resting on the desk, Jack was thoughtful for a moment before saying, "In a short while I shall phone Mark's mother, explain what's happened. Hopefully she will cooperate, if she knows anything, that is. But if we don't have anything new or know where Mark is by about six-thirty, then I'll have no alternative but to inform the North Yorkshire police. I will also call Gideon to tell him to go ahead and issue a news bulletin about Adele's disappearance. I can't leave it much longer than that."

Tessa pressed a hand to her mouth.

Linnet exclaimed, "Once the Harte media companies go public here, it will be on American television. Mummy will have to be told before she hears it from another source."

Jack gave Linnet a fleeting smile. "I'll be calling her after I've been in touch with the police, if that becomes necessary. You and Tessa can speak to her as well. But the main thing now is to find out whether Mrs. Longden knows anything." Jack leaned back in the chair, trying to relax his tense muscles, and glanced across at the grandfather clock.

There was a sudden silence in the room. They were all lost in their own thoughts.

Tessa's mind was in a turmoil, her senses swimming. It was almost five, she had no idea where her child was, and she was more frantic than ever. She felt nauseated, and making a snap decision, she jumped up. "I need some fresh air!" she cried. "I feel as if I'm choking."

Immediately India pushed herself to her feet and hurried over to Tessa, took hold of her arm. "Come on, darling, let's go into the garden. After ten minutes outside you might feel better."

"I think I might," Tessa mumbled, pushing down the sickly feeling.

After Tessa and India had left, Evan cleared her throat and said to Jack, "I didn't want to bring this up in front of Tessa, but what if it's neither Mark nor kidnappers but a pedophile?"

A long sigh escaped Jack, and then he said, "That had crossed my mind." At this moment his mobile began to ring, and he answered it. "Figg here," he said, pressing it to his ear. Standing up, he walked over to the windows and stood listening to his caller, eventually murmured his thanks, and clicked off. Walking back to the desk, he told them, "That was one of my operatives who's been checking every hotel in the area. Mark Longden was definitely in Yorkshire three nights ago. He stayed at the Queen's Hotel in Leeds. And last night he was at the Swan in Harrogate. However, he has checked out of both places. So far my chap hasn't found him registered anywhere else."

"Perhaps he's staying at a private home," Linnet said, narrowing her eyes, endeavoring to indicate to Jack that she needed to speak to him alone.

"I'm sure Adele's with Mark, not strangers, and therefore she's quite safe," India said.

Tessa shivered, and gooseflesh sprang up on her arms. "You don't know what Mark's become, India! A *drunk, a drug addict*! He's not been himself for a long time, and he's an abuser. I've feared for my life . . ." She peered at India. "Did you know that?"

"Yes, your mother told me he'd been violent with you. It's shocking when you think about it—that he could become somebody totally different almost overnight."

"When he's in control of himself, he's fine. It's when he's under the influence of drink or drugs that he's dangerous, and quite inadvertently he could hurt Adele. That's what worries me."

"I understand. But as I said, we've got to remain positive." As she spoke, India got up from the wooden seat near the cuttings garden and suggested, "Why don't we go down to the old oak and sit for a while? It's nicer there."

"All right—" Tessa stopped, turned to India. "Perhaps we ought to go back inside. I'm afraid of missing something."

"Linnet will come and get us if there's any news. It'll do you good to be out of that room for a bit. It was becoming claustrophobic."

Tessa nodded, and the two of them walked down the path past the long terrace; they crossed the sloping lawn and finally came to a stop under the ancient tree. They sat together at the wrought-iron table but remained silent for a few moments.

It was Tessa who broke the silence. "I don't know what I'll do if anything happens to Adele. I love her so much, she's my life. I'd just fall apart forever; everything would become so meaningless without her."

"Come on, Tessa, don't talk like this," India exclaimed briskly. "Jack's going to get her back, you'll see. And you'll settle things amicably with Mark, the divorce will go through, and things will normalize."

"Oh, India, I do hope you're right, but he's being very greedy, you know. He wants the house, a lot of money, and joint custody of Adele. I don't think I could agree to joint custody. The house yes, but not joint custody."

"Once you've got Adele back, I think you ought to try to settle matters with him quickly. You know very well you hate things hanging over your head."

"You're right," Tessa agreed, suddenly brightening. "I'll talk to my solicitor, perhaps we can get everything moving faster. But it's only a few months since I left Mark."

"That's true, but so what? Anyway, Linnet and I agree that Mark has always been avaricious, so he's got his price, in my opinion. Buy him off, Tessa, it's the only way." India peered across the table at her cousin. "That's a Harte rule, remember."

Jack and Linnet had walked into the Stone Hall and stood talking quietly near the fireplace.

"Mark has friends in Yorkshire, where he could stay with Adele? Is that what you're suggesting?" Jack asked, squinting at Linnet in the dim early evening light.

"Yes," she answered and moved to turn on several lamps.

He stood watching her for a moment, thinking how much she resembled Emma Harte—well, a young Emma—with her red-gold hair and English-rose complexion. He'd gone to work for Emma when he was eighteen, forty years ago, and he had loved, respected, and admired her, found her the most exacting, exasperating, charming, bossy, and brilliant woman he had ever known. She had been his favorite boss. Now here was Linnet, the spitting image of her, and just as smart. She was his favorite amongst this younger generation because to him she exemplified so much of her family's heritage as well as the present. It's as if she has a foot in both worlds, he thought, and that makes her unique and very special to me.

"What are you thinking about, Jack?" Linnet asked, sitting in a chair. "You look as if you've just had a most brilliant thought."

"Not all that brilliant, but yes, I've had a rather interesting thought. Actually, it's a thought I'd had earlier and now it's come back. Look, Linnet, Jonathan Ainsley's in Hong Kong, that we know for certain, but the world's a village today, and he could very well be masterminding this situation with Mark and Adele. By phone, probably. He wouldn't want to put it in writing, in an e-mail or a fax. *And,* and this is very important, he's got a former girlfriend in Yorkshire, and she—"

"Of course, my mother's secretary, Eleanor! And what you're suggesting is that Jonathan is manipulating Mark long distance in order to hurt Paula and us, and that Mark goes along because he wants to spite Tessa.

Good thinking." She gave him a penetrating look. "Are you wondering if Eleanor's in on it?"

"I am indeed," Jack answered, flopping down in the chair opposite her, crossing his legs.

"If she is, she's being very foolish," Linnet murmured. "My mother's on to her . . . she has taken all power away. But she *is* an old flame of Jonathan's, and they've recently been in contact. Look, I'm not suggesting she'd help Mark take Adele, but perhaps she's offering him—"

"A safe haven for a few days?" Jack ventured, cutting in, then smiling at her.

"Yes, that's *my* thought."

"But would she risk her job, I wonder? She might tittle-tattle about your mother, but do you think she would really help Mark? It would make her an accessory after the fact in a kidnapping. And it *would* be construed as a kidnapping if we have to go to the police."

"But not everybody's familiar with the law, or as astute as you are, Jack. Maybe she just doesn't understand. Also, there's another thing we have to think about. Ellie does rather fancy herself, and she's still a lovely looking woman . . . so perhaps she harbors the idea that Jonathan is going to get back with her. And if that's the case, does working for my mother at the Leeds store really matter to her?"

"You've got a point there, Linnet. And Mark could have taken Adele to Ellie's home without her knowing what's going on, if we're to give her the benefit of the doubt." Jack now peered at his watch and stood up. "Time to make that call to Mrs. Longden, I think. Come on, Beauty, let's go on a fishing trip in Gloucestershire. Also, let's keep this conversation to ourselves, all right?"

"Absolutely," she said.

5

The moment Jack walked back into the library with Linnet he immediately picked up on the tension in the air. Tessa sat as rigid as stone on the sofa, her face strained, her eyes filled with suffering. India was next to her, also stiffly erect, her expression one of worry and anxiety. Evan, standing next to a window, was talking on her mobile, while Emsie and Desmond huddled on the upholstered brass fender, whispering together.

Linnet gave Jack a quick, knowing look, then hurried across to the other sofa, where she was instantly joined by Evan.

Jack strode to the desk and stood behind it, suddenly conscious of six pairs of eyes riveted unwaveringly on him. I've got to get this moving along, he thought. Time is of the essence now. He knew he was going to have to bring in the police and the media if he didn't succeed with Mark's mother. And there was the possibility that she didn't know anything. If that was the case, he would have calculated wrongly. He prayed that he had been right in his assumptions, that she *would* be able to help them solve this.

In his usual businesslike way he told them: "I'm now going to call Mark's mother." Fixing his penetrating gaze on Tessa, he added, "I'm putting the phone on the speaker so you can hear her responses, but I want you to be perfectly quiet." His eyes swept over the others. "And that goes for everyone else, too, of course. One other thing, Tessa. Will you have a word with your mother-in-law? It might be necessary."

There was only a moment's hesitation. "I'll talk to her, yes. We're not close, but as I said, she's a decent enough woman." There was a little pause; Tessa frowned, then added, "Mark's her only son, and she dotes on him. She'll be on his side no matter what. Even though he leads her a merry dance. But if you think it's necessary, I'll certainly come to the phone."

Jack nodded and sat down. Picking up the receiver, he pressed the speaker button and dialed.

A few moments later a woman answered. "Camden Lodge. Hello?" Her cultured voice was heard by everyone in the library.

"Is this Mrs. Hilary Longden?"

"Yes, this is she."

"Good evening, Mrs. Longden. My name's Jack Figg. I phoned earlier but you were out. You don't know me, Mrs. Longden, but you do know my employer, Mrs. Paula O'Neill."

"Well, of course. Tessa's mother. Have we met, Mr. Figg?" she asked, curiosity apparent in her tone, her voice pleasant.

"Briefly. At Tessa's marriage to Mark. But to get to the point, we have a problem, Mrs. Longden. I'm at Pennistone Royal with Tessa, and the reason I'm here is because Adele, your granddaughter, disappeared around eleven o'clock this morning and she still hasn't been found."

"Oh my God! How terrible! Tessa and Mark must be out of their minds with worry. Oh dear, oh dear, why haven't they found her? Surely she's somewhere on the estate? Oh, my poor little Adele, she must be so *frightened*. This is very upsetting. Can I speak to my son? And Tessa?" Her voice had risen an octave or two; it was obvious she was genuinely distressed. "And how can I be of help, Mr. Figg?" she asked.

"By telling me where your son is, Mrs. Longden," Jack answered in a voice echoing with cold determination.

"*Mark?* Do you mean he's not there with Tessa?" She was obviously startled by this fact.

"No, he's not. I have reason to believe that it's Mark who took Adele without informing Tessa," Jack announced. "I believe he has abducted her, and I must put certain things into oper——"

"Mark would never abduct Adele!" she cut in with great indignation. "That's preposterous! He's her father. . . . What on earth are you suggesting, Mr. Figg?"

"An abduction. Which will be construed as a *kidnapping* by the police and the law. Kidnappers get tough sentences, you know. And I *will* have to go to the police in the next few minutes. I can't put it off any longer. We've been unable to find Adele on the estate after several searches, nor can we locate Mark. So I have no alternative but to bring in law enforcement and the Harte media companies. They can issue news bulletins on television and the radio. We must find Adele as quickly as possible. *It's imperative.*"

"You're serious, aren't you, Mr. Figg?" She sounded shaken.

"Very, very serious, Mrs. Longden."

"But I don't understand," she began, obviously more unhinged than before. "Why would Mark take Adele without telling Tessa?"

Jack knew the woman was telling him the truth, and he made his voice softer as he explained. "Because of the divorce. It's becoming extremely bitter, he's trying to use Adele as a weapon against Tessa."

"*Divorce!* They're getting a divorce? But I don't know anything about that. Oh, this is so absurd, Mark would have told me. My son tells me everything. It just can't be," she asserted.

"Oh, it's true right enough," Jack answered. "Would you like to speak to your daughter-in-law now?"

"Yes, please."

"Just a moment." Jack beckoned to Tessa, who was by his side in a flash. Covering the mouthpiece, he said softly, "Be careful what you say. We need her."

Taking the receiver from him, Tessa murmured, "Hello, Mrs. Longden." She was willing herself to be controlled. "Jack is correct. Mark *has* taken Adele. There is no other explanation for her disappearance. She must be so upset and confused, poor little thing."

"Yes, yes, I know, you're right. But is it *true* about the divorce?"

"Yes, it is. I've tried hard to keep the marriage together, but it's not been working between us. We've been separated since June."

"Mark never told me!" Hilary Longden cried, tears in her voice. "How could he do that to me?"

"I don't know, but he did. And we do need to find Mark," Tessa repeated tensely. "And Adele."

"I don't know where he is, and I am telling you the truth!"

"Would Mr. Longden know?" Tessa probed.

"No, no, of course not. Mark's not a little boy, he doesn't check in with us. You know that, Tessa."

Tessa looked at Jack, made a grimace, and handed the phone back to him without a word.

"Jack Figg again, Mrs. Longden. Since you have no knowledge of Mark's whereabouts, I shall call in the North Yorkshire police. I do know Mark was in Yorkshire over the last few days, including last night, and I'm quite certain they'll find him fast enough. It's a pity, really, that I have to resort to this. And then there's going to be all the nasty publicity. That can't possibly do his reputation much good. Well, thanks for your courtesy in hearing me out, Mrs. Longden. Good night."

"Mr. Figg, please, don't hang up! I promise you I have no idea where Mark is, nor do I know anything about Adele's disappearance. However, I do have a mobile phone number Mark gave me last week. I think it might be a new one."

"Please give it to me."

"Just a minute. It's somewhere on this desk." A split second later she was reciting the number to him and extracting a promise to keep her abreast of the situation.

Jack hung up and said to Tessa, "Do you know this number?" He showed her the pad he had written it on.

She shook her head. "His mother's right. I think it's a new one."

Jack lifted the phone and dialed.

It was answered immediately. "Hello?"

"Mark?"

"Yes." There was a hesitancy in the voice, wariness.

"If you cut me off I will immediately ask the North Yorkshire police to go into action. And I'll tell the media about your abduction of Adele."

"What?" Mark exploded.

"Don't start with me, Mark. We know you have Adele. You've been spotted."

"Who the hell *is* this?" he demanded, anger in the tone.

"Jack Figg here. I work for Paula O'Neill. I'm with Tessa at Pennistone Royal. We want Adele returned. *At once.*"

"I don't have her. It's the first I've heard about an abduction."

"You don't sound too upset about your daughter's sudden disappearance. Which means that you know exactly where she is. *She's with you.* How do charges of kidnapping sound, Mark? Should help your career and your reputation no end, eh?"

"I don't know what you're talking about," he cried.

Tessa came to Jack, gave him a hard stare, and motioned to the phone. He handed it over at once.

"Mark, this is Tessa. Please bring Adele back."

"Why am I being accused in this way?" he demanded, anger echoing again.

"Because you took her this morning. We know you did. Wiggs saw you. Please, please bring her back to me. For Adele's sake."

"I told you, I don't have her!"

"Yes, you do. Don't play games with me, Mark."

There was a silence, and she wondered if she had lost him when he suddenly spoke again. "You won't get her back until you meet my terms."

"Anything you want," she said swiftly, relief flooding through her.

"Joint custody, for starters," Mark intoned.

"The solicitors will work all that out. But you can have the house in Hampstead, the cars, a financial settlement, as you wanted."

"Joint custody," he repeated, icy cold.

Jack's cell phone began to ring, and he answered, walking closer to the window.

Tessa's eyes followed Jack; she said into the phone, "The solicitors will have to get together to work things out." She took a deep breath and against her better judgment added, "If not joint custody then certainly a lot of access."

Suddenly Jack was hurrying toward her, a grim smile on his face. When he came to a standstill, he took the receiver from her unceremoniously and said, "Jack Figg here. I've just been speaking to the North Yorkshire police on the other line. They are on their way to pick you up. We know you are at the Spa Hotel in Ripon with Adele. Registered under the name of William Stone."

Jack paused when he heard the surprised intake of breath at the other end of the phone. "If you leave now, you can be here at Pennistone Royal in half an hour and deal with me. Or you can wait for the police to pick you up in the next fifteen minutes. Your choice, mate."

"I'm leaving now," Mark said abruptly, the bluster gone from his voice.

"With Adele?"

"Yes, I'm bringing her," he mumbled and clicked off.

Jack replaced the receiver and looked at Tessa, a triumphant gleam in his light gray eyes. "That was one of my operatives on my mobile. When he discovered that a man with a little girl was staying at the Spa in Ripon, he double-checked with a contact he has there. The name William Stone didn't ring a bell with Pete, but he thought he'd better tell me, and of course I knew it was Mark at once."

"Thank God!" Tessa touched Jack's arm. "Thanks, Jack, thank you so much."

Jack stepped closer, pulled her into his arms, and

hugged her. "Before you can say Jack Robinson you'll have Adele back with you. Now come on, we've quite a lot to do before he arrives."

Tessa nodded and then burst into tears. "It's relief," he said to her gently and led her over to the sofa. Looking at India, he went on, "It's a normal reaction, she's been pent up with tension all day. Sit with her, she'll be fine soon."

Beckoning to Desmond and Emsie, Jack continued, "I need you two to do a couple of things for me."

"Yes, Jack!" Desmond exclaimed, rushing over with Emsie in his wake, her face eager, her dark eyes bright with earnestness.

"Desmond, please go and find Wiggs and tell him that Adele should be back within half an hour. But don't say anything else, and don't mention Mark. Okay?"

Desmond nodded, then volunteered, "And, Jack, when you talk to Mums, tell her we need to do something about security here. Anybody can come and go as they please."

"I've made a note to do that, Desmond. I've a plan for a proper security system in the works," Jack replied and then smiled at Emsie. "Go and tell Margaret and Joe that Adele is coming back soon, and please ask Margaret to bring in some ice and a tray of drinks. I certainly need a vodka, and I'm sure everyone else wants something, too."

The two youngsters hurried out, and Linnet walked across to Jack and hugged him. "Thanks, Jack, thanks for everything you've done."

"Thanks not necessary, Beauty." He stared at her intently, then said in a low voice, "I pushed the envelope a bit, but I felt I was doing the right thing. Thank God it worked out all right. Mark became scared when I said the police were on the way. It sobered him up."

"Why? Was he drunk?" Linnet asked swiftly, raising a brow.

"Just a manner of speaking."

"*Had* you called the North Yorkshire police, Jack, or were you bluffing?"

"Bluffing, Beauty. But when Pete, my operative checking the local hotels, mentioned the name William Stone, I remembered what you'd told me once about Mark using that name as a pseudonym for his client Jonathan Ainsley."

"I'm glad I told you."

He smiled, went to the desk, and looked at the pad where he had made voluminous notes.

A moment later Evan was standing in front of the desk, and he glanced up, his eyes questioning.

"Thanks for being such a calming influence, Jack. Would it be all right if I told Robin that Jonathan *is* in Hong Kong? He was wondering where his son was when I had lunch with him today. It will ease his mind knowing Jonathan's not in the country."

"By all means, Evan."

A moment later Linnet and Evan went to sit with Tessa and India, gently reassuring Tessa that everything was going to be all right. She accepted their words and tried to smile. But the tension was deeply embedded in her, and she was aware that her life had been changed forever by the events of the day, that she wouldn't feel peace until her child was safely by her side. Mark, obviously, was capable of anything.

Gideon Harte sat at his desk in the offices of the Yorkshire Consolidated Newspaper Company in South East London, not far from the famed Fleet Street. Although the renowned street of ink was still there, many of the great national daily newspapers had moved to quarters elsewhere.

Overlooking a portion of the Thames, Gideon's office was spacious and light filled, with lots of plate-glass windows shaded by silver metal-mesh panels. It was discreetly decorated in shades of white and gray, and there were lots of books banked in low-slung, black-lacquered shelves that rode across a long back wall. His black-lacquered desk was empty, the way he liked it, with a few memos in simple black trays, a dictionary, a thesaurus, and antique crystal ink pots on a silver tray.

Pushing his chair back, Gideon lifted his feet to the desk and leaned back in the chair, watching the large modern clock on the wall straight ahead. Once the hands hit six forty-five, he lowered his legs, sat up straight, and picked up the phone. He dialed The Peninsula hotel in Beverly Hills and waited.

When the operator answered, he said, "Toby Harte, please."

A moment later his brother was saying, "Hello? Toby Harte here."

"It's me, Toby. Gid. And it's good news. Jack's found Mark. He's admitted he has Adele, and he's on his way to Pennistone Royal now bringing her back to Tessa."

"Thank God! What a bastard he is, Gid, taking his own child that way, and all to get back at poor Tessa. He should be— Well, I can't think of anything quite bad enough to do to that shit!"

Gid laughed. "How about horsewhipped, to use an old-fashioned term? Or even better, what about hung, drawn, and quartered?"

Toby also laughed and said, "I'll punch him in the face a few times myself, and I'll be relieved when I know Adele is actually with Tessa at the house. Only then will I relax. I don't trust that bugger."

"I agree with you. But I promised to let you know as soon as I had *some* news, and I just hung up on Jack. Evan had called me a few minutes before to pass the word for him. But then Jack called himself, wanted to talk to me about security. Not only at Pennistone Royal, which is very vulnerable, as we now know, but at all of our homes, and I think he's right. They should have more protection."

"Agreed. And Jack's the right chap to set everything up. By the way, do Paula and Shane know anything yet, Gid?"

"God, no! And don't get involved. Don't tell our parents, because you know our mother will pass it on to Paula. They're as thick as thieves.

"Listen to this. Jack told me one of his operatives found out that a man with a small child was registered at the Spa Hotel in Ripon—your old hunting ground, if you recall. Anyway, the man had registered under the name William Stone. It meant nothing to Jack's chap, but the minute Jack heard it he knew it had to be Mark. William Stone equals Jonathan Ainsley. That's his pseudonym."

"Oh Christ, you're right! Was Jonathan involved, do you think?" Toby wondered.

"I've no idea," Gideon answered, "but it's crossed Tessa's mind and Linnet's, not to mention Jack's, so Evan told me."

"I see. Paula will have to be told eventually, you know; something like this can't be shoved under the rug."

"It couldn't be anyway, because Tessa's promised Mark Longden the earth to bring Adele back to her, and she's going to have to discuss all that with her mother and Shane. It could involve millions, according to Linnet. I guess right now Longden is harping on about joint custody, so Tessa is trying to buy him off. Everybody has a price. Emma's rule."

"Emma was right. And that joint custody bit won't sit well with Tessa. Thank God Adrianna and I don't have any kids, it certainly makes things easier."

"Are you and Adrianna definitely getting the divorce, then, Toby?" Gideon asked.

"We are, but at least it's amicable. We both want it, Gid. She's decided she prefers to live and work in Hollywood, and I want to be in London. Have to be, when you consider my responsibilities. The marriage was a big mistake, in all truthfulness. But she's being decent, believe it or not. . . . She's not a gold digger, far from it. Adrianna doesn't want alimony. She'd like me to buy her a small flat in London, so she can have a base. You know, one foot each side of the Atlantic, and I agreed. Actually, though, I'm thinking of letting her have our flat. I've never really liked it, and she has always loved it."

"I felt you wanted a divorce, so I'm glad for you, Toby. And Dad will be, too. He's looking for grandchildren from you, and he never thought Adrianna was the motherly type."

Toby began to chuckle. "Never a truer word spoken by our dear dad." There was a moment's hesitation before Toby went on. "Do you think I can call Tessa? I've been so worried about her, and I do want her to know I'm here for her, whatever she needs."

"Why shouldn't you phone her, Toby? You and she have been joined at the hip all your lives. And she knows you're there for her. But of course, give her a ring."

"I wouldn't want to call her just when she was getting Adele back. I wouldn't want to interrupt that."

"You've got a few minutes before Mark arrives at the house. So call her now and give her my love."

"I will. Everything's all right between you and Evan, isn't it, Gid?"

"Absolutely. Never been better. Talk to you later."

"Sure thing, Gideon."

Gideon leaned back in his chair after hanging up the phone, propped his feet on the desk again, and closed his eyes. He began to think about Evan Hughes.

Things *were* better between them, even though she was constantly worrying about her father's impending trip to England. But she's really worrying about what he'll think of *me,* and of Robin Ainsley, Gideon suddenly decided, and wished then that she wouldn't invent problems when they didn't exist. The problem was Evan herself, Gideon now decided. She needed everybody to like the people she liked, and that wasn't the way the world was.

He knew he wanted to make a life with Evan. And ever since the beginning of their relationship, he had felt she wanted to make a life with him. But he had come to the conclusion she couldn't make that commitment to him because of her father and his peculiar attitude about the Hartes.

Gideon sighed. He would be delighted when her father finally did arrive from New York. Then everything would be out in the open. In the meantime, he had a national daily to get out. With his father away, the *Daily Gazette* was under his aegis. Opening his eyes and swinging his feet to the carpet, he stood up, retrieved his mobile from the desk, and headed for the newsroom, one of the places he loved to be.

Tessa could hardly sit still, and finally she stood up and exclaimed to Jack, "I just can't stand it! I've got to go to the front door and wait for Adele there."

"I know, I know. Go ahead, Tessa. Mark should be arriving at any moment now. Come to think of it, I'd better accompany you." Jack took hold of her arm and led her to the Stone Hall.

After taking only one step into the Stone Hall, Tessa stopped dead in her tracks and stared at Jack. "The rag doll! The first thing she'll ask for is her Reggi. Hang on a minute, whilst I go and get it. I left it in the library."

He nodded, his eyes following her as she retraced their steps. She had hugged that doll to her for half the day, saying time and again to them all that Adele was undoubtedly heartbroken because she'd lost it. He sighed. This was one hell of a mess, a bitter separation that would only become more acrimonious.

When Paula had brought him in a few weeks ago to investigate Mark Longden, he had realized how troubled she was about her daughter's husband. Paula was not the type of person to pry into people's lives; she had great respect for privacy. Once he had begun to dig, though, Jack was glad she had taken the steps she had; he hadn't liked what he had discovered about Mark Longden, and he had lost no time in bringing the information to Paula.

Longden was very entangled with Paula's cousin Jonathan Ainsley, her great enemy and the enemy of the entire Harte family. Jonathan had hired Longden as the architect of his new mansion in Thirsk, and Longden had soon fallen under Jonathan's bad influence. Booze and drugs and other women were the perks Mark was offered. He had indulged and become addicted. Paula had been as appalled as Jack was and worried for Tessa because of Mark's violence toward her. Even though they had separated, there was no telling what Mark Longden might do to her. Witness today. Snatching Adele was both cruel and dangerous. It's blackmail, Jack thought, he set out to blackmail her and he succeeded. He's after money, big money, as well as joint custody. He won't get that, not with the evidence I have about his private life. But Paula will give him the money just to get rid of him.

"Here I am!" Tessa exclaimed, hurrying back into the Stone Hall, the rag doll in her hand. "You don't know how she loves this bit of nothing. To her it's the most precious thing in the world. . . ." Tessa paused, looked at Jack, and said softly, "As she is the most precious thing to me. Thank you again, Jack, for getting her back."

"I know that, Tess. And you ought to know by now that I'll always help you any way I can. Why, I've known you since you were Adele's age, and you looked just like she looks now."

"Mummy always says she's the spitting image of me."

They crossed the small entrance hall, Jack opened the front door, and they both stepped out onto the top step. The sky was pale blue and bright, the light crystalline on this August evening, and it was warm. Yet he noticed that Tessa shivered slightly as she stared toward the drive, and he saw the strain settling on her face once more. She had relaxed for only a moment, and he knew she could barely contain herself as she waited for Adele.

They glanced at each other as they heard wheels on the gravel drive, and within seconds a black Mercedes was turning the bend.

Tessa started to move, but Jack restrained her. "I know you long to hold her in your arms, but let us wait for a moment, Tessa. I need to see how Adele behaves when he takes her out of the car. I need to know if she's upset and, most important, if she's afraid of her father. Those things are significant for the divorce, you see."

"I understand," Tessa mumbled, but her agitation was growing.

The car finally came to a standstill in the area near the privet hedge that was used for parking. She wished he'd driven right up to the front door.

Mark alighted, glanced across at Tessa and Jack in the doorway, then went around and lifted Adele out of the car.

For a moment it seemed as though he was going to carry her over, but Adele began to struggle in his arms, and he had no option but to put her down. The child shot away from him, shouting, "Mumma! Mumma!" moving as fast as her little legs would carry her. "I lost Reggi," she shouted and began to sob loudly.

Tessa ran to meet her, afraid that the three-year-old was going to stumble and hurt herself, and as she drew close Tessa noticed how disheveled Adele looked; her silver-gilt hair was a mess, her face had black smudges on it and what looked like raspberry jam around her mouth, and her pale blue shirt and shorts were grubby.

A split second later Tessa was showing Adele the rag doll, exclaiming, "Look, here's Reggi, I found her for you, darling."

"Oh, Mumma. It's my Reggi!" Adele's sobbing instantly stopped, and she lifted her tearstained face to her mother, giving her a huge smile as she clutched the rag doll to her.

Tessa, who was kneeling, pushed away her daughter's tears, smiled back, and took Adele in her arms, filled with love for her defenseless little girl. And mingling with that love was enormous relief that she was now safely home. Out of the corner of her eye, Tessa saw Mark approaching. Instantly she let go of Adele and stood up. Then she scooped the child into her arms and took a step backward, wanting to put distance between herself and Mark.

When he drew to a standstill, he glanced at Jack and then addressed Tessa. "Shall we have our little talk?"

"Let's do it later. *Please*. Adele must be awfully tired, perhaps even hungry. Have you fed her today?"

"Of course I've fed her, you stupid fool! I love my child, why wouldn't I feed her!" he cried, glaring, his face flushed.

Tessa glared back at him, hating every fiber of his being.

"Now, now, Mark," Jack said quietly, stepping forward protectively, motioning for Tessa to go into the vestibule. "Angry words aren't going to get you anywhere. And certainly we shouldn't be doing business in front of your daughter. Or on the doorstep, for that matter." Looking over his shoulder at Tessa, who stood just behind him, he said, "Perhaps we could talk to Mark for a few minutes? Inside?"

Filled with anger, and anxious to bathe and feed her daughter, Tessa simply nodded, swung around, and walked into the Stone Hall. Jack caught up with her and said, "Why don't you take Adele into the library? She'll be all right with the others for a few minutes, and that's all this is going to take, I can assure you. Just leave it to me."

"All right, Jack, but I hope it *is* only a few minutes." She hurried across the vast hall, heading for the library. When she pushed open the door and went in, everyone clapped and laughed and surged around her, making a fuss over Adele, who laughed happily, her eyes sparkling, and accepted all their kisses.

A moment later, just as Tessa was turning to leave the room, Elvira rushed in, her face drained of color, her eyes filled with apprehension.

"Elvira!" Tessa cried when she saw the nanny. "Did you just get back from Leeds?"

"I did, Mrs. Longden, and Margaret and Joe told me what happened to Adele today. Oh, Mrs. Longden, I'm so sorry, I wish I hadn't taken the day off, I wish I'd been here . . ." Her voice trailed off, and she looked suddenly uncertain what to do next.

"Elvi," Adele said, smiling at her, "I lost Reggi. Mumma found her. Look." She showed Elvira the rag doll.

"I'm glad she's safe," Elvira murmured to the child, looking up at Tessa as she spoke.

"Take her for a few minutes, Elvira, please, I have to speak to Mr. Longden," Tessa said and handed Adele to the nanny.

Tessa's eyes then settled on Linnet. "I'll be right back. Jack's in charge out there, and he knows what he's doing."

"He certainly does," Linnet concurred. "He's the best."

Tessa found Jack and Mark sitting opposite each other near the Stone Hall fireplace. Mark was angry, while Jack seemed unperturbed. He's holding all the cards, she suddenly thought, remembering some of the things Jack had told her mother.

Not wanting to make it appear that she was ready to have a long discussion, Tessa remained standing, positioning herself near the soaring stone fireplace.

Jack looked across at her and said in a soft but distinct voice, "I told Mark you would be quite happy to reiterate the terms you had given him earlier on the phone. It seems he'd like to hear them again."

"You can have the house in Hampstead," Tessa began, "which is actually *mine*, since my mother gave it to me, not to us. You can also have the two cars which are garaged there. I'll throw in all of the contents of the house as well, except for a few paintings and other items that are mine, and my other personal possessions, such as clothes, that sort of thing. And I will make a financial settlement on you."

"I want the jewelry back. The pieces I gave you."

"That's certainly fine by me," she said, thinking that every piece was worthless.

"And I want joint custody of Adele."

"That I can't promise," Tessa replied, her voice sud denly trembling, "but I will give you fair access."

"Joint custody," he snapped nastily.

"No, Mark, I can't agree to that. Not after today."

"We'll see what the divorce courts have to say," he threatened.

Jack cleared his throat. "If you don't mind me saying so, I think the divorce courts will be in Tessa's favor."

"No way! A father has as many rights as the mother these days."

"But you *are* rather a problematic father."

"What the hell does that mean?" Mark demanded, staring at Jack through blazing eyes.

"I don't want to go into it now, since your solicitor and Tessa's will be discussing everything shortly. But perhaps I should just add that we have quite a lot of information about your indulgences, your rather . . . *decadent* lifestyle. Do I need to say more?" Jack gave the younger man a penetrating look, rose, and went to stand next to Tessa.

Leaping to his feet, Mark cried, "This sounds like bloody blackmail to me!"

"Call it what you will," Jack murmured. "But I do have the evidence to prove that I am speaking the truth. And by the bye, it's the kind of evidence that a judge would certainly be interested in hearing, especially since it concerns a child's welfare."

Glaring first at Jack and then at Tessa, Mark shouted, "You haven't heard the last of me!"

"Nor have you heard the last of me, mate," Jack retorted. "And now, under the circumstances, I think it's about time you left. I'll escort you to the door."

6

Paula O'Neill stood at one of the windows in the bedroom of the Fifth Avenue apartment, looking out at the view of Central Park. It was sunny and hot but not humid outside, and there was a sparkle to the day. The leafy domes of the trees in the park were brilliantly green against the azure sky, and rising beyond them the skyline of Manhattan looked superb. Bright sunshine glanced off thousands of windows, making the skyscrapers appear almost to shimmer in the clear light.

There's no city like it anywhere else in the world, she thought. She had loved New York ever since she had come here as a child with her grandmother; Emma had also been addicted to this electric, exciting, whirlwind city—where anything was possible. Emma frequently said this to her, often adding, "The sky's the limit here, Paula. And don't you ever forget it."

Turning away from the window, Paula walked across the bedroom and into the entrance foyer, her high heels clicking against the black-and-white marble floor as she headed toward the library, one of her favorite rooms in the apartment. It had been her grandfather's favorite, too, according to Emma, who had once confided that he had loved the dark wood paneling on the walls, the many books bound in red leather, the Georgian antiques she had chosen, the warmth of dark rose brocade hanging at the windows and used on the sofas. "He used to say it was masculine without being stuffy and heavy," her grandmother had explained, "but then he usually did like the way I decorated our homes."

Paul McGill had bought the Fifth Avenue apartment for Emma and himself in the 1930s; it was a spacious duplex designed by the renowned architect Rosario Candela in 1931. After Paul's untimely death in 1939, Emma had contemplated selling it, but only briefly. There was a war on, and she was far too preoccupied with the Blitz in London to worry about the apartment in Manhattan. "And I'm glad I didn't sell it," Emma had once told Paula, "because it means we can live here in comfort and privacy when we come to the States instead of having to stay in hotels."

Paula and her brother, Philip, had inherited the apartment jointly upon Emma's death, but it was also used by other members of the family when they came to America, particularly the cousins Emily and Winston Harte, and Emily's sister Amanda Linde, who flew in all the time. Everyone loved it, took great pride in its uncommon beauty; luxurious and comfortable without being ostentatious, it bore Emma Harte's imprint in every way and was a reflection of her critical eye for color and the finest in antiques and paintings.

Now, as she seated herself at the desk, Paula felt a sense of awe about her grandmother and her achievements. It was mind-boggling really when she considered everything that Grandy had accomplished in her life—and she a poor girl from Fairley, a mill village on the Yorkshire moors, who had started working at the age of twelve as a servant for the Fairleys of Fairley Hall.

However did she do it? Paula wondered. Where did it come from, this talent, this infallible taste, this understanding of art? And where did her drive and energy, her strength and stamina come from? How did she summon up that indomitability, that desire to scale the mountaintops? How on earth did that little servant girl become such a great lady, such a successful tycoon, so absolutely inimitable? Emma Harte almost single-handedly had created an international business empire worth billions of pounds today, and had left her descendants an extraordinary legacy of power, wealth, and privilege.

There has never been anyone like her, Paula thought, still gazing into space. Emma was a one-off; they threw away the mold after they made her.

The phone rang, and Paula automatically reached for it. "Hello?"

"Hello, Mummy, it's me, Linnet."

"Darling, what a nice surprise! How's everyone? How's the remodeling of the stores coming along?" Paula asked, her joy at hearing her daughter's voice echoing in her own.

"Oh, very well, I'm pleased . . ." Linnet paused, took a deep breath, said quickly, "Mummy, listen, something happened today. It's all right now, everything's fine. Honestly. But I thought I'd better fill you in. And—"

"What happened, Linnet?" Paula cut in swiftly. "I hope everyone's all right?" She had a sudden remembrance of the day her cousin Winston Harte had called Shane in Connecticut to break the news that her father and her husband were dead, killed in an avalanche in

Chamonix. Gooseflesh speckled her arms, and she tensed, wondering what bad news was coming now.

"Yes, yes, all's okay," Linnet exclaimed and told her what had happened.

"Oh God, no! Not Adele! But she *has* been found? You did say everyone was all right?"

"Yes, she's safely back at Pennistone Royal again, with Tessa." There was a pause, then Linnet added, "I brought Jack in, and here he is, Mummy. I'll come back to you in a few minutes."

"Hello, Paula," Jack said.

"Hello, Jack, I'm so glad you're there," Paula answered, and she thought her voice sounded unnatural.

"Everybody's quite safe," he went on in his most reassuring voice. He had always adored Paula; there were those in the family who believed he'd been secretly in love with her for years. "As Linnet just told you, the child is unharmed. Now, Paula, I must insist you do something about security here. You don't have much at all. Just burglar alarms . . . it's downright dangerous."

"Shane's mentioned it several times lately. I don't think any of us envisioned something like this . . . *kidnapping* happening, though. But you're right, security has become extremely important. Can you do it for us, Jack?"

"Yes, I'll get the best experts on it at once. Tomorrow, in fact."

"That's a good idea, and thank you for everything you've done for us. I'll be forever grateful."

"Just know I'm always here for you," he said.

"Can I speak to Tessa, Jack?"

"Yes indeed, she's standing right next to me, and I'll talk to you later, Paula."

"Hello, Mummy," Tessa began and stopped abruptly, choking up.

"Tessa darling, I'm so sorry this happened, so very sorry. You must have gone through hell today."

"I did," Tessa answered. "But I'm happy to say Adele is perfectly fine, and she doesn't seem at all upset, other than she thought she'd lost her rag doll. She's fast asleep now, and Elvira is sleeping in her room tonight. Mummy, Mark was beastly. He did this because he wanted to get at me. It was wrong that he used Adele in this way. Oh, and he wants joint custody."

"He'll never get it, Tessa, be assured of that. When Jack investigated Mark, he came up with quite a lot of unsavory information, and I feel certain he will be viewed as an unfit father by the courts. What did you promise him, darling, in order to get Adele back?"

"Only those things we'd discussed earlier. The Hampstead house, the cars garaged there, and a financial settlement. Nothing more, and I was wary about the custody. I said the lawyers will have to talk it through."

"Good girl. And do let the legal team handle things from now on."

"Oh, I will, Mummy, but I had to offer something to get him to bring Adele home."

"I know you did. I think you did very well indeed. And one thing we must do is make sure the price is right. You don't want Mark around your neck like an albatross for the rest of your life."

"Can I stay up here? Jack says it'll be perfectly safe, that Mark won't come troubling me again. And he has the front and back gates locked tonight. He can make it really secure here."

"Yes, I think you should stay, as you'd planned, and of course Jack is right about it being made secure, and also about Mark, who's probably already regretting that he did this terrible thing. How're Emsie and Desmond? I suppose they were there when this happened?"

"They were out riding. But they want to say hello. I'll pass the phone, Mummy."

After she had hung up, Paula sat for a while, mulling over everything Jack and her children had told her; she had also spoken to India and Evan. It seemed to be a general consensus that Jonathan Ainsley was involved somehow.

Jonathan Ainsley. Her first cousin and bitter enemy. Enemy of her immediate family. Enemy of the entire Harte clan. And the O'Neills and the Kallinskis as well, since they were all so closely connected. She knew he had hated her and Emily, Winston and Shane, since their childhood, when he had no reason to hate them. He was, very simply, a bad person, riddled with envy and greed.

Lately he had pulled Mark Longden into his orbit by hiring him to design his new home in North Yorkshire. Mark had taken the bait and quickly been lured into Jonathan's decadent social life, and inevitably, he had become Jonathan's pawn. Her cousin hadn't had to do anything himself to hurt her—simply whisper a few choice words in Mark Longden's ear about Tessa.

She did not know how to deal with Jonathan at this moment, though she would eventually find a way to out-wit him. But she did know how to handle Mark, render him powerless against her daughter and grandchild. And she would put her plans in motion tomorrow.

She glanced at the carriage clock on the desk, saw that it was after five, and wondered what had happened to Emily. She couldn't still be at the board meeting at Harte Enterprises, could she? But of course she could. Emily was diligent and—

"Sorry I'm so late getting back!" Emily exclaimed, hurrying into the library, her face slightly flushed. "Oh good, it's lovely and cool in here. It's a furnace outside—" Emily suddenly broke off, staring at her cousin and frowning. "What's wrong, Paula? You look quite awful."

"Hello, Emily," Paula answered, walking around the desk and kissing her cousin on the cheek. "I just had a bit of a shock actually, but everything's all right. I'll tell you about it in a moment. Shall we have a cup of tea? Or do you want iced tea?"

Sitting down on the sofa without taking her eyes off Paula, Emily said, "I think I'd like iced tea for a change. Shall I go and tell Alice?"

"No, no, I'll do it. And will Winston be back from Toronto? I need to tell her how many we'll be for dinner."

"It's still just you and me, darling. Winston won't make it out today. Maybe tomorrow, and I'm assuming Shane is coming on Friday as planned."

"That's correct. He's taking the morning plane from Nassau. So yes, we're a couple of grass widows tonight." As she spoke Paula glided out of the room, went to the kitchen, spoke to Alice, the housekeeper, and returned.

She went over to the seating arrangement, sat down in a chair facing Emily, and explained, "There's been a bit of a fuss at Pennistone Royal today." Speaking with her usual conciseness, Paula told Emily everything that had happened in Yorkshire.

"What a ghastly day poor Tessa must've had, and thank God it all ended well. Almost anything could have gone wrong, you know. And listen, Paula"—Emily leaned forward and continued in a much quieter, confiding voice—"I tend to agree with Linnet and Tessa, bloody Jonathan probably *was* involved. He *has* to be dealt with—somehow."

"I agree, but I'm not sure what to do about him at this moment, Em. However, I think I have a way to make Mark Longden toe the line. I've come up with a plan in the last half hour. And I intend to set it in motion tomorrow."

After Emily had gone to her room to relax until dinner, Paula sat for a while at the desk, going over her engagements for the next few days. But the striking of the clock in the hall made her sit up with a start, and her concentration fled.

Leaning back in her chair, she sat thinking about Tessa and her granddaughter, Adele, and the things that had happened at Pennistone Royal that day. Thank God they were safe. She wished Shane were here. Turning her head, she focused on the photographs on a nearby circular table, then rose, walked over to it.

Seating herself in the adjacent chair, she picked up a silver-framed picture of Shane, and a smile broke across her face. It had been taken many years ago, when he was about twenty-six, and she couldn't help thinking how wonderful he looked, so handsome, debonair even then. What was it Emma had always said about him? That he had an intense glamour. And that was the truth. She had never known anyone, man or woman, with that kind of glamour. Dark hair, dark eyes, he was Black Irish through and through, and she had always teased him, said he had kissed the Blarney Stone. "Inherited the gift of the gab from my grandfather," he answered back, and she usually responded, "Emma says Blackie's kissed three Blarney Stones!"

It's funny how life works out, she suddenly thought, her eyes settling on a photograph of Tessa and Lorne with Shane. He had brought them up as his own since they'd been toddlers, and she knew how much Lorne loved Shane, but she sometimes wondered about Tessa's feelings for him.

Of course she loves him, Paula told herself. Everyone

has always loved Shane. Grandy. My mother. Winston Harte, his best friend and sparring partner since they were boys. And Emily. And Sally and Anthony Standish. Shane, if the truth be known, was the most popular person in the three clans, and anywhere else!

Her eyes moved on, and she laughed out loud when they fell upon a photograph taken when they were all teenagers: a picture of them taken one summer at Heron's Nest, Emma's house in Scarborough by the sea. It had been the year the boys had formed their own band. The Herons, they called themselves, and of course it was Shane who was the leader. He also played the piano and was the vocalist. Alexander, her beloved Sandy, sadly dead these long years, had played the drums and cymbals. Michael Kallinski had warbled the harmonica, Jonathan scraped the violin, Philip blew the flute. But it had been Winston who considered himself the most important, the most talented member of the ensemble. He had modeled himself on Bix Beiderbecke, after seeing the film *Young Man with a Horn,* and thought he was the bee's knees. They had wondered out loud where he learned to play the trumpet, and Emma had smiled thinly and said he hadn't, and that was the trouble. What fun they had had together in those days.

Shane had been part of her life for as long as she could remember. She had become conscious of him when she was four and he was eight and had tagged along after him.

One summer afternoon Shane had told her he had a wonderful idea. He said she was to become Queen Boadicea, leader of the early Britons, and he would be her consort, her lord. "But we have to look right," Shane had confided. "How should we look?" she had asked him, her violet eyes full of love and pride at being his friend even then. "We have to be blue," the eight-year-old boy had explained. And then proceeded to paint her blue all over, after he undressed her. She had insisted on keeping her knickers on, being a modest child. And later Emma had been thankful she had. At least some pores had been allowed to breathe, and so she had not died. Somehow, Shane had coaxed her into painting him blue to match, keeping his underpants on, and there was hell to pay when Blackie came over at Emma's request to chastise his grandson. "Young scallywag," Blackie had pronounced.

Paula smiled inwardly, thinking of the turpentine baths Emma and Blackie had given them . . . worse than any thrashing.

Blue, she thought, seeing in her mind's eye her lovely blue marbles, which Shane had managed to lose. He had presented her with some new ones, but they weren't as nice, and she had been put out with him for a long time.

And then one day, when they were grown up, he had given her a small red leather box, and when she had opened it she had been entranced by the sapphire earrings inside. Leaning down, kissing her, Shane had said, "I hope these will satisfy you. . . . They are in place of those blue marbles I lost when you were six, or somewhere thereabouts."

And one day much later she had married Shane.

Yes, life *is* strange, she thought again. They had grown up together, been inseparable even as teenagers, and then he had gone off to boarding school, later university, and she had seen less of him.

And she had met Jim Fairley, who worked for Emma, and they had fallen in love. Or so she thought. And she had married Jim, had had the twins, Tessa and Lorne.

Shane had moved to New York to run the O'Neill Hotels chain on that side of the Atlantic. But he had never married, and one day, when her marriage was falling apart, they had suddenly understood that they were in love with each other and always had been.

They had discovered this in Shane's wonderful old barn in New Milford, an oasis of peace in the Connecticut countryside. And they had vowed to be together always. *Somehow.* Because it was meant to be.

Life plays funny tricks, she now murmured to herself. Jim Fairley and her father, David Amory, on a skiing holiday in Chamonix, had been killed in an avalanche. Winston and Emily had decided not to go skiing that day and so had escaped death. Their time wasn't up, Paula whispered. That's what Emma always used to say: "You go on living until your time's up."

For a long time she had grieved for Jim and her father, and suffered devastating guilt. She had sent Shane away because of her guilt. But eventually she had realized how much she loved him and needed him, had understood he was her entire life. He still was.

Evan's mother, Marietta Hughes, was furious.

Once again Owen had behaved in the most high-handed way, and she felt like strangling him. But because her mother had always told her no man was worth murdering because of the dire consequences to oneself, she had decided against this rather drastic solution.

Flight for several hours was the only way she could settle the score and calm herself. And so she grabbed her handbag, picked up the shopping bag she had just taken out of the wardrobe, where it had been hidden behind her clothes for days, and left the suite. She didn't even go into the bedroom to say good-bye to him. He would worry when he discovered she had gone.

As she took the elevator down to the hotel lobby, she prayed she wouldn't run into the hotel proprietors, George and Arlette Thomas, especially Arlette, who constantly wanted to take her for tea or coffee in order to gossip about Evan. She knew the Frenchwoman adored Evan and meant no harm, but Marietta usually felt a degree of discomfort if forced to discuss members of her family, particularly Evan, who was very special to her.

Fortunately she was not waylaid. It was a nice day, if a little too humid, but she was relieved it wasn't raining. It had poured yesterday. She hated the rain. Owen thought this was because she was from sunny California, but that wasn't the reason at all.

Although he did not know it, the unhappiest day of her life had been spent in London in the rain . . . on that awful day her life had crumbled into ashes, and she had felt as if her entire being had been washed away by the rain. Yes, her life had ended in the rain that day. Mere existence had begun. And that was how it had been ever since.

A cab slid to a stop in front of her, and she got in, gave the driver the address of her bank, then sat back. She was relieved that she had escaped from the hotel without having to deal with George or Arlette and, most important, that the shopping bag had gone undetected in its hiding place in the wardrobe.

Marietta placed her handbag on the cab seat next to her but kept the shopping bag on her lap. Ever since finding the package inside, she had believed it to be dynamite—and she must keep it safe. She wasn't sure if she could use it to her advantage, but she certainly was aware of its value.

It suddenly struck her how wise she had been to keep her account open at Barclays. There wasn't much money in it, but they knew her at this branch, and renting a safe-deposit box had presented no problem. How relieved she would be when the package was safely in the bank. Then she would go to Fortnum & Mason and have coffee in the restaurant, perhaps browse in the store. She might even buy herself a hat, although she knew she wasn't going anywhere special to wear it. But she'd always loved hats.

Normally she would have gone to Harte's in Knightsbridge for coffee, but she was afraid of running into Evan. They were supposed to be in Connecticut, and were not due in London until next week. Owen had decided to come earlier than planned. "To give us time to get over our jet lag," he had said, but she knew this was just a ploy. He had wanted to arrive sooner than expected in order to take Evan by surprise.

Marietta hadn't liked that at all, but she had kept quiet. Long ago she had learned not to argue with Owen. Most of the time she kept her own counsel; however, this did not prevent her from drawing her own conclusions, and she knew she was right when it came to his attitude toward their daughter.

Owen had always believed he owned Evan. Certainly he behaved as if he did. He had taken their daughter over when she was very young, and he had pushed *her* out. She had lost Evan because of his possessiveness, also because of her own mistakes perhaps. She gripped the shopping bag tighter, her knuckles whitening as she thought of the past. Sometimes you did something, just a small thing, yet it could have the most far-reaching consequences.

The cab came to a stop, and she alighted quickly, paid the driver, and went into the bank. It was all so easy . . . within minutes she was placing the precious package in the safe-deposit box and putting the key in her handbag. Now no harm would come to it, nor could it be lost or stolen.

It was only much later, when she sat sipping her coffee in Fortnum's, that a terrible thought occurred to Marietta. What if she got sick and died, or was killed in an accident, or became senile? What would happen to the package in the safe-deposit box? Only she knew it was there. She would have to tell someone. But who could she confide in?

Marietta's mouth twitched slightly in a wry smile. There was nobody she could make her confidant because she did not trust anyone she knew. A lawyer, she thought; I need a lawyer. To make a will. Yes, that's what I have to do. She had a few things of real value to leave. As well as the package in the safe-deposit box. For her daughter Evan. The person she loved the most in the entire world.

Tomorrow that would be her project. She would find a lawyer. It was imperative.

7

The four of them—Jack Figg, Gideon Harte, Evan Hughes, and Desmond O'Neill—walked slowly around the perimeter of the estate. Jack had a captive audience, and he was talking about his favorite subject, Security with a capital *S*. "For years all that's ever been needed here are burglar alarms, because there are so many people around most of the time . . . Wiggs and his gardeners, the stable lads, Joe and his estate workers. But it's very different now. We're living in dangerous times. England's changed and *not* for the better."

"You're right in everything you say," Gideon answered. "It's the same at Allington Hall, by the way. My father hasn't got proper security either, except for alarms, and it's downright neglectful when you think about it . . . all those valuable horses, for example."

Desmond said, "Uncle Winston *has* been talking about security with Dad. I heard them wittering on about it a few weeks ago. But I think Dad and Uncle Winston are very trusting, they're living in Dick's days."

Gideon burst out laughing. "Perhaps that's true when it comes to their homes. But I know for a fact that your father is extremely high on security for all the O'Neill hotels, and certainly Dad knows it's a priority at the newspaper offices, the television network, and our radio stations." He glanced at Jack. "I'm hiring you right now to overhaul the security system at Allington Hall. And I'd like you to tackle the newspaper offices, television studios, radio stations as well. Make sure we've got the latest."

"Thanks for your vote of confidence, Gideon," Jack said, "but I *will* be hiring outside companies, if that's all right. Of course I'll be working with them, supervising."

Gideon nodded.

"One thing's for sure, the store has huge security in place," Evan volunteered, smiling at Jack. "And I know you're responsible for that."

"Yes, it was always at the top of my list when I was head of security at Harte's."

Evan's mobile phone began to ring. Bringing it to her ear, she said, "Hello?"

"Hi, Evan honey, it's me," Owen said.

"Dad! Hi! It's nice to hear your voice." As she spoke she gave Gideon a wide smile, went to sit on a drystone wall. She watched the three men as they moved on, talking animatedly.

"I can't wait for you to get here. I'm dying to see you and Mom," she continued.

"We're here already, honey," Owen announced, a chuckle in his voice.

"You are! But why didn't you let me know you were coming earlier?" she exclaimed, startled but not unduly put out. "When did you get to London, Dad?"

"Wednesday night. Three days ago. I decided to change the date so we could recover from our jet lag before we started running around. Anyway, we'd love to see you today if you can make it. Your mother's excited about your new apartment, and so am I. We thought we'd come over later."

"Oh, Dad, it would have been great, but I'm not in London. I'm in Yorkshire."

"Oh, are you working up there?" he asked.

"No, not today, not on Saturday. I came up for a few days of rest, and I'll be here through next Wednesday, since I have to help India with certain things at the Leeds store. I guess I won't see you until Thursday, when I get back."

"I see." He sounded disappointed. "Too bad, honey," he added. "Thursday it is then."

"I'm so sorry, Dad. I made my plans around your original date. Gee, I don't know if I can change things . . ." Her voice trailed off as she wondered how to reschedule everything; but she knew she couldn't, at least not easily.

"Your mother wants to say hello, Evan."

"Put her on, Dad." A moment later she was exclaiming, "Hi, Mom, it's so good to hear you. How are you?"

"I'm very well these days, Evan," her mother said, her voice loving and warm. "I gather you're not around."

"No, I'm in Yorkshire. I didn't expect you until next week."

"I know, I know. I told your father you'd probably be busy, but you mustn't worry about us. We'll see you as soon as you return. At least, I hope we will."

"Absolutely. The hotel's nice and cozy, isn't it, Mom? I know George and Arlette must've made you very comfortable."

"Yes. They miss *you,* of course, now that you've

moved out. But I don't blame you. It's nice to have a place of your own, isn't it, Evan?"

"Yes, it is." She laughed. "Oh, Mom, I can't wait to get back to town now I know you and Dad are there." She meant this, and she was particularly pleased that her mother sounded so *normal.* That was the only word for it. Normal. And, yes, *happy.* Actually happy. She who was always depressed.

They went on talking for a few more minutes, and after promising to phone them at the hotel tomorrow, Evan clicked off the cell. She hurried after Gideon and the others, whom she could just see heading for the front gates.

It was true, she *was* glad her parents had arrived in London. She hadn't seen them since January, and it was now August. Eight months in which her life had changed in so many ways. And, in a sense, she had changed. She was a different person. She couldn't wait to see them, but at the same time she *was* slightly apprehensive. Although she and Robin had agreed, only a few days ago, that she would not tell her father about him, there were many other things she had to discuss. Difficult things.

Tessa stood at the window of her bedroom, her eyes focused on Jack Figg. He stood talking to Gideon, gesticulating, and to Desmond, who was with them.

She guessed it had to do with security. Jack had brought in a number of experts since Adele's disappearance on Wednesday. For the past few days scores of men had been digging, laying cable, hauling in cameras and monitors and all manner of other devices. Linnet said they had been invaded by an army, and that was how it seemed to her, too. Parts of the estate had been mangled, but she didn't care about the mess. Things could be put right once they had left; Wiggs had told Linnet and her not to worry about it. And so she wasn't going to; she kept reminding herself the most important thing was that Pennistone Royal was being made impenetrable.

Turning away from the window, Tessa went into her small sitting room, which adjoined the bedroom. She glanced around, as always filling with pleasure when she was in this intimate room. The walls were primrose, there were yellow-and-red draperies made of a *toile de Jouy* cotton, and the small love seat next to the fireplace was upholstered in a yellow-and-white flower print. The cheerful, sunny room had been hers since she was a little girl, and it was her safe haven still.

She paused in front of the Victorian mirror on the side wall, staring at herself and not liking what she saw. She felt totally drained, and she realized she looked it; her face was a ghostly white, and there were dark smudges under her eyes. Because she had not eaten much over the last few days, her face seemed narrower, and it was taut with lingering tension. Only her silver-blond hair was as beautiful as always.

Sighing as she moved away from the mirror, Tessa went and sat down at her desk, the French *bureau* which had stood in the same spot for as long as she could remember. Next to the big yellow porcelain lamp was a photograph of Adele taken earlier in the summer, and she reached out, touched the image with one finger. The most intense love for her daughter surged through her, and Tessa became more aware than ever that her child took precedence over anyone on this planet, certainly over anything else in her life.

Mark's abduction of Adele had changed her forever. Tessa had understood that within a few hours of her little girl's disappearance. Now she realized that she would have to start assessing her entire life, deciding what changes to make. And there would be changes. She wasn't prepared to sacrifice her daughter's well-being for her career. Suddenly, being the boss of Harte's one day had lost a great deal of its luster. At least for the moment. Perhaps her attitude would shift when everything settled down, when Mark had been neutralized, although she was sure—

A few gentle taps on the door interrupted Tessa's chain of thought, and she exclaimed, "Come in!"

The door opened, and Elvira's face appeared around it. "Could I have a word with you please, Mrs. Longden?"

"Yes, of course, Elvira." Noticing at once that the nanny was alone, she asked, "Where's Adele?"

"She's fine, Mrs. Longden, perfectly safe. She's with Margaret in the kitchen, giving a tea party for her dolls."

"I'm sorry, Elvira, you did tell me that was what you'd planned." Tessa forced a smile. "I think I'm getting paranoid."

"No, you're not, and anyway it would be natural, wouldn't it?" Elvira hovered in front of the desk, twisting her hands and looking worried.

"What's wrong, Elvi?" Tessa asked, using the diminutive to put the nervous young woman at ease.

"Mrs. Longden, there's something I need to tell you. . . . I saw Mr. Longden on Wednesday morning, just after leaving the estate. He was sitting in a car with another man, about halfway down the road, and he . . . well, he flagged me down. I think he recognized my car."

Tessa's eyes narrowed, and she asked in an urgent voice, "Who was the other man? Did you know him, Elvi?"

The nanny shook her head. "No, I didn't, Mrs. Longden. I'd never seen him before. Anyway, Mr. Longden just said hello, told me he was on his way to see Adele, and asked if you were about or had you gone to the Harrogate store? And I said no, that you were at Pennistone Royal, working in the library, and that Adele was on the terrace playing—" She broke off. Tears sprang into her eyes, and she tried to flick them away with her fingertips. "I wish I hadn't stopped. I feel so responsible for what happened."

"Oh, Elvira, you *mustn't*. It wasn't your fault," Tessa replied. "But why didn't you tell me before? After all, you were back on Wednesday evening, just when Mr. Longden returned Adele. Surely that was the time to say something?"

"It was, yes, but you were agitated, and exhausted, and I was very distressed myself, *thrown* if you know what I mean."

"Today's *Saturday,* Elvi."

"I know, but on Thursday and Friday you were ever so busy with Mr. Figg, I didn't really like to disturb you. I did keep trying to find the right moment, but there just wasn't one. Besides, I was a bit afraid, to be honest. I felt very guilty about talking to Mr. L. And I thought you'd be angry with me."

"Never mind all of that. Now tell me, Elvi, do you think Mr. Longden was parked down the road here actually waiting for you? Do you think he was expecting you to leave around the time you did?"

"I don't know, Mrs. Longden, but I have the same routine on my day off. I usually leave about ten or ten-thirty. And he knows Wednesday is my day off. I've taken Wednesday ever since Adele was a baby."

Tessa inclined her head. "I understand, and let's forget it. However, Elvira, if anything ever happens, anything at all, that you think is strange, you must tell me."

"I will, Mrs. Longden, I will, I promise." The nanny attempted a smile, but it didn't quite materialize, and she added, "Well then, I'd better get back to Adele." Without another word she scurried out.

Left alone, Tessa felt oddly chilled, and a little frightened once again. Mark had obviously planned the abduction carefully, waiting for Elvira on the roadside, quizzing her, and then swooping in and scooping up Adele. While his accomplice, whoever that was, did all that dialing on a mobile phone. She shivered involuntarily and bit her lip, and suddenly her eyes filled with worry.

After a few moments Tessa managed to calm herself, and she made a vow to outwit Mark Longden. Whatever it took, that was what she was going to do. *Outwit him.*

"My parents are here," Evan said, staring at Gideon.

A look of genuine surprise crossed his face, and then his brows met in a puzzled frown. "I thought they were coming next week."

"They were. Dad changed the date, he said he wanted a chance for them to get over their jet lag. Anyway, they're in London. At the hotel. That was Dad on my mobile when we were walking with Jack."

Evan and Gideon were seated at the wrought-iron table under the old oak tree. Gideon put down his glass of white wine and leaned across the table. "So when am I going to meet them?" he asked, a red-gold brow lifting quizzically. When she didn't immediately answer, he said, "I *am* going to meet them, aren't I?"

"Of course. But I thought I'd better see them by myself first. On Thursday, when I get back to London. It *has* been eight months, and there's a lot to catch up on, and I just think it's better that I see them alone." Evan didn't add that they might resent his presence, although she was thinking that.

"I understand," he said and went on swiftly: "Tell you

what, I'll take the three of you to dinner on Friday evening, or lunch on Sunday, somewhere really nice." He
spoke in a voice that forbade argument and looked at
her very intently. There was a steely glint in his eyes.

"That'll be great," Evan responded softly, realizing it
was better for the time being to acquiesce.

Gideon experienced a small stab of dismay at her obvious lack of enthusiasm, which made him feel suddenly awkward, and he reached out, took hold of her
hand. His green eyes bored into hers. "I know I've said
this before, but I'm in love with you, Evan."

"I know that."

"And what about *you*? How do you really feel about
me?"

"I'm in love with you, Gideon," she replied, her voice
suddenly intimate. "You know I am."

He realized she was being sincere, and he relaxed,
smiled, squeezed her hand. "I want to spend the rest of
my life with you, as if you didn't know that, and I want
to marry you. I know I've said that to you before, but
I'm asking you again. . . . Evan, please marry me."

There was only a fractional hesitation before she
agreed. "Yes," she said. "I will, Gideon."

"Let's tell your parents when we see them! Then it
will be official, and we'll phone my parents in New York
to give them the good news. Do let's get engaged."
Without waiting for her reply, he grinned and rushed on,
"I've got a confession to make. I've had your engagement ring for ages."

"You have?" Evan's gray-blue eyes sparkled, and she
began to laugh. "Gee, you are sure of yourself, aren't
you?" Her voice was teasing.

"I could only hope, my love, I could only hope. Actually, I can't give it to you this moment. Unfortunately,
it's locked up at Allington Hall."

"Well, at least it's in Yorkshire," she quipped.

"I'll give it to you tonight, and *can* we tell your parents next week?" he pressed.

Evan took a deep breath and blew out a few puffs of air. "I'd like to tell them when we have dinner, but I'm still a bit worried about the Robin-Dad situation. I don't know what to do about that yet." She frowned and shook her head, groping for words that would describe what she felt. "I'm so *ambivalent,* and having to tell Dad that his father wasn't his biological father is going to be—"

"Let's not go there, let's not get things confused," Gideon exclaimed impatiently. "Our engagement doesn't have anything to do with Robin, your father, and Richard Hughes."

"But it does, because my father—"

"Evan, please don't start with that whole business of us being related. My grandmother Elizabeth and your grandfather Robin are brother and sister, but that isn't troublesome. A genealogical chart would show that we are cousins a few times removed. So what! In this country it's not illegal to marry even a first cousin, so *we're* certainly within the law. And I don't believe those old wives' tales about children of cousins being born afflicted with something. My parents are cousins, yet Toby, Natalie, and I are perfectly all right. Not that you've met Nat yet, what with her being in Australia at the moment. But you can take my word for it, my sister's as perfectly healthy and sane as Toby and I."

"Oh, Gid, don't get angry, please don't. I do love you very much, and being related has nothing to do with it. I *do* want to marry you. It's just that my father seems to bear a grudge against the Hartes, and I want to find out *why* that is. Can't you understand that?"

"Yes, I can. I know it's important to you that my parents like you, and they do. In fact, they're very approving of you. However, please understand that even if they didn't like you, I would still marry you. They can't live my life for me, and I would never permit them to influence my choice of a wife." He frowned, his eyes scanning her face as he finished. "Don't you feel that way, too? Surely you believe in your own choices?"

"I certainly do, and I'm my own person. But I want to get to the root of his *dislike* of the Hartes, so please try to accept that. Ultimately, whatever he says, and what my mother says, won't alter my decision. I am going to marry you." A few moments ago he had released her hand, now it was Evan who grabbed his. "I think I know what it's about, Gideon."

"You do? Then for God's sake don't keep me in the dark."

"It's all to do with class differences, I think. Money, privilege, upbringing, background, those kinds of things. *Your* life as opposed to *mine*. Look, my family wasn't, isn't, dirt poor. Not a lot of disposable income, but my sisters and I never wanted for anything. We had decent if somewhat plain clothes, yearly vacations, and we went to good schools. But in my father's mind I come from a different world than you, Gideon, and he believes there will inevitably be a clash, that a relationship with you will only end in unhappiness for me. In a way, I think he believes that I'm not good enough for you, that I don't have the right pedigree."

Gideon was startled. Finally he said in a very quiet voice, "He sounds as if he's extremely prejudiced, Evan, and a little bit out of date."

"Dad *is* old-fashioned. Stubborn and opinionated as well. And, yes, you're right, he's very prejudiced."

"And what about your mother? How will she react to our engagement?"

"I'm not sure. . . . I think she'll be pleased if she

knows I'm happy. But to be truthful, sometimes I think I don't know my mother very well. All those years of . . . of her being ill, being a manic-depressive, those years took their toll on our relationship, Gid. We missed out on such a lot when I was growing up, and I regret that. I wish we'd been closer then, I really do."

"I can understand that. Did you speak to her this morning?" he asked.

"Dad put her on, and you know what? I thought she sounded *different*. Much more like a normal person, no hint of depression, at least not in her voice, and it struck me that she sounded really happy. I can barely remember her sounding, or being, *happy* ever in my life. I was taken aback. But I was happy that she was happy."

Gideon found this last statement so sad he didn't speak for a moment. How terrible for someone to have lived that way for most of her life, a prisoner of her own pain. A rush of sympathy for Evan made him exclaim, "It can't have been easy for you as a child. I'm so sorry, Evan."

There was a moment's silence; Evan stared up at Pennistone Royal, that stately home sitting atop the hill, thinking about her childhood in Connecticut. She had trouble talking about it. It had been so bleak in many ways, yet there had been her father and of course her grandmother, who were her great allies.

Evan's face brightened, and she exclaimed, "There was always Glynnis. She was there for me, my lovely gran. It was she who really brought me up, and she was—just *wonderful*."

"I bet she was. And she was truly beautiful, if that snap you showed me this morning is anything to go by," Gideon murmured.

Evan nodded. "It's amazing to think that Robin kept it all these years."

"It's obvious he had a real big *thing* about her, my

sweet, just as I do about you. I wish we could go back to Allington Hall and make love."

She laughed, shaking her head. "I do, too, but we can't."

"I realize that. I have a sinking feeling that we're stuck here for lunch. With Tessa."

"Yes, and Jack Figg. Just the four of us."

"Oh. Where're Linnet and India?"

"Linnet told me she was going to the Harrogate store, and later to see Sir Ronald. Julian's brought him up from London, but he's not well apparently. She was going over for lunch with them, and India's meeting a friend."

"Thank God Jack's here, he's good company," Gideon said. "Tessa can be hard to take. How is she, by the way? I guess it was some ordeal on Wednesday."

"It was. She really suffered, as I told you. There were moments when I thought she was going to pass out from anxiety. Yesterday she seemed a bit better, but so quiet. She seems to alternate between looking worried and being preoccupied. Linnet thinks she's changed a lot in three days, but I'm not sure."

"I hope it's for the better," he shot back succinctly.

They finished their drinks in silence, and then Gideon said, "I guess we'd better wend our way." They rose, picked up their empty glasses, and began to walk slowly up the hill. It was still scorching hot but not muggy, and the blue sky and brilliant sunlight combined to make it the most gorgeous August day.

Gideon stole a look at Evan, thinking how young and fresh she looked in her strapless cotton sundress and sandals. She was not wearing any makeup except for a touch of lipstick, and she suddenly seemed vulnerable and tender; he wanted to protect her, cherish her. He couldn't help thinking what a strange childhood she must have had. Several times she had expressed worry about her chances of inheriting her mother's illness. But after eight months he was quite certain she had not inherited that troubling disease. He had never met a woman like her. She had so many lovely attributes, and she was intelligent, caring, and most important, had a great sense of humor.

As for Evan, she was also thinking about her mother, wondering what had brought about this change in her, what had made her sound so . . . *upbeat*. There was just no other word for it. Her thoughts focused on her father, and she dreaded the idea of telling him that he was part Harte, that she was part Harte, and that she was contemplating marrying a Harte. I'm going to have trouble with Dad, she thought, especially about Gideon.

She stole a surreptitious look at him, and her heart seemed to melt. He was the nicest, kindest man she had ever met, not to mention charming and good-looking with his reddish blond hair and green eyes. Emma Harte's coloring, she thought, the same as Linnet's and his father's. He was a full-blooded Harte, and she was half Harte, but so what? She loved him very much, and she had every intention of marrying him, no matter what her father said. Well, I've finally made up my mind, she thought, at least about Gideon. And she smiled to herself.

"Where have you been, Emma? Dad's been looking for you all over the place. It's about Lady Hamilton Clothes." As he spoke, Sir Ronald Kallinski adjusted his glasses and peered at the couple standing in front of him. The sun was behind them, and he could not see them properly; he blinked several times, focusing first on the woman and then on the man.

"Is that you, Michael? What are you doing with Emma? You're delaying her."

"Grandfather, it's me, Julian, not my father. And this is Linnet, my fiancée, not Emma. You know Linnet, Grandfather, she's *Paula's daughter*, Emma's great-granddaughter. We're engaged, remember?"

"Yes," the old man said vaguely, sitting up straighter on the sofa.

"I think you must've been dozing, Grandfather, and having a dream perhaps—about the old days, eh?" Julian smiled at him.

Sir Ronald blinked again and peered at the couple. "Of course it's you, Julian, and Linnet! I suppose it's possible I *was* daydreaming about the past; that's what you do when you're over ninety, dream about the days long ago, live with the memories. I'm one of the last, you know, except for Bryan O'Neill, Linnet's grandfather, and Edwina, Robin, and Elizabeth. All of the others are gone now. Yes, I'm one of the last."

"That's true, but you're pretty *healthy*," Julian said in a reassuring voice, motioning for Linnet to sit down next to Sir Ronald on the sofa. He took the chair opposite them; he was worried about his grandfather, to whom he was close.

Sir Ronald turned to gaze at Linnet and said in a voice tinged with awe, "But my goodness, Linnet, you could be *her*. Now, when I look at you, I feel as if I'm seeing a ghost, a reincarnation."

"I know, Uncle Ronnie, everyone tells me that." She smiled at him and went on. "Julian and I have come to have lunch with you, and tell you about our marriage plans."

"Although I'm a bit doddery on my feet, I'll be there!" Sir Ronald announced in a voice all that much stronger. "You can be damned sure of that. I've not made any plans for dying, oh no. I still have too much damage to do." He began to smile. "It's going to be the joy of my life, seeing you two get married. It was always a dream of Emma's . . . that a Kallinski and a Harte would wed. And somehow she wanted an O'Neill in there. The three clans, started by her, David Kallinski, and Blackie O'Neill."

"And don't forget I'm also part O'Neill," Linnet reminded him. "So Julian and I *will* be linking the three clans when we tie the knot."

He nodded. "That's fantastic, my dear. And what's the date then? Last time I asked, you said you didn't know. Julian, do *you* know yet?"

"We haven't settled on the actual date, Grandfather. But it will be during the first week of December, probably the first Saturday. We'll make a final decision in a few days."

"And where will you be wed?" he asked, beaming at them. Their arrival had cheered him immensely. Nothing like the young to keep you young.

"Mummy wanted it to be at the church in Pennistone Royal village, but now we're not too sure about that . . . there seem to be a lot of people to invite. So Dad's been talking about Ripon Cathedral."

"Aye, that's a grand place, a very beautiful cathedral indeed. Your father sang 'The Minstrel Boy' there, long, long before you were born, Linnet."

"Yes," she said softly, "at Emma's funeral, wasn't it? He told me about it once."

"Aye, it was. Where's your father, Julian? I thought he was coming up here this weekend."

"He is. He said to tell you he'll be arriving in time for dinner, Grandfather. Now, would you like to go in for lunch? Mary told me when we arrived that we can sit down any time you wish."

"Well, all right, why not? Got to eat a bit, keep myself alive and kicking for your impending nuptials." He smiled benignly at them both. "I think you'll have to help me up," he muttered, staring at his grandson. "My bones ache, you know. I'm living on borrowed time, I suspect." He chuckled, and turning to Linnet, he said, "That's what your grandfather's always telling me, so it must be true."

8

Don't move!" Dusty exclaimed without looking up, his eyes focused on the canvas propped on the easel. "It'll just be another few minutes, and then you can have a stretch. Perhaps only a few seconds even."

"It's all right, I'm not going to move a muscle," India answered. "In fact, I'm fine, really I am."

"Good girl, good girl!" He still didn't look at her, concentrated on the painting, and then quite suddenly he exclaimed, "There, that's it! I've got it! Just those last few strokes were what I needed. Okay, sweetheart, you can stand up and stretch those lovely limbs of yours. I know you must be bloody cramped by now."

Dusty put down his brush and wiped his hands on a paint rag, then dropped it on the worktable and stepped around the easel. He walked over to the chaise where India reclined, and taking hold of her hands, he brought her to her feet. "You're a marvelous model," he murmured, pulling her into his arms. "Bloody marvelous. You didn't even flick an eyelash."

"I tried very hard to keep perfectly still," she said, laughing, looking up into his face.

"Oh God, are you luscious today," he murmured, bending toward her, finding her mouth with his own. His lips lingered on hers, his tongue slid alongside hers; she wrapped her arms around him, found herself leaning into his body, longing for him again even though they had made love only two hours ago. He devoured her mouth, slid his hands down her back and onto her buttocks, and pressed her even closer.

A moment later he brought one hand to her breast, played with her nipple, visible under the black chiffon top she was wearing. Carefully, he lifted the top, bent over her breast, kissed her nipple, then stopped abruptly, stared up at her, and said, "Let's go back to bed. I can't stand fooling around like this when I want you so badly."

"Yes" was all she said, and then she smiled at him and whispered, "but the painting will never be finished at this rate, Mr. Rhodes."

Holding her away from him, he looked down into her large, shining eyes and murmured, "Only too true, Lady India, only too true. But this lad wants to—"

She stopped his words with her mouth, kissing him deeply. Then, pulling away, she said softly, "I'll be here for the rest of the day. And tonight. I can stay as long as you want me to stay, Mr. Rhodes." Her smile was inviting, her eyes provocative.

He smiled back at her, enjoying the way she was flirting with him.

"It's the weekend, and I'm free as a bird. And whatever you want to do with me you can—paint me, feed me, talk to me, and love me, love me, love me," she finished. "Yes, please, to the last."

"You've got *that* exactly right, my lady." Dusty hugged her to him and added, "You're the best, India, just the best. I can't begin to tell you what it's like making love to you. . . . It's the nearest thing to ecstasy I've ever experienced." When she remained silent, he said in a low voice, "I mean that, you know."

"Yes" was all she could manage, feeling weak at the knees. His words filled her with happiness, thrilled her, actually. She wanted him to love her the way she loved him, with all his heart and soul and mind.

Dusty released her and looked down into those unique silvery eyes. "All right, a bit more work and then we'll have a lovely break. Later I'll paint you for another hour or two, and then I'll make you dinner. I'm glad you're not planning to abandon me, we've got the whole weekend together."

"I'm glad, too," she agreed, and reaching for the ceiling, she stretched her long, lithe body. She *was* a little cramped after reclining in one position for almost two hours, yet the time had passed quickly. She enjoyed watching him as he painted. She was so much in love with him she couldn't see straight; he was the only man she wanted forever, and that was the truth.

Dusty began to move around himself, stretching, breathing deeply, touching his toes, and saying, between movements, "Thank God for the air-conditioning. Just think how stifling it would have been on a day like this with all these windows. Are you all right, India? How about a glass of water?"

"Thanks, but I'm fine. This blouse is as light as air, and so are the harem trousers." She laughed and looked down at them, making a little grimace. "All I need are bells on my ankles, bells on my toes, and a tambourine and I'd be quite exotic."

"Don't knock it. You look very sexy in that outfit, and those trousers! *They* don't leave much to the imagination." He rolled his eyes theatrically.

"Oh, Dusty, you're priceless," she said and ran over to him, threw her arms around him. "I do adore you so—"

The door of the studio flew open with a noise so loud it startled them, and they swung their heads, gaped at the young woman who had appeared on the threshold. Her face was twisted in rage, her eyes blazing, her hair tousled; even her clothes seemed all awry.

"Get away from him, you bloody whore!" she shrieked at India. "Get away from him. He belongs to me."

The woman ran into the studio, her eyes taking in everything—Dusty's paint-stained T-shirt, India's flimsy costume, the rumpled bed at the far end of the room. Finally she spotted the canvas on the easel.

Rushing across to Dusty's worktable, she grabbed the first knife she saw, a jackknife he used for cutting canvas, and made a run at the painting, the knife raised. "Whore! Whore!" she screamed.

Dusty had been frozen in shock, but now he went into action. Pushing India to one side, he dashed over to the easel, stood in front of the painting, and took the thrust of the knife in his left upper chest. Blood spurted, then gushed, staining the white T-shirt vivid red.

India screamed.

The woman, who had the knife raised to strike again, began to wail when she saw the blood. Instantly dropping the knife, she swung around and flew out of the studio, banging the door behind her.

Dusty stepped over to the worktable, grabbed the paint rags, pressed them to his chest, and steadied himself against the table, cursing under his breath.

India raced to him, her face pale, her eyes wide with horror. "Oh God, Dusty, this looks really serious!" she cried and ran to the bathroom, rushing back with a pile of hand towels. "It's bad," she asserted, taking the paint rags out of his bloody hand, pressing two of the clean towels against his chest, then placing his hand over them. "Keep the pressure on," she instructed. "We must staunch the bleeding the best way we can."

"I think she's severed the artery just above my pectoral muscle," he said in a strangled voice, and suddenly his face crumpled. "Jesus! That's a bloody blinding pain!" He gasped and sat down heavily in the nearest chair.

"Get dressed, India. *Be quick.* I need to get to Harrogate hospital. I could bleed to death with a severed artery, and I'll certainly go into shock very soon."

"Give me a minute," India exclaimed, aware of the pain in his bright blue eyes, the agony twisting his mouth into a grimace. She threw off the black chiffon outfit, scrambled into her cotton trousers and T-shirt, grabbed her handbag, and rushed back to him.

Taking hold of his right arm, she helped him to stand. "Come on, let's go. I'll grab some more towels as we leave. Where did you put the door keys! I must lock up."

"Table. Near the door," he gasped.

He sounded so terrible India tightened her grip on his arm and glanced up at him. He was chalk white now, and beads of sweat stood out on his face.

"Don't pass out on me, darling," she said in a strong voice. "I've got to get you to the car and then to Emergency."

"I'll just about make it . . . I hope." He groaned.

Brilliant sunlight blinded India as she and Dusty came out of the studio, and she was glad she had parked just behind this building, instead of near the barns. She soon had Dusty seated in the Aston Martin, the seat belt across his chest and buckled. Groping in her bag, she pulled out two more hand towels she had grabbed from the bathroom, put them under the seat belt and on top of the towels already there.

Once she had finished, she looked at him. He was ashen, still perspiring profusely, and she knew she had very little time before he went into shock. And the loss of blood was frightening. After closing the door she ran around to the other side of the car and got in, put the key in the ignition.

"The studio door," he mumbled, partially turning his head to look at her. "Lock it."

"It's double-locked, Dusty, don't worry," she reassured him, turned the key and started the car, then backed up the dirt road and headed around the house to the main driveway. At one moment she said, "The seat belt's holding the towels in place, darling," but he didn't seem to hear her. His eyes were closed, and his right hand was still pressed on the towels covering the wound.

Slowing the car as she came to the main gates of Willows Hall, she took out her cell phone and punched in Linnet's number. It was answered after only a few rings. "Hello?"

"Linnet, it's India. Don't talk, just listen please. I've got a very serious problem. Dusty's been stabbed. Badly. An artery's been severed. I think. He's losing lots of blood. I'm just leaving Willows Hall. I should make it to Harrogate District Hospital in about twelve minutes, unless there's more traffic than usual. Call Emergency, would you please, Linny? Tell them I'm coming."

"God, how terrible! I'll call immediately. Then I'm heading there myself. I should make it in five minutes if I leave now. I'm at Uncle Ronnie's house."

"Thanks, Linnet." India clicked off and glanced at Dusty. His eyes were closed, and he seemed to have slumped down in the seat. Blood was seeping through the towels and trickling down his arm.

As she started up the car again, India noticed that her

hand trembled, and she had to take several deep breaths to steady herself. Now was not the time to panic. Gripping the wheel, she edged out onto the road to Harrogate, was filled with relief when she saw that it was empty except for a truck and a cyclist. She put her foot down on the accelerator and concentrated on driving.

She made it in exactly nine minutes, and as she slowed down at the hospital gates she could see several people clustered at the Emergency entrance next to a gurney. Linnet was with them, looking pale and anxious.

India braked and alighted, motioned to the doctors, then ran around to the passenger door. Before she had even opened it they were rushing toward her with the gurney, and Linnet was not far behind.

India stood to one side, allowed the professionals to lift Dusty out of the car, but she said to one of the doctors, "My friend thought the knife struck his artery, maybe even severed it."

He stared at her, frowned. "Is he a doctor?"

She shook her head. "No, he's an artist. But he studied the human body in art classes."

"I see." He nodded and added, "He's probably correct. Right now he's in shock, and there's obviously been enormous blood loss. Try not to worry." And with that statement he ran after the gurney, which was already being trundled inside.

Linnet came over, took hold of her arm, and said, "Let's go inside and sit down. I gave them as much information as I could, but they'll want to talk to you, India, I've no doubt."

She nodded. "I know. I suppose they've already called the police."

"It's routine, isn't it, with something like this?" Linnet murmured, eyeing her closely.

"I expect so." India suddenly began to shake uncontrollably and brought her hands up to her face. "It was so awful, Linny."

After leading her to a chair, Linnet sat down next to her cousin and asked in a low voice, "What the hell happened? Who stabbed Dusty?"

"A woman. I don't know who she was, so don't ask, and I certainly wasn't able to question Dusty under the circumstances. Perhaps he knew her, I'm not certain. She burst into the studio and just went berserk when she saw me."

India now told Linnet everything that had happened, not pausing for breath until she had finished, and then she let out a long, shuddering sigh. "Oh God, Linnet, I hope he's going to be all right. What if he dies? I couldn't bear it if anything happens to him." India took hold of Linnet's arm, stared at her intently, and then burst into tears.

At once Linnet put her arm around India and brought her close. "Dusty will make it, darling. He's young, strong, and they can work miracles today."

"But he's lost so much blood. It just . . . spurted out of him. It was frightening to see—" She broke off, her face underwent a sudden change, and then she exclaimed, "I could give him blood if he needs a transfusion. Would you do it, too, Linnet, if it were necessary?"

Startled, Linnet said, after the merest pause, "Yes, of course, if he needs it."

India now sat up a little straighter, and her face seemed to lose some of its tension. Giving her cousin a half smile, she murmured in a low voice, "I love him very much, you know. I've never felt like this about any other man. He's the only one I've ever wanted to marry."

This announcement did not surprise Linnet; she had known from the outset of India's involvement with

Dusty Rhodes that her cousin had fallen heavy and hard for the artist, and Linnet was pleased for her. Her only worry had been his reputation as a carousing and volatile rabble-rouser, but India had assured her this was a big put-on. But hysterical women wielding knives were another thing altogether and smacked of an unsuitable, perhaps even an unsavory background. This thought troubled her. Other women who had been rejected could cause untold problems.

Linnet looked up as a voice said, "Lady India, could you come and give us some details about Mr. Rhodes, please."

India rose at once, said, "Certainly," and followed a woman in a white coat holding a clipboard and a pen. A moment later two police officers walked in, and Linnet groaned. There was no question in her mind that they had come to talk to her cousin about Dusty's stabbing. And if Dusty died, it would be murder they were talking about.

The woman in the short white jacket holding the clipboard was Mrs. Anita Giles, and she led the way to her office off the Emergency entrance lobby.

Once they were seated, Mrs. Giles explained, "Now, Lady India, if you could fill in the gaps for me I'd be very appreciative. Your cousin Miss O'Neill just gave me the name Russell Rhodes and said he'd been stabbed. I'm making the assumption that Mr. Rhodes is the well-known artist. Am I correct?"

"Yes, you are, Mrs. Giles. His full name is Russell Cecil Rhodes, and he lives at Willows Hall in Follifoot. He's forty-two years old. Is that the kind of thing you want to know?"

Mrs. Giles nodded, continued to write; once she had jotted down these facts, she asked, "Does Mr. Rhodes have any medical problems that you know of?"

"No. At least, I don't think so. He's very fit as far as I know. He exercises, watches his diet, drinks very little." India smiled when she saw Mrs. Giles raise her brow and added, "His reputation for being something of a *roué* is quite false. Somewhat self-engendered, if you know what I mean, and wildly exaggerated." Leaning forward, India asked, "He is going to be all right, isn't he? I mean, he said he thought an artery had been severed."

The woman's face was quite unreadable when she said, "Everyone at the hospital will do their very best for him, Lady India, and I'm sure you'll understand that I can't hazard a guess under the circumstances. Now, could you tell me exactly what—"

There was a knock on the door, and Mrs. Giles stopped and said, "Come in."

The door opened to admit two policemen. "Hello, Mrs. Giles," one of them said; the other simply nodded and smiled at her.

"Good afternoon, Officers. This is Lady India Standish, a friend of Mr. Russell Rhodes, who is the victim of the stabbing reported earlier. Lady India brought him to the hospital."

India immediately stood up and shook hands with the policemen, who introduced themselves as Constables Hobbs and Charlton.

"If you'd be so good as to leave us alone with Lady India," Hobbs said, staring hard at Mrs. Giles.

"Oh yes, of course. I do realize you wish to speak to Her Ladyship alone." Smiling at India, she hurried out of the small office, closing the door behind her.

India said, "There's not much I can tell you."

"Just give us the details, Lady India," Charlton suggested and gestured for her to sit down.

"Thanks, but I'll stand," she answered and told them, "Mr. Rhodes is a well-known artist, as I'm sure you know, who lives at Willows Hall in Follifoot. He has his studio there, and he's painting my portrait . . . for my father, the Earl of Dunvale. A short while—"

"You're related to the late Mrs. Emma Harte!" Hobbs exclaimed, eyeing her with unconcealed interest.

"Yes, I'm her great-granddaughter. And another of her great-granddaughters is Linnet O'Neill, my cousin, who's waiting in the lobby."

"Both my mother and grandmother worked at the Harte store in Harrogate," Hobbs explained with a small smile, then continued, "So Mr. Rhodes was painting you, and suddenly someone came in and stabbed him, is that what you're saying?"

"No, it isn't what I'm saying at all," India answered briskly. "We had stopped because I'd been sitting for over two hours without moving, and I needed to stretch myself, and Dusty, er, Mr. Rhodes, was also a little stiff. Anyway, we were doing our exercises and chatting when the door of the studio flew open and this young woman came in. I don't know who she was, and I'm not certain that Mr. Rhodes did either."

"And she rushed up and stabbed him, is that it?" Charlton asked, sounding skeptical.

"Oh no, she saw me and started shouting at me, calling me names. She was a bit out of control. And then her eyes lighted on the portrait, and she seemed to go berserk, ran forward, grabbed a knife from the worktable, and made a beeline for the portrait, the knife raised."

"And she slashed the painting before stabbing Mr. Rhodes?" Hobbs asked, his brows drawing together in a frown.

"No, no, it didn't happen that way at all! Dusty and I, well, we were both sort of stupefied, yes, that's the best word. We were *utterly stupefied,* in fact, and then he realized she was heading for the portrait, and he ran forward, stood in front of it to protect it, and that's how he got himself stabbed. The woman meant to damage the painting, not Mr. Rhodes. It was an accident."

"I see," Hobbs murmured and glanced across at his colleague. They exchanged knowing looks, and Hobbs said to India, "We hope to speak to Mr. Rhodes soon, once he comes out of the operating room."

India clenched her hands, digging her nails into the palms, her anxiety rising. "Have the doctors told you anything, Constable Hobbs? He's not going to die, is he?"

"I dunno," Hobbs said, shaking his head. "I hope not. And Dr. Palmerton is a wonderful surgeon. If anybody can make Mr. Rhodes right, he can. But we'll just have to wait, won't we?"

9

Where is my beautiful other half?"

Tessa, buried in one of the big wing chairs in the library, threw the folder of balance sheets on the floor, jumped up at the sound of her brother's voice, and ran to him.

Lorne Fairley leaned nonchalantly against the doorframe, looking every inch the actor he was. "Hello, darling girl," he said in his beautifully modulated voice.

"Oh, Lorne, you made it! Thank God you're here!" She flew into his outstretched arms, and he held her tightly, filled with relief that she appeared to be calm and in control after her ordeal.

They stood together in a long and loving embrace, as close to each other emotionally as they had always been. They were of similar height, had the same blond coloring and sculpted, pristine features. There was no mistaking that they were twins, carried the genes of their late father, Jim Fairley, their mother's first husband.

Tessa, who had been born a few minutes before

Lorne, considered herself the elder and never let him forget it; Lorne, good natured and easygoing, simply laughed when she pulled rank. From childhood he had called her "the Ancient One," much to her irritation.

"I'm so sorry you had to come back all the way from Turkey, but—"

"My few days of holiday were almost over," he interrupted, standing away from her, his eyes roving over her face before he kissed her on the cheek. "And to be honest, I was getting bloody bored. Anyway, I wouldn't leave you in the lurch. We're always there for each other, aren't we?" Putting his arm around her shoulders, he walked her over to the seating arrangement and went on, "I gather Ma's not coming back just yet."

"No, she's not. I insisted she kept to her schedule, stayed on in New York with Shane."

"I know. I spoke to Dad, and he said everything was under control here, so they weren't making any changes in their plans. And how's my sweet Adele?"

"She's fine, Lorne, none the worse for what happened, thank heavens." At the thought of her daughter, Tessa broke into smiles and added, "She's such a happy child."

"And where is the little tyke? I want to see her at once."

"She's taking her afternoon nap, so you'll have to wait a bit."

They sat down together on one of the sofas, and Lorne peered at her again. "What's the latest on that bloody awful husband of yours?"

"He's about to become my ex!"

"So fast?" Lorne stared at her, a skeptical look crossing his face. "Don't tell me he's being acquiescent for once?"

"No, he's very demanding and arrogant, and naturally the divorce will have to take its course. But our solicitors, his and mine, are doing a lot of talking, and incidentally *his* are pretty annoyed with him for snatching Adele the way he did. Obviously it puts *him* in the *wrong,* and they don't like that one bit."

"It was a ridiculous stunt he pulled. As *you* well know, I've never really liked him, Tessa. I've always thought he was two bricks short of a full load."

She began to laugh. "You remind me of Jack Figg with all of your old-fashioned sayings. They're forever on *his* lips."

"They always were. Where do you think I learned them? At the knee of the master himself. Whom I just saw when I drove in. He was as usual warm and loving, but he's a tough bugger, Tess, and thank God for that. He told me he's making this place impregnable, and if the number of chaps around here installing things is anything to go by, I believe him."

Tessa nodded. "He told me he's staying on until Monday, then he's going back to Robin Hood's Bay for a couple of days. He'll be back in the middle of next week. Anyway, I thought I'd cook for us all tonight. I want Margaret to have the evening off. She and Joe have been so worried. All this trouble . . . it's sort of . . . done them in a bit."

"I'm not surprised, and talking of Margaret, I went to the kitchen when I got here and asked her to make me a sandwich. I stepped off the plane at Heathrow and drove straight up here. I'm famished. So come on, let's go see what she's managed to rustle up. And as far as tonight's concerned, I can't wait for one of your gourmet specialities."

As they crossed the Stone Hall together, they ran into the housekeeper. "There you are!" she exclaimed, and to Lorne she said, "I've put your sandwiches in the morning room, along with a pot of tea for you both." She nodded and hurried off toward the kitchen, thinking about Lorne. He had always been her favorite, and she was pleased he was back at home to look after his sister, if only for a short while. She wished he stayed longer. He was the kindest, sweetest of men, and his fame as an actor had not changed him one bit. He was the same as he'd been when she'd bounced him on her lap.

Until last winter the morning room had been an office which Emma Harte had used whenever she was at Pennistone Royal. But this past December, Paula had finally decided it was wasted space and had transformed it into a charming spot for breakfast and casual meals.

As they went in, Lorne glanced around, thinking how cool and restful it looked on this hot August Saturday. Very welcoming, he decided. The walls were a soft apple green, and there were rafts of white everywhere; the lovely curving bay window was treated to airy balloon shades made of a green-and-white-striped silk, while the chairs around the walnut table were covered in a green-and-white-checked fabric.

"Mother did a great job with this room," he remarked as they sat down at the circular table which Margaret had just set. "I'm going to take her up on her offer to redo my flat." Staring at the plates of sandwiches, Lorne now shook his head and smiled. "She's a wonder, that woman! Look, Margaret's made all of my favorite nursery sandwiches."

"Yes, she always did spoil *you*," Tessa said, giving him a knowing look.

Lorne did not rise to the bait, merely grinned, took an egg salad finger sandwich, and munched on it, watching his twin as she poured tea into his cup and added a slice of lemon. She had sounded so upset when she called him on his cell on Thursday; she had reached him in Turkey, where he was spending a few days with friends before starting a new film at Shepperton Studios, where they would be based. But first they would go on location to Paris. He had the male lead opposite one of his favorite actresses, and it was a good script.

Even if he had been having the best time in the world, he would have left immediately once he knew his twin sister needed him. As it was, he was fed up, itching to head back to London. Because of the heavy holiday air traffic, he had not been able to get a direct flight. So he had jetted to Paris, spent the night at the Paris O'Neill Hotel on the Avenue Montaigne, and flown to London today.

There was nothing he wouldn't do for his sister, and they were extremely close. Yet he was fully aware of Tessa's faults: her rivalry with Linnet for supremacy at Harte Stores, her terrible jealousy of their half sister, which he considered totally unreasonable. And then there was her snobbery about being a Fairley. This he found a bit silly. After all, they were Hartes and McGills and Amorys as well; in fact they owed everything they had to their great-grandmother Emma Harte, and to their great-grandfather Paul McGill.

Lorne wished Tessa could see things his way, but apparently she couldn't, or perhaps wouldn't. She was obstinate in her views, vociferous in her opinions, but he had ceased long ago to chastise her. There was no point really; he was convinced she would never change. And he continued to adore her as he had since their childhood, accepted Tessa as she was, tried not to make judgments about her. Or anyone else, for that matter. His motto had always been live and let live.

However, he now stared at his twin in surprise when she announced: "Linnet was on top of everything,

Lorne. She really was. I don't know what I would have done without her."

"*You're* suddenly singing a different tune!"

"Don't be mean."

"I'm not being mean, just truthful, my pet. You're the one who's constantly complaining about Linnet. I realize that you're determined to be the supremo at Harte's, but there's a place there for Linnet, too."

"I know, I know. Don't go on about it, Lorne. I'm really grateful that Linnet had the presence of mind to do the things she did, like get Jack Figg on the job. You see, there was no one here when Mark snatched Adele . . . well, only Wiggs and his gardeners."

"Where the hell was everybody?" Lorne's voice had risen. "This place is teeming with people usually. Odd that everyone was gone that morning, don't you think?"

"Nothing sinister, Lorne. Just a coincidence. Margaret had decided to go marketing, Joe had driven over to East Witton on estate business, and Elvira was on her day off." Tessa paused, sat back, and thought for a moment about her encounter with Elvira earlier. It still bothered her that the nanny had waited so long to mention Mark's conversation with her on the roadside.

"What is it? Something's troubling you, Tess."

"No, I'm fine. It's just that Elvira told me this morning that Mark had been waiting for her on the main road outside Pennistone Royal—"

"How the hell did *he* know she'd be leaving when she did?"

"Because it was *Wednesday*, and she always has that day off. Anyway, apparently he flagged her down, she stopped, and he asked her where I was, where Adele was, said he was on the way to visit us."

"And she gave him all the details." Lorne nodded,

and a reflective expression settled on his face. "They weren't in cahoots, were they? Do you trust her?"

"I'm quite certain they weren't in cahoots, and yes, I do trust her. She's a creature of habit, Miss Elvira is, and she has never changed her day off. Everything is done in the same way, almost by rote, although it's not really that . . . banal."

"And Evan? Where was she? You did say she's staying here."

"She'd gone over to Lackland Priory to have lunch with Uncle Robin."

"And where is the dastardly, elusive Jonathan?" Smiling acidly, not waiting for her answer, Lorne declaimed, in a highly exaggerated upper-class English accent, "They seek him here, they seek him there, those Frenchies seek him everywhere. Is he in heaven, or is he in hell, that damned elusive Pimpernel?"

Tessa began to laugh; her brother had always had the ability to bring a smile to her face, and she loved listening to him when he put on his actor's face and voice and adopted appropriate mannerisms. "Jonathan's in Hong Kong, according to Jack, who had him tracked by one of his top operatives. But as Jack pointed out, where he happens to be is of no consequence in this Age of Communication. Mr. Ainsley can direct the traffic from anywhere."

Lorne nodded his understanding and narrowed his eyes. "Mark and Jonathan, what a pairing up *that* is. My God, Mark's a bloody fool, Tessa, when one thinks about it. How could he let himself get . . . conned by Jonathan?"

"You just said it yourself, Lorne. He's two bricks short of a full load."

Lorne picked up his cup, took a swallow of tea, and

remarked, "I wouldn't want to be in Evan's shoes. . . . Jonathan must detest her."

"Absolutely true, I'm sure. She's very, very close to Gideon, you know. I think they might"—Tessa sat back, gave her twin a long, knowing look, and finished—"be very serious about each other."

"I thought they were at Dad's sixtieth birthday party, didn't you?"

She simply inclined her head, suddenly filled with a strange aching feeling, a sadness really, when she thought of Shane's birthday celebration. She had been alone that night, having left Mark two months before— and she'd felt empty inside, awkward and somewhat lost. It had been her cousin Toby Harte who had come to her rescue, looked after her just as he had done when they were little. They had been close all of their lives; Toby truly understood her.

Wasn't it funny how life worked out? He was in a mess now himself, getting a divorce from Adrianna.

Divorce. She rolled the word around in her head like a small glass bead. She hated the idea of failure; she had failed at marriage. But she wasn't going to fail at motherhood. Oh, no. Whatever it took, whatever it cost her, she was going to make sure Adele had a happy childhood and a wonderful life, and without any interference from Mark Longden.

Tessa picked up her cup, took a sip of tea, and with a small shock noticed her hand was shaking. Swiftly replacing the cup in its saucer, she turned and gazed out of the window, her mind awash with memories of Mark and the early years of their marriage.

She had had such great hopes for it. How had it gone so very wrong? Was it somehow her fault? Had she not pulled her weight? Why had Mark fallen under the influence of Jonathan Ainsley, a man he knew the entire family despised? Was he motivated by greed? The need for fame? Dissatisfaction with her? Or was he, very simply, a weak man? A man who needed drugs, alcohol, and other women to satisfy him.

Unexpectedly, her silver-gray eyes filled. She tried to choke back the tears, felt a burning sensation in her throat . . . now the tears were spilling unchecked out of her eyes. Bringing a hand up to her face, she attempted to hide behind it but didn't succeed.

Instantly Lorne noticed how upset she had become, and he was filled with a mixture of dismay and concern. Leaping to his feet, he went and placed an arm around her shoulders. "Oh, little pet," he said, using his child-hood name for her. "Don't, don't, Tess, he's just not worth it. Nobody is, you know." When she remained silent, he added, very softly, "Did you give him your heart, Tess?"

Clearing her throat, she wiped her face with both hands and shook her head, then looked directly at her brother. "I'm fine, do go and sit down, Lorne dear, and finish your sandwiches." Sighing, she remarked, "And no, I didn't . . . give him my heart."

"But you did fall in love with him," Lorne asserted, returning to his chair.

"I suppose I did. Well, I *thought* I was in love with him. Maybe it was just an infatuation."

"Perhaps it was. I've been there."

"Oh, you're thinking of your last girlfriend, are you? Did you give Miriam Delaney your heart?"

He smiled, and it was a rueful smile, barely settling on his mouth before it was gone. "Oh yes," he said.

"So what happened?"

"She trampled on it."

"I'm so sorry. I knew you were very much in love with her. I hadn't realized it was so one-sided."

"Neither did I, at first." He shrugged, then lifted his hands in a Gallic gesture. *"C'est la vie, chérie."*

A small silence fell between them, but it was an easy silence, and they were as comfortable with each other now as they had been since childhood. On the same wavelength, thinking the same thing.

Suddenly Tessa said, "I'll never get married again. It's not worth it."

"I do sincerely hope you don't mean you're going to remain celibate for the rest of your life."

"Why not? There are worse things."

Leaning across the table, Lorne exclaimed, "Listen to me, Tessa Fairley. I'm not going to permit you to lead a bleak, empty life without love. You must be fair to yourself. I agree that marriage might be too much for you after your recent hassles with Mark, but there has to be a lover. I won't let you spend the rest of your life without a man in it, a loving, caring man who will treat you the way you deserve to be treated. Actually, if it's anything to do with me, I'll see you have a string of devoted lovers," he finished on a teasing note.

Tessa had the good grace to laugh, and she managed to push her troubles to one side. "And that goes for you, too. Put Miss Delaney behind you and find yourself a gorgeous girl. Perhaps you'll meet somebody wonderful in Paris when you're over there on location. A beautiful *mademoiselle* perhaps."

Lorne was relieved that her mood had lightened, and he caught hold of her hand, kissed it. "Now you're sounding better, much better indeed. Like your normal self."

"This is an extraordinary studio, India," Linnet exclaimed, glancing around. "Dusty did a wonderful architectural job. You did say he designed it himself, didn't you?"

"That's right," India replied, sounding preoccupied as she let her eyes roam around the room, taking in everything. There were a lot of blood splatters on the floor near the painting. She hurried over to check the portrait and saw, with great relief, that none of the blood had hit it.

It was at this moment that she noticed the knife on the floor where the young woman had dropped it, and she said, "Look, Linnet! Over there! It's the knife." She pointed to it and immediately added, "I mustn't pick it up or touch it. *Her* fingerprints have to be on it, not mine."

"You're right about that," Linnet emphatically agreed. "And I just want to say this, India. I thought the two policemen were nice to us but just a little bit suspicious of you, wouldn't you say?"

"Yes. Constable Charlton was suspicious of my story. But not Hobbs. I know those who are closest to a victim, especially of the opposite sex, are usually suspected of being the perpetrators. So they most probably do have me in their sights."

Linnet glanced at the big clock on the wall. "Those two will be arriving soon. Are you sure you don't want me to ask Jack Figg to be here in case you need him?"

"No, no, honestly, it's fine. My prints aren't on the knife, and I know that when Dusty comes round he'll tell exactly the same story I've told. Because it's the truth. Also, Paddy Whitaker will be back by four, or thereabouts. And maybe he can throw some light on what happened. He's the house manager I mentioned earlier—"

"Isn't that simply Dusty's more plebian name for a *butler*?" Linnet asked, an auburn brow lifting.

India half smiled. "You're correct in that assumption. Anyway, Paddy had to go to Manchester this morning, but I heard him tell Dusty he'd be returning around teatime."

"And where did you say the housekeeper was?" Linnet probed as she continued to prowl the studio, filled with curiosity.

"I explained before, it's her weekend off," India answered, sounding slightly impatient. "That's why we'd been looking forward to being here together. *Alone.*"

"So you think the house manager might know who the young woman was, or rather, is?"

"Yes," India answered quietly, her sharpness receding. "If it was somebody from Dusty's past . . . or present. But she could have been a total stranger, you know."

Linnet glanced across at her cousin and shook her head. "That's stretching it, love. Why would a stranger attack him? Or rather, attack the painting?"

"Perhaps she was a deranged fan."

"India, really! He's not a film star or a rock star. Fans of artists aren't—*stalkers,* for God's sake. They don't go bursting into studios and stabbing people, or rather stabbing paintings." Linnet threw her an odd look, shaking her head.

"She *could* be a deranged fan. Or a former girlfriend, a lover, even. But I trust Dusty, and he would have told me if there was anyone important still hanging around in his life. I just know he would, Linnet." India's voice had risen several octaves.

"Okay, okay, don't get upset. And I trust you and your judgment, India, so if you say he's aboveboard, then of course I'll take your word for it." Moving toward one of the tall side windows, Linnet continued, "I think

I'd better call Julian, he'll be wondering what's happening." As she spoke she pulled out her mobile and punched in her fiancé's number.

India half smiled, nodded, and walked over to the portrait, stood looking at it, her head to one side. Her thoughts went to Dusty in the hospital, strung up with wires and drips and God knows what else. He had rushed to protect this painting, and that was why he was where he was at this moment. He could have died for it actually, and the terrible thing was it was still in the early stages. He had only been working on it for three days, and he could have surely started it all over again, couldn't he? Perhaps he had acted on impulse, his reflexes automatic.

Fortunately, he was going to be all right; the doctors had told her that before she left to come to the studio. The "crime scene," the police called it, but there was nothing here of real importance to them, except the jackknife on the floor and Dusty's blood. Just before she had left the hospital, they had allowed her to see Dusty in the ICU. She had stood alone by the side of the bed, looking down at his drawn face, chalk white, as if his essence had been drained away. Well, it had, she supposed. The blood loss had been acute; he had had to have transfusions. Fortunately, the artery had been successfully repaired. Since he was still unconscious from the anesthetic, she had simply leaned over him, touched his face gently with two fingers, whispered that she loved him. And then the nurse had put her head around the door and beckoned for her to leave.

India's relief was enormous, and her anxiety had begun to ease. *He was going to live.* And so, after seeing him, she had been quite willing to drive over to Willows Hall and open up the studio for the police.

Who was the woman? This question hung in midair, as it had for hours. Was she a stalker intent on doing harm? Or a former lover? And would she come back to do more damage?

10

Gideon expected the kitchen door to be locked. But when he turned the knob it opened at once, and he walked straight in, anticipating a cheery greeting from Margaret and Joe, who were usually sitting here having a cup of tea at this hour. Much to his surprise, the room was empty.

He paused in his tracks, glancing around, then stood inhaling the marvelous smells. The air was redolent with the scent of mixed spices that brought memories of North Africa rushing back, of meat simmering and vegetables steaming and other glorious, mouthwatering aromas of a special gourmet meal being made. He was certain it would be a delicious feast because Tessa was the best chef he knew, bar none. *She* missed her calling, he thought offhandedly as he hurried across the kitchen and into the back service corridor.

A back staircase led to the first floor, which was mostly Paula's domain, then continued to the second floor, where so many of the bedrooms were located. No security here, he decided; anybody could've walked right in, just as I did, and made it to the main part of the house. They were all going to have to get used to locking outside doors, or they would have Jack Figg to contend with. He sighed as he climbed the back staircase, which had been used by servants when the house was staffed to the hilt.

It was a steep climb, and he thought of those little housemaids of long ago carting breakfast trays up to the rooms. They must have been worn out by mid-morning. But the world was full of genuine inequities in those days; in certain ways, things *had* changed for the better.

On the second floor every door had a small brass plate with the name of the suite engraved, announcing Yellow, Blue, Crimson, Gold, and so on; this way of identifying each room by a color had been Emma Harte's invention, and he had always thought it was a charming idea. Finally he arrived at the Yellow Suite, tapped on the door, and walked in before he was bidden to enter.

"Oh my God!" she exclaimed, "you startled me!" She clutched the towel to her naked body as she stood and gaped at him.

"Sorry," he apologized and walked toward her. When he came to a standstill he took hold of her hand and pulled her into his arms in the most proprietary manner. Holding her close, he kissed her deeply, then led her across the room.

She endeavored to keep the towel around her; the expression on her face was one of uncertainty. "What's going on?" she demanded quietly, staring at him, trying to break free of his tenacious grip.

Not answering her immediately, he went on maneuvering her toward the bed. "Now sit there, and stop struggling. I'm not going to rape you."

"Are you sure you're not?" she asked but dutifully sat on the bed, and watched him as he struggled out of his clothes. When he walked toward her, she realized that they were going to be on this bed for some time, and that would mean they would be late for dinner. But she didn't have a chance to protest because he was on the bed next to her and kissing her passionately before she could even blink. And, of course, she immediately responded, ardently so, since she did love him with all her heart.

After a moment or two they stopped kissing, and he pushed himself up on one elbow, looked down into her face. "I know what you're going to say, that we'll be late down to dinner and all that stuff. But I haven't been alone with you for over a week, and I do have the need to be close to you like this, and *very* intimate."

"I know, I know," she murmured, her hand going to the nape of his neck, then reaching into his thick hair. "I've missed you, too, missed being with you, making love like this."

Gideon looked down into her luminous blue-gray eyes and smiled at her; then, quite unexpectedly, almost involuntarily, he sat up, jumped off the bed, and went over to his clothes piled on a chair. A moment later he was back on the bed and taking her hand in his. "I wanted you so much I couldn't wait to get you into bed, but we've got the rest of our lives to make love. It's only once that a girl and a boy get engaged." He began to laugh. "Well, let's hope it's only *once*," he said and slipped the sapphire ring he was holding onto her finger, then announced, "Now we are really engaged, Evan, and that's all that matters."

She sat bolt upright and stared at him and then at the third finger of her left hand, her eyes brimming with surprise and delight. "Thank you for such a gorgeous ring," she said, and leaning forward, she kissed him on the lips. "And, yes, we really *are* engaged." There was laughter in her voice as she added, "Whether my father approves or not, we're engaged! *I* certainly approve! Oh, yippee!"

Gideon laughed with her, enjoying her happiness, and enthusiasm. "I'm glad you like your ring."

"I love it. Oh, Gid, you really have taken me by surprise, and it's all so great, and I'm so happy."

"So am I." He beamed at her. "Now, let's seal our bargain with a kiss, shall we?"

She smiled back at him and slid her arms around his neck, pulled him down so that he was laying on top of her. They kissed deeply, hungrily, touched each other in intimate places, and swiftly his passion soared. She felt sudden heat rushing through her, and she clung to him, loving him so much; then her legs went around his back as he entered her, and she cried out as she always did, as if she were taken by surprise. This thrilled him, and when she began to thrust her body vigorously against his, he thought he would explode with excitement. Within seconds they were moving in unison, had found their perfect rhythm. It was a rhythm that swiftly increased, and the faster they moved the more excited they both were. And as she came in ecstasy, she cried out his name, and he called hers a split second later, telling her over and over again how much he loved her.

After they had calmed down they took a shower, stood under the running water wrapped in each other's arms. It was as if they were unable to pull apart.

But they finally did so, and Evan went into the bedroom to dry her hair and brush it into shape. She was still wrapped in a towel, putting on a few touches of makeup, when Gideon came back into the room and quickly got dressed. Then he sat down in a chair and watched her, counting his blessings that he had found her. Yes, he had found his true love in this uncertain world, and he felt very lucky. This woman was a perfect fit in every possible way; they were in tune with each other.

After she had put on a pretty muslin frock and a pair of sandals, Evan swung to face him and said, "What is it? You sure are staring at me. *Hard.*"

"Just admiring, darling, that's all," he murmured languidly.

She walked toward him, holding out her left hand. "It's gorgeous, Gideon, isn't it? The most perfect engagement ring."

"I think so, and you *are* wearing it tonight, aren't you? Downstairs, I mean?"

"Yes, if you want me to. . . . Everyone will know we've become engaged." She paused, looked at him carefully, waiting for his reaction.

"Naturally. But since we *are* actually engaged, why shouldn't they know? They're family, yours as well as mine. And listen, I don't want you taking it off, not even when you see your parents next week. Okay?" His green eyes were piercing as they gazed at her.

"Okay, okay," she answered quickly, meaning it but also detecting something in his voice and in his eyes that would brook no argument. And he was right. Since they were engaged to be married, why should they hide it from her parents? Her father wouldn't be pleased, she was fairly certain of that, but it was her life, not his; conversely, she knew Gideon's parents would be delighted, because Emily and Winston had already told her they hoped she would marry their son. Suddenly she exclaimed, "Can we go over to see Robin tomorrow and tell him, Gid? I'd really like him to know we've made it official."

"Why not? Anyway, he's a bit of a romantic, isn't he? He'll be so happy that we've told him first. Imagine, Evan, he kept that snap of your granny all these years."

Evan started to chuckle. "She was no *granny,* not my Glynnis! Not even when she was old. And, anyway, over fifty years ago she was one helluva glamour girl."

"I saw the picture, didn't I? She was a true beauty, and so are you. *My* beauty. *My* beautiful wife to be."

Tessa stood at the stove, hovering over several pots, and so concentrated was she there was no way she was going to turn around at the sound of footsteps. She simply called out, "Where have you been? I thought you were coming to chat to me ages ago, Lorne."

"It's not Lorne," Jack Figg said as he drew closer. "Lorne sent me to ask if you'd like a drink."

Now Tessa swung around and nodded. "That would be nice, Jack."

"Lorne's busy opening a bottle of champagne in the Stone Hall. Is that all right? Or would you prefer something else?"

"Champagne, and thanks for going to get it."

"Back in a moment," he replied.

Tessa busied herself with her pans once more, stirring the meat gently, lifting lids, nodding to herself, then turning some of the pots off. A moment later Jack returned, offering her a flute of champagne. "Thanks," she said, taking it from him.

Bringing his glass to touch hers, he said, "Cheers."

"Cheers," she answered and took a sip. "That's crisp. Tastes great."

"All of this smells mighty good. What're you making for dinner?"

After turning off several more burners on the stovetop, Tessa walked over to the kitchen table, sat down, and sipped her champagne; Jack followed, stood looking at her. "Or is it a secret?"

"No, it's not. I've steamed a batch of white asparagus to start with, and I'm going to serve it warm with hollandaise sauce. The main course is couscous. I know it might sound like a strange dish on a hot night, but it's not really. After all, couscous is Moroccan in origin, and Morocco's a warm country. The couscous grain is very light, a type of semolina, you know, and I've used veal, which is a much lighter meat, instead of lamb. I've made a sort of Moroccan-style *blanquette de veau*, but with a brown sauce, not a white one. You'll enjoy it, Jack."

"I know I will," he answered, sitting down at the table. "The aromas are wonderful. What exactly am I smelling in here?"

"Lots of spices melding together, for one thing. Turmeric, ginger, saffron, cumin, and I've used onions, so you can smell those, as well as vegetables steaming, and meat juices. I hope you're hungry because I've made loads of it."

Jack laughed. "Sitting here inhaling these many aromas has certainly got my taste buds going. My mouth's really watering. If I was starving before, I'm now *ravenous*."

"It's almost finished. Is everybody downstairs?"

"Gideon and Evan haven't appeared, nor has India, but the others are out there in the Stone Hall quaffing cocktails."

"Gosh, I'd better get back to my pots and pans." She half rose.

Jack put his hand on her arm. "Give me a couple of minutes, Tessa. Or is something going to spoil? I'd hate to be the one to ruin a dinner you've spent innumerable hours preparing."

"No, no, nothing will spoil, as long as it *is* only a few minutes." She threw him a curious look and sat down again. "You want to talk to me about Adele, is that it?"

Now it was his turn to give her an odd look. "How did you know?" he asked.

"Because you've not mentioned her since Thursday, not asked me anything about her, and I thought that was very strange. You see, Jack, no one's asked me what happened when she was with Mark, and I suppose this struck me as rather peculiar. Maybe not the family being quiet, but I wondered why you hadn't brought it up."

"I wanted you to calm down. Also, I knew you would tell me if there was something I ought to know. And, to be honest, you've seemed very much on . . . an even keel, and I realized if Mark had treated her badly, or hurt her in any way, you would have come running to me."

"That's true, and you're right, nothing much happened according to Adele. He drove her around the countryside for a while, then he took her to Harrogate, to Betty's Cafe for lunch, and after that they went to Ripon. I think mostly she was bored, and upset, crying about the loss of her doll. And of course she became tired in the afternoon, so he had to take a room at the Spa Hotel so she could have her afternoon nap. God knows what he was thinking, pulling such a stunt. Well, to upset me, scare me, I must presume."

"That's absolutely correct. Did Adele mention the other man in the car? Did she know him?"

"No, she didn't know him, and she seems to have a good memory for a little girl. She said there was a friend of Daddy's with them. His name was Buddy. But I'm not sure that really *was* his actual name."

"Oh, what do you mean?" Jack asked, looking at her alertly.

"Because when I questioned Adele about the man, she said her father told her, 'This is my buddy,' and I suppose she thought that was his name, because he called the man *buddy* several times later. I've no idea who it was, Jack, unless it was one of his sidekicks from the office."

Jack nodded. "That's a thought. I'll have it checked out on Monday morning first thing, ascertain if any of his assistants were off on Wednesday."

Tessa jumped up and exclaimed, "I've got to start getting the food onto the platters, Jack, otherwise everything will fall apart. Is that it, more or less? I mean what you wanted to ask me?"

"Yes, it is, Tessa. Now can I help you?"

"Not really, but you could carry the food into the dining room in a few minutes."

"I'd be delighted." He took a sip of his Dom Pérignon, sat watching her empty pans, scoop food onto the big platters she had taken out of the two ovens. Lithe, efficient, totally in control. He thought she had never looked better. Normally as pale as a ghost, tonight she seemed to glow. Her milky complexion had a shell-pink tint which obviously came from exertion and the heat of the kitchen, yet it was becoming to her. Also, she had been busy all afternoon, and he was aware she was usually in much better spirits when she was working hard. In this she was like her mother. Paula functioned best under great pressure. When she had nothing to do, she became morose, lost all of that superwoman energy. Tessa and Linnet both took after their mother, but he also knew it was a characteristic all three of them had inherited from the founding mother of the dynasty. As long as he had known and worked for Emma, she had been pulled down by inactivity and boredom; she was at the top of her form and full of energy when she was working like a galley slave.

And there was another thing—Tessa did love cooking, drew enormous satisfaction from preparing gourmet meals for the family and friends. In his experience, someone who loved her work was bound to thrive. And she looked as though she were thriving tonight, despite her worries about Mark and the impending divorce.

Tessa interrupted his thoughts. "Jack, would you mind going into the dining room and lighting the candles on the table? And perhaps you could check the hot plates on the sideboard. I put them on low about half an hour ago, so they should be pretty warm by now. Then you can help me with the platters."

"Yes, General, sir!" he exclaimed, jumping up swiftly, saluting her, and hurrying out, chuckling to himself.

Her gaze followed Jack as he left the kitchen. If he loved her mother and adored Linnet, whom he had always called Beauty, he nonetheless did *like* her, that she knew for a certainty, and he was kind to her, had been since her childhood. But he was an enigma, a man who spoke little about his personal life. Her mother had told her that he had been married years ago, and there had been some kind of tragedy. He had let things drop from time to time—how much he loved sailing in Robin Hood's Bay, the picturesque Yorkshire seaside town where he lived, that he was keen on the theater and was an amateur painter in his spare time.

She knew he was devoted to the Hartes, on a retainer

with Harte Stores, and he had been around a lot lately, since the trouble with Mark had started. She was glad about that. He was a reassuring presence, comforting, very reliable, and like a member of the family. Yet there was so much she didn't know about him. Some mystery man, she thought, and began straining the vegetables.

Jack returned to the kitchen as she was heaping couscous onto an extra-large platter; he stood watching her as she formed it into a grand mound. "What are those other things in the couscous?" he asked, leaning forward, in order to see it better.

"Chickpeas and large raisins, which is the traditional way of preparing it. Now I'm going to add the steamed vegetables around the outside." As she was speaking, she had begun to spoon carrots, turnips, parsnips, zucchini, and pearl onions around the couscous, then turning to him she explained, "I'd like you to pop this in the big oven over there to keep warm, please. I've got to dish up the veal stew and warm the hollandaise sauce for the asparagus. Then I'm all set."

"Glad to be of help, Tessa, and congratulations, the dinner looks splendid." He walked over to the oven with the platter of couscous, then thought to ask, "How do you plan to serve?"

"After we've had the asparagus, I thought you and Desmond and Linnet and I could carry the big platters into the dining room and put them on the hot plates. The dinner will be buffet style, everyone can help themselves."

"It's the only way," he answered, "and certainly the easiest."

The room was unfamiliar. So much so he felt completely disoriented.

He blinked in the dim light and looked around,

slowly began to make out shapes and objects against one another: a chest, a chair, a clock on the wall, and to the right, a window. Where the hell was he?

Dusty Rhodes blinked again and adjusted his eyes. Very slowly he began to get a better picture of the room, a whole picture, not fragments. It was a hospital room. And he was in a hospital bed . . . hooked up to a drip. Or something.

For a moment he could not remember anything. Then with a flash he saw himself in the studio that morning, rushing to stand in front of the painting, protecting it from the raised knife.

Once again he felt the sharp pain of the blade entering his body. Excruciating. Blood. A lot of blood. Spurting out. Covering his shirt. On his hand. Running down his arm. On the floor.

She had driven him here. Harrogate District Hospital. That was where he was. Now he remembered it all. *India.* Lady India Standish, daughter of an earl, a lady in her own right. A wonderful girl. An angel. She had saved his life. No question about that. She had remained calm. He could see her in his mind's eye. Calm. Controlled. Practical. She had wadded him up with towels. Driven him here. At breakneck speed. He remembered cringing at the speed. She had delivered him in one piece to Emergency. Yes, that was why he was still alive, hadn't bled to death. Because of her.

She had come back to see him a short while ago. He had still been out of it. He had opened his eyes once and seen her sitting there. Next to the bed. Holding his hand. Mouthing soothing words. White and ghostly, the pale hair in disarray. He had tried to speak to her. But he had been too weak. Then he had passed out again.

Now she was gone. Forever? He hoped not. He wanted her in his life. Would she stay?

It would all come out now. About his long affair with Melinda. The press would know about his child. Atlanta. A very little girl. Beautiful Atlanta. He didn't want that to happen. But he knew it would. And the police would be on top of him. They hadn't talked to him yet. Because he had been incapacitated by the anesthetic. But they would be back tomorrow. Sure as God made little apples they'd be back. With their notebooks. Writing everything down. It would all read so badly. But Melinda hadn't meant to hurt him. It was an accident. She'd been after damaging the painting. Incensed by the sight of another woman in his studio. How had she managed to get out of the hospital? Get into his studio? His fault, that. He hadn't locked the door this morning.

What to tell India? All of it, that was the only way. Real honesty. *How* to tell her. That was the question. Find the right time. Tell her about Melinda. Tell her about Melinda's sickness. Her drug addiction. Tell her about their child. He loved her. Atlanta. India. He loved them both.

What to do about Melinda? How could he get her well? Get her on her feet? And get her out of his life? Thank God he had never married her. Still, he had to be responsible. Help Melinda. Get Atlanta. Keep India . . .

When the nurse looked in a short time later, she saw that Russell Rhodes, the famous artist, was sleeping soundly again. Best thing for him, she thought, knowing that it had been touch and go for a while. There was a moment when he might easily have died. Thank God he hadn't. Luck was on his side. Everyone needed luck sometime in their lives, she thought and quietly closed the door and went about her other duties.

II

The buzzing of the intercom brought Evan's head up with a start, and her eyes flew to the clock on the mantelpiece. It was twenty minutes to seven, and her parents weren't due to arrive until seven, but she knew it was them. A moment before, she had pulled on a pair of black linen pants; now she slipped her feet into black patent high-heeled mules and quickly buttoned her white cotton, sleeveless blouse as she ran to the door.

The buzzer was shrilling again, and she snatched up the small wall phone and said, "Hello?"

"It's us," her father's slightly disembodied voice informed her from the street.

"Hi, Dad! I'll buzz you in. Just push the door open. I'm on the third floor."

"See you in a minute."

She replaced the receiver, ran back to the bedroom, put pearl studs on her ears, turned to run out again, then dashed back to the dressing table to get her sapphire engagement ring, which she slipped onto her finger. Finally she hurried back to the front door, opened it, stood on the threshold—waiting for her mother and father to get out of the elevator. It was almost but not quite opposite her front door, and as they appeared she broke into smiles; she ran to greet them, hugging her mother first and then her father.

After a big bear hug, Owen Hughes held her away from him and searched her face, his own wreathed in smiles. "It's great to see you, Evan!" he exclaimed. "Just wonderful."

Her mother, also smiling, said, "We missed you, honey."

"And I've missed you. It's lovely to see *you* both after all these months," Evan responded, glancing first at her mother and then back at her father.

She stared at him intently for a split second, her stomach lurching, instantly thought: My God, he's a younger version of Robin Ainsley. I always believed he resembled Richard Hughes. How peculiar he should resemble both men. One his biological father, the other the man who adopted him as a newborn. Except that Robin and Richard *were* exactly the same type—tall, lean, almost rangy, with bright blue eyes and dark hair. Well, Robin's wasn't exactly dark anymore, and Richard's had turned pepper and salt long before his death.

It seemed her grandmother Glynnis had fallen for men of similar physical appearance, as most women do. Suddenly aware of the growing silence, Evan said, "Well, let's not stand here in the hall. Come in, come in." She turned and led them into her apartment.

They followed rapidly, and she was instantly aware that their eyes were taking everything in as she closed the door and joined them. "This is the living room," she explained, "and there's a small kitchen down at the far end. That's where the room turns into an L shape and becomes a small dining area. I have a bedroom and bathroom, and that's it. It's not very grand, I know, but I love it."

"Somehow I thought it would be much larger," her father murmured. "The way you spoke about it . . ."

Evan thought he sounded slightly critical, and somewhat defensively she exclaimed, "It's a lovely flat, Dad!"

"Oh yes," he said, nodding, and walked the length of the room, still looking around. He remained silent, as if he were at a loss for words, then made for the sofa near the fireplace.

Her mother said in a warm and confident tone, "I think it's very nice, very nice indeed, Evan. Comfortable, cozy even, and perfect for you."

"Yes, it is, Mom." Evan was really surprised that her mother sounded so firm, positive, perhaps not quite as intimidated by her husband as she had been in the past. Taking hold of her mother's arm affectionately, she led her over to the chairs placed opposite the sofa, where they both sat down. "I didn't want a large apartment, Dad. Anyway, I was extremely lucky to get this. It's a sublet, furnished, and it doesn't need a lot of upkeep. Besides, it's near the store. I can walk to Harte's every day."

Once again it was her mother who spoke up. "I like it very much, honey, and I can see so many of your own little touches. Lots of plants and flowers, which you always love to have around you, the photographs of us all, your favorite books, the fashion and news magazines you enjoy, and bits and pieces I recognize. And I bet all of these cushions are yours, that you just bought them recently. Yes, you've really made it your own." When Evan was silent, Marietta asked softly, "I am right about all those things, aren't I, Evan?"

"Yes, you are, Mommy, and thanks for your kind words." She grinned at her mother. "And I *did* just buy those cushions. I tried to put my stamp on the flat. You see, the owner had taken out all of the small objects and accessories, so it was quite impersonal. I had what I thought of as a blank canvas to work with. Anyway, it's not forever, just a temporary place."

"The furniture's very nice," her father remarked, obviously wanting to make amends for his first rather churlish words. "That's an extremely good-looking Georgian desk over there, and I'm sure the bookcases are Georgian, too." He walked over to the bookcases, looked at them with an expert eye. "Yes, just as I thought." He glanced at the mirror hanging on the long back wall and added, "That's definitely a Georgian mirror. All very valuable pieces. Who owns this place?"

"I don't actually know," she answered swiftly, deciding that a small white lie didn't matter if it kept the peace for the moment. "I made the deal through a real estate agent. The young woman who owns it is living abroad."

"I see. Well, yes, it's very nice," he murmured, obviously impressed by the antiques and returned to his seat on the sofa.

"Now can I get you both a drink?" Evan asked, rising. "A soft drink? Scotch or vodka? Wine? I've even got champagne."

"I'll have a glass of white wine, Evan," her father said. "Thanks."

"And I'll have one, too, please," Marietta announced in a light, clear voice.

Startled though she was by her mother's request, because she never drank alcohol, Evan kept a neutral expression on her face. "Coming right up," she said and made for the kitchen.

Once she was alone, Evan took off her engagement ring and slipped it into the pocket of her pants, hoping her parents hadn't spotted it on the third finger of her hand. But her father would have remarked about it. He would have been unable to resist asking a few probing questions.

As she opened the bottle of Sancerre, she admitted to herself that she was afraid to discuss her engagement to Gideon with her parents. And how furious *he* would be if he knew she had taken off his ring. But she felt easier holding back this news. At least for the moment.

Pouring the wine into the elegant crystal goblets she had taken out of the cupboard, she thought about the changes in her mother. They were startling.

First, Marietta looked very different. Her general appearance was much smarter than usual, her hair better groomed, her makeup nicely applied. Also, the navy blue linen dress she wore was superbly cut and styled, and more than likely it had cost much more than her mother was used to spending on herself. No, this was not her mother's normal way of dressing, she who favored T-shirts and slacks, and often looked sloppy and disheveled.

Second, her mother was managing to assert herself with Owen. Evan had never seen Marietta stand up to her father. Certainly not in the way she just had, overriding his comments with opinions of her own. Why, she had practically pooh-poohed his opinion of the flat.

It struck Evan now that her mother seemed not only better in health but much more independent, even *spirited*. Evan couldn't help wondering what had brought about this extraordinary change. It pleased her, made her happy inside for her mother. It's amazing, she thought. And puzzling. Was it a new medication finally kicking in? Or something else?

Opening the refrigerator, Evan took out the platter of hors d'oeuvres she had made and began to peel off the plastic wrap, focusing now on her father. She had known Owen would spot the genuine antiques in the flat; after all, he was a leading antiques dealer in Manhattan and Connecticut, and a well-known expert in Georgian furniture, even gave lectures about the period.

And everything in the flat *was* Georgian and valuable. It all belonged to Emily Barkstone Harte, Gideon's mother; she also owned the flat, which was normally occupied by Gideon's sister, Natalie. Since Natalie was doing a stint at the Harte newspaper company in Sydney, Gideon had arranged for Evan to move in until his sister returned to London.

Evan had been anxious to leave the charming little hotel where she had lived until a few weeks ago. And Gideon had wanted her to have a place of her own and blessed privacy. The hotel belonged to her father's great friend George Thomas, and they agreed that while Arlette, George's wife, was a lovely and motherly woman, she was far too keenly interested in their relationship for comfort. Evan had the feeling that her comings and goings were constantly noted by Arlette and reported to her father, albeit in the most innocent way.

There was no reason for her parents to know about her reasons for leaving the hotel, other than that she wanted a place of her own. Or to know about the ownership of this flat filled with beautiful Georgian pieces. It was nobody's business but hers. She was, after all, free, white, and twenty-one. Twenty-seven actually, self-supporting, and therefore her own boss.

Feeling more comfortable now that she had removed the engagement ring, Evan carried the tray of drinks into the living room and put it on the coffee table near the sofa.

After handing her mother and father their glasses of wine, she went back to the kitchen, saying over her shoulder, "I made a few little snacks, I'll only be a moment."

Placing the platter on the coffee table, she sat down next to her mother and reached for her glass. "Cheers, Mom, Dad, and welcome to London."

"Cheers," her parents said in unison, and both of them took sips of their wine.

"Help yourself to the smoked salmon and little sausage rolls," Evan instructed, love and warmth echoing in her voice. "I made them myself."

Her mother beamed at her. "You've gone to a lot of trouble. Thank you, honey."

Her father said, "So fill us in, Evan. We're dying to hear what you intend to do for the rest of the year."

Evan stared at him in surprise and exclaimed, "But I talk to you every week, and you know my plans, Dad. I love working at Harte's, and that's what I'm going to do for the rest of the year." She felt like adding, and the rest of my life, but refrained. She sat back, her eyes riveted on her father.

"I see. But a moment ago you said this flat was only temporary. . . ." His voice trailed off, and he looked baffled, uncertain.

"I did say that, yes, but what I meant was that this flat was only temporary until I find a place I really like, which I will then buy."

"That's a good idea," Marietta said. "It will be a good investment."

Her father threw her mother a reproachful look, then said in a rather subdued voice, "Do you mean you're planning to live in London indefinitely, Evan?"

"Yes, I do."

"But when you came here in January, it was my understanding it was only for a year, a sort of sabbatical, like the one I took myself years ago."

"Perhaps that's what I meant *then*, Dad, but I do love working at the store. In fact, I love the store. It's probably the greatest department store in the world, thanks to Emma Harte and her heirs, and I'm thrilled to be a part of it."

"I hope they're not working you too hard there. You look to me as if you've lost weight. You're very thin."

Something inside Evan rose up like bile, and sharp retorts sprang to her lips. But she knew it was wiser not to respond to her father's comments. The anxiety suddenly clouding her mother's face was another reason she avoided sarcastic remarks. Instead, she said, "No, they're not working me too hard, Dad. In fact, they all work much harder than I do, or than any other employee. And they're wonderful people, the Hartes. I can't understand why you have this hatred for them." There, it was out. She hadn't meant to say it, at least not yet, but she had, and she wasn't going to retract it.

"I don't hate the Hartes!" he cried. "I don't even know them. Why would you say a thing like that? You're being silly, overimaginative."

"No, I'm not, Dad. You've made remarks about them ever since I started working at the store, and you continue to make strange comments about Gideon, a man you don't even know."

"Is that what this is all about? Your boyfriend?" he asked, his voice suddenly chilly.

"No, it isn't. You started it by implying that my bosses made me work too hard, that I look like I've lost weight. Maybe I have, because I want to be thin and elegant, wear the nice clothes I have with self-confidence. Anyway, I've always been pretty slender. As far as

Gideon's concerned, he's a very nice young man. And he's been kind to me every day since I arrived, which is when I met him."

Marietta, sensing a row brewing, said, "I think it's nice that you have a boyfriend, Evan, a man who is kind and understanding, and obviously devoted to you. I hope we're going to meet him while we're here."

Evan gave her mother a loving smile, thankful that she had poured oil on troubled waters. "Of course you are. I *want* you and Dad to meet Gideon. In fact, he would like to take you out to lunch on Sunday—"

"Oh, I don't think we can do that," her father cut in. "I promised George and Arlette we would join them for lunch on Sunday. At the hotel. You know how much they care about you, Evan."

"I suppose it'll be all right," Evan murmured, disappointed but glad the tricky situation had been diffused. "I'll tell Gideon about the change in plans. I think he'd enjoy seeing George and Arlette again."

"Oh, but I don't believe George was including your friend," her father said. "He meant just the three of us."

Evan sat back, furious. She was about to remind her father that they had come to London to see her, not the friend of his youth, when her mother put a hand on her arm, cleared her throat, said quietly, "Don't be upset, Evan dear."

Leaning forward in her chair, Marietta focused all of her attention on her husband. "No, Owen, I'm afraid we won't be accepting George's invitation for lunch on Sunday. At a later date perhaps, but not this Sunday. We are going to go out to lunch with our daughter and her boyfriend. We don't need other people along, not if we're going to properly get to know Gideon Harte."

"I don't wish to offend George," Owen began, glaring at his wife, but before he could finish his sentence, Marietta was speaking again.

In a firm voice, she said, "Oh, it won't offend him. He'll understand, I'm sure. Anyway, I can always go alone with Evan to meet Gideon, you know. And you, Owen, can have lunch with George and Arlette if you prefer."

Evan was once more surprised, and delighted. Her father had opened his mouth, then promptly closed it. He looked mortified, but she didn't care. She was silently applauding her mother. God knows what's happened to her, but she's a different woman. And quite wonderful, Evan thought, smiling to herself.

Suddenly her mother was continuing in that lovely, newly confident voice. "Now, Evan, you said yesterday that you'd booked a table at a special place for dinner tonight. So . . . where *are* we going, honey?"

"To Rules, Mom. It was Glynnis's favorite restaurant, and she and grandfather used to take me there when I came to London with them. And you and Dad came with us once. I thought it would be lovely to go back to a place of shared memories."

12

You two Stormy Petrels have lived up to your name this week, and then some," Gideon said, looking from Linnet to India, his two favorite cousins.

Linnet frowned, repeated, "*Stormy petrels?* Now where did that come from?" and stared at Gideon, then looked across at India and raised an auburn brow quizzically.

India said, "Don't look at me, I don't know what he means. But actually I do happen to know what a stormy petrel is. It's a rather beautiful bird that spends most of its life on the sea, and it follows ships quite a lot. I think it comes ashore only to breed, and it does that in the remote western islands around our shores."

Julian Kallinski began to laugh, shaking his head. "What short memories you two have. And, Linnet, you also seem to have forgotten what your mother told us . . . the legend of the stormy petrel, that the name *petrel* is supposedly a diminutive of Peter. You see, when it's feeding, the bird appears to hover just above the water, and its feet look as if they're pattering on the surface of the sea. One gets a sense that it's *walking on water,* the way St. Peter did in the Bible story, hence its name petrel, for Peter."

"Oh gosh, Jules, I think I do remember that now," Linnet murmured. "My mother *did* tell us about the stormy petrel. We were all very small and staying at Heron's Nest in Scarborough for the summer, and there were stormy petrels flying around. And, very vaguely, I remember you saying, Gideon, that the Harte girls were stormy petrels . . . but it's such a long time ago."

"Yes, you're very ancient," Julian remarked, chuckling as he spoke.

"*We're* not ancient. It's Tessa who's the Ancient One, at least that's what Lorne has always called her," India reminded them.

Gideon smiled at India and remarked, "Tessa's a stormy petrel, too, and I'm paying you all a compliment. You see, I thought you were beautiful birds who could walk on water even when you were little girls. And I still think that."

"Thank you, Gid," India answered, smiling back at him. He had always been one of her favorites. He was there for her whenever she needed him. "It's a charming way of describing us," she went on. "From now on we'll call ourselves the Stormy Petrels and remind the world we can indeed walk on water."

"Tessa came through her ordeal very well, and Linnet, you were superb, and what a good idea you had when you brought Jack in to help with the abduction. As for you, India, I think you're quite remarkable the way you handled the situation with Dusty." Gideon sat back, reached for his glass of wine, and took a long swallow.

The four of them, best friends since childhood, were enjoying a drink before going out to dinner. It was something of a ritual, this weekly dinner, although sometimes one or another of them was missing because of business commitments or travels. But they endeavored to get together even if they were not a full complement, because they cherished their lifelong relationships with one another.

Linnet began to fan herself with one hand and remarked, "It's terribly hot in here, Jules, are you certain the air-conditioning is working?"

"I know it is, but I'll check it, darling," he murmured and went across to the unit, bent over and examined it. "It's okay," he told her, his dark blue gaze full of love. "Talking of Heron's Nest, I wouldn't mind being by the seaside in Scarborough right now. Oh, for a weekend on the beach, and the pleasure of a few salty sea breezes."

India, who had been looking off into the distance somewhat pensively, exclaimed, "Heron's Nest! Gosh, that's a good idea for Dusty, the perfect place for him to recuperate. What do you think? Would it be all right if I took him there?"

"I'm sure it's fine, but how will you manage?" Linnet asked, then reminded her, "There's no real help there these days, India. Only Mrs. Hodges keeping an eye on it."

"I'm a Stormy Petrel," India shot back. "I can walk on water, remember? So I'll certainly be able to manage a house and a man who's recuperative, wouldn't you say?"

Linnet laughed, as always enjoying India's pithy comments.

"How *is* Dusty?" Gideon asked, focusing on his cousin.

India sighed, bit her lip, and then her face clouded over. "It's been worse than I expected, but he's going to be all right. To be very honest, it was a lot more serious than he or I realized at first. The wound I mean. The brachial artery is where the pectoral muscle goes up into the shoulder, and that artery was almost severed completely. It was really touch and go for a while during surgery. And there was an enormous loss of blood. He could easily have bled to death—"

"It's thanks to you that he didn't!" Linnet pointed out swiftly. "If you hadn't acted immediately, he'd be dead by now."

India nodded but remained silent, hardly able to countenance the idea of Dusty being dead.

Julian leaned forward and asked, "What's your feeling about the stabbing, India? Any new thoughts on it?"

She shook her head. "Not really. But my common sense tells me that he must have known that woman at some time. A stranger is not going to find his studio, burst in unannounced, go berserk at the sight of me, stab a portrait of me, and then run away. For me to think the woman was unknown to Dusty would be pretty ridiculous, don't you think?"

"Yes, it would," Gideon agreed. He knew a lot about Russell Rhodes now. He had had two of his crack investigative reporters on the story for the past week. Not that he intended to tell India much of what he knew. But to properly protect her, and the family, he had put the top journalists to work at once.

Now he said, "Your practicality serves you well. Dusty did know her. I'm not going to lie to you, India, I put reporters on the story, but I'm not running anything in any of our papers. Let's hope the nationals don't either."

India was sitting bolt upright, staring at Gideon, and she exclaimed, "Who is she? What did you find out?"

"Not as much as we'd like to know, you and I. She was his girlfriend for a while. A model and an actress. From what I gather, she's had problems with drugs and has been hospitalized somewhere for quite some time now. Trying to get detoxed."

"I see," India murmured, looking suddenly morose.

Picking up on her mood at once, Gideon added swiftly, "From what I've been told, their relationship had been over for a long time. But it seems she's been . . . well, a bit obsessed with him."

"What's her name?" India asked softly.

"You don't really want to know. . . . Oh well, I can see you do. It's Melinda Caldwell."

"I can't imagine why Dusty didn't tell me about her!"

"I think that's understandable under the circumstances, darling," Julian interjected. "If she's been bothersome to him, he wouldn't want you to become upset. Also, men tend not to talk about old lovers to new ones." Julian looked at Gideon for support.

Gideon said, "Julian's right, there was no real reason for Dusty to talk about other women, now, was there?"

"I suppose not," she muttered, brushing her hair away from her face, which was suddenly much paler.

"Have you discussed anything with Dusty?" Julian asked. "I suppose he's well enough by now to talk to you."

"Actually, he's not been in top form. In fact, the doctors have been a little worried about him," India explained. "I didn't want to upset him unduly, so I decided to wait until he's out of hospital."

"I see. When is he going to be able to go home?" Julian continued.

"Next week. Either Monday or Tuesday. Hence my thought about Heron's Nest. If the heat keeps up, it might be nice by the sea. On the other hand, it may be wiser to take him back to Willows Hall, where there's a staff, and it's only ten minutes away from the hospital. In case of any emergency."

Linnet said, "I'm glad you made that decision, I think

Heron's Nest probably needs a thorough cleaning. None of us has been there for ages."

"We should go, though," Gideon exclaimed, his eyes lighting up. "I'd like to take Evan there for a weekend. Actually, we might all go and spend a weekend there. It would be like old times."

"Why not? And I'm sorry Evan's not with us this evening," Linnet murmured, standing up. "But I suppose she felt obligated to take her parents to dinner. After all, she hasn't seen then for eight months."

"That's right," Gideon replied. "She booked a table at Rules. Apparently her grandparents used to take her there when she came to London with them years ago."

"And where are we going?" India asked.

"I booked a table at the Ivy," Gideon told her. "Because I know how much you like it."

"Thanks, Gid," India said and sighed as she, too, got to her feet. "It's lovely to be with all of you. The last few days have been awful, worrying about Dusty, and when I think about last Saturday, I go cold all over."

"I can certainly understand why. It was the most bizarre stabbing I've ever heard of!" Linnet exclaimed, shaking her head. "Incredible really."

"It was surreal," India announced. "I still can't believe such a thing happened."

"It did, but let's forget it for tonight at least." Gideon took hold of India's arm and walked with her to the door. "I know the police now have the full picture, the right picture, and they won't be bothering you again, thank God."

Things were better in the cab going through the park, the Mall, and down the Strand to Rules. For a few minutes, just before they left the flat, Evan had decided her father was going to be grouchy and argumentative all evening. His expression was grim and discontented when they left; but he had grown lighter when the cab was on its way and even made a bit of small talk.

And her father's mood only improved once they were being welcomed at the restaurant. Rules was still one of Evan's favorite restaurants in London; she came here often, and the staff knew her well, so the greetings were warm, the table the best in the house.

Evan ordered a bottle of Pouilly-Fuissé, and they all had a glass of the dry white wine while they studied the menu. After much discussion about various dishes they had enjoyed in the past, they ended up choosing the same—dressed crab to start, followed by grilled Dover sole and a mélange of summer vegetables.

As the three waited for their food, they chatted briefly about the restaurant and the fond memories it evoked of Glynnis and Richard. Then both of her parents asked her about her job and she regaled them with details about her daily routine and amusing stories. There was no mistaking how much she loved her job.

It was over the crab salad that Evan suddenly remarked, "Dad, do you remember that you said you thought your mother had known Emma Harte during the Second World War, here in London?"

"Yes, I do, Evan."

"Is that all you know? That Grandma had been acquainted with Emma at that time?"

"Why yes, it is," he answered swiftly, staring at her in puzzlement. "Why?"

"Because the beautiful Glynnis Jenkins, as she was called then, the girl from the Rhondda Valley in Wales, was actually an employee at Harte's, just as I am today. Your mother was Emma Harte's private secretary, Dad, and very close to her lady boss."

"Heavens to Betsy!" her father exclaimed. "I never realized that."

"Well, it's true," Evan went on, "and your mother was quite a favorite with the whole family." When her father remained silent, Evan glanced at her mother and saw the strangest expression on her face. She quickly realized it was contempt in her mother's eyes. And she knew, intuitively, that her father had just deliberately lied to her, and her mother knew he had.

Clearing her throat, Evan changed the subject at once. "I hope you'll come and have lunch with me at the store one day next week, Mom. And I'll give you a full tour as well."

"Why, Evan honey, I'd love that."

"Let's do it on Tuesday, because I have to go to Leeds on Wednesday. We're revamping some of the stores, and I'm in charge of the Leeds overhaul with India."

"Who's India?" Marietta asked.

"She's Linnet O'Neill's other assistant, and her cousin. Lady India Standish is her full name, and she's a great girl."

"I'm so happy you made some nice friends here," Marietta murmured, smiling at Evan. There was a moment's hesitation, and then she said slowly, "It's an unusual name, *India*. I've never heard it used as a first name before."

"It's a Victorian name," Owen announced before Evan could answer and explained, "It came into popularity because of England's involvement in India and its influence over the country for hundreds of years. During those years of the Raj, the English loved so many things of Indian origin, and of course there were a lot of British troops stationed there. Anyway, I suppose someone had the bright idea of calling a child after the coun-

try. India became a favorite name for girls when Queen
Victoria was on the throne and Empress of India as well,
and it's still used today."

"Gee, Dad, I didn't know you were so well versed in
British history!" Evan exclaimed, glad they were off the
subject of Emma Harte and his mother. If he was reluctant to admit that he'd always known his mother worked
for Emma Harte, then he would surely not like to hear
that his *real* father was Robin Ainsley, Emma's favorite
son. No way, Jose, she thought, and nodded to the waiter
when he began to clear the plates away.

The conversation progressed normally from then
on; they talked about her sisters, Elayne and Angharad,
and her mother spoke rather proudly about their
adopted daughters, who were having successes with
their work and in their personal lives. Both of them had
new boyfriends, and Marietta explained that she was
quite certain Angharad would settle down with her current beau.

Evan nodded and smiled, said very little, not wanting
to become embroiled in a discussion about *her* love life.
And it seemed to her that her mother felt the same way,
because within seconds Marietta had moved on, was
talking about some of the day trips they planned to take
while they were in London. Then her father launched
into a long story about going to France to look for country antiques and finished up by asking her to join them.

"I just can't at the moment, Dad," Evan told him and
then talked about getting the Leeds store up to par; he
appeared to accept this explanation with good grace; in
fact, she decided he was in a wholly different mood by
the time they were selecting desserts.

He's calmed down, she thought, eyeing him over the
top of her menu, thinking suddenly how handsome he

looked in his gray linen jacket, pale blue shirt, and darker blue tie. God, he's the spitting image of Robin, at least the way Robin must have looked when he was the same age . . . fifty-seven. He's got Robin's elegance, his refinement. I wish I could tell him the truth. But I don't dare. At least not tonight. *And maybe never.*

"Do you think she's swimming in dangerous waters?"

Linnet swiveled her head and looked up at Julian; a small sigh escaped before she settled back in her fiancé's arms, leaning her head against his bare chest. "I don't think so," she answered, after considering his question for a moment. "In any case, there's not much any of us could do about it. India's got a mind of her own, as you well know."

"Yes, that's true. But I've got to admit I'm a bit worried about her, darling. Russell Rhodes has quite a reputation."

Struggling up in the bed, Linnet crouched next to Julian, looking into his face intently. "Don't worry so much," she murmured. Since they were children he had always worried. "India told me weeks ago that the reputation is somewhat self-manufactured. You know, for the publicity it gets him. She told me that the rabble-rousing is merely a great deal of noise about nothing. And he hardly drinks at all. Nurses a Stolichnaya all night."

Julian frowned. "Gideon seems to think he's a bit of a womanizer, though. And Gid's got great insight."

"But India says there are no other women around, and haven't been since she's known him, which is several months now. Also, she told me he confided that he'd been on his own for quite a while before he took up with her." When Julian was silent, Linnet continued, "Listen, an artist who paints with the precision he does has to have a steady hand every morning, and his paintings are glorious, you know that."

"They're *magnificent*. But I was talking about his *womanizing,* not his drinking."

"I know. Gideon didn't seem to have much information about that, though. He only knew about this Melinda Caldwell," she reminded him.

"He probably wouldn't want to talk about other women in front of India anyway."

"Did Gideon confide something in you?" Linnet probed.

Julian shook his head. "He didn't. All he did say, when you and India went to the ladies' room, was that the Harrogate police had seemingly buried the incident."

"Oh." Total surprise flickered on her face. "Why on earth would they do that?"

"Local-boy-made-good syndrome, that's what Gideon calls it. From what I understand, the police have wiped the slate clean, and the hospital has done the same thing. The incident never happened. Also, Gideon's quite certain that Dusty's not bringing charges against the woman."

"India *does* say it was an accident."

"I suppose it was. And in a way, Linny, that's what I was getting at a moment ago. Is India swimming in dangerous waters because of Melinda Caldwell? This woman is apparently obsessed with Dusty. How do we know she won't stalk him, make life hell for him, and for India as well? And there's another thing, how serious is their relationship?"

"It's serious as far as India's concerned, that I do know. Actually, she'd like to make it permanent. But he's not so keen about marriage."

"What chap in his right mind would turn his nose up at India?" he exclaimed.

"Dusty Rhodes, the poor boy from the back streets of Leeds."

"But why?" Julian shook his head, his expression a mixture of puzzlement and disbelief.

"*Why?*" Linnet repeated, and she couldn't prevent a small smirk from settling on her mouth. "Because of *who* she is. He doesn't like her family, which is all of us as well as her parents, whom he's never met. He's against the Hartes because we're too posh and well-to-do, apparently, and even more against her parents because Anthony has a *title*. It's a kind of reverse snobbery, I suppose. For instance, he won't call his butler 'the butler,' but insists on referring to him as 'the house manager,' if you can believe that one."

"Oh, I can all right, I've met chaps like Dusty. But I suppose he'll come round when he's met us. We're not so bad."

"I think *you're* wonderful, Julian Kallinski, husband to be, light of my life. Since we finally decided to get married on December the first, I put the invitations into work earlier this week, by the way."

Julian beamed. "That's great." He touched her face lightly. "That'll please my grandfather." It also pleased him. He'd wanted to marry her since she was twelve.

"It'll please mine, too." Linnet cocked her head to one side and said, "The last ten days have been sort of . . . hellish, wouldn't you say? What with one thing and another, I sometimes think this family's cursed."

"That's a silly thing to say!" Julian exclaimed. "The Hartes are a big family, and more things happen in a big family than they do in a small family . . . so it just seems overwhelming at times. But the Hartes are not cursed, neither are the O'Neills or the Kallinskis." He shook his head. "Very simply, life can be catastrophic at times—"

"For some families more than others, though," she

cut in. "Currently there are two divorces pending, and one is going to be supremely unpleasant. There's been an abduction, failed, of course. But nonetheless it's put the fear of God in Tessa, changed her life to a certain extent. India's been involved in a stabbing, and let's face it, she could have been hurt—"

"That's what I was getting at when I mentioned *dangerous waters*," he interrupted.

"I know that. And this Melinda Caldwell is a problem for Dusty. He's going to have to solve that one, Jules, because India won't put up with any nonsense. Which means her future with him is even more dubious than I thought."

"I agree with you. Back to Tessa for a moment. Do you think she means it when she says she wants to spend more time with Adele? That her career must come second?"

"Yes, I suppose I do believe she means it . . . at the moment. It's hard to really know with Tessa, she can change her mind so easily. But I believe she *is* afraid of Mark Longden or, rather, what he might pull next. Her solicitors met with his during the week, and there's now some sort of financial negotiation going on. But it doesn't make her feel any easier, from what she said to Mummy on the phone the other day."

"Does your mother know you and I set the date for the wedding?"

Linnet smiled at him. "Yes, and she's happy we've settled the matter. But to be honest, I'm wondering if we shouldn't have planned it for earlier, maybe for November."

Julian nodded, understanding what she meant immediately. "Because Grandfather's old, and not up to par," he murmured, pulling her into his arms, stroking her hair. "That's what you're getting at, isn't it?"

"Yes," she murmured against his chest. "And mine's getting on in years, too. Mind you, Grandfather Bryan's not showing his age."

"Not at all, and it'll be fine, Linnet. The grandfathers are not going to die before we're married." He chuckled. "You know they've always wanted us to tie the knot, because Emma loved the idea of uniting the clans. They're going to *will* themselves to stay alive until after the event."

Linnet laughed with him. "That's what Mummy said."

"When is she coming back from New York?"

"The first week of September, as planned. Dad's going to the Bahamas for a few days and flying back from there. Emily and Winston will be returning to London with Mums."

"What did she say about the reception?"

"She wants to have it at Pennistone Royal, she's never changed her mind about that, nor will she."

"I'm glad."

Julian held her closer, and they lay together like this for a while. It was Linnet who broke the silence. "Two good things happened in the past week to counteract the bad. You and I finally set the date, and Evan and Gideon became engaged."

"That's right! He's going to meet her parents on Sunday, make it official, then he plans to phone Emily and Winston to tell them."

"They'll be so happy, they love Evan." There was a pause, and then Linnet said softly, "I'd like us to have a baby straightaway, Julian. I don't want us to wait to start a family. Is that all right with you?"

"Of course it is. I think it's best to have babies when we're young."

"Especially women who work. A baby and a job are easier to handle when you're in your twenties."

"Oh, you can handle anything, darling," Julian pronounced in a confident voice. "After all, Gideon has anointed you . . . you're a Stormy Petrel who can walk on water."

There was a hint of laughter in her voice when she answered. "Oh, Jules, darling, let's start practicing now."

"Walking on water?"

"No, silly! You know very well what I mean . . . making babies." She loved to tease him.

"It'll be my pleasure," he whispered against her hair, bent over her, and began to kiss her passionately.

13

Evan sat at the desk in her office at Harte's on Saturday morning, staring at the simple sketches she had made for Linnet. She had started them last week, and they showed her suggested changes for the various fashion departments in the Leeds store. She was pleased with her ideas and hoped Linnet would be, too; she knew the changes were good, could be made without a large expenditure.

When Linnet had given her the task of revamping three fashion departments on two separate floors, Evan had been flattered by the confidence in her as well as excited by the challenge. Now her eyes swept over the sketches. They were somewhat rough, but certainly they would help a draftsman come up with more finished plans. What was more, they were accurate in details and measurements.

Setting the drawings aside, Evan turned on her computer to check her e-mails, made a few notes about the Leeds project, then sat back and took a sip of coffee. All manner of things began to run through her head, but within seconds she was focusing on the dinner with her parents.

It had been successful in the end, but it had certainly commenced with a strange undertone. Her mind veered to her father. He had seemed difficult when he arrived. Her mother had been perfectly all right. But it was almost as if her father were spoiling for a fight.

Perhaps he had been nervous, and maybe he had imagined, perhaps even worried, that she had somehow changed in the eight months she had lived in London. In certain ways she *had* changed, Evan knew that, but not very drastically, certainly not in her character. It seemed to her that once he had realized this he had calmed down, become his normal self again.

She had always been close to her father. She loved him, adored him really. And they had been a team of two when she was growing up. Inseparable. Grandma Glynnis had joked about that, the way they did everything together, like two old buddies, Grandma always said.

And then last night something truly odd had happened. She had spent the night tossing and turning, thinking about Owen Hughes, who and what he was. He was still her father, but he had lied to her, she was positive of that, and suddenly he had become no longer the man she had believed him to be.

In the end, in the early hours of the morning, she had convinced herself it didn't matter. She still loved him. You loved people despite their faults. After all, no one was perfect. He had told her a lie, but it was a white lie, and perhaps there had been a reason for it.

Actually, Evan wouldn't have known he'd lied if she had not happened to glance at her mother at that precise moment. Her expression had been one of contempt. Or had it been disgust? Whichever, it had announced in no uncertain terms that Owen was lying.

There was a sudden knock, and before Evan could say anything the door flew open. Linnet came hurrying in, looking disturbed. Evan instantly straightened in the chair, bracing herself for trouble.

"Do you have a minute, Evan?" Linnet asked.

"Of course. What's wrong? You look upset."

"*Perplexed* is a better word." Linnet sat down heavily in the chair near Evan's desk and continued. "I just had the strangest conversation with Tessa, and I'm still taken aback."

"What was it about?"

Leaning forward, Linnet said in a low voice, "She asked me to look after Adele while she goes to Paris with Lorne."

Evan herself was momentarily startled; then she exclaimed, "But why *wouldn't* she ask you, Linnet? You're her sister, she trusts you and has confidence in you. She's very nervous about Adele's welfare right now, concerned for her."

"I know, but I was a bit surprised she didn't ask our grandmother Daisy Rickards. They're actually rather close, and Daisy would be much better looking after little Adele than me."

"Obviously Tessa thinks *you're* the best choice while your mother is still in New York. I'm sure she would have asked Paula to babysit Adele if she'd been here."

Linnet puffed her cheeks, blew out air. "Gosh, that's one tremendous responsibility, looking after another person's child, and especially Adele under the circumstances. Mind you, Elvira's going to be with us, and it *is* only for a long weekend," Linnet explained. "At Pennistone Royal; Tessa's insistent about that location. Anyway—" Linnet paused, gave Evan a small smile, and asked, "I was wondering if you'd come with us, spend the weekend in Yorkshire? It would be fun if our chaps were with us. Please say yes."

"Yes." Evan laughed and added, "I'd be happy to be with you and Adele at Pennistone Royal, it's one of my favorite places. And you're right, it would be great if Gideon and Julian joined us."

"Thank you so much, I do appreciate it, Evan. Anyway, before I accepted to do this for Tessa, I suggested she take Elvira and Adele to Paris with her, but she dismissed the idea out of hand. I can't say I blame her. I happen to agree that it's better if Adele remains in England with some member of the family, that she doesn't travel abroad until this nasty divorce is over. I fully understand Tessa's worry about Mark Longden. I don't trust him either."

Evan said, "And I have my suspicions about him, and his friend and client Jonathan Ainsley. I think *he's* a rotten piece of work. He's been a lousy son to Robin."

"Jack Figg's on top of Jonathan," Linnet told her, "breathing down his neck. At least Jack's operatives in Hong Kong are, and we'll know exactly where he is from now on. By the way, Tessa's become a convert to Jack Figg's religion of total security."

Evan burst out laughing. "You say that in such a droll way, Linnet. I also think Jack's a pretty terrific guy."

"He is, and he's turned Pennistone Royal into the most secure house in the British Isles. Want to bet?"

"Oh, no way! I think you're correct."

"There's one thing that does puzzle me," Linnet announced, walking over to the window. Without turning around, she went on, "I just can't get over the fact that Tessa asked me to look after her child. I mean . . . she's always been so competitive with me, calling herself the Dauphine, wanting to take over from Mummy *now.* And Mummy doesn't even want to retire, for heaven's sake, won't retire until she's old and decrepit. Not that I think she'll ever be that. Oh well, I guess times have changed."

"Or Tessa has changed," Evan suggested softly.

Linnet swung to face Evan. There was a quickening in her green eyes when she said, "There's a certain truth there. I do believe that the abduction frightened her. And perhaps she does put Adele before anything else. *At the moment.*"

"I wouldn't be surprised if she did retire, and sooner than you think."

"I'm not so sure she'd do that, Evan. You see, Tessa's far too ambitious. She wants to run the stores, thinks it's her right. But she wants to manage them in her way, not the way Mummy has run them for over thirty years." Linnet laughed lightly. "You know what, Evan, Tessa would love *me* to retire, and that's the truth."

"I know how she is, but it's a bit silly to discuss all this, since nothing's going to change as long as Paula is in charge."

"Agreed."

"Why is Tessa going to Paris with Lorne?" Evan asked, her curiosity getting the better of her.

"Because he's making a film there, starting in about another week. The whole cast and crew are going over, according to Tessa, and they'll be in Paris for about six weeks. Then they come back to work for two months at Shepperton Studios. He invited Tessa for the first weekend he's there because he thought the change would do her good."

"He's a really lovely man," Evan said, then glanced down at the sketches on her desk. "I was just going over these before you came in and was about to bring them to your office. My ideas for the Leeds store." She handed Linnet the sketches.

Linnet looked at them quickly, then started at the be-

ginning again, studying the six sketches more carefully.
Eventually she looked up. "How clever you've been.
Bringing all of the fashion departments onto one floor
and designing an open plan so that they flow into each
other."

"With the small boutiques for accessories in various
corners and smaller areas," Evan pointed out, "there is a
wonderful flow. And the customer doesn't have to go to
another floor for shoes or bags and other accessories.
Everything is *there*."

"I think it'll work perfectly. You've done a good job,
Evan."

"Thank you," she answered, pleased. Evan then explained, "Actually, what I've done is borrow from your
mother's idea on the fifth floor here, the way she has put
lingerie, sleepwear, at-home clothes, casual and exer-
cise clothes, hosiery, and casual footwear in different
boutiques next to each other."

"That's right, I see that now. But I think this open
floor plan works much better, Evan. Let's go to the fifth
floor and take a look, shall we?"

One of the things Evan loved most about her job at
Harte's was the store itself. Many a morning she came in
early so that she could traverse some of the floors before
the doors opened to the public. Being on the floor was
thrilling to her, especially when she was alone except
for the odd maintenance person, or another early bird.

Linnet felt the same way; they often compared notes,
and now, as they walked through Lingerie together,
Evan confided, "I love all the floors, all the departments,
but my favorite is Cosmetics. What's yours, Linnet?"

"Cosmetics, too, but I'm also crazy about the Food
Halls. You know when my great-grandmother, I should
say *our* great-grandmother, first started, she had a little

shop in Upper Armley, on the outskirts of Leeds, and her mainstay was her food products. My mother told me that Emma Harte also loved the Food Halls here, and perhaps I inherited that inclination from her. Let's face it, they're wonderful . . . meats and fish, shellfish, chickens and turkeys, and all those gorgeous hams and tongues. And the fruit stalls, and the cakes. I think they're the best in the world."

"Who wouldn't love our Food Halls? They're fantastic. I'm afraid I have to dodge them, they're so tempting. I often see Tessa browsing around, buying there, but then she's very much into food. Gideon says she missed her calling, that she ought to be cooking for the world."

"I bet he said, 'just like Paula,' because my mother thinks she has to feed the starving multitudes, truly believes she's Mother Earth."

"I know she does, and yes he did say that, and meant it in the nicest possible way."

"Oh, I know Gideon adores my mother."

"Who doesn't? Anyway, getting back to my sketches, in particular I took this area as my model, Linnet, but instead of self-contained boutiques I made an open floor plan." Evan glanced around and added, "That way, with no real walls or entrances, the customer feels no constraints, can see everything—well, almost. Oh goodness, there's my mother!"

"Where?" Linnet asked, glancing around. "I don't see anyone who could possibly be your mother, Evan."

"Over there, the woman looking at the negligees. The blonde."

"The blonde! That's your mother? Gosh, I can hardly believe it. She looks like your sister."

"Not quite." Evan giggled. Then, taking hold of Linnet's arm, she hurried her across the floor, exclaiming, "Hello, Mom! Fancy seeing you here!"

Marietta's face lit up at the sight of her daughter. "Hi, Evan honey. I was going to call you on your cell when I'd finished here."

"Mom, I'd like you to meet Linnet O'Neill. And Linnet, this is my mother."

The two women, both beaming, shook hands; then Marietta said, "You look very young to be the boss."

Linnet began to laugh. "I *am* too young to be the boss, and anyway, I'm not. My mother runs Harte's, Mrs. Hughes."

"Oh, I know that. I mean Evan's boss. That's what she always says, 'Linnet's my boss.'"

"I bet I know why you're browsing through all these gorgeous nightgowns, Mom. You're looking for something special for Angharad, who you're convinced is going to be a bride soon."

Marietta gave her daughter a bright smile and shook her head slowly. "Why no, I was browsing for myself."

This comment startled Evan, but she managed to keep a neutral look on her face and answered, "Oh, well, there are some lovely things here, Mom. Linnet does a lot of the buying." She turned to Linnet and went on, "What do *you* think would be suitable for my mother?"

"Let's go down to the other end, Mrs. Hughes, I know just the designer for you."

"Thanks, Linnet, and please call me Marietta."

Linnet inclined her head, smiled, and taking hold of Marietta's arm, led her to the other end of the section.

Evan followed. Today Marietta was wearing a pale blue cotton skirt, matching shirt, and high-heeled blue sandals. Evan couldn't help thinking what great legs her mother had. Funny, but she'd never noticed her legs before. Of course not. Her mother had been in a dressing gown or trousers for most of her life.

Once more, innumerable questions ran through Evan's head. What had wrought this extraordinary change in her mother? She made up her mind to find out. As soon as she possibly could.

Tessa sat at her desk thinking about her impending trip to Paris, feeling suddenly ambivalent about it. She wondered if she'd made a mistake, agreeing to go with her twin when he went to start the movie.

The thought of leaving Adele alone with Elvira worried her, even though they would be at Pennistone Royal, which was now a fortress thanks to Jack Figg and his security systems. When she had voiced her worries to Lorne yesterday, he had suggested she ask Linnet to spend the weekend at Pennistone Royal in order to keep an eye on Adele. "She'll never refuse you, Tess," Lorne had said, reminding her how much Linnet loved her little girl.

And so this morning she had approached Linnet, admittedly a little tentatively, and been happily surprised when her half sister so readily agreed. *Half* sister. That was the way she always thought of Linnet. Just as she thought of Shane as her *step*father, which he was, but he had treated her like his own, and she knew how much he loved her. But they were O'Neills and she was a Fairley, and somehow she could never forget that. Still, Linnet had behaved like a true sister when Adele was stolen. She had taken charge, done all the right things, and because of Linnet everything had been handled with the minimum of fuss for the maximum of success—

The phone on her desk interrupted her thoughts, and she reached for it. "Hello?"

"Is that you, Tessa?" a woman's voice asked.

"Yes, it is. Who am I speaking to?"

"It's Great-Aunt Edwina," the Dowager Countess of

Dunvale announced, bellowing like a British general about to lead his troops into battle. "Have you forgotten me, Tessa Fairley?" she went on. "I certainly think so! I haven't heard from you in the longest time."

"I haven't forgotten you at all, Great-Aunt Edwina. In fact, I was talking to India about you the other day, and we—"

"How is that granddaughter of mine? It strikes me she's become decidedly elusive lately. Haven't heard from her either. Never mind, you're both very young, no time for an old lady like me, what?"

"Please don't say that!" Tessa exclaimed, feeling guilty about neglecting her great-aunt and wondering why Edwina was phoning her. There was always a reason when she made a call. Suddenly Tessa thought of Dusty Rhodes and the stabbing, wondering if Edwina had got wind of it. But how? *Easily.* She lived near Harrogate, just outside Knaresborough, and news traveled fast, bad news traveled faster. And there was Uncle Robin, who lived nearby and spoke to Evan all the time; no doubt she'd filled him in about everything.

Clearing her throat, Tessa said, "India and I were talking about giving a dinner party for you, Great-Aunt Edwina, and the only reason I haven't phoned you is because—"

"Adele was abducted," Edwina interrupted knowingly. "I'm glad Linnet managed to foil that terrible husband of yours. And the child is safe. Now, what's this about a dinner party? Why would you and India give a dinner party for an old lady like me? And who would come, eh? Answer that one, Tessa Fairley."

"Your son and daughter-in-law would certainly come—"

"Bah! Rubbish. All the way from Ireland. Forget it.

Anthony never moves too far from those damned bogs of his."

"They *would* come, Great-Aunt, and so would your grandchildren, and Mummy and Shane, and I'd come, and what about your brother and sister, Robin and Elizabeth? And there's Emily and Winston. The whole family would come, I'm sure of it."

"And would my darling India bring her new boyfriend, do you think? The famous artist."

"You'd have to ask her," Tessa murmured noncommittally, afraid to be drawn into a discussion about Russell Rhodes.

"I want to see you and India. And as soon as possible," Edwina said.

"*Oh.* Is something wrong, Great-Aunt?"

"No. Well, not that I know of, but I am ninety-five, you know. Still in fine fettle, mind you, ready to tackle anything or anyone. So, how about it? When are you two likely to be in Yorkshire?"

"We both have to be there this coming week. We're revamping the Harrogate and Leeds stores," Tessa explained, more worried than ever now.

"Then I'd better see you then. You'll come to dinner at Niddersley House. Please be good enough to inform India. *I* can't reach her on the phone. And let me know tomorrow at the latest which evening you'll come."

"Yes, Great-Aunt Edwina. What about our dinner—"

"We'll discuss *that* when I see you next week."

"I'll try to find India. She must be somewhere in the store."

"When you *do* find her, please have her telephone me. And thank you, Tessa. Good-bye."

" 'Bye, Great-Aunt. I'll tell India to give you a buzz, and we'll see you next week."

Tessa hung up, sat back in the chair, and wondered what this was all about. She couldn't help asking herself if Edwina knew about the stabbing. How could she know? *Robin could have told her.* After all, they were siblings.

My God, she's the oldest of the lot, Tessa suddenly thought. Emma Harte's first child, born when Emma was only sixteen, out of wedlock. Only daughter of Edwin Fairley. And a Fairley right down to her boots, even though she was illegitimate. Aunt of *her* father, Jim Fairley, who had been Edwin's grandson. God, what complications in this family, she thought.

Opening her engagement book, Tessa turned to the coming week, looking for a night to go to Niddersley House. She noticed at once that she was due to fly to Paris on Thursday evening with Lorne. Thursday, August 30, 2001. And her mother was coming back from New York on September 5.

We'll have to go to dinner with Edwina on Monday or Tuesday, Tessa decided, because she would need to return to London on Wednesday afternoon.

Closing the book, she stood up, grabbed her cell phone, slipped it in her jacket pocket, and went out into the store, looking for her cousin India.

14

ᔥ

I'm pleased we bumped into each other the way we did,"
Marietta said, smiling across at Evan. Mother and
daughter were having lunch together in The Birdcage,
one of the restaurants in the store. Chatting away, sipping their water as they waited for their food, they were
completely relaxed with each other.

"So am I, Mom," Evan responded, "and Saturday is
always a good day for me, I'm usually working on my
computer, catching up on paperwork. It gets really hec-
tic during the week."

"I was going to call you after I'd strolled around the
store, but I'm afraid I got caught up admiring the nightgowns," Marietta explained with a girlish laugh. "Imagine that, at my age."

Evan merely nodded, sat gazing at her mother, thinking that Linnet's words of an hour ago had been so true;
Marietta didn't look old enough to be her mother. She
was forty-nine, soon to be fifty, yet she appeared much
younger. Did she look suddenly youthful because she

was not suffering from depression? Or was it something else as well? A face job maybe? No, her father didn't have the kind of disposable income to pay for plastic surgery. Well, yes, he did actually, since his mother's death; Glynnis Hughes had left both Evan and her father small legacies.

"You're staring at me, Evan, and you look very puzzled. Have I got dirt on my face? Or don't you like the way I'm dressed?"

Evan blinked, swiftly exclaimed, "Don't be silly, Mom, of course you don't have dirt on your face! And to be honest, I think you look great. Just as you did at dinner the other night. If you want to know the truth, that's why I'm staring at you like this. You've undergone such a change. It's fantastic. You're such a different woman I can hardly believe it."

"Sure you can, you're seeing it, and seeing is believing, isn't it, Evan Hughes? Remember I used to say that to you when you were little . . ." Her mother's voice trailed off as she saw the sudden puzzlement on Evan's face.

Then Evan cried, "Of course I remember! When I doubted there was a Santa Claus you said, 'Seeing is believing,' and you and Grandma took me to the local department store to meet him."

Pleased that she had remembered, Marietta broke into smiles, took a sip of her water, and remarked, "You were such a lovely child."

Evan leaned across the table and said in a conspiratorial whisper, "Come on, Mommy, 'fess up, tell me what's happened." When Marietta remained silent, Evan volunteered, "You're on a new medication, aren't you? And it's changed your life, hasn't it?"

Marietta still didn't say anything, and after a moment Evan sat back and waited. As the silence dragged on, she wondered if her mother resented her probing, and she reached out, took hold of her hand, squeezed it. "I'm sorry, I shouldn't pry this way. It's just that I'm thrilled you look so great, that you seem a bit better in health."

"I'm a *lot* better, and you're not prying. And I do want to talk to you, Evan, but I don't know where to begin."

"Begin at the beginning," Evan suggested, "and take as long as you want. I'm pretty much finished for the day. And naturally I'm all ears."

"The beginning, yes. . . . It started last February, just after you left. I don't know whether you remember Auntie Dottie. She was my mother's sister, and she lived in L.A., not far from my mother. They were very close until Mom died."

"I remember her vaguely, you used to talk about her sometimes. She'd worked as an actress in films when she was young, in the forties."

"That's correct," Marietta said, looking surprised. "I can't believe you remember that, you only met her a couple of times when she came east with her husband on business. You were very small at the time. I was her only niece, and she usually made a big effort to see me. Auntie Dottie was married to Howard Kempson all her life. He was head of publicity at Ardent Pictures until his death about ten years ago."

"Do you know, I recall his death. You were upset, and they must have made an impression on me. Or you did, telling me stories about her working in pictures and how she and Howard met."

Marietta laughed. "She was only ever a bit actress, but the family loved to boast about her movie career."

The waitress arrived with their tomato salads and iced tea and hurried away.

After a forkful of salad, Evan urged, "So continue the story."

"In February, Auntie Dottie came to New York, to attend the fiftieth wedding anniversary of a girlfriend from her Hollywood days. And we got together. She was pleased I was doing relatively well but thought I should be doing much better. She told me about her friend Doctor Anna Marcello and insisted I make an appointment to see her."

Marietta put down her fork and leaned toward Evan. "I'll never forget Auntie Dottie's parting shot. She said, 'Get up, get going, and get a life. Before it's too late, Mari.' I guess her words . . . just galvanized me."

"Sometimes we all need that kind of push from someone we trust."

"I went to see Doctor Marcello, who did take me in hand," Marietta said.

"I'd guessed the change in you had to do with your health."

"Doctor Marcello gave me new medication and superior care. But it wasn't only *that* which helped me to change. Something else occurred."

"Tell me," Evan urged.

"Not long after Auntie Dottie's visit to New York, she died. She was in her eighties but seemed very fit to me, and she wasn't a bit senile. She'd only been back on the West Coast a week or so when she had a fatal heart attack. To cut to the chase, as she would've said, she left me everything. Her apartment in Brentwood, some stocks, and her jewelry. It's mostly costume, but some of it is vintage and it's very nice. Anyway, as it said in her will, I received 'all her worldly possessions.'"

"Just imagine you becoming an heiress, and so unexpectedly."

"I didn't inherit a fortune"—Marietta laughed—"far from it."

"What did Dad say?"

"Not much."

"Wasn't he pleased?" Evan asked, nonplussed for a moment.

"Not really."

"But why not, Mom?"

"Because by dying and leaving me her money and all, Auntie Dottie had changed the circumstances of my life. She'd made me independent."

Evan gaped at her mother. "Dad didn't like it? Because you didn't need him anymore? Financially, that is. You're saying exactly that, aren't you?"

"Yes, I am."

"But you've been married all your lives. He couldn't possibly think you were going to walk out on him *now*, because your aunt left you money. Or could he?"

"I don't know what he thought then, or thinks now, Evan. Your father never discusses it with me," Marietta answered and drank some of her iced tea. "You know, I did take Auntie Dottie's advice last February and went to Doctor Marcello. And I was glad I had listened to her. So after her death and receiving the inheritance, I decided I must absolutely take charge of my life. And my inheritance as well."

"Because you knew that's what your aunt wanted you to do."

"Exactly. I contacted a real estate broker on the Coast and put Auntie Dottie's apartment up for rent. Furnished, of course. The broker had a deal for me within the week, and I now have a regular income from that. I didn't sell the stocks, I kept them, and what money my aunt had in her bank account I transferred to a bank in Manhattan."

"Mom, I'm so proud of you! You've been efficient, businesslike, and very practical. Congratulations!"

"Thanks, and that's praise indeed, Evan, coming from you."

"I mean every word."

"I just want to say this. I haven't gone mad with the money, you know. I've only bought a couple of new things. It's nice to have some pretty clothes to wear. For a change."

Marietta sounded so wistful, Evan looked up and stared at her alertly. Hadn't her mother ever had any nice things in the past? Not really, not that she could remember. Was that her father's fault? Hadn't he given her mother money to buy pretty things? Maybe he hadn't been able to afford it in those days. Don't blame him, Evan cautioned herself. Mom was very *sick*. A manic-depressive, remember that. Yes, Dad did his best, I'm sure of it, but he was awfully discouraged at times.

Evan concentrated on her salad for a few minutes, but looking at it more than eating. Suddenly she didn't feel very hungry, and she put her fork down and straightened in the chair.

A silence fell between Evan and her mother, but it was an easy silence, and there was affection flowing between them. Evan began to wonder if she had been unfair to her mother all these years, always blaming her, applauding her father. Perhaps her mother had needed a bit of praise, too, and applause at times. And love from *her*. Guilt settled on her.

The waitress arrived, removed their plates, said she'd be back in a moment with their crab cakes, and hurried off once more.

Evan said quietly, her eyes focused on Marietta's face, "I want to tell you something, Mother. You really looked lovely at dinner, just as you do today. Dad must be pleased that you're so much better, and in every way. And looking so beautiful."

"I don't know. . . . I hope so, honey. But he doesn't really pay much attention."

Evan shook her head. "I can't figure him out, Mom," she muttered, feeling suddenly annoyed by him and his behavior.

Oh, I can, Marietta thought but murmured, "The money's not that important to me, as I said. I'm not going to rush out and buy lots of things. But I do like the feeling of independence it gives me. I like knowing that if I had to, I could support myself."

For a moment Evan was at a loss for words. She understood what her mother was saying. What she couldn't understand was her father's attitude, apparently grudging to say the least. Was he jealous? Threatened? Did he really think her mother would leave him? But why? With a small shock, Evan realized that she didn't know much about her parents' marriage. After all, she had left home nine years ago to live with Glynnis and Richard Hughes in Manhattan. Had her mother been too ill for too long? Did her father resent the lost years? Still, her father had become a success as an antiques dealer. He enjoyed his home, a lovely old farmhouse in Connecticut.

"Please don't judge your father too harshly," Marietta was saying.

Rousing herself from her thoughts, Evan replied, "I don't judge him at all. However, I do want to ask you something. You had a strange look on your face when Dad said he hadn't known that his mother worked for Emma Harte." She took a deep breath and plunged. "It was contempt I saw, Mother, wasn't it? Contempt on your face."

"Not contempt, Evan honey. Merely dismay."

"He lied to me, didn't he?"

Marietta couldn't bring herself to confirm this verbally, so she simply nodded.

"But *why,* Mom? Why does it matter that she worked for Emma? And why does Dad hate the Hartes?"

"You've asked me three questions at once, and I will answer them in three words . . . *I don't know.*"

"Let me ask you another question. If Dad knew Glynnis had worked for Emma Harte at the store, and he disliked the Hartes so much, why did he encourage me to go to London in January?"

"Because he didn't know about Glynnis and Emma then. Oh yes, he did remember that his mother had met Emma in the war years, and that they'd stayed in touch for a bit after the war. But he had no idea she'd been Emma's secretary."

"He found that out after Grandma Glynnis died last November, didn't he?"

Her mother nodded.

"Did he discover some of his mother's papers?"

"A reference Emma had given Glynnis all those years ago, singing her praises as a secretary."

"And that's all he found?"

"Oh, yes."

"It still doesn't explain why he's taken this attitude with me."

"No. Unless—"

"Unless what?" Evan interrupted.

"Unless he's just terribly upset. From the moment you walked into this store you've been madly in love— with the store, with Linnet O'Neill, with Paula O'Neill and India Standish. And with Gideon Harte as well. Maybe your father feels abandoned by you, Evan. Perhaps he thinks you'll never come home."

"Oh, Mom," she said softly.

"I know you're not coming home, at least not to live. I know you're going to stay in England. You see, women are intuitive and so much more practical than men. And we see things as they really are, not as we'd like them to be, the way men do." Marietta sighed. "I know you're very much in love with Gideon, and I'm happy for you, honey. You certainly have my blessings."

"And not Dad's, is that what you're saying?"

"No, not at all. It's as I said, he doesn't want to lose you completely. You were always—the favorite, let's face it."

Changing the subject, Evan asked, "Why did you and Dad adopt Elayne and Angharad?"

"I couldn't have more children."

"But you were a manic-depressive, you found it hard to look after *me,* never mind two more."

"Your father wanted a bigger family, Evan."

Evan took hold of her mother's hand and held it very tightly. Intently, she looked into her face, saw its loveliness, its calmness, the curved contours, the wide brow; her face had always been unlined and full of repose. She had the most unique eyes, not blue, not green, but a subtle turquoise. Her mother's hair was a shining blond halo around her face, and Evan suddenly realized that Marietta had always looked like this, perfectly beautiful in a quiet, very soft way.

Evan said, carefully, "It was *you,* Mommy . . . you who wanted another child . . . because he took me away from you. He pushed you out, took me for himself, didn't he?"

Marietta blinked and turned her head, made no response.

"I love you, Mom. I really do love you. I always have," Evan whispered in a gentle voice.

"And I love you, Evan," her mother answered, and Evan saw the tears glistening in those extraordinary eyes.

The sudden arrival of the waitress interrupted this conversation, but once they were alone again, Evan said, "I didn't mean to upset you."

"I know that. And after lunch I'd like us to go to your office for a moment or two. There's something I need to explain to you."

Evan didn't ask what it was; she just nodded.

"I want to tell you something about your grandmother," Marietta said to Evan an hour later, after they had settled themselves in her office.

"Tell me then. And will it make me understand things better?"

"I hope so, honey. Last summer, before she got really sick, Glynnis asked me to come into New York to have lunch with her. I was happy to go because I knew she cared about me, and I loved her. Actually, I thought she wanted to discuss my health or hers, I wasn't sure which." Marietta stopped, wondering for a moment if she should continue. Was she not opening Pandora's box, releasing terrible secrets?

Evan, waiting, her eyes on her mother, cleared her throat several times and pressed. "And why did Grandma want to talk to you?" When Marietta remained silent, Evan exclaimed, "I bet it was about your *health*. She was always concerned about you. Glynnis loved you, you know."

"Yes, she did. However, that day she didn't want to talk about me. Or even about herself. It was *you* she was fretting about."

"She was?" Evan seemed taken aback by this revelation.

"Yes, your grandma thought you were in a rut, going nowhere."

"She was right. I'd told her how I felt. That I was in a dead-end job. Bored. Fed up with New York."

"She told me you must go to London," Marietta said. "She was going to give you money and ship you off. When I argued against this, asked her what you'd do there all on your own, she said you could work at Harte's. She explained that she'd been close to Emma Harte once, knew the store because she herself had worked there during the Second World War. She told me that Harte's in Knightsbridge was the perfect place for you."

"My God, Mom, she was planning it then! Didn't she know Emma Harte was dead?"

"I'm fairly certain she did, Evan, but she didn't mention it to me that day. Glynnis said she wanted to put you amongst the Harte family, in their orbit, because that's where you belonged. When I asked her what she meant, she became rather quiet, almost withdrawn. After a moment, she did start to talk about them once again, told me that she had a long history with the Hartes and that I should trust her. When I still opposed the idea of you leaving New York, she said that children were only ever lent to us for a short time, and then they must leave, have lives of their own. 'Let her go,' she said, 'send her to London. She's irresistible.' Those were her exact words."

"She meant I was irresistible to the Hartes?"

"Yes."

"What did Dad say?"

"I never told him about the conversation. Your grandmother made me promise not to."

Evan leaned back in her chair, stared at her mother, wondering just how much Marietta knew. It was on the tip of her tongue to ask her mother if she knew that

Glynnis and Robin had had an affair, then she changed her mind. It would be wiser to probe a little more first. She was still uncertain about telling her father the truth. So she said quietly, with a little smile, "Well, Grandma got her way in the end, didn't she?"

"That's right, on her deathbed," Marietta murmured. "When she told you to go to London to find Emma Harte, because she held the key to your future, Glynnis surely knew exactly what she was doing."

"That's true. Because she was certain that I would do what she said, that I wouldn't be able to resist going to London."

"I know you don't have any regrets," her mother said, lifting a brow, her eyes not leaving Evan's face.

"That's true, Mom, I don't. Did Grandma tell you anything else about her connection to the Hartes? Whether she knew all the family?"

"No, she didn't," Marietta answered, asking herself if she was doing the right thing by lying. Well, she had no choice, at least for the moment. Perhaps later she would come clean with her daughter, confide the truth.

Evan, scrutinizing her mother intently, exclaimed, "Mom, you look worried. Is there something you're not telling me?"

"No, of course not," Marietta lied.

"If there is something on your mind, you could tell me, you know. I wouldn't tell Dad."

"Good God, you mustn't tell him what I've just revealed to you, Evan! I never said anything to him, not even after Glynnis died and you came to London. I promised his mother *on my honor,* and you must promise me now, the same thing."

"I do. I won't tell Dad about your conversation with Grandma, I promise. *On my honor.*"

Marietta let the tension ease out of her body. She

smiled at her daughter and said in a low voice, "Thank you for today, honey. I've so enjoyed being with you . . . sharing. And I'm sorry."

"Sorry for what?"

"Being *absent* from your life when you were growing up. We missed so much, you and I . . ."

"You were sick such a lot. But there were times when you were there for me. . . . I remember them all, Mom."

"I'm glad. About lunch tomorrow with Gideon, your father and I are *both* coming after all. I think he's now quite looking forward to meeting Gideon."

"And George wasn't upset that you can't keep the date with him and Arlette?"

"Of course not. That was just something floating around in your father's head. Now, where shall we meet, and at what time?"

"At the Dorchester at one o'clock. I'll be waiting for you in the lobby," Evan replied, filled with happiness and relief that her parents were finally going to meet the man she loved and had promised to marry.

It was two-thirty when India hurried into Tessa's office exclaiming, "I'm sorry you couldn't reach me. I got your message about my grandmother. Is she all right?"

"She's fine, India, in fact she sounds like a British general at the head of an army about to quell the natives, as she usually does. Great-Aunt Edwina must be made of cast iron."

India burst out laughing. "I agree with you. Did she tell you what she wanted?"

"Yes, you're to phone her. But she also wants us to go to supper with her next week at Niddersley House. I said we would. But it will have to be Monday or Tuesday, because I need to come back to London on Wednesday afternoon. I'm going to Paris the next day with Lorne."

"That should cheer you up a bit," India said. "And I wonder why Grandmother wants us to go to dinner with her? Did she give you a clue?"

"None, but she sounded determined, feisty, and in a funny way, rather nice. I've often thought she was kind of—*cool.* Especially for a very old lady."

"I know what you mean," India concurred. "She doesn't seem old, nor does she act it. Bustling around hither and yon like a youngster."

Tessa smiled. "I'm to let her know tomorrow which evening we're free."

"I'd like to make it Monday, if you don't mind, Tessa, mainly because I'm hoping to take Dusty back to Willows Hall on Tuesday afternoon, and I'd be spending the evening there. Fortunately, he's very much on the mend, and the hospital's going to discharge him."

"I'm happy to hear he's better, and Monday's fine with me. When are you going to Yorkshire? Tomorrow afternoon?"

"Yes. And you?"

"The same. I'm taking Adele and Elvira with me. I want to get them settled before I leave on Wednesday. Linnet's arriving at Pennistone Royal on Wednesday evening to keep an eye on everything."

"I understand," India murmured, flopping down in a chair. She was convinced there was nothing to worry about now, since Jack Figg has turned the house and grounds into something akin to Fort Knox. She said, "They'll be perfectly safe, to be sure they will. Any news of the dreaded Mark?"

"Ugh, no," Tessa responded with an involuntary shudder. "Thank God. His solicitors are talking to mine, but it seems to be slow going. Mummy says it won't be for much longer, since once she gets back to London she's going to light a fuse under them all."

"Knowing Aunt Paula, that's *exactly* what she'll do." India stood up again, moved over to Tessa's desk, and said, "Do you mind if I call my grandmother from here? And you can tell her a day early that we'll see her on Monday."

"Be my guest," Tessa answered.

India dialed, waited for the number to ring through, and when it was answered she said, "May I speak to the dowager countess, please."

"You're speaking to her, India, dear. It's me."

"Hello, Grandma. I'm with Tessa, she tells me you've been trying to reach me."

"Correct. I wanted to talk to you about your boyfriend. How's he doing? Is he out of the hospital yet?"

India stared at Tessa, rolling her eyes and looking surprised. "He's better, Grandmother, and coming out of the hospital on Tuesday."

"Glad to hear it. You'd better bring him over to Niddersley House to meet me when he's up to it. All right?"

"Yes, that's fine."

"He has a giant-size talent. Correction, it's more than great talent. The man's a genius."

"Oh yes, he is," India exclaimed, relieved that her grandmother was sounding positive about Dusty. "Tessa wants to talk to you, today instead of tomorrow."

"You've settled on a date for supper, have you?"

"Yes, Grandmother."

"When?" Edwina barked.

"Monday evening, if that's all right with you."

"Naturally it is. I'm hardly leading the social life of a debutante, India. Oh, and by the way, what's all this nonsense about you and Tessa giving a dinner for me?"

"She mentioned it then? We just thought it would be nice to . . . *honor* you, as the oldest living member of the Harte family."

"Don't remind me of that!" Edwina exclaimed, and then she chuckled. "Since you're both part Fairley, as indeed I am, I'll consider the idea. Do you think you can drag your father out of the bogs of Ireland? Will he come?"

"I'm certain of it, Grandma."

"Let us discuss it on Monday. Seven o'clock sharp, India. Good-bye."

" 'Bye," India said, but Edwina had already slammed the phone down. India stared at Tessa and said in a puzzled tone, "She knew about Dusty. Who could have told her?"

"You didn't?" Tessa asked, her face bland as usual.

"No. I hadn't told anyone except Linnet. It was after the stabbing that it all came out in the open."

"Then there's your answer. The whole family suddenly knew," Tessa pointed out.

"She probably got it from Uncle Robin, because Evan chats to him every day, well, practically," India remarked.

"Do you care she knows? Anyway, what was her reaction?"

"She says he's a genius . . . she wants to meet him." India returned to the chair, leaned back against the cushions, and muttered, "The problem is, *he* won't want to meet her."

"Why ever not?"

"Because he thinks the family's stuck up, all that silly stuff, just because Daddy has a title."

"I bet he will meet her if you paint the right picture—oh, do excuse the pun. You must make her sound like a real eccentric, which she is." As she was speaking, Tessa turned off her computer, reached for her handbag, and said, "I'll meet you at Niddersley House on Monday evening, and now I'm going home to be with my child."

India jumped up, saying, "I'm going to call it a day, too. Do you have your car, or can I give you a lift to your mother's house?"

"I was going to walk, but that'd be great, India, thanks. It's so dangerous in London lately . . . even in daylight."

On the way to Paula's house in Belgrave Square, India spoke for a few minutes about Dusty and the portrait he was painting of her. Then she suddenly asked, "How long are you going to live with your mother and father, Tessa?"

Glancing at her swiftly, Tessa replied, "Until the divorce is final and everything's settled with Mark. Then I'll find a flat. I don't want to live at the Hampstead house, even though it's actually mine. I can't bear the place. Mark turned it into something so ugly, cold and grim. He can have it and he's welcome."

"I know he wants a lot."

"He does. My mother seems to have some sort of plan, but I won't know about it until she gets back at the beginning of September. In the meantime, the Belgrave house is rather large, and there's the downstairs flat, Paul McGill's old quarters. I have a bit of privacy down there, if I need it."

As they turned into the square, India said, "Can I pop in for a minute? I'd love to see Adele, give her a hug."

"Of course. Oh, my God, India! That's Mark on the doorstep, ringing the bell. What does *he* want?"

India said firmly, "Don't panic. *We* can deal with him," and a moment later she brought the car to a standstill outside the house. "Keep calm," she murmured as Tessa made to get out of the Aston Martin.

"I will." Tessa hurried across the pavement, exclaiming, "Mark, what do you want?"

He swung around on hearing her voice. "I want to see my daughter, that's what. You're keeping her from me, and that's not fair," he said in a belligerent voice, his face turning red.

"You know you're supposed to make an appointment. You can't just show up like this," Tessa cried, drawing to a stop at the bottom of the steps, staring up at him, trying to hold her emotions in check.

"Well, here I am, Mrs. Longden. It's my right to see Adele, she's my child. I love her, and she loves me."

"You forfeited the right to see her the day you abducted her," Tessa told him.

"I didn't abduct her, I just took her out for a drive, and lunch. I brought her back unharmed. I would never harm her, whatever you might think, and have said so to your solicitors. You're unconscionable, the way you've bad-mouthed me."

"You cannot see her until we have an ironclad agreement," Tessa announced coldly, glaring at him. "You're the one slowing it down."

"You're such a bitch, and—"

At this moment the door flew open, and Harriet, the housekeeper, stood on the threshold.

"Oh, it's you, Miss Tessa," she said and waited for instructions, since like the rest of the staff, she knew the situation.

India hurried to join Tessa and took hold of her arm. "I think it might be better if we let him come in for tea. You can't stand here having a shouting match."

Tessa walked up the steps with India at her side and said to him in a lowered voice, "Come in then, Mark. We'll have tea with Adele."

Harriet hesitated for a split second, then opened the

door wider for Tessa. "It's all right," Tessa murmured. "There's no problem, Harriet. Is Ben here?"

"Yes, thank God," Harriet muttered, relieved that her husband was in the house watching TV.

Once they were inside, Tessa turned to Mark and said in a voice dripping ice water, "Just this once I'll overlook the rules you agreed to last week. But this is it until we have the settlement worked out. Do you understand?"

He nodded and quietly followed her up the stairs to the playroom which had been used by the rest of the family when they were young. Now it was Adele's favorite place.

When Adele saw her father, she smiled and waved, but it was Tessa to whom she ran, crying, "Mumma, Mumma, I'm glad you're home."

Tessa bent down, hugged the running child to her, kissed her cheek, and hugged her again. Then straightening, she said, "Here's Daddy and Aunt India. We're going to have a tea party. With you, Elvira, and your dolls."

"Oh, that's lovely, Mumma. And Reggi has just put the kettle on," Adele said inventively, pointing to the rag doll which was always with her.

"Well then, let's all sit down and wait for Harriet to make the tea," Tessa murmured lovingly.

An hour and a half later, Tessa escorted Mark down the stairs to the marble entrance foyer. "Thanks," he said softly, and before she could stop him he had pulled her into his arms, begun to kiss her face and stroke her silver-blond hair. She struggled with him, finally managed to push him away, and exclaimed, "Don't ever do that again! *Ever,* do you hear me?"

"I'm sorry, I didn't mean to grab you so hard."

"Just don't touch me. Not ever," she cried, her voice shrill.

"Tessa, I'm sorry. I know I surprised you, I surprised myself. Look, I love you. Let's start over, forget this divorce. Let's be a family again. The three of us."

Tessa stood in the middle of the hall gaping at him in amazement and fury. The gall. Suddenly something in her snapped, and she cried, "Start again! After all you've done to me—humiliated me, abused me, mentally *and* physically, stolen Adele? You're insane to think I'd even consider it!"

"Tessa, please, you're exaggerating as usual."

"Please leave," she said, her tone icier than ever; she walked over to the front door and opened it. "Leave, Mark. *Now.*"

He left without uttering another word, the set of his mouth mean and ugly, his eyes filled with anger.

She slammed the door behind him and slid the bolt, then turned and ran upstairs. She was shaking, and still furious, but she managed to put a bland expression onto her face before she went back into the playroom.

India rose when she saw her and hurried across the floor. "Is something wrong?" she asked, knowing there was.

"He just suggested we get back together. Can you believe that bastard? He tried to pretend *he* didn't do anything to ruin our marriage."

15

Gideon Harte stood in the lobby of the Dorchester Hotel waiting for Evan. Glancing at the clock above the revolving door, he saw that it was ten minutes to one, and he knew she would come rushing in at any moment. Evan was punctual. It was another characteristic they had in common, one which pleased him.

He wished they were having lunch alone. The idea of meeting her parents had suddenly lost its appeal, perhaps because it had assumed such enormous proportions in the past few days. In fact, he wished they hadn't come to London at all. She hadn't been herself since their arrival, and she was growing more ambivalent about telling her father the truth about Robin Ainsley.

Initially he had said whatever decision she made about that was all right with him. But he had come to realize how much the truth mattered. He felt it was important for her father to know he was part Harte, as she herself was.

This train of thought dissipated as she came barreling

in through the revolving door, a smile illuminating her face when she saw him. He thought how pretty she looked in a loose, rather floaty frock of pale blue cotton. She had on very high-heeled blue sandals, which made her appear even more willowy; there were smoky blue beads at her neck and on her ears, and these echoed the color of her eyes.

"I'm not late, Gid, am I?" she asked as she drew to a standstill next to him, her smile wide and warm.

He shook his head. "Early, in fact. But where are your parents?"

"I told them to meet us here at one-fifteen. I just wanted a few minutes alone with you. I've missed you."

"Me too, you." Taking her arm, he went on, "Let's go and sit over there on the sofa, shall we?"

"I told Mom that we'd be in the Grill, so we might as well go in."

After they were seated at Gideon's favorite table in a corner, he ordered a bottle of Veuve Clicquot and then sat back and looked at her, a smile on his face. "You look wonderful, Evan," he began, then stopped abruptly. The smile slipped. "You're not wearing your ring," he said, staring at her left hand.

She stared back at him, her face suddenly a bright pink.

"Evan, you haven't told them, have you?"

"Look, Gideon, please don't be angry, but I just didn't dare say anything the other night. I hadn't seen them for months, and Dad was in a peculiar mood, to say the least. I didn't want to hit them with that straight-away. I wanted to wait until after they met you."

"Oh, and does that make a *difference* to you? What they think of me? Will you change your mind about me if they don't approve?"

"Don't be silly, of course I won't," she said in a low

voice, leaning closer to him. "You know I love you, that I want to spend the rest of my life with you. But my father's always been a bit . . . well, possessive of me, and he's got to adjust to the fact that I'm not going home, that I'm going to be living in London. He'll have to come to terms with that."

"Yes, he certainly will." His green eyes narrowed.

"Please try and see it from my point of view, Gideon. Please, darling."

He sighed. "I suppose I understand . . . well, a little bit. And what about Robin? Have you told your father he's actually a Harte, a member of the family he loves to hate?"

She bit her lip. "No, I haven't. I felt it was better, kinder, not to bring up all of this stuff when he'd just seen me for the first time in eight months. Mom was great, of course, and I had lunch with her yesterday. She knows how much I care for you. I know she's expecting me to marry you, Gid, and she gives us her blessings. She said so."

"That's good to know," he muttered, the tension in his shoulders relaxing. "I'm not being difficult, Evan, I simply want them to know about our engagement so that I can tell my parents before someone else does. After all, the cousins are in on our secret, which of course isn't one anymore."

Always cued in to his moods, she was sorry his voice wasn't calmer. "I promise I'll tell them soon, and I'll talk to my father about Robin as well—"

The arrival of a waiter with the champagne interrupted this conversation, and once it had been poured and they had clinked glasses, taken a sip, she said, "I hope he understands about Glynnis and Robin. . . . I hope he won't be terribly upset."

"I suppose it will be a shock," Gideon murmured a

little grudgingly, and then he started to talk about the newspapers, and his plans for the next few months.

Gideon was surprised. Owen and Marietta Hughes were pleasant, and her father didn't seem to be quite the curmudgeon Evan had made him out to be.

Gideon had done a double take when they had arrived at the table. It was something of a shock to see the strong resemblance to Robin Ainsley. It was much more pronounced in her father than it was in Evan. There was no doubt that Owen Hughes was actually a Harte. Tall, slender, good-looking, he had Robin's aquiline features and dark hair flecked with gray. It took Gideon only a moment to recognize that he bore a very strong likeness to his own great-grandfather, Winston Harte I, the brother of Emma.

Her mother was a bit of a surprise, too. A pretty woman in a soft and feminine way, she looked very young, and there was no hint of the manic-depressive about her. In fact, she was full of smiles and good humor. That was the medication kicking in, Gideon decided.

After the waiter had served them champagne and they had all toasted each other, there was a bit of small talk, which suddenly seemed endless to him.

Eventually Gideon said, "I had hoped to take you out to the Waterside Inn at Bray for lunch, but unfortunately I'm working today. I have to get back to the papers fairly early, and it's a bit of a drive there and back. Another time perhaps. I know how much you like the water and sailing, Mr. Hughes."

"I do, yes," Owen said, "and it would've been great on a hot day like this. On the other hand, I've always had a soft spot for the Grill here at the Dorchester. My mother brought me here when I was a little boy."

"Did she really!" Gideon exclaimed and threw a

pointed look at Evan, who glanced away, not wanting to have prolonged eye contact. Also, she was truly startled. She hadn't known her father had come back to London as a child. What else didn't she know? she wondered.

"I came to England with her several times in the fifties," her father was telling Gideon, and Evan pricked up her ears; her mother gave her a knowing look.

Evan ignored this and said, "I was telling Gideon you were planning a trip to France, Dad, and he wondered if you were intending to go to the south?"

"Probably. I'd like to take your mother to Monte Carlo, she's never been there."

"It's very built up these days," Gideon murmured, "a pile of concrete, to be exact. But if you do go, perhaps Evan and I could join you for a couple of days."

"That'd be nice," Owen responded, in a voice so low it was almost inaudible. It was obvious he was taken aback by Gideon's suggestion.

"It would be absolutely lovely," Marietta jumped in, smiling hugely. "We haven't had a vacation together for years, have we, Evan?"

"No, Mom."

"I thought you couldn't get away from work," her father said, his eyes riveted on her.

"I can't, at least not when you're planning to be in Paris and visiting Normandy and such. But later on I think I can swing a long weekend."

"Sounds good," her father answered in a clipped fashion.

Gideon said, "Shall we order? I'm not rushing you, but I do like to have a leisurely lunch on Sunday, don't you, Mrs. Hughes?"

"I certainly do, Gideon, and please call me Marietta."

"I will, thank you very much."

"I know this is one of your favorite places, Gideon,

Evan told me that. So what do you recommend?" Marietta asked, looking at her daughter's boyfriend, liking
his clean-cut good looks, his straightforwardness. She
prayed Owen wouldn't spoil things by being grumpy
and grudging with Evan, because she knew that these
two were very much a couple. But had Owen picked that
up? She wasn't sure.

Gideon, studying the menu, looked up and smiled at
Marietta. "I tend to have the same things," he explained,
"usually smoked salmon or potted shrimps, something
like that to start with, and then I'm afraid I always fall
for what's on the trolley, either roast lamb or roast beef."

"And Yorkshire pudding," Evan interjected. "However, Gideon says there's only one place where they
make real Yorkshire pudding and that's Yorkshire."

Gideon laughed. "I'm prejudiced, I'm afraid, being a
Yorkshireman born and bred. They do a sort of popover
here, and it's very good, really."

"I think I'll have the roast beef," Evan said. "What
about you, Mom? And Dad?"

"The same," her mother answered.

Owen nodded. "That's my choice, too, and I'll start
with the Morecambe Bay potted shrimps." Looking at
Marietta, he murmured, "Why don't you try them,
dear?"

"Thanks, Owen, but I'd prefer the asparagus. Cold
with vinaigrette."

Once all of the orders had been taken, Gideon said,
"Talking about Yorkshire pudding, I do hope you'll
come up to stay with my parents at Allington Hall, or
perhaps at Pennistone Royal with my aunt Paula
O'Neill and her husband, Shane. I know they'd love it."
When there was no response, Gideon pressed on. "It's
such beautiful country, most especially the Dales, where
we all live. Have you ever been to Yorkshire?"

"Yes, I have," Owen said without thinking. In order to cover his embarrassment at blurting this out, and wanting to cut off any further discussion about Yorkshire, he swiftly added, "I did quite a lot of touring around with my mother when I was a little boy. She wanted me to know her country. And so she took me up to Scotland, and also to Wales. She was Welsh, you know."

"So I'd heard," Gideon murmured and gave Evan a sly look.

Evan ignored Gideon; she was almost afraid to look at him. So instead she said to her father, "Fancy that, Dad. You *are* secretive! You never told me you'd toured the length and breadth of Great Britain. Did he tell you, Mom?"

"No, he didn't," Marietta said, and she spoke the truth.

"You'd like Pennistone Royal," Gideon went on, determined to make Owen say something about the Hartes if he could. "It's a wonderful house, one of England's great stately homes. But what you'd love about it, I think, is the furniture. My great-grandmother Emma Harte was an expert on Georgian furniture, and she collected it. I understand from Evan that you're also an expert on this period."

"Yes, I am considered such," Owen said, afraid to say too much in case he let something slip.

During the first course, as she cut into her thin-sliced smoked salmon, Evan looked first at her mother, then at her father, and said, "It would be great if you could visit Yorkshire. We could have a nice weekend there together."

"I'm not sure," her father murmured in that very low voice again.

"I think it would be wonderful," Marietta exclaimed, flashing a bright smile at Gideon and Evan. "And you know, Owen, you could do a bit of business up there perhaps, go to a few antiques shops. I've heard they're very good. You might find some Georgian pieces."

"Oh yes, especially in Harrogate," Evan interjected. "Think about it, Dad."

"I will," he muttered and concentrated on his potted shrimps.

Halfway through the first course, Gideon asked, "Would anyone like wine? Since we're all having the roast beef, I think a full-bodied red would be excellent."

"Thank you," Marietta said, once more taking the lead, wanting to put this nice young man at ease.

Gideon motioned for the wine waiter, and after studying the wine list he finally ordered a Château Duhart-Milon, one of his father's favorites. To Owen he explained, "Dad likes this wine very much, and I'm sure you will, Mr. Hughes. It's from the Domaines Barons de Rothschild, and it's superb."

Owen merely nodded. He had a sinking feeling that this young man, with his looks, magnetism, self-confidence, and charm had conquered his daughter. It made him sad that she was lost to him, and in a funny way he resented Gideon for being who and what he was. A Harte, and a superior Harte at that. The chatting went on around him; he was lost in his morose thoughts.

It was toward the end of the lunch that Gideon suddenly lifted his glass, and looking at Owen and Marietta, said slowly, "I would like you to join me in a toast to Evan."

All three of them, especially Evan, were startled, but they picked up their glasses and stared back at Gideon.

He said softly, in a loving voice, "Here's to you, Evan, the most unique woman I've ever met, and my future wife."

There was a stunned silence.

Gideon, aware that he had dropped a bombshell, glanced at Owen and Marietta and said, "One of the reasons I wanted to have lunch with you both today is to tell you that Evan and I are engaged. I do hope you approve."

Owen looked at Evan furiously, then cleared his throat several times. Finally he said in an uptight tone, "Why yes, if that's what Evan wants."

He scrutinized his daughter with intensity, and so did Gideon, who noticed at once how pale her face had become. Otherwise her expression was unreadable.

Marietta, aware of the discomfort between her husband and her daughter, jumped to the rescue yet again. "Congratulations to the two of you! You have our blessings. We're delighted for you." Disregarding her husband's obvious disgruntlement, she asked, "And when will you make it official?"

"Why right now, Marietta," Gideon responded. Then, turning once more to look at Evan, he said in a light, bland voice, "What a pity you're not wearing your ring, darling."

Knowing that there was no use fighting him, she murmured, "Oh, but I have it with me, Gideon," and fumbled in her handbag.

A moment later it was gleaming on the third finger of her left hand and being admired by her mother, who was impressed by the size of the sapphire and the surrounding diamonds. "It's beautiful, Evan," she said. "You're a very lucky girl."

Done, Gideon thought with a spurt of satisfaction. And done in the best Harte style.

Gideon was just leaving his office for the late afternoon editorial meeting when his cell phone began to shrill. Realizing he had forgotten to put it in his pocket, he rushed back to his desk and grabbed it. "Hello?"

"It's me," Evan said.

"Hi, sweetheart, I can't really talk now. I'm running late for the editorial meeting. The traffic was lousy from the Dorchester. Is it important?"

"I think so. Gideon, how *could* you?"

"How could I what?" he asked mildly, although he knew exactly what she meant and he could tell she was annoyed.

"Just announce like that, so unexpectedly and so bluntly, that we were engaged. I'm really upset about the way you handled this."

"Well, you shouldn't be. Your mother is thrilled, and your father didn't look all that unhappy. Anyway, be—"

"He was really upset that I'd been what he called sneaky, that I hadn't told him anything in advance. Actually, the afternoon fell apart, and he went off in a snit."

"Really. What a sudden change of mood. He was very cordial with me when I left. In any case, it's over and done with, so now let's move on."

"It's hard for me to do that. You didn't even give me a hint you were going to pull this—"

"I didn't pull anything, Evan, I simply spoke the truth," he snapped. Then, softening his voice, he added, "I think you *must* move on, darling, and push your father's resentment to one side. Look, in a few days you should tell him about Robin Ainsley being his father, get that out of the way as well. Wipe this slate clean so there are no secrets. I think we'll all be the better for it."

"I can't tell him about Robin now!" she cried. "It'll be too much for him."

"I doubt it," Gideon said coldly. "I have to go, I'm late for the meeting. They can't start without me. Talk to you later, darling." He clicked the phone off, slipped it in his pocket, and left his office, wondering how a woman as bright and intelligent as Evan could be so weak-kneed when it came to her father.

He couldn't help wishing she'd behave like a true Harte. He wanted her to be bold and strong, like his female cousins. But then she hadn't been brought up a Harte, had she?

This unexpected and troubling thought did not hinder his rush to the meeting. But later that night it gave him reason to pause, and ponder long and hard on his relationship with Evan Hughes.

Tessa stood in the entrance foyer of Niddersley Hall watching Great-Aunt Edwina walk slowly down the grand staircase. She wore a dress of purple silk, her favorite color, a royal color, and she looked both regal and royal, Tessa thought. Her silver hair was swept up in an elegant style, and as usual she was carefully made up, looked twenty years younger than her age.

"There you are, Tessa!" she exclaimed as she glided toward her great-niece, who came to meet her. "You're looking much better than I expected after all you've been through lately. Such an ordeal."

"Thank you, Great-Aunt Edwina, and *you* look fantastic!" After kissing her aunt on the cheek, Tessa stepped back, and eyeing Edwina she couldn't help asking, "Are those pearls *real*?"

"My dear girl, the whole world knows I never wear anything that's artificial. Of course they're real. I just bought them a few weeks ago. South Sea pearls, perfectly matched. I thought I'd give myself a treat, you see."

Tessa and her aunt walked into the drawing room; a relatively small room, it was nevertheless elegant with a beautiful Adam fireplace and several tall windows which overlooked the garden.

"Shall we sit over there?" Tessa suggested, indicating an arrangement of chairs near an open window. It had been another hot day, and even though it was now early evening and the sun had set, it was still balmy; Tessa preferred to sit in a cool spot like this.

"Certainly," Edwina answered, making her way to the chairs grouped around a low coffee table. "I told Frome to bring us champagne. Or do you prefer something else?"

"That's lovely, thank you." Tessa seated herself opposite her great-aunt and said, "India will be here momentarily. I only had to come from the Harrogate store, she's driving over from Leeds."

"Yes, she phoned me and said she'd be a bit late, but that's all right, my dear, we can have a little chat while we wait. Ah, there you are, Frome," she continued as the butler came in carrying an ice bucket and bottle of champagne on a tray. "We'll both have the champagne, thank you."

"Yes, m'lady," Frome answered, and within seconds he was carrying two crystal glasses to them. They each took one and thanked him.

Edwina lifted her glass, and smiling at Tessa, she said, "Here's to you, Tessa, and a sparkling future."

Smiling back, Tessa clinked her glass to her aunt's. "And to your sparkling future, too, Great-Aunt."

Edwina burst out laughing. "Well said, little Tessa, well said. Thank you. I certainly don't intend going anywhere just yet."

"Obviously," Tessa shot back, laughing with her. "When you buy yourself a string of pearls like those, you plan to wear them. I think it's marvelous that you treated yourself, it shows a most positive attitude."

"I suppose it does." After taking a sip of the champagne, Edwina settled herself against the needlepoint cushions in the French armchair and went on. "Now what's afoot with that fool of a husband of yours? He's got a few screws loose, in my considered opinion."

"He's very difficult, Great-Aunt, and I agree with you, I think he is a bit off the wall, and—"

"He must be to treat a wonderful girl like you so shabbily. I'm appalled at his behavior toward you and extremely glad you've taken the steps you have to get a divorce," Edwina said rather forcefully.

Tessa explained, "He'll soon be my ex."

"Whatever it costs, just get rid of him. He's caused you far too much heartache already. I'm a great believer in divorce, you know. It's ridiculous for a couple to stay together if they're making each other unhappy. I understand he wants a lot."

Tessa nodded. "Yes, he does. Mummy's going to get things moving along a bit quicker once she returns from New York next week."

"Well, as I said, just pay him off, get him out of the way." Edwina took a sip of champagne and continued, "You know, Tessa, everybody has a price, and it isn't always money, there—"

"As your mother always said," Tessa cut in. "I know Emma Harte's credo, too."

"I'm glad to hear it. She was the most remarkable woman, a legend in her own time. You can't go wrong, following her rules. Anyway, I was going to say that there are often other considerations, and several ways to skin a cat."

"Not with Mark, Great-Aunt Edwina, all he's interested in is money."

"And a few other things, from what I've heard. Such as wine, women, and song, to put it in a polite way."

"That's true. But I don't care about him anymore. I just want him out of my life."

"It was rather foolhardy of him to kidnap Adele in that way."

"It hasn't done him any good in the eyes of my lawyers—or his own, I might add."

"I'm sure not." There was a small pause. Edwina stared at Tessa intently and finally said in a kindly voice, "I hope he hasn't made you afraid to have another relationship with a man, Tessa. You're young, a very beautiful woman, so you must get over this hurdle as quickly as possible. You must find a way to quell your fears about him taking Adele again and move on to greener fields."

"How did you know I fear that?" Tessa asked, studying her great-aunt thinking how extraordinary she was for her age.

"Because it would be natural for any mother to fear another kidnapping when she's dealing with a fool like Mark Longden. But I doubt he'll do it again, once he's been paid off by Paula."

"I do hope you're right."

At this moment India came hurrying into the room, looking flushed and a little out of breath. "Sorry, Grandma, but the traffic from Leeds was quite impossible tonight."

"We're not going anywhere," Edwina murmured and lifted her face to be kissed. "Now relax, India dear," Edwina continued, "and pour yourself a glass of champagne. It'll be quicker than if we ring for Frome. He's getting a bit old."

India laughed. "Grandma, he's all of fifty if he's a day! Much younger than you."

"Maybe, but he's a bit of a slow coach. I'm a lot more sprightly. Do you prefer something other than a drop of bubbly?"

"Champagne's great, thanks," India told her and

walked over to the chest where the drinks tray stood, still laughing. Her grandmother was a hoot: blunt to the point of rudeness at times, and a true eccentric. But she was very special, and India adored her. Her father always said they'd thrown the mold away after making his mother.

Returning to the group of chairs, India sat down next to Tessa, lifted her glass, said "Cheers," and took a sip. Then she leaned forward slightly from the waist and said to her grandmother, "Who told you about Russell Rhodes, about my involvement with him, and the stabbing, Grandma?"

"As a matter of fact, it was someone who works at Harrogate District Hospital, but I did promise to keep a confidence, and so I must, my dear."

India, taken aback, exclaimed, "So it wasn't anyone in the family?"

"Not at all. I haven't spoken to Robin or Elizabeth for weeks, and you younger lot don't bother too much with me these days."

"Oh, Grandma, don't say that, it makes me feel awful."

"Well, it shouldn't, because I don't mind really, except for you and Tessa, India. You two are my best girls, part Fairley like I am, and I do miss hearing from you both. I feel left out of your lives."

India looked at Tessa, knowing her cousin felt as guilty as she did.

Before India could say anything, Edwina went on. "I know he's recovered and that he's going home to Willows Hall tomorrow, and perhaps later this week, if he's up to it, you'll bring Dusty here to meet me. Lunch, tea, or dinner, whichever you prefer, my dear."

"I'll try for dinner, Grandmother, but he's not an easy man."

"Do your best. I know I bluster a lot, and boast that

I'm not going anywhere, but you never know what can happen. Life has a funny way of hitting you in the face when you least expect it."

"Don't say that!" India cried. "You'll be here for a long time yet."

"Let's hope so. Now, do you love this man enough to want to spend the rest of your life with him?" Edwina asked briskly.

India nodded and opened her mouth to say something but changed her mind and sat very still, staring at her grandmother.

Edwina nodded. "Not sure about *his* intentions, eh?"

"You're right as usual, Grandmother," India admitted ruefully.

"If you want him, then it's up to you to get him! That's the way it always is. Most men can't make up their minds about women, or about a long-term commitment. Anyway, my dear, if you love him, then I trust your judgment. I know he must be a decent man, a man of honor, if you have set your sights on him."

"Yes, he is. At least, *I* believe he is."

"Now . . . one of the reasons I invited you to dinner is to give you both a gift." Pushing herself to her feet, Edwina added, "Follow me, girls," and marched forward toward the hall. She crossed it in the same majestic way and went into the library; India and Tessa followed, exchanging baffled glances.

Taking a key out of her pocket, Edwina sat down behind the huge Georgian partners desk in front of the bay window and unlocked one of the drawers.

"Don't stand around like that, like a couple of sucking ducks," she instructed sharply. "Sit down, both of you. On the sofa."

They did as she asked without uttering a word; they knew it was wise to leave the floor to the Dowager

Countess of Dunvale, who obviously was in crackling form tonight.

A moment or two later, after taking various items out of the drawer, Edwina beckoned to India and Tessa. "Come and help me carry these things to the coffee table," she said, rising and picking up one of the items herself.

The two young women joined her, and then they all three of them sat down. Edwina was quite certain her granddaughter and great-niece were riddled with curiosity, and she smiled, thinking of the shock they were in for.

Well, it's a nice shock, she said to herself, knowing she would enjoy these next few moments. She hadn't enjoyed much lately, in actuality; also, she had been disconcerted by the abduction of Adele and, so soon after that, the stabbing of Russell Rhodes, who happened to be her favorite living painter.

Her lovely girls had been at the receiving end of some bad goings-on, much to her dismay. She loved them both very much and was exceedingly protective of them; now she wanted to show them her love in a very real way.

Sitting up a little straighter, Edwina ran her hands over her knees, smoothing the purple silk dress. Then she looked at Tessa.

Slowly, Edwina said, "You are a few years older than India, and therefore I shall talk to you first. Your great-grandmother Emma Harte was the most extraordinary woman, and everything you are, everything you have in this world, you truly owe to her, to her brilliance as a businesswoman and entrepreneur, to her stamina, hard work, and determination to succeed. And her foresight, of course. You must never forget that, Tessa. Well, let me proceed to another matter. . . . Many, many years ago my mother gave me a gift. She knew it would be very meaningful to me because I thought of myself as a fully fledged Fairley, rather than an illegitimate one, which I was. I was also a Harte, but I was a bit of a snob in those days and liked to think of myself as an aristocratic Fairley, as if such a thing really matters in the long run. Who cares these days?"

Edwina glanced at the items on the coffee table, let out a long sigh, as if remembering something from long ago, and then continued softly. "The gift my mother gave me was for Christmas. She knew its meaning would not be lost on me, because it had once belonged to my grandmother Adele Fairley."

Reaching for an extremely old black leather case, Edwina opened it and then placed it on the coffee table again.

Both Tessa and India gasped, then leaned forward to get a better look.

Placed on the black velvet inside the worn circular box was the most beautiful diamond necklace either of them had ever seen. In a lacy pattern, it fell almost like a bib and was composed of hundreds of diamonds. Glittering like white fire in the lamplight, it was a magnificent thing to behold.

Both young women looked up at Edwina, who was scrutinizing them in the most thoughtful way. It was India who spoke first. "It's simply gorgeous, Grandma, but how did Emma come by it if it belonged to Adele Fairley?"

"Many years before my mother gave the necklace to me, she had bought it at an auction of Adele's jewelry in London. In fact, she bought the entire collection."

"Why was it being sold at auction?" India wondered aloud.

"Because Gerald Fairley needed money to keep his

businesses running, and he had inherited his mother's jewelry collection from his father."

"So Gerald put it up for sale, and Emma bought it," Tessa murmured.

"Yes. I think she saw the irony of it all, as only she could, and with a great sense of humor. This neck-lace"—Edwina indicated it with a finger—"was Adele's favorite, and when Emma was a little servant girl at Fairley Hall, she used to fasten the necklace around her mistress's neck. Years later, she was the owner. What a reversal, eh, girls?"

"Yes, indeed," India said. "And did Emma enjoy wearing it, too?"

"Oh, she never wore it. Oddly enough, it was never worn by anybody after Adele until my mother gave it to me. I wore it a few times, and now, Tessa, I am giving it to you."

"Oh, Great-Aunt Edwina, I can't take it! The neck-lace should go to India, she's your granddaughter. Thank you, but—"

"No thank you, is that what you're saying?" Edwina asked.

"Absolutely."

"No, Tessa!" India exclaimed. "Grandmother should do as she wishes, and she wants you to have it." Looking at Edwina, she added in the most sincere way, "You must do what you want."

"There's a real reason why Tessa should have it," Ed-wina replied, looking from India to Tessa. "Jim Fairley was a *legitimate* Fairley, grandson of Edwin, and he was your father, Tess. I think Adele's necklace should there-fore be yours. And there's another reason. . . . Your mother was very close to Emma. Since Emma ulti-mately owned the necklace, she might easily have given it to Paula one day, rather than to me."

"But I—"

Edwina held up her hand. "Please don't argue with me, Tessa dear. This is my gift to you, because of who you are, a true Fairley through your father. But you must never forget that you are also a Harte, Tessa. Never. I did once, and I lived to regret it. I love you, and it's yours."

"Thank you," Tessa said a little tremulously. She tried to swallow, but her throat suddenly ached and she flicked the tears from her lashes.

"Now to you, my beauty," Edwina went on, looking over at her granddaughter. "The rest of the jewelry in those old boxes belonged to Adele, too. It's the collection Emma bought at that auction long ago, and she left everything to me in her will. You can choose anything you want, India, but I thought you might like this." Bending over the coffee table, Edwina picked up a tall red-leather case and opened it.

Again the two young women gasped in surprise and stared at each other and then at the old dowager countess.

"It's for me, Grandma?" India whispered, her eyes wide in astonishment.

"If you want it, my dear."

India was silent. She simply bent over the coffee table and picked up the choker. It was made entirely of pearls, and it was very wide, in the Edwardian style. At its center was a huge sapphire, surrounded by five rows of rose-cut diamonds; the whole centerpiece was oval, and like the diamond necklace, it was a truly magnificent piece.

"I thought it would suit you, India, since you have a long, swanlike neck. There's another box there containing the matching sapphire earrings. Oh, and Tessa, there are diamond drop earrings to match your necklace. Now why don't you rummage among the smaller cases and find them?" Edwina sat back, smiling.

"Is this really for me, Grandma?" India asked, her voice quavering slightly.

"It is, my darling, because I love you very much. You, too, are a Fairley through me, and you should also have something that belonged to your great-great-grandmother."

"Thank you, thank you so much," India said, and putting the necklace down in its box, she went to her grandmother and embraced her, her eyes tearing up.

Tessa followed her and kissed her aunt. Edwina began to laugh, delighted to witness their shock, their pleasure, and their obvious gratitude. "There's a mirror over there. Why don't you girls try them on?"

India, who was wearing a black dress with a scooped-out neckline, found that the choker went on easily, and she turned and said to her grandmother, "How does it look? It's so beautiful, isn't it?"

"It suits you perfectly, India, I was absolutely right, choosing it for you. Come here, let me look at you properly."

Hurrying back, India stood in front of Edwina, who nodded her approval. "It's absolutely perfect on that long neck of yours, my dear."

"Thank you again, Grandmother, it's so generous of you."

"I'm having trouble with this necklace," Tessa said, over her shoulder. "It doesn't seem to fall properly."

India ran across the room and unzipped the back of Tessa's white dress. "Slide the dress down a little bit, off your shoulders, then the necklace should sit properly." Tessa did as her cousin told her, then went to show Edwina.

"What do you think, Great-Aunt Edwina? Does it suit me?"

Edwina nodded, and unexpectedly her eyes welled. "Why the two of you suddenly look like ethereal beings from a long-ago age, and you know something, you both look more like Adele than ever. It's your blond hair and silvery eyes . . ." Edwina groped in her pocket for a handkerchief and blew her nose. Recouping quickly, she said in a more businesslike tone, "The jewelry is my legacy to the two of you, and the rest of Adele's collection I will give to Sally. Your mother will inherit the most. But I shall give something to Paula."

Now Edwina stood up. "Let's go in for supper," she said in a quiet voice. "I think I'm really quite hungry."

"Yes, let's do that, Grandmother," India agreed. "But perhaps we ought to lock the other leather cases away?"

"Good idea," Tessa said, taking off the diamond bib, placing it in the box, and then fastening her dress. She suddenly threw a pointed look at India and turned to Edwina. "Don't you have a safe here, Great-Aunt?"

"You don't think I keep all of this priceless stuff lying around, do you, you silly girl? Jack Figg would have my guts for garters if I did."

Tessa and India burst out laughing, and India asked, "So who sent Jack to see you?"

"Gideon Harte. Who else? He's got a soft spot for me. And Jack was very pleased to see I had three safes. One for documents, one for jewelry, and one for the silver. He was most impressed."

"I bet he was." Tessa laughed.

"Oh, Grandma, you're such a scream." As she spoke, India began to carry the cases over to the desk, and Tessa helped.

Edwina watched them, her face glowing with pleasure.

16

The paintings were beautiful, landscapes Dusty had done earlier in his career, and they dominated the walls of the drawing room at Willows Hall. India stood in front of each one for several minutes, studying it intently before moving on to the next. There were four altogether, one on each end wall and two on the long back wall, which was intersected by French doors leading out to the terrace and the gardens.

She loved these landscapes, with their lush, dark greens and pale blue skies, light filled and luminous. His skies reminded her of the sky in the Turner painting that hung at Pennistone Royal. She knew how hard it was to capture light on canvas, and how brilliantly Dusty had done it here, and continued to do it. She admired the style he painted in, classical realism, and he had once mentioned to her that it was hard to master. "Painting landscapes and people as they are exactly seen is not an easy thing to do," he had pointed out. She had nodded her understanding, wanted to tell him how his land-scapes of the English countryside resembled the great classical paintings of Constable. But she hadn't dared for fear he'd think she was saying he had copied Constable, which he hadn't, of course. He could be touchy.

Over the beautifully carved white marble fireplace hung a fifth painting. This was a portrait of a beautiful woman dressed in the clothes of the Georgian period, and it looked as if it had been painted in the 1700s, but there was Dusty's small signature in the right-hand corner to prove otherwise. It brought to mind George Romney's famous portrait of Lady Hamilton that hung in the Frick Collection in New York. Her maiden name had been Emma Hart, without the *e* at the end. Because of that odd coincidence of the same name as her great-grandmother, Lady Hamilton, Lord Nelson's mistress, had always been of interest to India.

She went and sat down on the sofa facing the fireplace, gazing up at the portrait of the young woman, but her mind was filled with thoughts of the artist, not the subject.

She had driven to the hospital in Harrogate this morning, picked him up, and brought him home. After a light lunch, which the housekeeper Angelina had prepared, Dusty had gone to the studio. "To reacquaint myself with it," he had explained, "to banish the hobgoblins."

He had not had to tell her he wanted to go there alone; she understood that. This was one of India's great assets, her awareness of another person's moods, her ability to understand them, even to second-guess them, to empathize.

She heard footsteps in the marble hall, and she turned her head toward the handsome walnut doors, which stood open. Her face lit up at the thought that it was Dusty, but the smile faltered slightly as Paddy Whitaker hove into view.

"I'm not disturbing you, am I, Lady India?" he asked from the entrance, his manners scrupulous as usual.

"No, you're not, Paddy," she answered. "I was just sitting here admiring the portrait over the fireplace."

"Yes, it is rather lovely," he agreed, now stepping into the room. "Mr. Rhodes was wondering if you could come over to the studio. He just buzzed me on the intercom in the butler's pantry. There isn't one in here, you see."

"Of course," she replied.

"This is the first opportunity I've had to thank you for putting me in touch with Jack Figg," Paddy said. "He came over to look at Willows Hall, then sent in a team of specialists. Remarkable blokes. You know, I've long been after Mr. Rhodes to spruce up the security here. Anybody can wander in whenever they want. At least they could. Things have already improved." The house manager looked directly at her and added, "You saved Mr. Rhodes's life, Lady India, and for that we are all grateful, very grateful indeed."

Dusty Rhodes was standing near the easel when she walked into the studio, and he stepped forward and stretched out his hands to her, smiling broadly. "It's all right in here, India, after all. Perfectly all right. No hobgoblins, therefore no bad vibes."

She took hold of his hands, smiling back, allowed herself to be pulled closer to him. Dusty leaned into her and said against her cheek, "Thank you." Then he moved away, looked into her face, and added softly, "It's been such a difficult time for you. I'm sorry."

"Dusty, there's nothing to be sorry about! It happened. Thank God you're all right. You are all right?"

"Yes. Are you?" he asked carefully.

"*Absolutely*. I'm fine . . . as long as you're fine."

"I thought I might feel uneasy in here, but I don't. So I can happily go back to work tomorrow, India my sweet."

"Are you sure of that?"

"Oh, yes, very sure. Anyway, I paint with my right hand, not my left."

She nodded and walked across the studio, sat down in one of the armchairs.

After a moment loitering near the easel, Dusty came, took the other chair, and stretched out his legs. There was a small silence before he said, "I haven't felt up to talking about the stabbing before now, even though I know you've been anxious to discuss it."

"Yes, I *have* needed to talk it through with you, Dusty."

"The day it happened it wasn't possible, and since then I haven't been in the right frame of mind to explain, but it's okay now. There's one thing I must make clear, India. I *do* know her . . . the woman who stabbed me."

India simply nodded.

He said, "We were involved once, but only for a short while. We split up about a year and a half ago. She's a drug addict, very self-destructive, and to be honest, try though I did to help her, she just couldn't stay away from heroin. I hadn't seen her for a year, until about six months ago, when her mother phoned me up. Melinda, that's her name, was really bad, and her mother needed help to get her into a clinic. I did my best to find the right place, and fortunately she agreed to go into detoxification. I thought it was all going well until she showed up here, then went berserk when she saw you."

"She must be still involved with you," India suggested, her eyes focused on his.

"I dunno, maybe. And how she ever got out of the clinic I'll never know," he answered, slightly embarrassed.

"Is she back there now?" India probed.

"Yes. Her mother's a good woman, and she found Melinda within a day, convinced her to go back to the clinic. She put herself under the care of Doctor Jeffers again."

"Can she get better, Dusty?"

"If she wants to, and if she works at it. I hope she can, for her sake."

"Well, so do I." India cleared her throat, gave him another direct look, and asked, "You didn't press charges, did you?"

"How could I? India, she was off her head that day! I'm convinced she had access to drugs of some kind, and you know full well she was going for the painting, not me."

"Yes, I do," she replied softly. Biting her lip, she added in a low voice, "I think you did the right thing, actually."

He looked at her alertly and held himself still, conscious of the worried expression on her face, the lack of energy when she spoke. He hoped she wasn't going to tell him that she was going her own way. He wanted her to stick around, to be part of his life; he had known that in the hospital, and now he truly understood that she had become rather important to him. He leaned across the space between the chairs, took hold of her hand. "It wouldn't have been a good idea to bring a case against her, darling."

"I know that, and I also know that stabbing you was an accident." India swallowed hard before asking, "Do you think she's going to be a pest, though? She could make your life miserable."

"And yours, too. That's what you're getting at, isn't it?"

"Yes, it is. I'm concerned for both of us, Dusty."

"She's going to be in the clinic for a long time. Also, thanks to your bloke Jack Figg, there's no way she, or anyone else, can get onto the estate without being spotted. Security's tight."

India began to laugh. "Poor Jack undertook to do something for Linnet, and now he's become the security expert for the entire family, and you, too. Oh dear, Jack must be cursing us all to himself."

Hearing the laughter, seeing the sudden cheery smile, Dusty immediately felt a lightening of his spirit. Everything was going to be all right with India and him, he felt certain of that. Wanting now to please her, he said, "What was it you asked me earlier? About going to have dinner with your grandmother?"

India exclaimed, "Would you go?"

"She sounds like a gutsy lady, just my type, don't you think?"

"She is. And she'll be thrilled. Whenever you feel up to it, she'd love us to go to supper. She's not far away, between Harrogate and Knaresborough. Can I tell her yes? Maybe over the weekend?"

"You can tell her yes," he responded, smiling and then standing up. "Come on, let's go back to the house."

They left the studio hand in hand and walked in the direction of the back terrace. India was thinking how pleased her grandmother would be to meet Dusty.

And Dusty was thinking how cowardly he had been not to tell India he had a child by Melinda. He hoped to God the press wouldn't find out and make splashy headlines out of the story.

Fingers crossed, he said to himself. *Fingers crossed.*

• • •

"I do like this suite," Lorne announced in his mellifluous voice, walking through the large sitting room and opening the door at the other end. "Oh, Tessa, *look,* here's another bedroom. Well, my darling, this is a treat." He swung around to face his twin sister and added, "When I spoke to Dad in New York the other day, he said he'd made sure we had a large suite we could share, and he's done us proud."

"And then some," Tessa agreed, glancing around the beautifully furnished sitting room of the Paris O'Neill Hotel at the very end of Avenue Montaigne. "And it's nice to have that bird's-eye view of the Eiffel Tower."

Hurrying to her brother, she hugged him. "I'm glad I came with you, Lorne, thanks for making me. I've been very down, so I think this trip *will* cheer me up, like you said."

"Just as long as you're going to relax and not worry about Adele. She's absolutely as safe as houses with Elvira and Linnet at Pennistone Royal, and Evan's there as well, isn't she?"

"Yes, she been working at the Leeds store with India, but I suppose India's staying with Dusty Rhodes at the moment, and not at Pennistone Royal. Gideon and Julian will be spending the weekend with Evan and Linnet. They're arriving tomorrow night, Linnet told me. So I'm fine with it, honestly. Now, which bedroom do you want?"

Lorne glanced over his shoulder into the room he'd just discovered and said, "I think this is the more feminine of the two, and the larger. Why don't you take this one, Tessa, and I'll use the one at the other end of the sitting room."

The doorbell rang, and Lorne went to answer it. He ushered in the bellboy with the bags, directed him on the placement of the luggage, and tipped him.

Alone again with Tessa, Lorne said, "Now, Tessa my darling, I want you to get all spruced up. We've got a special evening ahead of us."

"We do? Where are we going? You didn't mention anything on the plane."

"I thought it would be a nice surprise. First we're going to a book party—a sort of cocktail party and book signing combined—and after that we're going on to dinner as guests of the author."

"Who's the author? I suppose it's a beautiful woman, knowing you, brother of mine," Tessa murmured, throwing him a pointed look.

"No," Lorne said, shaking his head, smiling at her, his eyes full of mischief. "It's Jean-Claude Deléon."

Staring hard at him, Tessa frowned. "You say his name as if I should know him. Do I?"

"You did meet him once. Briefly. At an opening of mine. But I don't know that he registered on you that night. However, you should know him, Tessa, since he's the most famous intellectual in France after Bernard-Henri Lévy."

"I've never heard of him either. Who's Bernard-Henri Lévy?"

"Oh, Tess, don't be such a dunce. Lévy is the *first* most famous intellectual in France, and look, both men are renowned, they're celebrities."

"I don't think I want to go. This party's *pas ma tasse de thé*."

"It *is* your cup of tea, don't be so silly. Anyway, the party's seven to nine. So we'll go at eight-fifteen for forty-five minutes, then go on to dinner with him and a small group of his friends."

"Even forty-five minutes sounds too long to me. Can't I come for the last ten minutes?"

"No, you can't," he exclaimed sharply. "It's about

time you got out and about. We're in Paris, you agreed to do whatever I wanted before we came, so we're going to the book signing. At eight-fifteen."

"All right, all right, don't get your knickers in a twist!" she exclaimed and glanced at her watch. "It's six-thirty, an hour earlier in England, so I'm going to phone Elvira and Adele, and then I'll get ready."

"I want you to look gorgeous and glamorous," Lorne instructed and hurried to his bedroom to get ready himself.

An hour later Tessa stood staring at herself in the bathroom, the walls of which were entirely mirrored. Turning this way and that, she was wondering if she had chosen the right outfit. Perhaps she should have worn something a little more dressy. Lorne had told her that Jean-Claude Deléon was a national celebrity, and a special favorite amongst the chic in the worlds of literature, theater, and society. Therefore the party would be full of sophisticated writers and intellectuals and the *beau monde* of Paris, as well as actors. And certainly this outfit was understated, to say the least.

Yet her reflection now told her that she looked pretty, and this pleased her. She hadn't felt pretty in the longest time, weighed down by worries about the divorce, her sense of failure that the marriage had ended. And then there had been Adele's abduction; she could not deny that the fear had taken its toll.

One of the reasons she had chosen the outfit she was wearing was the weather. It was as hot here as it was in London, so she had settled on this skirt and top made of white voile. The voile was gauzy and light as air; the skirt, which fell to just above her ankles, was relatively full and intersected with bands of narrow lace. The bands were set in at intervals from the hip down, and the same narrow lace trimmed the hemline. The top was sleeveless and had a draped neckline that was very becoming, she thought. A white leather belt clinched her waist and matched her high-heeled sandals, and her only jewelry was a watch and chandelier earrings made of pearls.

Glancing at herself one more time, she decided she'd done the best she could and went back into the bedroom. Picking up a small white leather purse, she opened the door to the sitting room.

Lorne was on the phone, and he looked across the room as he heard the door opening. "Got to go, Phil. My date's arrived. See you tomorrow," he murmured and hung up.

Coming toward her in long strides, her brother let out a low, wolfish whistle and exclaimed, "You've done me proud, Ancient One! You look bloody wonderful!"

Tessa laughed. "And you don't look so bad yourself, Lorne Fairley. Now isn't it great that you're wearing black? We blend very well, wouldn't you say?"

"I would. And thank God I didn't wear my white shirt and trousers, we'd have looked like some awful double act."

"Never," she shot back. "We could never look *awful*, Lorne. I might, but not you, sweetie pie."

"Oh, you're just prejudiced because you're related to me. Little *me*, a famous actor," he said in his usual self-deprecating way, laughing. "Now, come on, let's get a move on, I don't want to get there any later than eight-fifteen."

"But it's early, only twenty to eight—"

"Ah, but the traffic is worse here than London," he cut in. "And we have to get to the Faubourg Saint-Germain."

"So come on then, slow coach, let's get going," Tessa

replied and hurried toward the door of the suite. "I'm assuming you arranged for us to have a car."

"Of course we've got wheels, silly girl," he exclaimed, taking hold of her arm and opening the door at the same time. "I'm very well organized. The Harte training, you know."

She looked up at him and began to laugh, feeling happy for the first time in ages, happy to be with someone who loved her as Lorne did, and to be in Paris, a city she had a soft spot for. Their mother had brought them here when they were quite young, and they had been coming ever since, often on their way to the South of France and the Villa Faviola, which they visited several times a year. As they went down in the elevator, she felt a sudden sense of anticipation and wondered why.

Once they were settled in the car and the driver was edging away from the hotel, Tessa said, "I like the seventh arrondissement; in fact, I've often thought I'd like to have an apartment in that district. Actually, anywhere on the Left Bank would be fine by me, I've always enjoyed it, felt at home there."

Lorne looked at her in surprise and exclaimed, "Anywhere around the Faubourg Saint-Germain costs an arm and a leg, but those private houses are quite beautiful."

"I wasn't talking about a private house, just a little garret for me and my child. It might be a nice escape from time to time."

"Well, why not," he murmured, wondering if she was serious. Then he said, "I like the area, too, because it's such a great mix, an enclave for aristocrats and a haven for students, artists, and writers. And aside from all the historic buildings, such as Napoleon's tomb, the French Academy, and the Rodin Museum, there are two of the most famous hangouts for writers and artists, the Café aux Deux Magots and the Café de Flore. Both of which I love."

"I know, and what about all the antiques shops and bistros and art galleries? It'd be a wonderful place to have a little hideaway—because it's charming."

"If you mean it, we can look at some real estate in the next few days. Actually, I'd enjoy it," Lorne remarked, still wondering if she was merely daydreaming.

"Maybe we can do that. It would be fun, a little adventure," Tessa murmured, then said, "When actually do you have to check in for work?"

"Shooting starts on Monday, but I'm not on call until Wednesday morning. Why?"

"No reason, you hadn't really said, and I just wondered. Anyway, Lorne, tell me about Jean-Claude Deléon."

"I've told you."

"No, you haven't. All you said is that he's famous, a celebrity, an intellectual, and a good friend of yours. Tell me a bit more about him, so I don't feel a total fool when I meet him."

"Let me see . . . he's a journalist as well as an author of books, and he lectures. He's considered one of the great thinkers in France today, and he's certainly thought of as a philosopher, ranks second to Bernard-Henri Lévy. He's genial, charming, a great bloke. You'll like him, and I think you'll enjoy the evening."

"How do you know him?"

"I met him a few years ago, when I was staying at Villa Faviola with Gideon, Toby, Uncle Winston, and Dad. If you remember, we had that all-male weekend together. Jean-Claude came over with one of Toby's friends, and we hit it off. Spent a lot of time talking about the theater and films. And then whenever he was in London he called me, and we got together if we could."

"And is there a Madame Deléon?"

"No, there isn't. And I don't think there ever has been. Mind you, Jean-Claude does have a reputation . . . as being something of a ladies' man."

"Oh, so he's young then?" Tessa asked.

"Maybe he's forty-nine, fifty, I'm not sure."

"And where are we going to dinner?"

"Tessa, darling, I've no idea. He simply said, 'Bring your sister to the book party, and afterwards you'll both join me for dinner with a few friends.' So your guess is as good as mine."

17

He saw her the moment she walked in. A vision in white. Ethereal, almost otherworldly. He moved his head slightly to see her better. He knew at once who she was: Tessa Fairley, Lorne's twin sister. Lorne was holding her elbow, moving her through the group clustered near the door, bringing her to him.

He was sitting at a *bureau* at the far end of the grand entrance foyer, in one of the great private homes in the Faubourg Saint-Germain, signing his latest book. Except that he wasn't signing at this moment. He was sitting waiting for the woman in white, the most beautiful woman he had ever seen.

As she drew nearer, her eyes met his, registered his concentrated stare, and she blinked, appeared to recoil for a split second, but she continued to walk toward him, and her eyes never left his.

The chattering around him became just a dim noise in the background; no other person present interested him any longer. Only this girl, for that was how he saw her, so young, so fresh, so innocent-looking, a little un-worldly even.

He was suddenly on his feet, walking around the writing table, waiting for her to come to him.

"Jean-Claude, good evening," Lorne said as they drew to a stop.

"Ah, Lorne, *quel plaisir de vous voir.*"

The two men shook hands; then Lorne went on, "This is my sister, Tessa." As he spoke Lorne moved her forward slightly, closer to Jean-Claude.

"Enchanté," he said, and switching to English he added, "I am happy you could come." To Jean-Claude his voice sounded gruff, even hoarse.

"I'm pleased to meet you, too, Monsieur Deléon," Tessa answered in a clear, light voice, offering her hand to him.

He took it in his, held it tightly. She smiled at him. The smile, her silvery eyes, that pale, silken hair were heart-stopping. His gaze fastened on hers. Mesmerized by each other, they stood staring.

"I think I've got to break this up, people are staring at the two of you," Lorne said with a slightly embarrassed laugh.

Jean-Claude blinked and murmured, "Excuse me, I must continue with the signing." Reluctantly he let go of her hand, smiled at her, and walked back around the desk. To Lorne he said, "I shall now sign books for the two of you, *mon ami.*" As he spoke he pulled one toward him, signed it, and handed it to Tessa.

"Thank you," she said as she opened her book. After reading the inscription she stared at him, her eyes questioning.

Jean-Claude looked at her intently. A small smile struck his mouth when he saw the bafflement on her face, and then he looked at Lorne, gave him his signed book. "Take Tessa to meet our hostess, Marie-Hélène; you've met her with me before. She's in the salon. I have more books to sign. After, we go to dinner."

"Thanks for the book, Jean-Claude, and that sounds great," Lorne murmured.

Jean-Claude nodded and glanced around. It seemed to him that all those who had crowded around had dispersed, and he shrugged and wondered if he could bring the book signing to a close sooner rather than later. But no . . . here they came, once they saw he was alone. His friends and acquaintances flooded around the desk once more, wanting the book, his signature, and so he smiled and signed, and wished he were alone with the young woman who had disappeared from his sight. Later, he thought, I will be with her later.

Lorne had propelled Tessa through the marble foyer, with its wall-hung tapestries, crystal chandeliers, and elegant furniture, and once there was enough distance between them and Jean-Claude, he whispered, "My God, what happened back there?"

"I don't know," Tessa muttered and thought: I met Destiny. I met the man who is my destiny. As bizarre as she knew this thought was, she knew she was right. A strange calmness settled over her, like a soft, transparent veil. And her heart was suddenly perfectly still. Tessa thought of the words he had written in the book and suddenly knew what they meant. He felt the same as she did. *Of course.* But hadn't she known that before reading his words? She had seen it on his face . . . and in his eyes. They had reflected what she was feeling exactly.

"You've suddenly gone very quiet," Lorne murmured, searching her face. "Are you all right?"

"I'm perfect," she replied and gave him a small but loving smile.

"Then let me take you to meet the hostess of this event."

"Who *is* Marie-Hélène?"

"She's a socialite, married to a French industrialist, Alain Charpentier, and they're old friends of Jean-Claude's. I think they're coming to dinner, along with another couple, and Jean-Claude has invited his editor as well. We're eight."

"He said you'd met Marie-Hélène before, but do you know any of the others?"

"I've met Alain, her husband, and Jean-Claude's editor, Michel Longeval, several times before, but I don't know who the other couple are. Anyway, we'll soon find out. In the meantime, there's Marie-Hélène over there near the fireplace. Let's go and say hello."

A moment later Tessa was shaking hands with one of the chicest women she had ever seen, including her mother. It was the kind of elegance that only a French-woman knew how to achieve. Marie-Hélène, a slender blond of medium height and indeterminate age, wore a simple black linen sheath with a round neckline and no sleeves, which was obviously haute couture. On her ears were pearl-and-diamond studs, and around her neck a single strand of large pearls—South Sea pearls. They're not as beautiful as Great-Aunt Edwina's, Tessa thought, and this made her smile to herself. She couldn't help wondering, all of a sudden, what Edwina would make of Jean-Claude Deléon.

Their hostess was charm personified and chatted away to Lorne and Tessa in the most entertaining way, while they sipped from their flutes of Dom Pérignon. Lorne was the one who mostly chatted back and, Tessa vaguely noticed, flirted in a mild way with the woman, who on close inspection looked to be in her late fifties.

Tessa herself nodded occasionally and said only a few words because her concentration was elsewhere. Her mind was focused on the man in the entrance foyer signing his latest book.

He elected to sit in the front seat with the driver, while Lorne, the editor, and she lined themselves up in the back of the car.

Alain and Marie-Hélène had taken the other couple to the restaurant with them. They were called Natalie and Arnaud; Tessa hadn't caught their last name, but they had seemed very pleasant when they were introduced in the house.

Tessa sat staring at Jean-Claude's head, thinking that it was very shapely and that he had good hair. Suddenly, as if her eyes had bored into him, he glanced over his shoulder and stared at her. And she stared back. Then without saying a word, he swung his head rather abruptly and looked straight ahead through the windshield, remaining silent as they drove to the restaurant.

Tessa sat very still, saying nothing, just thinking about him, asking herself what was happening to her. And why now? She half listened to Lorne and Michel discussing an old French movie they both loved, *Belle de Jour*, but mostly she was thinking about Jean-Claude Deléon, replaying in her head their meeting just over an hour ago. Was that all it was? An hour? She felt as if she'd known him always . . . how curious to feel that. . . .

Quite innocently she had gone with Lorne to that grand private house on the Faubourg Saint-Germain; a *hôtel particulier* it was called, as were all these grand private homes in Paris, each hidden behind forbiddingly high stone walls. They had entered the inner courtyard through a black-painted door set in a narrow side wall, crossed the large cobblestone yard, gone through the front door of the house, and mounted an imposing staircase, which led to the handsome foyer.

Since Lorne had not told her very much about his old friend, she had not known what to expect; much to her astonishment she had found herself mesmerized the instant she set eyes on him.

He had moved slightly when he had caught sight of her walking toward him with Lorne, and their eyes had locked and held. Immediately she had been drawn to him. Perhaps it was his eyes, which were magnetic, amber-brown in color and deep set below shapely brows that matched his dark hair. His face was well defined, with a strong jaw, broad brow, aquiline nose, generous mouth, and full lower lip. She wasn't sure how old he was, a lot older than she certainly, but she didn't care, and it was instantly apparent to her that he was all male, masculinity personified, in fact.

Suddenly her legs had felt weak, and she had trembled inside. She had met his intense gaze head-on and found it impossible to look away. When they shook hands he had not let go, and she hadn't minded that. They had just stood there, oblivious to everyone, gazing at each other. She had felt the irresistible pull of sexual attraction. Yet it was so much more than a purely physical thing. She felt as if he were looking deep into her soul, seeing her innermost self, and she had understood something else . . . that they were making a pact with each other, albeit unspoken. At that moment, something profound had happened, and she was aware there was already an undercurrent of intimacy between them even though they had only just met.

Now, in the back of the car, an involuntary shiver ran through her. Automatically she straightened on the seat as she admitted to herself that there was something inevitable about them. The fates had brought them together.

• • •

He took them to Taillevent on the Rue Lamennais, a restaurant she was familiar with but did not know well. It had been closed for summer vacation since mid-July, had just reopened, so there was a flurry of greetings and friendly chatter when they arrived. And he was treated with such deference, as though he were a king. Yet there was a warm familiarity between him and the staff which he appeared to encourage, and she realized he had humility despite his fame. This pleased her.

At the table, Jean-Claude began to seat them, just as Marie-Hélène, her husband, and the other couple arrived. Tessa noticed she would not be sitting next to him; he had placed her at one end of the table, flanked by Alain and Michel, while he took the other end, between Marie-Hélène and Natalie.

This meant he was looking directly at her, and although he was the perfect host, cosseting them all, talking to everyone, motioning to waiters, being the bon vivant, his eyes came back to her face every few minutes.

It seemed to Tessa that the evening passed in a blur. She did everything by rote, ordered food, barely tasted or enjoyed it. Occasionally she sipped her wine and made conversation with the two men on either side of her.

Sometimes she looked across at Lorne, half smiled or spoke a few words to him, but mostly she remained quiet, listening. And she rarely took her eyes off Jean-Claude. Once or twice he asked her if she liked the food, or gave her a faint smile, but mostly he spoke eloquently about the things which interested him and the others at the table—theater and film, literature, and politics.

As he talked she began to understand more about him. She hadn't realized he had covered wars—in Bosnia, Kosovo, and Afghanistan. That he was a journalist of some standing quickly became apparent to her;

she also learned he had been a protégé and favorite of President Mitterrand; that the French elite thought of him as another André Malraux; and that he had made documentaries and written a play that had run at the Comédie-Française, one of the great theaters of Paris.

The only thing she didn't know was his exact age. Lorne had said he was about forty-nine, but she thought he was wrong. Jean-Claude looked to her to be in his fifties, although she had to admit she'd never been very good at guessing people's ages.

And so the evening went until it was time for them to leave the restaurant. Once more Jean-Claude came with them in the car but insisted that she and Lorne were dropped off first. When they arrived at the hotel, Jean-Claude got out, came to say good night to her on the steps. He took one of her hands, brought it to his lips, and kissed it. Then he stepped back and gave her a long, penetrating look, as if committing her face to memory.

"*À bientôt,*" he murmured and stepped to one side, shook Lorne's hand, and said good night. A moment later he was gone.

As she and Lorne walked through the lobby to the elevator, her brother said, "That was an abrupt departure. I was about to ask him to come in for a nightcap. I know he likes a good Calvados."

"Obviously he wants to get home," she responded softly.

"He's very taken with you, Tess."

"Is he?"

Lorne gave her a swift, peculiar look and exclaimed, "Come on, you know he is!" When she was silent, he asked, "What about you?"

"What about me?"

"You know what I mean. Are you interested in him?

Stupid question, isn't it, when you were practically swooning at his feet."

"Is that what I was doing?" She looked up at her brother, her silvery eyes questioning.

"Yes, you were. I've never seen you like that before. But then I've never seen him like that either."

"So you've seen him interact with women, have you, Lorne?"

"Occasionally."

"And how did he seem then?"

"Laid-back. Cool."

"And how was he with me? At the actual book signing, I mean?"

"Bowled over. Very taken. Actually, I think the word I'm looking for is *intent.* He was very intent and intense."

Tessa sighed but said nothing more as they got into the elevator. Once they were inside their suite, she swung around and said to her brother: "I'm going to say good night, darling. I'm tired. You don't mind, do you?"

"No, of course not, Tess." He kissed her cheek, watched her as she walked to her bedroom. He thought: She'll be all right.

Once she was in her room, Tessa sat down in the chair near the bed and looked at the book in her hands, which she had clutched all evening. Its cover showed a collapsed suit of medieval armor. *His* name blazed across the top, and at the bottom was the title. One word. WARRIORS. She turned to the inside back flap, studied his photograph for a moment, started to read about him.

The phone began to ring, and she reached for it. "Hello?" she said.

"C'est moi."

"I know."

"When can I see you?"

"Tomorrow?"

"That's good. For lunch?"

"Yes," she said, her heart beginning to clatter against her rib cage.

"I hope Lorne will not feel—how shall I say? Left out."

"He has other plans tomorrow," she improvised.

"*Bien. Je vous enverrai une voiture.* At noon."

"Thank you."

"*À demain,*" he said and was gone.

Tessa stared at the phone for a moment, put the book down on the bed, and went out into the sitting room. Lorne was nursing a balloon of Calvados and watching a political show on CNN, but he swung his head as she came in. "Do you want one of these?" he asked, lifting his glass.

"I don't know . . ." She paused when she came to the sofa and stared at her brother. "Jean-Claude just phoned."

"I guessed it was him."

"I'm having lunch with him tomorrow."

Lorne nodded. "He told me he was going to phone you about lunch."

Seating herself on the arm of the sofa, she exclaimed, "He did! Was he asking your permission? I hope not. I'm thirty-two, for heaven's sake, a mother, and about to become a divorcée."

Lorne threw back his head and laughed. "Don't sound so indignant. Of course he wasn't asking my permission. He's not like that. As we were leaving Taillevent, he told me he intended to call you when he got home, that he wanted to take you to lunch. And I suppose he wanted me to know that, since I'm your brother and we are here in Paris together. Also, he and I are good friends."

When she remained silent, looking worried, Lorne

added, "He's a grown man, Tessa. He'd never ask my permission to take you out. He was simply being courteous. He's very gentlemanly, always has been, and about everything."

She merely nodded, murmured, "I understand," and walked over to the bar, where she poured herself a small glass of apple brandy.

As she returned to the sofa, Lorne lowered the volume of the television set, raised his glass, and with a smile said, "Cheers."

"Cheers." Tessa sat down opposite him and asked, "What did he write in your book?"

"He said he admired my talent as an actor, called me his *cher ami,* and wished me luck with the film. What did he put in yours?"

"Something rather odd."

"What?"

"He wrote my name, and then *Je suis là.*"

"'I am here.' That's what he wrote? It does sound a bit odd. I am here *what?*"

Tessa shook her head. "I am here . . . *waiting.* I am here . . . *for you.* That's how I interpreted it."

"I think you're correct. And I was right, he is full of *intent.*"

"I find him very compelling."

"Yes, he's extremely charismatic."

"And you don't mind that I'm having lunch with him? You're not warning me about him?"

"No. I wouldn't warn you about a man like Jean-Claude Deléon. He's . . . *true blue* as our mother would say. And a giant of a man, very serious, very responsible. He's what Uncle Ronnie would call a *mensch.*"

"But *you* said he was a ladies' man," she reminded him.

"I did, but I didn't mean he was a *womanizer,* because I don't believe he is. Oh, there've been lots of women in his life, I know that. But he's not a philanderer. What I meant when I said he was a ladies' man is that he likes women, *admires* women. He's not a misogynist like some men I know who are red-blooded but don't *like* women."

"I see." She leaned back in the chair and sipped her drink. After a moment she said, "He's sending a car for me tomorrow at noon."

"I told you he was a gentleman. Anyway, my Tess, you should be flattered. Before he meets you for lunch he's going to be at the Élysée Palace with the president of France."

Not far away from the Paris O'Neill Hotel, Jonathan Ainsley sat in a small bar on a narrow street just off the Champs-Élysées.

He was waiting for Mark Longden, wondering where he was, and sipping a glass of Napoleon brandy. He kept glancing at his watch, cursing the other man under his breath. He was a stickler about time, loathed unpunctuality in others. Lately, he had come to wonder if Mark had become something of a liability, a hindrance. He had expected the man to have done much more to destroy Paula through her children.

While it was true that Mark had managed to bring Tessa to her knees, there was still Linnet to take care of, and then Emsie. Jonathan wanted these three Harte women ruined along with Paula. He hated all Harte women, except for his cousin Sarah; she was the exception to his rule. Paula and her three daughters reminded him far too much of his grandmother Emma Harte, whom he had detested throughout her life. And he continued to harbor hatred for her, even in death. He believed she had cheated him out of his inheritance, favoring Paula. He had been jealous and envious of Paula since childhood.

Mark suddenly pushed through the door, came hurrying into the bar. Watching him cross the floor, Jonathan was instantly struck by Mark's pallor, his strained look, the tired eyes. After they greeted each other, Mark sat down and motioned to a waiter. He ordered a Napoleon, a cup of black coffee, and a pack of Gauloises cigarettes.

"Started smoking again, have you, Mark?" Jonathan asked, a brow lifting sardonically. "I thought you were one of the true believers, that you condemned out of hand secondhand smoke."

"I still do, but I *need* a smoke tonight. I suppose you could say I need to indulge myself a bit after a hard week."

"My dear Mark, I've plenty of things available which you can indulge yourself in, you just have to say the word. And certainly things that are much more pleasurable than a mere cigarette."

Mark looked at him sideways and shook his head. "No women tonight, my friend. Or anything else. I'm too damned tired. It was a rough trip down from Thirsk to London, and I just made the plane to Paris."

"I told you to fly from Manchester. You could even have taken a flight from Yeadon. Well, never mind. How's my house coming along?" He asked this in a warm voice even though the topic was of no real interest to him.

"If I say so myself, it's looking wonderful. I know you're going to like it, Jonathan," Mark said. "More than that, you're going to love it. You won't want to leave. *Ever.*"

Now Jonathan merely smiled, inclined his head, knowing very well he would want to leave it, and leave it a lot. There was his luxurious apartment here in Paris, and his palatial house on a hill overlooking the harbor in Hong Kong, not to mention his farm in Provence, the latest acquisition. Of course he would continue to travel to these homes, which were much more splendid than the country house in Yorkshire. The building of Thirsk was only a ruse, wasn't it? A ruse to delude Mark into thinking he needed an architect, when he had only needed a man to do his dirty work . . . ruining those ghastly Harte women. With his inferiority complex, his desire for fame and money, and his innumerable weak spots, Mark had been an easy target. He was lustful and loved tarty women, and he couldn't get enough of Ecstasy, even smack at times, although he was a bit more cautious when it came to heroin. And he liked to booze it up.

He is my creature, Jonathan thought, looking at the younger man. I have him totally in my control. He needs all the things I can offer. Jonathan sat back, a satisfied smile playing around his mouth.

Mark drank the coffee, took a gulp of the cognac, and then lit a cigarette, inhaling deeply. Once he had smoked for a few seconds, he said, "I heard on the grapevine up in Yorkshire that your father's other son, Owen Hughes, is in London. Staying at that Welshman's hotel in Belgravia. Brought his wife with him from New York. Is seeing his daughter Evan, your father's only grandchild, and has even had lunch with Gideon and Evan. It seems like there's a family gathering going on. How about that?"

Jonathan was furious when he thought of Evan Hughes. The grandchild his father had always craved. *She would have to be dealt with as well.* He laughed silently. But *she* was a Harte, too, a descendant of the dreaded Emma. He would deal with *her* himself.

Before he could stop himself, Jonathan said, in a boastful voice, "I have a son, you know."

Mark was flabbergasted. "You have a son! Jesus

Christ, man, why isn't he visiting your father with you in Yorkshire? That would certainly put Evan Hughes's nose out of joint."

"My son lives in another country," Jonathan answered, which was the truth. Then, realizing that more of an explanation was required, he added, "He has not been well for some time. He has to live in a warm climate, a special environment." This was not true. The truth was the son his wife had presented him with some years earlier had actually not been his but that of his Chinese partner Tony Chiu. It was his eyes that had given her game away. Damn and blast his wife, too.

"Who told you all this about Owen Hughes, Mark?"

"I picked it up here and there. I have my sources. Anyway, how long are you staying in Paris?"

"I'm not sure. That's why I needed you to come to see me, rather than meeting you in London. I have to pop down to the South of France. I've bought a rather nice old farm. . . . I'm going to need you for that, you know, Mark, as well, need your input, for which, of course, you will be very well paid. But we'll get to that later. Right now I'd like to know how your divorce is coming along. You know how much your separation from that dreadful girl has meant to me. We can't have you, such a talented architect, hampered in your rise by a mere Harte, now can we? And she is something of a bitch, isn't she?"

"*Bitch* is not a strong enough word to describe Tessa Fairley. She's impossible. I wish I could get Adele away from her," Mark cried.

"Well, my dear boy, why don't we try? Money's no object as far as you're concerned. I'll give you anything you need in this fight to . . . the death, shall we say."

Mark glanced at him swiftly and exclaimed in a low voice, "I don't mind bashing her around a bit, but I'd never kill her, Jonathan. I'm not a murderer, and I'm not going to take a dive for any woman."

"Listen here, my friend, I have a few ideas." As Jonathan spoke, Mark leaned closer, and slowly a smile spread itself across his face.

The two of them sat talking and drinking for another hour or so, and then Jonathan paid the bill and he and Mark left the bar together. Still embroiled in their plotting, they did not notice a nondescript couple in a corner of the bar who had been watching them for the entire time they had been there. The man and woman followed them into the street and kept them under surveillance until Jonathan located his car and chauffeur. The couple were just behind in their own vehicle, bracing themselves for a long night.

It was noon on Friday, and Lorne was alone in the hotel suite, studying his lines. Next week he had to report to the studios outside Paris, and he wanted to be word perfect.

He was on his fifth reading of the first few pages of his part when the phone on the desk cut into his concentration. He had barely said "Hello" when his half sister Linnet exclaimed, "Hello, Lorne, it's me."

"Little Bird, how lovely to hear your chirps. Where—"

"I do think our mother should have known better, not named me after a bird, of all things! And I'm here, at Pennistone Royal."

"How's the weather?" he asked.

"It's cooler, in fact it's very pleasant, and I'm sitting here on the terrace, taking it easy for once in my life."

"You taking it easy! Balderdash. I'll believe that when I see it." He laughed, full of affection for Linnet, who had always been a favorite of his. "All is well there, I presume?"

"Yes, nothing untoward is happening. I can see Adele, playing with her dolls, Elvira is with her, and Evan is due here for lunch. She, too, is taking the afternoon off, it's been quite a week for her at the Leeds store. Anyway, how's Tessa? I hope she's not worrying too much."

"No, she's not, and I'd put her on but she just left a few minutes ago for lunch with a friend."

"No, no, I didn't want to speak to her, it was you I was looking for, Lorne."

"What's the matter? You suddenly sound strange."

"Everything's okay, more or less. But I wanted to alert you to the fact that Jonathan Ainsley's left Hong Kong. He's in Paris—"

"How do you know?" he cut in quickly.

"Jack Figg phoned me a short while ago. His operatives are all over the place, have their sights on Mr. Ainsley. Anyway, he was spotted in Paris last night with the horrible Mark Longden. They were in a bar together, looking very cozy indeed."

"Oh, hell, that's the pits."

"Lorne, don't worry, and please don't tell Tessa. There's no need for her to know about them being there together. You can say I called to tell her all is well here, which it is."

"I hope those two buggers are not plotting something nasty," Lorne muttered. "I don't trust either of them."

"Neither do I," Linnet agreed. "But it could be just a meeting about the house Mark Longden designed for Ainsley in Thirsk. He was up in Yorkshire for a couple of days, so Jack tells me. Try not to be alarmed, and as Dad would say, keep your eyes peeled."

"I will, and thanks for alerting me. When is Mums actually coming back? Tessa said she would be back next week, Dad a few days later."

"That's right, Mummy's coming with Winston and Emily, around September sixth, but Dad has some more meetings in the Bahamas or Barbados, and another in New York. From what she said, Mummy wants to get the divorce moving for Tessa, and she feels her presence is required."

"I think it probably is, so listen, chickadee—"

"Hey, stop all this bird stuff, dearest brother of mine, I had enough of it as a child."

He smiled into the phone and said, "Sorry, but old habits die hard, you know. Big kiss, Linnet."

"Big kiss to you, big brother. And break a leg next week."

18

After helping her into the back of the car, the driver gave her an envelope. Sitting comfortably against the leather seat, Tessa looked at the envelope, on which Jean-Claude had written: *Madame Tessa Fairley.*

She gazed for a moment at the handwriting. His penmanship was beautiful, she thought—bold and flowing. Opening it, she took out the note. *Dear Tessa:* he had written, *The chauffeur will take you to my home. If I am a few minutes late, my houseman Hakim will serve you refreshment. JCD.*

After reading the note again, she put it in her handbag and glanced out the window, wondering where he lived. But the driver had not volunteered any information, and she decided not to ask. There had been many questions on the tip of her tongue this morning when she had breakfast with Lorne, but she had resisted asking them. She wanted to find out about this man herself; the opinions of others, even Lorne, were not important.

In any case, she knew her brother would not say anything about the writer that was not laudatory.

Tessa straightened the black linen tunic she was wearing over matching narrow pants and settled herself comfortably in the corner of the car seat. Uncertain of where they would be going to lunch, she had chosen this simple tailored outfit because it could go anywhere—to a bistro or a much more elegant restaurant. A pair of pearl studs and a pearl-and-gold flower pin on the shoulder added a certain chic, yet all could be removed if necessary to play down the outfit.

The heat had hit her when she came out of the hotel, and now she was glad she was wearing the sleeveless linen top and strappy sandals on her bare feet. It was obviously going to be a sizzler, this last day of August, and the black linen was cool and comfortable.

As the car pushed through the traffic, Tessa began to realize that they were more than likely heading to her favorite part of Paris, the seventh arrondissement, and sure enough it was not very long before the driver was turning onto the Rue de Babylone. He eventually came to a stop in front of a turn-of-the-century building with a massive *porte cochere*, those huge wooden doors where horse-drawn carriages used to pass into the courtyard in days gone by.

After helping her out of the car, the driver indicated the small door cut into one side of the porte cochere and bid her good-bye. She smiled, thanked him, and went through the door into the cobbled courtyard of the building, which obviously had been a *hôtel particulier,* a grand house, before it became apartments.

The concierge immediately stepped out of his small office, greeted her pleasantly, and asked how he could help her. She told him that Monsieur Deléon was expecting her, and he nodded, led her into the apartment building, and showed her to a pair of double mahogany doors to the right of the small, cagelike elevator.

Thanking him, she walked over to the doors, rang the bell, and waited; a moment later one side of the doors was opened by a smiling middle-aged man in a white butler's jacket. From his olive skin and dark hair, she thought that he was probably North African.

"Madame, bonjour," he said at once, opening the door wider, ushering her into the apartment. "I am Hakim," he added in accented English.

"Bonjour, Hakim," Tessa replied, her high heels clicking as she followed him across the marble floor of the entrance foyer.

Showing her into a large room that was obviously a library, Hakim said, *"Madame . . .* an *apéritif?"* and added, by way of explanation, *"Monsieur sera de retour dans dix minutes."*

"Un verre d'eau, s'il vous plaît," Tessa murmured.

Left alone, she surveyed the library from the doorway, not moving for a moment, taking everything in eagerly, wanting to know as much as possible about Jean-Claude Deléon.

It was unlike any room she had ever seen, elegant in an understated, rather masculine way. It bespoke great taste, especially evident in the antiques, which looked like museum pieces to her. It was a monochromatic room based on a play of soft creams and beiges, and this mix of pale colors made a subtle background for the mellow wood tones of the various antique pieces. The walls matched the full-length cream wool draperies at the windows and the cream-and-beige upholstered sofas and chairs, while the wood floor, devoid of rugs, shone like glass.

From the entrance Tessa faced two tall windows at

the far end. A large antique mahogany desk stood in front of the windows, and it was partnered with a mahogany chair which she thought was French Empire. On the desk were a pair of gilded-wood column lamps with square black shades and various other things she couldn't quite make out, except for the back of a tall clock.

Glancing to her left, Tessa saw that this wall was dominated by a white marble fireplace, over which hung a *trumeau,* an antique mirror. The main seating arrangement, grouped in front of the fireplace was composed of four Louis XV *bergères,* elegant wing chairs, and two matching sofas. They surrounded a glass coffee table, which did not seem out of place to her at all amongst the antique furniture.

On the opposite wall, floor-to-ceiling bookcases of dark polished wood ran the length of the room; they were filled to overflowing. Just in front of the bookshelves was a lovely eighteenth-century library table, and in one corner, to her right, stood a *guéridon,* an antique pedestal table, and next to it a straight-backed chair and a standing lamp.

At this moment Hakim reappeared, arriving on silent feet with her glass of water, and after taking it and thanking him she walked down to the windows and stood looking out.

Much to her surprise there was a wide terrace immediately outside, and beyond, a lawn and flower beds filled with white flowers; growing against a high stone wall were a variety of large trees, shrubs, and bushes, all creating a shady green bower. Underneath the trees were several metal garden chairs, and she couldn't help thinking what a lovely spot this was in the very heart of Paris. Such a luxury, a garden in the city.

Hakim now came onto the terrace and began to set

the table, and she suddenly understood that she and Jean-Claude were going to have lunch here and not in a restaurant, and this pleased her.

Turning around, she glanced at the desk. The antique clock was by the famous Paris clockmaker Le Roy et Fils; there was an elaborate gilded-bronze box close to it, two crystal paper knives with bronze-filigree decoration on the handles, and a black leather desk blotter with white blotting paper untouched by ink. And that was it. There was a paucity of clutter on the desk, which looked elegant and masculine.

She went to look at the books on the shelves. So many philosophers . . . Descartes, Aristotle, Plato, Sophocles; books by French writers such as Victor Hugo, Céline, André Malraux, Jean-Paul Sartre, Émile Zola, and Colette; volumes of French, English, and American history; some of her own favorite novels by Dickens, the Brontë sisters, and Jane Austen. Politics were covered from all aspects, as the books by Charles de Gaulle, Winston Churchill, and others attested. There were a variety of political biographies of Churchill, John Major, de Gaulle, John Kennedy, Ronald Reagan, and Franklin Roosevelt, and histories of Napoleon, Talleyrand, Nelson, the Duke of Marlborough, and Cromwell, as well as Elizabeth Tudor and Charles II. And, she noticed, a collection of Churchill's famous speeches from the Second World War years, plus his *History of the English-Speaking Peoples* in its many volumes.

Every religion was represented, with books on Christianity, Judaism, Buddhism, and Islam. In fact, she realized there were a lot of volumes on Islam lined up alongside a collection of newer books on terrorism. Next to these were volume after volume covering the hundreds of wars which had been fought over the centuries. Conversely, on yet another shelf, there were many recent novels, and she recognized a number of titles with colorful jackets by well-known British authors.

Further along, she stared at a number of art books, which featured the work of Renoir, Picasso, Manet, Monet, Degas, Gauguin, Turner, Constable, Gainsborough, Bernard Buffet, and Rodin. Resting on another shelf were books on the music of Massenet, Bizet, Ravel, Bach, Beethoven, Mozart, Puccini, and the operas of Wagner.

She couldn't help wondering if Jean-Claude had read all of these books and decided it was more than likely that he had. She could not fail to understand that he had wide-ranging tastes as well as an interest in art and music.

Having sipped most of the water, Tessa put the tumbler on the glass coffee table, deeming it the safest place in a room full of valuable antiques. Now she began to wander around, looking at the art on the walls. An arresting portrait of Napoleon and another of Napoleon and Josephine together were hanging to the right of the mirror over the fireplace, and on the other side there was a lovely painting that appeared to be very old of an elegant woman in a blue dress. Tessa wondered if it was by Ingres. On either side of the door leading to the foyer were framed antique panels of a man and a woman in seventeenth-century clothing, depicting autumn and winter, she thought, in the style of Fragonard.

Finally, she returned to the fireplace and allowed her eyes to roam. Taking in everything once more, she acknowledged that this was not only a room of taste and refinement but a reflection of the extraordinary man who occupied it. A brilliant man who was highly educated, cultured, an intellectual and a philosopher, a man of immense accomplishment.

Suddenly she heard his footsteps coming across the foyer. A second later he was in the doorway, regarding her. He wore a dark suit and a white shirt, and as he stood there looking at her so intently, he loosened his tie. Then he walked toward her.

An unexpected attack of nerves froze her to the spot, and she realized she was curiously intimidated.

He came to a standstill in front of her and stretched out his hand. She took it. He brought her hand up to his mouth, barely brushed his lips against it, and let it go.

"My apologies. I kept you waiting," he said.

"That's all right," she answered, wondering why her mouth was so dry.

Jean-Claude stepped away from her, saying, "Would you excuse me, please? I want to put on different clothes . . . more comfortable. *Je reviens tout de suite.*"

Then he was gone, and she was alone once more, and she sat down on one of the *bergères*, feeling slightly weak in the knees.

Jean-Claude moved rapidly across the foyer, went up the staircase two steps at a time, and hurried into his bedroom. After shedding his clothes, he put on a clean white cotton shirt, rolled up the sleeves, went into a walk-in closet, and found a pair of beige cotton pants. He slipped his bare feet into a pair of brown loafers, feeling better already. The attire he had worn for the meeting at the presidential palace had been stifling, and he was glad to be rid of it.

Walking across his bedroom, he picked up the phone and dialed Lorne Fairley's cell phone number.

Lorne answered it almost immediately with a brisk "Hello?"

"*C'est moi,*" Jean-Claude said. "I am now at my home. Tessa is here, and we shall take lunch in the garden."

"That's a good idea, Jean-Claude. I don't think it would be wise for her to be seen in Paris with another man. I doubt that two Englishmen would stray into your world, but you never know."

"I have a question. I forgot to ask you when you phoned me a bit earlier."

"Ask me now."

"Is the presence of her husband a coincidence? Or is he stalking her perhaps? Should I get security for Tessa?"

"That's not necessary, but thanks for thinking of it. I'm pretty certain Mark Longden's in Paris to report in. Actually, he's probably been summoned by Ainsley."

"*Bien.* I understand. And be relaxed, Lorne, she is safe with me. I will stay in touch with you . . . and you must do the same."

"I will. Thanks, Jean-Claude. And remember, don't say a thing to Tessa. If she knows Longden's in Paris, she'll be upset."

"Not a single word. *Au revoir, mon ami.*" Jean-Claude crossed to the chair where he had thrown his jacket, retrieved his cell phone and slipped it into his trousers pocket, then proceeded into the bathroom. After washing his hands, he slapped cold water onto his face, patted it dry, added cologne, and ran a comb through his hair. He turned away from the basin but instantly turned back, stared at himself in the mirror. It struck him that he looked a little weary today.

Am I too old for her? he asked himself, seeing Tessa Fairley in his mind's eye. He sighed deeply. He had long understood that the question of age did not play in matters of the heart.

He felt as if his life had been turned upside down since meeting her last night. Even though he had been very focused at the meeting at the Élysée Palace, there had been a moment when his thoughts strayed to her. How to handle this situation? He who was so adept at handling every kind of problem was suddenly at a total loss.

I will let it handle itself. . . . I will simply let it come at me like a speeding train. What else is there to do? he asked himself. And as he walked back into the library a moment later, he acknowledged that matters were out of his hands. He was a man and she was a woman, and something intimate, profound, and deeply moving had passed between them last night. . . . He must let things take their course.

19

Tessa was standing at the window, looking out at the garden, when Jean-Claude returned to the library. At the sound of his determined steps on the parquet floor, she swung around to face him.

He came to stop at the glass coffee table, and his eyes met hers; he studied her for a moment, and a smile began to play around his mouth.

She returned his smile and felt impelled to walk over to him.

"Champagne, I think," he murmured, lifting the bottle out of the silver bucket which Hakim had brought in a few seconds before. "It's Rosé Billecart-Salmon, a favorite of mine," he told her. "I find it smooth. . . . I hope you like it."

"I love pink champagne," she answered, speaking the truth; it was her favorite even though she was not a big drinker. As she stood there watching him open the champagne, Tessa swallowed several times, discovering that she was feeling intimidated again. But then who wouldn't be intimidated by him? she asked herself. He was an accomplished, celebrated man, the darling of the French elite, and seemingly the favorite of presidents.

This aside, Tessa realized that a mixture of other emotions were swirling around inside her. For one thing she felt awkward, even slightly nervous being in such close proximity to him. She wanted to reach out to touch him, wanted *him* to touch *her,* wanted his arms around her. Strong-looking arms, she thought, and with a quick intake of breath moved to the other side of the coffee table before she made a fool of herself.

But he was standing next to her again within a split second, handing her the glass of champagne. His hand brushed against hers, and it was like an electric shock. She sat down in the chair without a word. And she did not fail to notice an amused smile on his face as he went to fill his own glass.

A moment later he raised the flute to her across the coffee table. *"Santé,"* he said.

"Santé," she answered and took a long swallow.

There was a silence, and then he asked, "And so, Tessa . . . how are you?" His dark, mesmeric eyes rested on her reflectively as he waited for her answer.

His question had startled her. She stared at him, frowning, and before she could stop herself she said, "Intimidated."

"By me?" He sounded taken aback, and now his brows drew together in a frown.

Somewhat thrown by her own honesty, Tessa shook her head and replied, "Yes, well, by your accomplishments and achievements, your standing in this world. I'm not used to famous men like you."

"But I *am* just that . . . *a man,* Tessa. Like other men."

"No, you're not. You're very celebrated."

"Fame is meaningless to me." He sat back in the

chair and once more looked at her thoughtfully before continuing. "You are nervous perhaps, you even feel awkward. Yes, that I think you are. Because I am."

"*Oh,*" she said, surprised, looking at him over the rim of her glass.

"It is natural. Of course we feel this way. Suddenly we are alone together. We do not know how to handle ourselves with each other."

"Perhaps . . ."

Leaning forward in the chair, Jean-Claude pinned his eyes on her and began to speak softly, almost gently. "Last night something happened between us. I looked at you in that grand foyer in Marie-Hélène's house, and you looked back, and we made a connection. The most intimate connection there is between a man and a woman. We understood each other *exactly.* Moreover, if we had been alone, I would have done something about it."

"What do you mean?" Her gaze was riveted on him.

"I would have said . . . *Come home with me.*"

"You should have asked," she murmured. "I would have come."

"*C'est dommage.*" Jean-Claude lifted his hands in the Gallic manner, lightly shrugged, smiled at her rather ruefully.

"So why didn't you ask me?" she pressed, her eyes still on his face.

He did not respond.

"Was it because your friends were with you?" she ventured, a brow lifting questioningly.

"*Non, non,*" he replied. "Not that at all. I do not live my life by or for the world. It was because of Lorne."

"But he wouldn't have minded! He adores you!" she exclaimed.

"That is a strange word to use, no?" He gave her an odd look.

She shook her head. "He idolizes you, thinks there's no one like you in this world. You can do no wrong with my brother."

"I am flattered. *Naturellement.* You must understand how much I value his friendship. I would never do anything to undermine it."

"He says you are a true gentleman," Tessa thought to add and took several quick sips of the champagne. She wondered if she was getting a bit tipsy.

"I am not sure if that factors into this equation" was his quiet response.

Tessa gazed at him but said nothing.

There was a silence, although it was not at all awkward. Talking in such an open way had eased the tension between them. Tessa was fully aware that she had never had this kind of honesty with Mark. The very thought of him made her cringe inside, and she pushed it away. There was no place for memories of *him* in this apartment with this man, who was a real man and not a poor excuse for one. A giant of a man . . . Jean-Claude Deléon.

For his part, Jean-Claude was glad that he had encouraged her to speak about her feelings, as he had about his. He hated long, drawn-out games between men and women. He found them childish and ridiculous. Only honesty and the truth were acceptable to him.

Suddenly standing up, he took the bottle of champagne, went to fill her glass, and topped off his own.

Settling back in the *bergère,* he savored the champagne before saying, "Are you afraid?"

"A little bit," she was quick to respond.

"Not of me? Surely not?"

"No, not really . . . of what might happen, though. Between us."

"Ah, yes, embarking on a love affair *is* risky."

She was quiet; her silver-gray eyes were suddenly pensive.

He said in a warm tone, a hint of laughter in his voice, "A *centime* for your thoughts, Tessa Fairley."

"How old are you?" Her words fell into the middle of the room like a lump of lead.

Jean-Claude stared at her. It was apparent he had not expected such a question.

Tessa could have bitten off her tongue. "I'm so sorry. How could I be so *rude*?" She felt herself coloring. "You don't have to answer that question because it—"

"Much too *old* for you," he cut in, smiling at her, a look of regret striking his face momentarily.

"No, you're not."

Ignoring her comment, he told her, "Last night, here alone, contemplating the evening, I asked myself why the sight of a woman should bring me up with a shock. That is something I must fathom out." But he already knew the answer. It was the shock of recognition, of knowing this was the one woman in the world who could solve the riddle of his life.

"It's your turn to look introspective," Tessa said, cutting into his thoughts.

"Ah, yes. I was thinking of you. What are your plans?"

"Do you mean this weekend? Or in the future?"

"Both."

"I have no plans for the weekend."

"Would you spend it with me?"

"Yes."

"What about Lorne? I cannot take you away from him. You came to Paris together. To abandon him would be . . . *unkind*."

"My brother's so serious about his work, but you know that, Jean-Claude, and he'll be happy to study his lines. He always wants to be totally prepared when he performs."

"*Mais oui*. That I do know. We must include him, however."

"We can ask him, yes. Why not?"

"You sound more relaxed, Tessa."

"I am. I think I feel a bit better."

"And what about the future?"

"I must push my divorce through. Once my mother gets back from New York next week, I think everything will move much quicker. She's very good at dealing with problems, and especially good at dealing with lawyers. Have you met her with Lorne?"

"I have. She's an exceptional woman." And I'm afraid she won't approve of me for you, he thought, but decided it wiser not to voice this.

Hakim appeared at the door of the library. *"Monsieur, s'il vous plaît."*

"Merci, Hakim." Pushing himself to his feet, Jean-Claude said, "Come, Tessa. Lunch is ready. We shall go to the garden through the dining room."

The dining room was next to the library, and Jean-Claude managed to usher her through it without actually touching her. She was aware that he felt as she did . . . that any physical contact would precipitate an explosion.

When they stepped out of the air-conditioned apartment onto the terrace, the heat hit them with a blast, and Jean-Claude paused. "I think this was a mistake. It's very hot out here."

"I know. But look, the sun has moved over there." Tessa indicated the far end of the garden. "I'm fine with it if you are. It's nice to eat outdoors sometimes."

"Very well," he agreed and led the way to the table. He pulled the garden chair out for her, and once she was seated he moved the large umbrella closer so that they would be completely in the shade. Sitting down opposite her, he picked up the bottle of water and filled their glasses. After taking a sip, he asked, "Shall we finish the champagne, or would you prefer white wine with lunch?"

"I'd like the champagne, please," she replied, knowing that the wine would go to her head, and that was the last thing she wanted.

"Excuse me, I will only be a moment," he said, rose, and strode toward the French doors to retrieve the champagne.

Tessa's eyes followed him, and she thought he looked very fit. He was tall, muscular, and well built, with broad shoulders, but there was no fat on him, and he appeared much younger wearing the white shirt and cotton pants than he had in a suit. Perhaps he *is* in his forties, just as Lorne said, she thought. Still, he *had* said he was too old for her. But what exactly did that mean? How could anyone calculate something like that? Some people were mature for their age, others rather juvenile. She was thirty-two but considered herself very mature for her age. But would he? This was a man unlike any she had ever known.

He returned almost at once, carrying the silver bucket that contained the pink champagne, and fast on his heels followed Hakim, holding a tray with two clean champagne flutes on it.

"Voilà!" Jean-Claude exclaimed, putting the ice bucket down on the flagstones while Hakim placed the flutes on the table, then hurried off. A few minutes later the houseman came back carrying a small metal table; he put the champagne and the water on this, nodded politely, and disappeared once more.

Pouring champagne for her, Jean-Claude said, "Lourdes, my cook, has prepared a simple lunch. It's far too hot to eat anything heavy."

"Yes, it is," she agreed, wondering whether she would be able to eat at all. She was unexpectedly nervous once again. She had begun to relax after their rather honest conversation, but now, suddenly, she felt at a loss, inadequate, she who was normally so self-assured. In fact she felt like a schoolgirl as she sat opposite this sophisticated man in his elegant garden in the middle of Paris . . . overwhelmed by him, the situation, and her reaction to him.

As if reading her mind, Jean-Claude suddenly said, "It is very difficult . . . getting to know a person, feeling at ease with them. I understand that, I am part of this . . . but it will be all right . . . trust me."

"How did you know?" she asked softly, staring at him. "It's as if you read my mind."

"I have no magical powers, I can assure you," he murmured, shaking his head.

Oh, but you do, she thought, making me so nervous, I've never, ever felt like this before. But she remained silent, picked up the crystal glass and sipped the pink champagne. Not wishing to speak about their feelings, she changed the subject. "Your library is one of the most elegant and beautiful rooms I've ever seen. But you don't work in it, do you?"

"No. However, I often sit there and think."

"So where *do* you write? Do you go to an office somewhere?"

"No, I work here in the apartment. I have an office upstairs. I'll show it to you later if you like, it's somewhat special."

"I'd like that. Did you write *Warriors* up there?"

"I did—" He broke off, drank some of the champagne, and then said rather rapidly, "I gave you my book as a courtesy, because you were at the party. You don't have to read it, you know."

"Oh, but I've started it already," she answered, and then blurted out, "I couldn't sleep last night." Instantly embarrassed by this admission, Tessa sat back with a jerk, color flooding her face. Then she went on, very quickly, "Anyway, I picked up your book and discovered I couldn't put it down. You know a lot about wars and terrorism and politics, don't you?"

He nodded. "Why couldn't you sleep?"

She swallowed several times and was about to tell him some ridiculous lie, then opted for honesty. "I was thinking about you."

Jean-Claude took a deep breath. "I know. I had the same problem." His gaze rested on her unrelentingly until she finally blinked and looked away.

Wanting to draw her back to him at once, he said, "I'm glad you understand French, it's important to me."

She wished to ask him why but did not. "Where did you learn to speak English?" she said instead and, striving for normalcy, added, "It's perfect."

"I took lessons when I was very young, and I studied, worked hard. When I was twelve or thirteen, I'd decided to be a writer, and I longed to travel, especially to America and England. For that reason I wanted to have total command of the English language."

"Well, you do." She wondered what was wrong with her. Why did she keep telling him what he knew?

The arrival of Hakim with the cold vichyssoise curtailed their conversation for a moment. When he had served her the soup, she picked up her spoon, took a mouthful, but discovered she could hardly swallow it even though it was delicious.

Once Hakim went hurrying off, Tessa said, "You've covered many wars as a writer, but surely that's dangerous."

"Life is dangerous."

She did not respond.

"*You* know that, Tessa."

Her eyes narrowed slightly. "Lorne has told you things about me," she asserted.

"No, he has not. I saw him several weeks ago, when he was flying from Istanbul to London via Paris. We had dinner together, and it was then he told me about the abduction of your child. But that's all."

"I see."

"He was worried about you."

"I know." She sighed. "But putting yourself in the middle of a war is like asking for trouble, isn't it?"

"No. I don't take risks . . . at least not in wars."

There was a long pause. A suggestive look entered his eyes, and they lingered on her face. He smiled at her, a warm, loving smile.

The magnetism of him was a palpable thing, and in an effort to break the spell he had cast on her, she picked up her flute of champagne. Much to her dismay, her hand trembled badly. Endeavoring to stop the shaking, she took a few deep breaths and put the flute down without spilling the champagne.

She knew he had noticed. How could he not have?

Hakim came and cleaned the table, returned with the omelettes, and departed yet again. She tried to eat without much success, and after a few seconds she realized that Jean-Claude was not eating either.

Becoming aware of her rather fixed scrutiny, he said, "I'm not hungry."

"Neither am I."

"I think we'd better get it out of the way, deal with it."

"What?"

"The physical aspects . . . of this situation. Come, Tessa, come with me." He stood up, and so did she and together they left the garden.

In the entrance foyer he turned to her and said, "I told you I would show you my office. It's up there." He indicated the staircase and led the way to the second floor.

After opening the door for Tessa, Jean-Claude followed her into his office. But just as he was about to take her in his arms the phone rang. *"Merde,"* he muttered, pushed the door closed with his foot, and hurried to his desk. Picking up the receiver, he discovered it was his sister Marie-Laure.

As he spoke to her warmly, listening for a moment or two, his eyes came to settle on Tessa, who was looking at the photographs on one of the walls: photographs of himself with other writers, politicians, actors, philosophers, painters, friends, the *beau monde* of Paris, of the world. Endeavoring to make the conversation with his sister brief, he explained he was in a meeting; he had been on the phone for only a few seconds, yet it seemed like a lifetime to him. At last he managed to hang up, and as he did so Tessa turned, stared at him. At once he saw the pent-up longing on her face, the yearning for him in her eyes, and he recognized she was as overwhelmed by desire as he was.

He came around the desk quickly, found himself rushing toward her, and she fell, almost stumbled, into his arms. A small cry escaped her as she clung to him, and then a second later she buried her face in his shoulder. She was trembling so much Jean-Claude was alarmed, and he tried to calm her, stroking her back, holding her very close to him, murmuring gently. "Tessa, it's all right, relax, *chérie,* relax," he whispered against her silver-gilt hair.

Finally, she raised her face to gaze into his. He felt swamped by those unique silvery eyes. Looking down at her, being so close to her, made him catch his breath, and yet again he was struck by her heart-stopping ethereal beauty. She parted her lips ever so slightly but most seductively, then licked her lips with the tip of her tongue.

No longer able to resist, he brought his mouth down on hers, crushing it, and then his tongue went into her mouth, and she met it with her tongue, and they savored each other. A thrill ran through him, and he held her closer than before. Finally their tongues lay still, but they went on kissing, lost in each other, oblivious to everything except themselves and their feelings.

A moment later, still clinging to each other, they sank onto the sofa, and he continued to kiss her passionately, just as he had wanted to the previous evening and every minute since then. At last she was exactly where he wanted her to be, in his arms, about to become part of him as he would make himself part of her. To be possessed by her, to possess her in return, that was what he craved.

After a short while he got up impatiently, began to unbutton his shirt as he strode to the door and locked it. When he came back she had undressed, her long, lithe body stretched out on the sofa for him. How beautiful she was, he thought.

A second later he, too, was undressed, his clothes thrown carelessly on the floor. He lay down next to her, overwhelmed by desire, and took her in his arms. He held her as close to him as possible, listening to his heart slamming against his rib cage in unison with hers.

Eventually, pushing himself up on one elbow, he

looked into those extraordinary eyes again, and she returned his intense gaze, touched his face.

"Jean-Claude," she said in a low voice.

"Yes, darling?"

"I want you so much."

"No more than I want you." He kissed her brow, her eyes, her small, firm breasts, stroked her long body and her stomach, taking his time. His hands fluttered over every part of her until she was moaning softly, her pleasure apparent as she responded to his touch and touched him in return.

When his hands and mouth came to rest in the silky hair between her legs, she could no longer restrain herself, and she cried out in pleasure. It was with tenderness and expertise that he brought her to a climax, felt her cresting on wave after wave. Moving onto her, positioning himself between her legs, he entered her swiftly, murmuring against her hair, "*Chérie*. Ah, my Tessa, my love . . ."

"Jean-Claude, Jean-Claude." She sighed and put her arms around him. She held on to him tightly, wanting all of him.

It seemed to him that they were rising and falling together in slow motion. Their bodies fit perfectly, and they moved in rhythm, as though they were one entity. Passion spiraled upward, and they began to move faster and faster, panting, gasping as they came together in an explosive climax. He felt as though he were falling into some silvery, light-filled space, taking her with him, knowing he could never, ever let her go.

They lay together on the sofa in a soft haze of pleasure, both of them slightly dazed. Pent-up longing for each other had been assuaged, all tension had fled, and there was only joy and fulfillment between them.

Against her hair, Jean-Claude said, "Are you all right?"

"Very all right. Except I'm thirsty."

He kissed the tip of her nose, pushed himself up off the sofa, and crossed the room.

She watched him, thinking how well he moved. At one moment last night Lorne had called him a man of action, because he was always rushing off on assignments, covering wars, taking on foreign projects, and she could indeed see him in action.

He had gone into another room, and when he came back out carrying a bottle of water and two glasses, she asked, "Do you have a kitchen up here?"

He laughed. "No, it's the bathroom. But I put in a refrigerator for water and soft drinks, and there's a coffeepot." Placing the glasses on his desk, he fiddled with the bottle, poured the water, and carried the two glasses over to the sofa.

Tessa sat up, swung her long legs to the floor, and took the glass from him. "Thank you. I'm very dry. It must be all that champagne you gave me."

Sitting down next to her, glancing at her quickly, he exclaimed, "I suppose you're now going to say I got you drunk and seduced you."

"No, I'm not. You did that last night, in Marie-Hélène's foyer. In front of half of Paris."

He laughed out loud. *"Touché."*

"Do you have a robe or a shirt I can put on? Oh, look, I can wear this," she said, reaching for his white shirt on the floor.

"Let me get you something else, that shirt's not clean, I've worn it."

"That's why I *want* to wear it." She buried her face in the shirt. "It smells of your cologne." Standing up, she slipped the shirt on, fastened a couple of buttons, added, "And it smells of you."

He chuckled as he went back to the bathroom and re-turned a moment later wearing a navy blue silk robe. "Are you hungry?"

"A little bit. But I don't think those omelettes will still be hot."

Laughter tugged at his mouth again, and walking over to her he put his arms around her, held her close. "I think I can rustle up some sandwiches. However, I want to talk to you first."

"What about?" she asked, pulling away slightly as the seriousness of his tone registered. Giving him a very direct look, she hesitated for a moment, then said quickly, "Is there something the matter?"

"Sit there," he said, sounding a little imperious, indi-cating the sofa. She promptly did as he asked.

He turned around, pulled a chair closer to the sofa, and sat down opposite her. For a moment he remained silent, looking contemplative.

She studied him surreptitiously. No wonder women fell at his feet. Well, hadn't she also? *And instanta-neously.* He was virile, with a strong, hard body. His amber-brown eyes were soulful, at times brooding as well as mesmeric. There was a sensuality to his fine mouth, yet it was kind as well. Yes, that was it. That elu-sive thing about him was the kindness in his face. But now, as he stared back at her intently, she saw a grave-ness settling over him, and once more she asked rather worriedly, "*Is* there something wrong?"

"No." He took a long swallow of the water, put the glass on a nearby side table, settled himself in the chair. "I'm a fifty-three-year-old man, a grown-up. This"—he paused, waved his hand between them airily—"is not a sport for me. This is not a game I'm playing."

"I think I know that, Jean-Claude."

"I've seen too much, done too much, lived too hard in

many different ways. Pain, heartache . . . they're old fa-
miliars. I have grappled with disillusionment and despair, I have borne many sorrows, and I suppose you
could say I've experienced most things. There are those
in Paris who think I am weary, jaded even, and in some
ways perhaps I am." He reached for the water again, obviously as thirsty as she had been.

"And so now, at my age," he went on, "I cannot afford
to squander my time, because I still have much to write,
to study, to achieve, and to do. Do you understand what
I'm saying, Tessa?"

"I think so, yes."

"Last night when I came home after dinner I felt
bludgeoned. That's the only word I can think of . . .
bludgeoned. And by you. By our meeting. You had an
enormous impact on me. And I believe I had the same
impact on you. Am I not right?"

"You are. I feel exactly the same way you do. Haven't
we just proved that to each other, Jean-Claude? But—"
She cut herself off.

"But what?"

"I'm a bit frightened."

He smiled at her. "And I am *terrified.*"

Clearing her throat, she said, "What you meant a moment ago is that you don't want *me* to waste your time,
isn't it?"

"That is correct. I've managed to waste a lot of my
time over the years, and quite often with women who
turned out not to be the women I thought they were."

"What about me then? What do you think I am?"

"The woman I've been searching for all of my life."

"In your book, the one you inscribed for me, you
wrote, *'Je suis là.'* What did you mean?"

"What do you think I meant?"

"I am here for *you . . . waiting* for you."

"That's very perceptive of you, Tessa."

"Lorne said he'd never seen me behave like that. He told me I was swooning at your feet, and I was. At least that's how I felt."

He nodded but made no comment.

She went on, "He said he'd never witnessed you behaving like that either."

"Lorne is right, I don't think I ever have." He suddenly chuckled. "I just wanted to grab you, bring you here and take you in my arms, hold you close to me forever. And it was such an overwhelming feeling I was stunned."

"You said you didn't want me to waste your time. . . . What is it you expect of me?"

"A fair shake, as my American friends would say. At this moment, right now, I would like to know if you are ready to embark on a relationship with me. But there is one other thing. . . . I must know that you will always be honest with me, always truthful."

"I would never lie to you," she exclaimed, then said in a softer voice, "As for a relationship with you, of course I want that. Haven't we just started one?"

"There are some who might consider it . . . a one-night stand."

"A one-afternoon stand," she corrected and began to laugh.

He had the good grace to laugh with her, shaking his head.

Tessa adopted a very low voice when she pointed out, "We live in different cities. I have a three-year-old child. And I also have a career, responsibilities."

"I know all of those things, Tessa. But let us try, shall we?"

When she did not answer, he pressed. "Are you willing?"

"I'm willing," she answered.

20

Brushing the hair away from her face, Tessa remained seated on the sofa, staring at the door. Jean-Claude had gone downstairs to get sandwiches. She was wondering why she felt suddenly out of sorts, and within a few seconds it hit her . . . she missed Jean-Claude's presence most acutely. His absence made her feel deprived. And he had been gone for only a few moments.

This knowledge amazed her, and then she remembered last night, how she had not been able to sleep, how thoughts of him had crowded out everything else in her head. And because she had been restless, she had finally turned on the light, picked up his book, and begun to read it. Aside from making her feel closer to him, it told her a great deal about him; the brilliance of his writing had amazed her. He was a remarkable thinker, and she had been bowled over by the chapters she read.

Last night she had silently thanked her mother for insisting she learn to speak French. If she couldn't understand his language, she wouldn't be able to read his books, and that, it seemed to her, was an imperative.

He's larger than life, she thought. It struck her that when he was in a room he dominated it with his physical presence and personality, and that was why she missed him now. His office was lifeless without him in it.

He also made love in a way she had never experienced before. There had been only one other man before she married Mark, and he had been a disaster in bed. As for Mark, he was always in a hurry; never considering her, never satisfying her. And then he had turned violent, actually hurt her during sex, and finally raped her in such an ugly manner that she had left him, lucky to have escaped with her life.

Don't think about Mark, she instructed herself, and immediately blocked him out. Think about Jean-Claude Deléon instead. She lay back on the sofa and closed her eyes, relived their lovemaking . . . an hour of such bliss. . . .

She knew how serious he was about her, he had made that perfectly clear. Well, he *was* a communicator, wasn't he? He wanted a long-term relationship. And so did she, she understood that already. Did that mean marriage? She wasn't sure. How could they make it work? Paris was his domain, where he was one of the philosopher kings. He rushed off to cover wars and uprisings, to interview politicians and presidents all over the world . . . he put himself in danger. Could she handle *that*?

And then there was *her* life . . . and Adele. Wherever she went, Adele came, too, but that did not present a problem. Jean-Claude would immediately fall in love with Adele, everyone did. But there was her career to consider as well, her responsibilities at Harte's. How could she work in London and live in Paris? And she would have to live here if their love affair progressed the way he wanted, no, actually expected it to.

After Mark had abducted Adele, she had suffered so much pain she had truly understood that her daughter came before everything else in her life. And she still felt that way. Her career had been moved to second place in her mind. Might it now take third place because of Jean-Claude?

She sat up with a jerk.

She had fallen in love with him.

Instantly, last night.

She had looked into that face, so handsome yet full of character and kindness and gravity, and she had fallen heavily. Just like India fell for Dusty Rhodes, she thought, and with a rush of clarity she understood about her cousin and the artist.

Jean-Claude said he had felt bludgeoned; she had been dumbstruck. And the emotions he had aroused in her were manifold. There was no question that she had never felt like this before.

Once again needing to understand more about Jean-Claude, she got up and began to wander around his office, looking at a selection of photographs on another wall, finding a line of books on a shelf, books bearing his name as the author. Twenty-five in all. Then she noticed that some of them had been translated into English, and other languages as well, and this pleased her. She laughed to herself. Why had she felt that sudden stab of pride? After all, she had only met him last night. It didn't seem possible . . . *only last night.* Her life had been turned upside down, changed irrevocably.

Unexpectedly, Tessa experienced a flash of panic. How was she going to *handle* all of this? For a moment she felt overwhelmed; then she took a deep breath and forced herself to relax. The only thing she *could* do was to let it happen and deal with everything one day at a time.

Now her eyes swept around his office, and she understood why he had said it was unique. A gallery encircled the entire room and fronted bookshelves rising to the ceiling on several walls, and there was a polished steel-and-brass circular staircase that twisted up to the gallery.

It was a spacious room, with a high ceiling and a tall window at the far end, and the colors were warm and masculine, a deep brick red and fir green mixed in an arresting combination. A brick red woolen fabric upholstered the walls, a matching velvet covered the sofa, and the rug was a combination of red and green. His desk was spectacular, a huge slab of heavy glass set on thick polished steel-and-brass legs, and the two lamps on the desk were made of stainless steel with dark green shades.

She glanced at the desk with enormous interest, saw that the surface was empty except for a blotter, an inkstand, and several metal trays for papers. Instantly she knew he was a tidy man with a tidy mind, and she liked that. She was a neat person herself and couldn't stand mess.

Along another wall, off to one side of the desk, there was a worktable, and on this stood his typewriter, computer and printer, and two steel lamps matching those on the desk. Serious work goes on here, she thought, nodding to herself. She had the feeling he was fast and efficient.

Tessa meandered back to the center of the office and glanced at her watch; to her amazement she saw that it was almost three o'clock.

At this moment the door opened. "I am sorry it took so long," Jean-Claude muttered, bending to pick up the tray on the floor. He walked to his desk and placed the tray in the middle.

Beckoning, he said, "Come, Tessa, come here, sit in this chair behind the desk. You will be more comfortable."

Bossy as well, she thought, but gave him a wide smile and hurried to join him. He put his arms around her, hugged her to him. *"Chérie,"* he murmured, stroking her hair, and then, releasing her, he went and brought a chair over, sat down facing her.

The tray had been beautifully set, she noted, obviously by Hakim. There was a sparkling white organdy cloth on it, matching napkins, and pretty china. Tessa took a plate and a napkin, and sat back until Jean-Claude insisted she start to eat. He poured the tea, took a sandwich himself, and they were both silent until they had finished.

After drinking his tea, Jean-Claude looked across at Tessa and smiled. "So preoccupied was I with you I didn't realize how ravenous I was."

"I know, I was starving myself," she replied. Then she cocked her head to one side, staring back at him intently.

"What is it?" he asked, putting his cup down.

"I've just had the most curious thought. Do you think my brother set us up?"

Jean-Claude was startled. His eyes narrowed slightly, and then he began to laugh. After a moment, he said, with another chuckle, *"Mon Dieu!* What a thought that is. And I must say this to you, if he did then I shall be eternally grateful to him." He shook his head, still amused. "What induced you to think this?"

"Well, I recently had a conversation with him, and I said I would probably never get married again after this debacle with—"

"Lorne's response?" he asked, cutting her sentence off.

"He said that was all right, but he wasn't going to allow me to lead a celibate life, that he was going to make sure I had lots of lovers."

"Only one, *ma chérie*." He reached out, put his hand over hers.

"*Oui, absolument.* Only one. *You.*"

His face was illuminated by a bright smile, and his dark eyes were warm as he said, "You had this thought about your brother, and I had one, too, when I was downstairs getting the sandwiches. It occurred to me that it would be nice if he came to the country with us tomorrow."

"We're going to the country?" she asked, surprised.

"You did agree to spend the weekend with me, didn't you?"

"Yes, I did."

"I have a house outside Paris, small but comfortable." He made a gesture and continued. "You would enjoy it there. You will come, won't you, darling?"

I would go anywhere with you, she thought and said, "It would be nice. And perhaps we should speak to Lorne now. I'm not sure what his plans are."

"I thought he was learning his lines," Jean-Claude responded, picked up the phone on the desk, and dialed the hotel number.

A moment later he was speaking to Lorne. "*C'est moi, mon ami. Comment vas-tu?*"

"Hello, Jean-Claude," Lorne exclaimed. "I'm fine, and you? Is everything all right with you and Tessa?"

"*Bien sûr.* Are you busy tomorrow?"

"No, just studying my part. Why do you ask?"

"I thought it would be a good idea to take Tessa out of Paris for the weekend, and it would be a great pleasure for me if you would come also. To my little house . . . you've been there."

"Little house!" Lorne exclaimed, laughing. "Haven't you told her it's a château?"

"Ah, my dear friend, you exaggerate always, it's hardly a château. But you *will* accompany us, won't you?"

"Thanks for your invitation, Jean-Claude, and I think it is a very good idea to get her out of Paris while those two scoundrels are skulking around."

"That was my thought exactly," Jean-Claude replied. "And so you will join us?"

"If she wants me along."

"Let me put her on," Jean-Claude murmured and handed the phone to Tessa.

"Hello, Lorne," she said. "You are going to come with us, aren't you? If not, I won't go either."

"Of course I'm coming, I love that house of his. Are you all right, sweetheart?"

"More than that, I'm . . . *great.*"

"He's a fantastic man, a really wonderful person, Tessa. It makes me feel better knowing you are with him. You'll always be safe with Jean-Claude."

"I realize that. I suppose Jean-Claude will call you later with the exact plans. No news?"

"None. Have you heard from Linnet?"

"No, but I didn't expect her to phone. I spoke to her this morning, and all was well. I have my mobile, and it's on all the time."

Jean-Claude took the tray back to the kitchen, and while he was gone Tessa put on her clothes. She was standing looking at a photograph of him on the wall when he walked back into his office, and she swung around to face him, puzzlement reflected in her eyes.

"Who's this child with you? It is *you,* isn't it?"

He came to join her, stood with his arms around her

"Yes. And that's my son," he said, looking down at her. "When he was ten."

"Oh" was all she could manage.

"He's grown up now, he's almost your age. I told you I was too old for you. I'm old enough to be your father."

"No, you're not! I didn't know you had been married." She cleared her throat. "You *were* married to his mother?"

"Very briefly. When I was young, it was a long time ago. I was twenty-one, and Philippe was born when I was twenty-two."

"I see. Does he live in Paris?"

"No, the South of France, he's an artist," Jean-Claude explained.

Tessa hesitated, then she said, "Are you still married?"

He burst out laughing. "Of course not. I'm divorced, and I have been for many years."

"And you never got married again?"

"No . . . there have been plenty of women . . ."

"So I gather."

Turning her toward him, he held her by her shoulders. "I cannot erase the past," he said, looking down into her upturned face. "Neither can you, *ma chérie*. We both bring . . . a certain amount of baggage to this relationship. And we have to deal with that the best way we are able. I can say this to you in sincerity . . . I believe you are *right* for me. I think you can fill all the empty places in my heart, as I will fill those in yours. So don't ever dwell on my past. Or yours. The past is gone, we have the future."

She laid her head against his shoulder and thought of Lorne's words a short while before . . . "You'll always be safe with Jean-Claude." And she knew her brother had spoken the truth.

. . .

Jonathan Ainsley sat at the Louis XVI desk in the study of his sumptuous apartment on Avenue Foch, one of the most elegant streets in Paris. The phone was pressed to his ear, and he listened attentively to the woman on the other end of the line. Once she had finished speaking, he said, "But are you sure Tessa Fairley is in Paris?"

"Yes. With her brother, Lorne Fairley. And they are bound to be staying at the Paris O'Neill Hotel, where else but at their father's hotel?"

"Only too true, my dear," Jonathan replied, playing with the piece of jade in his hand. "When did they arrive?"

"Thursday evening, and she's not expected back in London until Wednesday of next week. Her brother is staying on, he's filming in Paris. She's coming back sooner, no doubt because her mother is returning from New York on September sixth."

"Well done, well done, there'll be a really nice surprise for you when I see you in London. A little gift, and of course a rendezvous, a reunion. You'd like that wouldn't you, sweetie?"

"You know I would, Jonathan."

"Very well, I'll let you know when I am coming over. In the meantime, thanks for the information, it's very useful."

They said good-bye and hung up, and Jonathan immediately dialed the Ritz Hotel, where Mark Longden was staying. But he was not in his room. The phone rang and rang, and nobody picked up. Slamming the receiver down, Jonathan next dialed the Paris O'Neill Hotel and asked for Mrs. Tessa Longden.

A split second later the operator was back on the line and told him in slightly accented English, "Mrs. Longden is not registered."

"Perhaps her brother, Mr. Lorne Fairley, is staying

the hotel and she is with him. Can you please try his suite?"

"Mr. Fairley is not here, sir. None of the family are in residence at the hotel at this time."

Jonathan muttered his thanks and hung up, an ugly grimace clouding his face. Settling back in the chair, he brought his hand up to his chin and pondered for a moment or two. Obviously they were not at their father's hotel after all, but it was hardly likely they would be staying somewhere else. Since Fairley was filming in Paris, he could have rented an apartment for a few weeks, perhaps even a few months. Jonathan wondered how to find out if that were the case. Mark Longden would have to do the dirty work. He loathed to miss an opportunity to do Tessa harm; how easy it would be to arrange an accident of some sort if he knew where she was staying in Paris.

Since Longden had vanished for the moment, Jonathan decided to call his cousin Sarah Pascal. She probably wouldn't know anything, since she was on equally bad terms with the Hartes. But occasionally he did get a little sadistic pleasure making digs at Sarah about their cousins. His taunts always seemed to rile her.

Once again he was out of luck. He telephoned Sarah at her office, only to be told that she had left Paris for the weekend. Of course, it was Friday afternoon at four o'clock; she had no doubt gone to join her husband at their country home.

Too bad, he thought, and dialed his mistress, Yvette Duval. Her housekeeper told him that Madame had gone to Rome. "Rome!" he spluttered and banged the receiver into the cradle in fury and frustration.

What the hell was *she* playing at? He wondered if she was going to be as faithless a bitch as his wife had been. Suddenly he saw her in his mind's eye—*Arabelle Sutton.* A woman he had loved to distraction, who had betrayed him, cuckolded him in the most foul way, by sleeping with his Chinese partner Tony Chiu. How he loathed her. He had often thought of putting *her* on his hit list with the Harte women and Evan Hughes. Yet somehow he had balked at that. Maybe because he had once loved her. But what the hell? She deserved to suffer after what she had done to him.

As for Yvette Duval, he was finished with her. Tonight he would resort to one of the high-priced whores from Madame Simone's. And next week he would start courting Yvette's daughter Chantal. What better form of revenge? He would dump the mother and start up with the delectable daughter, only nineteen but a hot number.

The mere thought of this intrigue brought a smile of delight to his face. Picking up the phone once more, he dialed the Ritz Hotel, asked for Mark Longden.

When there was still no answer, he left a message. Eventually he would hear from him. Weak, depraved, gasping for money, Mark would do his bidding. For as long as he needed him. When Longden was of no further use, he would simply throw him to the wolves.

Jonathan was not at all surprised when Mark Longden telephoned him later and invited him to dinner. With nothing better to do, he decided to accept the invitation and the two men met for cocktails at the Ritz in the Place Vendôme.

As they sat together in the bar drinking dry martinis, Jonathan told Mark what he had heard earlier in the day. "That beautiful wife of yours, the delectable Tessa, is in Paris. Bet you didn't know that."

Mark was obviously startled, and he stared hard at Jonathan. "How do you know?"

"A little dickey bird told me. She's here with her

other half, her twin that is, the handsome actor Lorne Fairley. He's going to be making a film here."

Mark merely nodded, took a slow sip of the drink.

Irritated at the lack of response, Jonathan said, "Pity you're not in England. You could have a visit with your *adorable* child."

To Mark's ears this sounded sarcastic, and he stiffened and said, "Adele *is* adorable, the most beautiful child in the world."

Softening slightly, remembering one didn't catch flies with vinegar, Jonathan continued, "She is *beautiful,* Mark, I'll grant you that. You miss her."

"I do," Mark confided. "She's such a little chatterbox, loves to tell me about the things she does. She's going to be a bridesmaid at Linnet O'Neill's wedding, and she's very excited to be included along with the older girls."

Jonathan leaned forward, his eyes alert and shining with glee. "And when is the famous wedding? I've forgotten." He lied, never having known the date; Eleanor was no longer forthcoming with information. She would have to go, no two ways about that, he decided.

"The first Saturday in December. It's the first, I think."

"Really. And all the clans will be there, I've no doubt. All of the Hartes, the O'Neills, and the Kallinskis. Imagine that, Mark. All of them in Yorkshire at the same time. And where is the wedding taking place?"

"The little church in Pennistone Royal village, and the reception is at Pennistone Royal, at least that's what I've gathered."

"I'd love to be there . . . as a fly on the wall, I mean, Mark. Wouldn't you?"

Mark made a face. "Not on your life. Not with that snobby bunch."

"Just imagine, all of the clans. . . . What a pity we can't drop a bomb on the church. Blow it up. Or set fire to it. Oh my God, just imagine that!" He began to laugh hilariously.

"You're joking, aren't you?" Mark said, eyeing Jonathan warily.

"Of course I am, dear boy. Do you think I'd put myself in that position . . . having to swing for a bunch of Hartes. Not on your life. But you know, sometimes, Mark, I wish I could upset the applecart a bit. Just for fun."

"No, you don't," Mark said swiftly. He laughed and added, "You merely love to say outrageous things."

"Yeah, I do, that's true," Jonathan agreed. "I read a story recently in the *Daily Mail*, about a bunch of yobbos, you know, skinheads, hooligans, who went in a van to one of those picturesque villages in Somerset and camped on the village green. They claimed it was public land and they had squatters' rights. The police couldn't get them off that village green for months. It disturbed the life of the village no end. Just *imagine* that."

Motioning to the waiter, Mark ordered two more dry martinis, then said quietly, "You shouldn't joke about such things, Jonathan. At least not to anyone else. Someone might take you seriously."

Jonathan merely smiled again, sipped the second drink, which had suddenly materialized at his fingertips. But I *am* serious, he thought, smiling inside, deadly serious. A nice little fire in that church will fry all of the Hartes, O'Neills, and Kallinskis. I could kill three clans with one stone, or rather one fire. Now all I need to do is hire a bunch of yobbos, get them a van, and send them up to Pennistone Royal village to create chaos and mayhem on December first. Well, what a good idea that is. A very good idea indeed.

21

〜

Lorne was packing a bag for the trip to the country when his cell phone rang. He answered it immediately. "Hello?" "Mr. Fairley, it's Vincent."

On hearing the hotel manager's voice, Lorne exclaimed, "Hello, Vincent! I must have had some phone calls. Or are you calling about something else?"

"About a phone call, Mr. Fairley. A few minutes ago a man telephoned asking for Mrs. Longden, then for you. As you instructed us earlier this afternoon, the operator said none of the family were in residence."

"Good. And incidentally, that now happens to be the truth. My sister has left Paris, and I'm going away myself in half an hour. I'll be back after the weekend. However, keep our names off the register and the phone blocked. To all intents and purposes, we're not here."

"I understand, Mr. Fairley. Have a nice weekend."

"Thanks. Oh, Vincent, I suppose the man who called didn't leave a name, did he?"

"No, he didn't, but the operator who took the call said he was an Englishman."

"I see. I'll check in with you over the weekend. Please have the telephone operators monitor any calls for us. And keep a record."

"I will, sir."

The manager hung up, and Lorne finished packing. Then he went into Tessa's bedroom, took out a small suitcase, looked at the list she had given him over the phone: nightgown, dressing gown, underwear, flat shoes, flat sandals.

Within a few minutes he had gathered all of these items and laid them on the bed. Perusing the list again, he noted that she wanted the white outfit she had worn on Thursday, the white Manolo Blahniks, and the pearl chandelier earrings. He located everything, decided to add a couple of other pieces of clothing he liked on her, and began to pack the suitcase.

In the bathroom he found her makeup bag on the floor, scooped up certain cosmetics she had requested, plus her toothbrush and toothpaste, a few other essentials, and put all of these things in the makeup bag, along with her hairbrush.

Within half an hour he was finished with her bag and his own. Returning to the living room of the suite, he dialed Pennistone Royal on his cell phone.

"Pennistone Royal," Margaret answered.

"Hello, Margaret darling," Lorne answered in the special voice he reserved for her. "How're you feeling? Not overdoing it, I hope. You know you've got to take it easy these days."

"Oh, Lorne, how luvely to hear your voice," she said in a warm tone. "How's Tessa?"

"We're both fine, Mags, enjoying Paris. I assume everything is all right at the house?"

"Not a blessed thing out of place," Margaret reassured him. "Now, I suppose you're looking for your sister."

"Yes, I am. Thanks, Margaret."

"I'll tell her you're on the phone, and give my luv to Miss Tessa. Now don't be going away, I'll just put you on hold. Take care of yourself, luvy."

It's funny how she veers between calling Tessa by her first name and adding a Miss in front, he thought, but she never does this with me, thank God. I'm always Lorne. Margaret had known them since they were toddlers, and she was part of the family. Yet there were moments when she became quite formal with them, as if she'd suddenly remembered she was the housekeeper.

"It's Linnet," his sister said.

"Hi, sis!" he replied. "I'm just checking in."

"Nothing to report here. All is quiet on the Western Front. And I like this sis bit, far better than all those chirpy names you dig up for me."

He chuckled. "Listen, I just wanted to tell you what's happening here."

"Everything *is* all right, isn't it, Lorne?"

"Absolutely. I decided to take Tessa away for the weekend. We're going to stay with my friend Jean-Claude Deléon, you met him again last year, if you remember. Here in Paris with Ma and Pa, en route to the south."

"How could any woman forget *him*? He's dishy, to say the least. Okay, so you're going to spend the weekend at his country place. I think that's a splendid idea."

"He'd invited us, and I hadn't actually accepted, but then when you alerted me to Mark Longden's presence in Paris, along with Ainsley's, I decided to take him up on his offer. We might never run into either of these two buggers, but you never know. Best to be on the safe side."

"You don't think they'd try to do anything to you and Tessa?" she exclaimed. "Or do you?"

"Who the hell knows, Linny? Jack has a bit of a bee in his bonnet about them right now, so I'm not going to take any chances. I can't tell you how glad I am that I accepted the invitation, because the hotel manager just told me an Englishman has been calling, asking for Tessa and then me. I know it's not anybody from the family, because everyone has my mobile number. Anyway, they would have left their names."

"They would. And Tessa was happy to tag along?"

"Of course. She didn't want to deprive me of the peace and quiet of the country. She knows I've got to learn my part."

"I'm glad you're getting out of the city. Is it still hot?"

"Very. Anyway, my mobile's on all the time, and so is hers—because of her worries about Adele."

"I know that. Listen, this was a brilliant idea of yours, bundling her off to the country."

"Yes. Big kiss. Talk to you soon, Linny."

"Lots of love."

Lorne sat for a moment staring into space after they had hung up, thinking of Jean-Claude. It had been his idea to cart them off to the country. Not long ago he had phoned again and said he thought they should leave that evening in order to have longer in the country. Jean-Claude had suggested Lorne pack their bags before coming over to the apartment for a drink. When Lorne had hesitated, pointed out that Tessa would wonder what was going on, his friend had persuaded him otherwise. A little later Tessa had phoned and sounded perfectly normal when she rattled off the items she needed for the weekend. So that was that.

Jumping up, Lorne put the script, his notes, a pad, and a few other small items in a carryall, then went to the desk. He dialed the concierge, asked for a bellboy to bring the luggage down, and hurried to the bedroom to grab a jacket. Ten minutes later he was being driven across Paris to the Rue de Babylone.

Clos-Fleuri was in a private park on the edge of the Forest of Fontainebleau, and as Jean-Claude drove in through the iron gates, Tessa caught her breath in surprise. The house stood at the end of a short driveway, and now, in the fading light of day, it looked perfectly beautiful, silhouetted against a deep pavonian blue sky. Lights had been turned on, and the windows glittered brightly. What a lovely welcoming sight, she thought.

She saw at once that it wasn't a château at all, just as Jean-Claude had insisted earlier. Lorne had disagreed, teasing him. But Jean-Claude had been accurate in calling his house just that—she saw that now. It looked compact from the outside, and it had rounded towers at the four corners, each topped with a conical-shaped, dark blue slate roof. There were four chimneys, and all those tall, slender windows, far too numerous to count. To the left of the house were buildings Tessa thought were old stables, and to the right a copse of trees. It was an ancient property, she could see that from the time-worn stones and pale rose bricks. Possibly it dated back to the eighteenth century.

As they drew closer, Tessa admitted to herself that she had never seen a house so appealing, and she knew she would never forget this first impression. Her attraction had taken her by surprise, since she was not one to be bowled over by any building. But then again, Clos-Fleuri was *his,* perhaps that explained her liking for it.

A few minutes later Jean-Claude was parking at the front door, which was opened, almost before he'd pulled on the brake. A youngish man, in a white butler's jacket like Hakim's, came down the steps rapidly, greeting them all with enthusiasm. Once they had been introduced to the houseman, Gérard, Jean-Claude led them into the house and Gérard went to retrieve their luggage.

"Let me take you to your rooms," Jean-Claude said, leading them both across the well-furnished hall and up the wide central staircase with highly polished mahogany banisters. "I must then go to the kitchen and unpack the hamper so that we can decide what we are going to have for dinner."

"Tessa's a great cook," Lorne announced rather proudly. "She'll cook dinner for us."

Jean-Claude seemed surprised to hear this and said, "I don't think there *is* anything to cook. Lourdes filled the hamper with a number of cold dishes for this evening. And of course she'll be here tomorrow to cook for us."

"But I'd like to make supper, I really would!" Tessa exclaimed. When he didn't answer she added, "If that's all right with you."

"*Mais oui* . . . what a nice idea."

She glanced at him as they stepped onto the landing and thought that he hadn't sounded at all enthusiastic, but she said nothing further, followed him along the carpeted corridor with Lorne.

Halfway down he opened a door, turned to Lorne and said, "Here we are, *mon vieux,* I know you like this room," and ushered her brother inside.

Tessa peered in, saw how charming it looked with a blue-and-white *toile de Jouy* documentary-print fabric on the walls, at the windows, and on the bed, and a blue carpet on the floor.

"Thanks, Jean-Claude, it is my favorite. See you downstairs in a few minutes." Smiling at them both Lorne closed the door.

When they came to the end of the corridor, Jean-Claude stopped. "You're in here, Tessa, I hope you like it." He turned the knob, led her inside.

The entire room was covered in an unusual parchment-colored print patterned with pink roses and green leaves, but it had long since faded, and there was an old-world feeling to it now, a hint of days long gone. As in Lorne's room, the fabric had been used everywhere. She turned around slowly, noting the large four-poster bed, the pretty dressing table, the chaise.

"Well, what do you have to say?" he asked, scrutinizing her intently.

"It's beautiful," she murmured and gave him a smile, but it was a smile that quickly faltered. He instantly saw her downcast expression and understood what was amiss. Striding across the room, he opened a door and said, "I am in here if you need me. This is my room, Tessa. Do you wish to come in?"

Immediately her spirits lifted, and she ran after him into his bedroom. He was waiting for her in the middle of the room, a faint smile flickering on his sensitive yet sensual mouth. He wrapped his arms around her, and against her hair he murmured, "Does this make you feel better?"

"I thought you were banishing me," she whispered.

"That is something never to be considered, *chérie, je suis là. Toujours.*"

"Am I going to sleep in here with you?" she asked, her voice still a whisper.

"You had better not think of sleeping anywhere else. But I think it's important to be discreet, for your sake rather than mine. That is why I gave you your own room. You'll use it as a dressing room, of course." Moving her slightly away from him, he bent down, kissed the tip of her nose. "My father taught me that discretion is the better part of valor."

A short while later Tessa went down to the kitchen, and her face lit up when she walked in. It was spacious, built entirely of pale stone, with Provençal tiles in certain areas and a beamed ceiling, truly country style. But she saw all of the latest modern appliances and exclaimed, "I'd love to cook in here, Jean-Claude!"

Turning around, he laughed, nodded. "I know it is very conducive to creating a gourmet meal. However, I'm afraid that tonight we do have supper already prepared by Lourdes."

"I know." She joined him at the big oak table and looked down at the items he had unpacked from the hamper. Country pâté in a stone dish, cornichons, sliced country ham, a creamy potato salad, a tin of Beluga caviar, and a large glass bowl of luscious dark red cherries. "It's quite a feast," she murmured.

"And Gérard just told me there is a wheel of Brie in the pantry and fresh baguettes, so I don't think we're going to starve."

"That's true." She laughed and then glanced at the door as Lorne strolled in looking rather debonair in a pair of white slacks and a black linen shirt. "Gosh, you changed, and I didn't even think of it," she muttered, shaking her head. "Perhaps I should go—"

"It's not necessary, *chérie*," Jean-Claude said, putting a hand on her arm lovingly. "You look beautiful the way you are."

She glanced at him and smiled, then said, "I need glass of iced water, I'm very thirsty."

"I'll be bartender," Lorne offered, walking over to the refrigerator, taking out a bottle of water. "What about you, Jean-Claude? What would you like?"

"Pink champagne, I think." Jean-Claude swung around to face Lorne. "I believe you will find a bottle in there, Gérard usually has one cooling."

Opening the refrigerator again, Lorne peered inside, took out the bottle of Billecart he found. "Yep, here it is, and I think I'll join you. Now scoot, the two of you, I'll bring the drinks out to the terrace."

"That's a good idea." Jean-Claude took hold of Tessa's hand and drew her across the kitchen floor. "Don't worry about the food, Gérard will attend to it in a moment," he said to her.

A side door led out to the terrace which ran along the back of the house, and Jean-Claude and Tessa walked over to a group of chairs casually arranged around an old wrought-iron coffee table painted white.

"What a truly beautiful evening it is, Tess," he murmured as they sat down together. "I am so glad we left Paris when we did. There's nothing like a summer evening in the country. I must admit, I do forget how lovely Clos-Fleuri is when I'm away from it."

"It is lovely here, and I agree with you, it was a good idea to leave Paris tonight. It's a pretty name, Clos-Fleuri . . . it means field flower, doesn't it?"

"Exactly. When I found the house it was called that. But it was terribly neglected, a broken-down old place; however, my sister Marie-Laure helped me bring it back to life. You will meet her tomorrow; she is coming to lunch with her husband."

"I can't wait," Tessa said, smiling inwardly. She wanted to know as much about him as she could, and his sister would certainly offer a few more clues.

Tessa settled back comfortably in the chair, looking up at the sky. It was a very deep blue now, and a few stars had already come out. They seemed so close to the earth she felt as though she could reach up and pluck one down. The gardens surrounding the house were quiet; the only sounds she could hear were the rustling of the trees under the light breeze and a strange noise she couldn't quite place.

Glancing at Jean-Claude she asked, "What's that odd sound?"

"*Les grenouilles* . . . the frogs . . . in the pond at the edge of the lawn."

"Of course, I knew it sounded familiar. There's a frog pond at my mother's house in Yorkshire."

Gérard came out onto the terrace and said, "*Monsieur, s'il vous plaît, c'est un appel téléphonique pour vous.*"

"Oh. Excuse me," Jean-Claude murmured and got up.

Tessa closed her eyes, let herself drift with her thoughts while he went inside. Had she ever felt so peaceful? So complete and content? She doubted it. There had never been much peace with Mark Longden. He was always rushing around like a whirling dervish. Nothing had ever pleased him. Nor did he ever stop to think . . . about anything; he had no idea what was going on in the world, so self-involved was he. She couldn't wait to be free, a divorced woman.

Lorne and Jean-Claude came walking along the terrace talking. She sat up, took the glass of water Jean-Claude handed to her.

The three of them clinked glasses, and as he sat down Lorne said, "You know, I've been meaning to ask you something, Jean-Claude. Why did you call your book *Warriors,* using the English word rather than the French?"

"It struck me that *warriors* has such a good ring to it. . . . I think it is more descriptive, so does the publisher, and everyone does know what *warrior* means. Don't you think it is more international than *querrier,* the French word?"

"I do. And you're right, it works in any language."

Tessa said, "Earlier today I asked you why you cover wars, put yourself in danger, but you know you didn't really answer me. So . . . why do you, Jean-Claude?"

"Most probably because I like to be where the action is. Also I have been doing it since I was young. In a way I think of myself as a war reporter."

"But those wars you covered were hellish," she said softly.

"All war is hell, Tessa, yet we keep going to war." He shook his head, and a small sigh escaped. For a split second he looked perturbed, but he threw it off, then continued, "Will we never learn? I suppose not, unless man undergoes a radical change in his nature, which I consider most unlikely. War seems to be . . . an integral part of this planet, and I never stop wondering why that is so. I have the need to understand this and understand myself and the human race. I think that is why I keep constantly testing myself."

A small silence settled over the three of them.

Jean-Claude finally cleared his throat, forced a light laugh. "Enough of war. Let us relax here and count our blessings." He turned his head, looked at Tessa, and added, "Unexpected blessings."

She smiled at him.

Lorne thought: It has worked between them. I knew they were right for each other. And he smiled to himself in the twilight, knowing he had done the right thing in bringing them together.

Before she could stop herself, Tessa blurted out, "I shall worry about you if you go off to cover another war."

Jean-Claude did not respond. Instead he took her hand in his, brought it to his mouth, kissed it. Then he launched into a discussion about the film Lorne would be starring in. He was still holding her hand when Gérard came to tell them supper was ready to be served.

• • •

Much later that night, as she lay asleep in his arms, Jean-Claude remained awake, staring up at the ceiling, innumerable thoughts crowding his mind. He knew that he wanted her with him at all times.

He remembered how once, long ago, he had asked himself if anyone could ever know whether a happy marriage would follow love at first sight. A love affair was a risky business. Yet he was sure of the way he felt, and sure about her and the two of them together. Still, it was a frightening prospect, because it would have to be serious, he had no time to waste, not at this stage in his life. He was fifty-three after all.

She was too young for him, wasn't she? Only a year older than his son. Yet she was mature for her age, intelligent, educated, cultured, civilized. These were all attributes which he found seductive in a woman.

They had seduced each other in a day . . . drawn together as one soul, as one entity. What did age matter?

Wasn't she his destiny?

22

Gideon Harte picked up his briefcase, slipped his mobile phone into his jacket pocket, and walked across his office. As he reached the door, the telephone on his desk began to ring.

Hurrying back to the desk, he leaned over and picked up the receiver. "Gideon Harte."

"It's Andy. Can I see you for a moment?"

"I was just leaving. Is there some kind of problem?"

"Maybe."

"Okay, come on down to my office."

"Righto. Be there in a minute."

Gideon went over to the plate-glass window, put his briefcase on the floor near his desk, then turned and stood looking out at the rooftops of London. The sky had a peculiar dull glow along the edge of the horizon like a fire in the distance, except that he knew there was no fire. Gideon sighed. He was very tired; it was almost ten o'clock on this Monday night, and he had had a long day. He was glad his father was coming back from New

York at the end of the week. In his absence he had had the entire newspaper chain to supervise, and it had been quite a job since he also ran the *London Evening Post.*

Now his mind zeroed in on Andy McHugh, and he hoped his top investigative reporter was not coming to give him news he had been half expecting—and dreading—for some time.

A moment later Gideon swung around as Andy knocked and came barreling in, exclaiming, "Sorry about this, Gid, but I felt you had to know tonight." Closing the door behind him, Andy joined Gideon at the window.

"Okay, give it to me straight, no frills please," Gideon said, looking Andy in the eye.

"It's about Dusty Rhodes."

"Oh shit, I knew this was going to hit us in the face sooner or later. What's happened? Who's got the story?"

"Look, it's not a breaking news story, thank God. As you well know, the Harrogate police and the hospital conveniently forgot that stabbing ever happened. But there's going to be a special piece in the *Daily Mail* tomorrow or Wednesday. An in-depth interview with Melinda Caldwell."

"Well, thank God it's not about the stabbing. India's name would have been all over that story!"

"You're right, and she probably isn't mentioned in this one, although we don't know that for sure. But listen, Gideon, there's something else. This Caldwell girl has a child with Dusty. A little girl, Atlanta, three years old."

Startled, Gideon stared at the reporter. "Oh God, and he never told India. That I know for sure. She would have confided in me or one of her other cousins, we're all very close. This is going to be a big shock to her. It changes the picture for India. He's been duplicitous."

"Maybe not. I do believe that the relationship between Dusty Rhodes and the Caldwell girl is over, and has been for a long time. Harry Forster and I really did do a lot of digging into Dusty's past, and he'd definitely broken up with Melinda Caldwell by 1998, actually maybe just after the child's birth. He's been truthful with India about all that."

"He just failed to tell her he has a three-year-old child. Lying by omission, I would call it."

"That's true."

"How did you find out, Andy?"

"As you know, I have a contact at the detox clinic, well paid by us, a male nurse I asked to keep me informed about Melinda. He just phoned tonight. About two weeks ago, a friend of Melinda's, Carrie Vale, went down to see her, as she has over the past few months. But this time she brought another woman, who was passed off as also a friend of Melinda. I say passed off because the other woman is a writer for the *Mail*. Obviously, the two of them induced Melinda to sell her story. 'My Terrible Life with Britain's Greatest Living Artist,' or something like that. My contact, Barry, told me that Melinda opened up to him tonight, boasted that she'd been paid a lot of money to tell her side of the story, although Barry believes she's been motivated by revenge, not money. Wants to get her own back on Dusty Rhodes for dumping her. You know how it goes . . . hell hath no fury like a woman scorned."

Gideon sat down at his desk, pondering for a moment, then said to the investigative reporter, "Come and sit here for a minute, Andy," indicating the chair at the other side of the desk. "Let's try to assess the damage . . . to India."

Andy nodded, lowered himself into the chair, also looking thoughtful. "I don't think there'll be any real damage to her, Gid, I mean as far as the story goes.

There's nothing wrong with her having a relationship with Dusty Rhodes. He's single, available. However, I'm fairly certain she herself won't be too favorably disposed toward him *if* he hasn't told her about his child. And I do say *if*. He may have explained the whole situation."

"I doubt it! She'd have confided in one of us. But I agree with you as far as the actual story's concerned." Gideon blew out air, slumped down in the chair. "I shall have to alert her, especially since you said it might appear tomorrow."

"That's right, and one of the reasons I wanted to talk to you tonight is that there could be repercussions as far as certain tabloids are concerned. Once the story appears, other papers may do follow-ups about Dusty and his kid. If India is with him at Willows Hall, she'll be exposed to them, maybe even in the middle of the feeding frenzy. You know what they're like, some are real buggers," Andy finished.

"Damnation!" Gideon exclaimed, sitting up. "I can just imagine the tabloid headlines . . . playing up their different backgrounds. Anyway, it was smart of you to pay off that male nurse. At least we're not going to be taken completely by surprise."

"I'll stay on top of it, Gideon, but there's not much we can do about other papers picking it up, running with it."

"I realize that. However, let's be thankful for small mercies. I shall call India to warn her, and if she's staying at Willows Hall I shall advise her to beat a hasty retreat at once."

Linnet was sitting in the upstairs parlor at Pennistone Royal, studying the sketches for her wedding gown as well as those for the bridesmaids' dresses. She had spread them out on the coffee table, and suddenly, glancing up, she focused on Evan, who sat at the other side of the room near the oriel window.

"I know you're going over the list of tomorrow's chores at the Leeds store, Evan, but can you spare me a couple of minutes?" Linnet asked.

"Of course. What do you need?"

"Your eyes. I just can't make up my mind about my wedding dress. Maybe you can help me, you've got such good taste."

Evan came to join Linnet on the sofa, picked up one of the sketches, and gazed at it for a few minutes. She suddenly made a face. "No, not this one. Far too modern." Slowly, paying great attention to the details, she went through all the sketches, discarding every one. Then she turned to Linnet and said, "I'm not really crazy about any of these, Linny, to be honest. This one isn't too bad." As she spoke she selected a sketch, handed it to Linnet, and added, "Even so, it isn't the kind of gown I picture you in on that very special day."

"How do you see me?" Linnet asked, sitting back against the cushions, staring at Evan with interest.

"I think you should look elegant yet romantic." Evan moved her hands around in front of her, as if trying to draw a shape in the air. "I think you should wear a medieval dress— No, not that, but something that hints of . . . the Tudor period! Yes, that's it, and not white, it's too sharp for your pale skin and red hair. I think the gown should be cream-colored, *rich,* like clotted cream, and made of satin. *Heavy* satin. There should be pearl embroidery on it, too. The style I envision is with a high bustline, *Empire,* perhaps even with a high neckline and long sleeves. A full skirt, almost a crinoline. Elizabeth Tudor style, I think. That's how *you* should look, like a young Tudor queen . . . and you *are* a queen that day, you know."

Linnet was staring at her, her bright green eyes sparkling. "I love what you're describing. Listen, you're a fashion designer, design it for me! Oh, please say yes, Evan. There's just enough time, if you start immediately. Today is September fourth, my wedding is on December first, that's a good three months."

"Do you really want me to design your wedding dress?" Evan asked, eyeing her warily. "Are you sure you don't want a gown from Balmain or Yves Saint Laurent? A big-name designer?"

"No, I want Evan Hughes. Say you'll do it. *Please*."

At this moment the phone on the desk began to ring, and Linnet went to answer it. "Hello? Pennistone Royal."

"It's Gideon," he said.

"Hi, darling! Are you looking for Evan? She's right here."

"I'll speak to her in a minute, Linny, but first I want to have a word with India."

"Oh, Gid, India went over to Niddersley to have dinner with her grandmother. Great-Aunt Edwina's been wanting to meet Dusty Rhodes, so they drove over there at six-thirty. Have you tried her on her mobile?"

"It's off. Hmmmm. Is she staying with Dusty tonight? Or is she coming back to Pennistone Royal, do you know?"

"Oh, she's definitely coming back here. She told Evan they could drive to Leeds together tomorrow morning, since they're in the middle of the renovations at the store. That's their baby."

"I'm glad about that!" he said somewhat sharply. "I mean that she will be with you."

"Gideon, you sound ever so put out. Is there something the matter?"

"Sort of," he responded, sighing heavily, and then repeated everything Andy McHugh had told him.

When he had finished, Linnet said, "I doubt she knows Dusty has a child. Because she once made a reference to the fact that he hadn't been married, that he had no children. *Phew!* She's not going to like this omission, is she, Gid?"

"Not at all, she's so straight and open, and she can't abide duplicity in others."

"He may have just been embarrassed to say something," Linnet pointed out, as usual trying to find the best in others.

"Perhaps you're right. On the other hand, don't you think he could have mentioned it after the stabbing? Let's face it, his affair with Melinda Caldwell had suddenly come to light—why not tell the whole truth? Shouldn't he have trusted India to understand?"

"I suppose so, but we don't know Dusty Rhodes, now do we?" At that moment India walked in, a look of puzzlement on her face.

"Hi, India!" Evan exclaimed, smiling at her, then turned to look at Linnet, signaling with her eyes. "Here's India!" she added, putting great emphasis on her name.

"I know that. Gideon, India just arrived. I'm going to put her on before you speak to Evan."

India walked to the desk, frowned, and muttered, "Why were you talking about Dusty?"

Linnet remained silent, thrust the receiver at her, and went back to the sofa, grimacing to Evan. She knew India was going to be upset . . . and why shouldn't she be?

The two other women said nothing as India stood at the desk, listening to Gideon, her face impassive. But

Linnet and Evan both saw the little vein pulsing at one side of her temple, and her eyes had narrowed perceptibly. She was angry, but the anger was contained.

At last Gideon finished, and she replied, "Yes, absolutely. Of course I'm not going to stay with him at Willows Hall, Gideon, that would be asking for trouble. Anyway, it happens that I was planning to stay here at Pennistone Royal all week because of my work at the store. Evan and I are on a project together, oh, and here she is. Thanks, Gideon, for the warning and the advice."

Evan rushed to take the phone. "Gideon, how are you?"

"Worn out tonight, bloody knackered, actually. I can't tell you how happy I am that Dad's going to be back at his desk on Monday."

"I know it's been rough, and most especially this month." Turning around, facing the windows, Evan lowered her voice and asked, "You're not still angry with me, are you, honey?"

"No, that's all been blown away by hard work." He laughed. "I love you, Evan, you mustn't forget that. Just because we have a disagreement now and again doesn't mean I've fallen *out* of love. Just out of bed on the wrong side. Anyway, on some days, that's what's really making me irritable."

She laughed with him, although she knew he didn't mean this. He had been annoyed with her all last week. But now, tonight, he sounded more like his old self. "By the way, I think I might have to stay up here this coming weekend, Gid."

"Because of work?"

"Partially. I also promised Robin I'd go and see him. It's not a problem for you, is it?"

"No. As a matter of fact, I think my parents will come straight up to Yorkshire, they usually do when they've been abroad. I'll be there, too. So, how do you like them apples?"

"I positively love them apples." Stepping further away, she dropped her voice another octave and whispered, "From what I heard Linnet say to you, there are problems with Dusty."

"Linnet will tell you all the gory details, but the bottom line is that Dusty has a child by the woman who stabbed him, and he never told India."

"He's been a bit stupid, hasn't he?"

"Oh, yes. And I've got to go, darling, I'm beat. I'll ring you tomorrow. Big kiss."

"Big kiss. I love you, Gideon."

"Me too you."

Evan put the phone down and went to join her cousins, who were seated together on the sofa. India looked unusually pale, and her face was strained.

"So, Evan, what do *you* think?" India asked softly, a silvery blond brow lifting.

Sitting down opposite Linnet and India, Evan answered, "Well, I don't actually know the whole story. What's happened?"

Linnet explained everything, mentioned the feature which was about to appear, and finished, "Gideon's worried about the aftermath, the tabloids having a field day with it. You know they love scandals, especially those involving well-known people."

Evan looked at India sympathetically. "And you never had an inkling?" she asked softly.

"No, I didn't. And I don't understand why he didn't explain after the stabbing. Gideon's right. He told me about Melinda, so why not mention his little girl?"

"He may very well have felt embarrassed," Linnet murmured, taking India's hand in hers, squeezing it reassuringly.

"I agree with Linny," Evan remarked. "I think that's the only possible explanation. And where is the little girl, by the way? Since her mother's in rehab, who's looking after her?"

"Presumably the child's grandmother," Linnet volunteered.

"I do wish he'd told me. I feel rather foolish." India leaned back against the sofa, looking saddened. "And he misjudged me."

"How was Great-Aunt Edwina tonight?" Linnet now asked, wanting to distract her for a moment. "And how did the dinner go?"

"Fine. It went well."

"Did she like him?" Linnet probed.

"Oh yes, very much. If you'll pardon the expression, he charmed the pants off her."

Evan couldn't help it; she started to laugh. Linnet joined in, and after a moment India was laughing with them. For a few seconds they were hilarious.

Finally coming to a spluttering stop, wiping her eyes, Linnet cried, "Oh, India, you do say the funniest things sometimes. I had this wonderful picture of Great-Aunt Edwina without her knickers. But seriously, what *are* you going to do?"

"I'm going to call him on it. What else is there to do?"

"When are you going to do that?" Linnet asked, as usual like a dog with a bone.

"Tomorrow morning. On the way to Leeds. Evan and I are driving over very early, so we'll stop off at Follifoot to see him. Are you game, Evan?"

"Absolutely, India. You can throw down the gauntlet and I'll be right there at your side. Harte rule number one, isn't it?"

* * * *

Dusty Rhodes was still half dozing, on the edge of sleep. But as more daylight filtered into his bedroom, he began to bestir himself, knowing he should get to his studio, attempt to paint. As he finally sat up, he became conscious of another presence in the room.

Blinking in the dim light, he saw a figure standing at the bottom of the bed, although it took him a moment to determine who it was.

"India!" he suddenly exclaimed, standing up, moving toward her rapidly. "What are you doing here, sweetheart?"

For a moment she didn't answer, merely stared at him, until at last she said, "I came to warn you."

"Warn me? About what?"

"Melinda Caldwell has sold her story to the *Daily Mail*." As she spoke she handed him the newspaper.

He felt as if his insides were going to drop out, even though he had known that one day something like this was sure to happen. He took the paper, threw it on the bed, stood gaping at her speechlessly. He saw how cold her eyes were, noted the severity of her mouth, became aware of her contained demeanor, with anger hovering below the surface.

Feeling suddenly vulnerable and stupid, standing there stark naked when she was dressed for work, he snatched his robe and pulled it on hastily.

"It's not in the paper today," she continued in that icy voice of hers. "But the feature is announced inside. It's going to run for two days, starting tomorrow. I thought you should know my cousin Gideon thinks that some of the tabloids will want to rehash it, try to interview you, so I suggest you go somewhere for a week until it dies down."

"But there's a lot of security here now, thanks to you

and Jack Figg," he protested. "I'm protected behind the gates."

"I just wanted to alert you. It's up to you what you do. I'd also like to ask you a question."

"Yes, ask me, sweetheart." He stepped toward her, but she immediately backed away, and he knew that winning her over wasn't going to be easy. "India, you know you can ask me anything," he repeated.

"Why didn't you tell me you had a child with Melinda Caldwell?"

He stared at her, at a loss for words; he had no excuse really; he should have told her, explained. He felt suddenly embarrassed, so he shrugged, looking helpless. "I guess I thought it might come between us."

"And it has, but only because you didn't trust me enough to confide in me. You've totally misjudged me, Dusty, and that makes me feel very sad. Because I realized last night that you don't really understand me or know who I am, where I'm coming from . . . emotionally and philosophically. You've just no idea about *me,* and I don't think it's possible for us to continue our relationship."

"Don't say that!" he exclaimed. "I do know you and understand you. And I care for you, India. You're very important to me, surely you realize that."

She shook her head. "I do know one thing . . . you're totally wrong in your attitude toward my family. You've dismissed them as snobs whom you don't care to meet, when in actuality they're not. They're very nice, normal, hardworking people. But you never bothered to find that out. And that leads me to believe that you are arrogant, self-centered, and a coward."

"How can you say such things! I met your grandmother last night, didn't I?" he blustered.

"Oh, don't be so ridiculous! A lady of ninety-five whom you had eating out of your hand in five seconds because you flirted with her. I'm talking mostly about my cousins, my closest friends. You don't want to meet them because they're more your size, and not so easily manipulated."

"India, listen to me, you're going off at the deep end. I *was* going to tell you about Atlanta when I got out of the hospital, but to be honest I didn't want to spoil our little romantic interlude and—"

"It's certainly spoiled now," she snapped and headed toward his bedroom door.

"Hey, wait a minute! Are you breaking up with me because I have a child, for God's sake?" he exploded.

"No, I'm not. I certainly have enough compassion to understand about your little girl, understand that she's part of your life, that you have a commitment to her. I am leaving you because you don't trust me, don't know me, and make no effort to see things from my point of view."

"You're being very unfair, India," he chastised, but his voice was lower.

"And so are you, Dusty. You know how much I love you, and actually I think you love me. Yet you don't want the relationship to move forward, certainly you don't want to make a commitment." She shrugged. "So what's the point? . . . I think it's time for me to move on, frankly."

She started down the staircase.

He ran after her. "India, wait!" he begged from the top of the landing.

"It's over, Dusty." She continued down the stairs without looking back.

"But listen, what about your portrait?"

"Fuck my portrait," she shot back, crossed the hall, and went out the front door. She slammed it so hard he thought the glass panes on either side would shatter, but they merely rattled.

Dusty was unable to move for a moment. Finally he turned away, went back to the bedroom, filling with a sense of desolation. Could he win her back? She was furious with him, and he understood why. He cursed himself for not trusting her more. But then he had never been able to trust those who truly loved him. Would he never learn from the mistakes of the past?

Once she was outside the house, India ran all the way to the Aston Martin, which she had parked near the big barns. She scrambled into the driver's seat and immediately turned to Evan.

"Are you all right?" Evan asked, touching her arm lightly, her face ringed with concern. "You're awfully white, India dear."

"I'm okay," India replied and promptly burst into tears.

Evan put her arm around her and endeavored to soothe her, offering her tissues, murmuring kind words. After a moment, India pulled herself together. She blew her nose and turned on the ignition. "Let's get out of here," she said. "I want to put some distance between myself and Mr. Rhodes."

"I understand," Evan murmured and decided not to ask any questions for the moment.

Once they were on the road to Leeds, India told her what had happened, adding, "I do love him, you know." Her eyes focused on the busy road as she explained, "But I can't be with a man who doesn't know where I'm coming from as a person. So that's it. I'll get over him. Eventually."

"I'm sure you will," Evan agreed, but she couldn't help wondering if India would.

23

⁓

Paula looked up as the door to the upstairs parlor opened, and her face broke into smiles at the sight of her eldest daughter. "Good morning, Tessa darling," she said. "I see you're bringing me a very welcome pot of coffee. Don't stand there hesitating, come in. And you've brought a cup for yourself, that's good, we can have a little chat, catch up."

"I know you've been up since the crack of dawn, working, and I didn't want to disturb you before. But it's almost eleven, and I thought you could use some refreshment by now." Tessa walked over to the coffee table standing between the two big sofas and set the tray down, lowering herself onto a sofa.

Pushing back her chair, Paula left the timeworn Georgian desk, once her grandmother's, and sat facing Tessa, pouring the coffee. After putting milk and a sweetener in her cup, she took a sip, then sat back, eyeing her daughter, affection written on her face. "You look lovely, Tessa, and very well indeed. I thought so at dinner last night. Paris must have done you good."

"It did, yes, and Lorne is always so kind, thoughtful. We had a nice time together."

"So he told me," Paula murmured, immediately thinking of Jonathan Ainsley and Mark Longden and their troubling presence in Paris together last weekend. First Linnet and then Lorne had filled her in, and Jack Figg had given her a full report yesterday. The information he had supplied had only made her more determined than ever to deal with Tessa's husband once and for all.

Leaning back against the cushions, Tessa said, "Last night you told me that you are having the meeting with Mark and all the lawyers on Monday afternoon. And that I have to be there. But do I really?"

"Yes, actually you do, Tessa," Paula replied, leaning forward. "I know you can't abide him, and neither can I, but it *is* necessary. Christopher Jolliet is rather insistent about that, and he's one of the best lawyers I've ever had. I do listen to his advice, you know, whatever you might think about me 'running the show.'"

Tessa laughed. "Then I'll be there, Mummy . . ." She did not finish her sentence but frowned and hesitated before asking, "Will I have to do anything? Say anything?"

"Not unless you're asked any questions by Christopher, or Mark's lawyers. Then you will have to answer," Paula explained.

"I see. A couple of weeks ago, when I spoke to you in New York, you told me you had a plan. What is it?"

"I'd prefer not to discuss it with you today, Tess, if you don't mind," Paula answered swiftly. "I have a few things to talk over with Christopher this weekend, before it will be all settled in my mind. But I am certain my plan will work."

"If you say so, Mummy. It's all right, we don't have to talk about it now. I trust your judgment; in my opinion there's nobody smarter than you."

"Probably your father." Paula laughed. "But thank you for your confidence. By the way, I had a little visit with Adele early this morning, in the kitchen. She's so adorable, perfectly fine, and as happy as a lark." Paula paused, then added, "Thank God she wasn't hurt in any way on that awful day. And I'm so sorry I wasn't here to share your burdens—"

"But Linnet was," Tessa interrupted, "and she handled things extremely well. Actually, I don't know what I would have done without her. It was so smart of her to bring in Jack, but I've told you that."

"Yes, you did, and you're quite right. She used great judgment."

"I've agreed to be Linnet's matron of honor, Mummy."

"You changed your mind?" Paula was taken aback.

"Yes I did, because I think she was a bit hurt when I refused."

"So now it's going to be India, Evan, and Emsie as bridesmaids, and you as matron of honor? Is that it?"

"Not exactly. I've changed my mind about Adele being part of the wedding. I told Linnet the other day that Adele can be a bridesmaid after all, just as she wanted her to be."

Harmony at last between them, Paula thought. It's hardly believable. "I think that's lovely of you, darling, and I'm so glad you decided to participate. I know Linny was truly disappointed when you said no."

"Did she tell you that Evan's going to be designing her wedding gown?"

"No, she didn't, but it's only Saturday, I've hardly caught my breath since arriving in Yorkshire. Do tell me all about it, Tess."

"Linnet didn't like any of the sketches she'd had from

various designers, and she asked Evan's opinion the other evening. Evan came up with some superb ideas, like heavy cream satin, pearl embroidery, a style reminiscent of the Tudor period, and Linnet loved her suggestions. So Evan's been busy sketching, in between tearing down the Leeds store and rebuilding it with India."

"You *are* joking? About the Leeds store?" Paula asked, looking askance at her daughter.

"Of course. But they are doing a lot of innovative things. You'll be surprised, Mummy. They've certainly been much more radical there than I have at Harrogate." Tessa drank some of her black coffee and added, "Much to the annoyance of that old harridan of a secretary of yours apparently."

"Which secretary do you mean?"

"Eleanor. At the Leeds store."

"She's not really an old harridan," Paula answered. She knew Eleanor was not spying for Jonathan. There was nothing to find out anymore. Her private papers had been taken away.

"It's just a manner of speaking, Mums, but she is a grumpy, bad-tempered woman."

"Now, you mentioned India. How is she?" Paula asked. "Linnet told me there's been a bit of trouble between her and the artist, Russell Rhodes."

Tessa filled her mother in and finished, "I do feel sorry for her. India's so good, such a straight person, I suppose it's only natural she feels let down."

Paula nodded and poured another cup for herself. As she put the pot down, she gave Tessa a long, concentrated look, understanding as she had last night that there had been a remarkable change in Tessa's demeanor. It was particularly pronounced at this moment.

Her daughter was not as prickly or aggressive as she so often was. In fact there was a softness about her, something Paula had never seen before. Tessa appeared much more feminine, more relaxed. She had a wonderful glow about her, the kind of glow that usually emanates from a woman who has been well and truly loved, who is sexually satisfied—that was the only way Paula could describe it.

Oh my God! Paula sat bolt upright on the sofa, scrutinizing Tessa carefully. *She's fallen in love.* And it's obviously reciprocated. Love had caused this most extraordinary change in her daughter.

So startled was she by this realization that Paula instantly got up, walked over to the window, and stood looking out at the moors, not wishing Tessa to see the expression on her face. Who can it be? she asked herself. When did it happen? Paula had been absent for almost two months, so she had no real answers. And if anyone else in the family had known, they would have mentioned it to her on the phone, she was quite positive.

Tessa was in love but no one knew. Did that mean there was some kind of problem attached to the relationship? A married man perhaps? She hoped not.

"Mummy, I forgot to tell you about the dinner India and I had with Great-Aunt Edwina. Please come back to the sofa, I want you to hear all about it."

Arranging a neutral expression on her face, Paula straightened her navy linen shirt and walked back to the seating arrangement. "I'm all ears," she murmured, sitting down opposite her daughter.

Tessa told her mother the entire story of the evening with Edwina and the gifts of jewelry to herself and India.

Tessa went on, "Great-Aunt Edwina told me that I shouldn't dwell on my marital problems, that I should get the divorce and move on to greener pastures. She said she hoped the debacle with Mark wouldn't put me off men, that I had to get over that hurdle. And immediately."

"Did she now?" Paula gazed at Tessa, her head to one side, and after a slight pause, she said, "I'm making the assumption you took her advice to heart."

"Yes, I did." Jumping up, Tessa came and sat next to Paula on the sofa. "The most wonderful thing has happened to me—"

"You've fallen in love," Paula interrupted.

"How did you know?"

"It's written all over your face, darling. I noticed a great difference in you last night, and it's more marked than ever today. I'm assuming he's fallen in love with you?"

"Yes," Tessa said, blushing. "At first sight."

"And who *is* this man who has wrought this change in you?"

"It's Jean-Claude Deléon, the French writer. You met him in Paris . . . he's Lorne's friend. Do you remember him?"

Although she was rarely at a loss for words, Paula was speechless. Then, taking a deep breath, she said, "Of course I remember him, and he's an extraordinary person. Very attractive, very celebrated. And when did this happen?"

Before Tessa could respond, Margaret appeared in the doorway, clearing her throat and murmuring, "Excuse me, Mrs. O'Neill, but I was wondering how many we'll be for lunch today."

"Goodness, Margaret, I'm afraid I've no idea," Paula answered, turning to Tessa. "There's you and me, and Grandfather Bryan, right, Tess? What about Linnet and Evan?"

"Oh, yes, Mums, they'll be here, because right now they're working downstairs on the designs for the wedding gown and bridesmaids' dresses. At least Evan is, and Linnet's going over other details for the wedding."

"Very well, Margaret, it looks as if we'll be five. Oh, and there's Emsie and Desmond. So we'll be seven."

"No, no, wait a minute," Tessa interjected. "Linnet mentioned something about Julian coming for lunch with Uncle Ronnie."

"Oh, that'll be lovely, I can't wait to see them. Why don't you think in terms of ten for lunch, Margaret? There's always the possibility that Gideon might end up here as well."

The housekeeper nodded, and glancing at the piece of paper in her hand and then at Paula, she said, "I've made your favorite Mrs. Beeton's mulligatawny soup for the first course, and I'd planned to make a cottage pie—Mr. O'Neill likes it so much, you know—and a steak-and-kidney pie as well. Plus steamed fresh vegetables, and I've also got a luvely Yorkshire ham baking in the oven, Mrs. O'Neill. For dessert I'm going to make bread-and-butter pudding. And fresh fruit for those on a diet," she thought to add, glancing at Tessa.

"It sounds like a delicious feast. I must admit, I've missed your wonderful cooking, Margaret."

"Thank you, Mrs. O'Neill, and I'm ever so glad you're back."

Once they were alone again, Tessa hurriedly went on, "Getting back to Jean-Claude. We met last week, Mummy, when I went to Paris with Lorne. It was one of those instantaneous things, we responded to each other on a lot of different levels immediately, and well, what can I say, we both feel as if we've been hit by a bus."

Paula nodded. "Is this a flash in the pan on your part, Tessa dear?"

"No, and it's not on his either. Jean-Claude wants a serious, long-term relationship."

"Are we talking marriage here?"

"Well, he hasn't used that word, but yes, I think that's

what he means when he says long-term relationship."
Noting the worried look setting on her mother's face,
she asked quickly, "Don't you approve of him?"

Paula was silent for a moment, then she murmured,
"There's something of an age difference, isn't there,
darling?"

"Yes. But it doesn't matter to me, nor does it matter
to him."

"How old is he?"

"He's fifty-three."

"Really. He certainly doesn't look it, and I'm sure
he's serious in his intentions, he's that kind of responsible, caring man, from what I've observed."

"So it's all right then?"

Paula fixed her eyes on Tessa. "Would it matter if I
said it wasn't?"

"Yes, because I want you to approve. But it wouldn't
make me change my mind. . . . How can I change what I
feel for him?"

"You can't, not if you really love him. And you are
thirty-two, a mature adult, and therefore you can do
anything you wish with your life. But it just so happens
that I don't disapprove of Jean-Claude. Quite the contrary, in fact. I always thought he was a rather charming
man, and your father likes him, too."

Tessa sat back, relaxing her taut muscles. "That's a
big relief, Mummy. After the horrible problems we've
all had with Mark, it's important to me that you like the
man I'm involved with now."

"I do. And I just want to say this. I think you must be
careful at the moment, while we are trying to settle the
details of the divorce."

"Do you mean I shouldn't see Jean-Claude?" Tessa
asked, appalled at the thought.

"No, that'll be all right, providing you don't flaunt yourselves."

"We wouldn't do that, in fact we didn't do it in Paris. We ate at his apartment, and on the weekend Lorne and I went with Jean-Claude to his country house. We'll be circumspect."

"There's another thing, Tessa."

"Yes, Mummy?"

"You're looking exceptionally pretty and happy at the moment. But on Monday I'd prefer you to look miserable and a little bit plain, if you can manage that. For the meeting with the lawyers and Mark, I mean."

"I'll make myself look drab, use hardly any makeup; that should do the trick, I think."

"It will. You must play the victim, which indeed you are. And that's the last thing you look at this moment."

Tessa left the upstairs parlor intent on playing with Adele before lunch, and Paula returned to the Georgian desk near the window. She picked up her pen, thinking she would do some more work, but it instantly struck her that she was no longer in the mood. No, not this morning, she decided, I've become too distracted.

Putting the pen down, she sat back in the chair and gazed out of the window. Already the heather was blooming on the moors, and by the middle of September the hills would be an undulating sea of purple as far as the eye could see. How beautiful it was out there today, the sky a soft, light blue with puffy white clouds skimming toward the horizon. Paula loved the moors best at this time of year, when the bees hovered in the sunlight where the heather bloomed. Linnet, by contrast, was addicted to them all year round, just as Emma had been.

Suddenly Paula realized how truly happy she was to be back here at Pennistone Royal, the house in which she had grown up and which she loved so much; she was glad to be sitting here at this window, at the desk where Grandy had worked for so many years, savoring the memories, thinking of her enduring love for Emma. But a moment later her thoughts veered away to her firstborn child.

Smiling to herself, Paula understood how brainwashed she was; they all were, because for years Tessa had drilled something into them: *She had been born five minutes before Lorne.* And so, Tessa pointed out to anyone who would listen, *she* was the eldest of Paula's children.

Tessa McGill Harte Fairley Longden. A rather unique young woman.

Forget about the Longden, Paula reminded herself. Her daughter had already dropped *his* name, had gone back to her maiden name, of which she had always been inordinately proud.

How tragic it was that Tessa had been physically and mentally abused for years, and none of them had known because she was too ashamed and afraid to confide in them. Until the day had come when she couldn't take it any longer, and fearing for her life she had fled the marital home. She had found the strength, courage, pride, and will to survive—all of which Tessa had inherited through her mother from Grandy. And so Tessa had saved herself and her child.

And now a man called Jean-Claude Deléon had arrived on the scene. If he stayed, nothing would ever be the same again. He was the catalyst to end all catalysts. In a sense, the family's future was in his hands. But this did not alarm Paula.

She sat pondering him . . . a man of such stature, intellect, ethics, and vision most of France was at his feet. She knew full well his prominence, his celebrity, not only through the media but from Lorne, who idolized him, and with good reason.

Jean-Claude had impressed her on numerous occasions. She liked his humility, his lack of pomposity. He had a wonderful sense of humor, and he had frequently made her laugh uproariously; she had also been impressed by his wisdom and his kindness, and she knew very well the potency of his considerable charm.

He was twenty-one years older than her daughter, just three years younger than she was, but it struck Paula now that his age was an advantage. He was mature, serious-minded, responsible, and trustworthy. Should their liaison last, Tessa would be in safe hands for the rest of her life, and for that Paula was thankful.

Yes, the advent of Jean-Claude was a serious matter for the family, and for her especially, to consider. She had already seen the effect he had had on Tessa; suddenly she was a much nicer person, or so it seemed to her mother. And if Tessa were with him on a permanent basis, there might be other meaningful changes in her personality and in her life.

Would her eldest child push her overweening ambition to one side? Could she give up her dream of running the Harte stores to be the full-time wife of the writer-philosopher? Or would she remain determined to be the heir apparent? The Dauphine, as she called herself?

Funny that she would choose a French name to describe herself, Paula now thought, gazing absently out of the window but seeing nothing except Tessa's face . . . how softly beautiful she was today. If that was the effect this man had on her daughter, then he would be welcomed joyfully by her.

If Tessa gave up her dreams of being the great merchant princess, then the way would be open for Linnet. She could run Harte's without fear of interference. Would Emsie want to join her sister one day? Where did India fit in if Tessa was gone? And what about Evan? Paula was fully aware of Evan's ferocious desire to play a major role at Harte's. And if Evan married Gideon, would he object to a working wife?

No, not Gideon. He was a true Harte, since both of his parents were Hartes, and he had grown up understanding the female work ethic. His mother, Emily, had run Harte Enterprises since before he was born.

We're all women at Harte's . . . and it's the women Jean-Claude will affect the most if he marries Tessa. Because so many things turn around her, Paula thought, her eyes narrowing. I have to meet him again, and soon. I need to see him through a mother's eyes. And through the eyes of the head of a major corporation, because he could so easily change the balance of power. . . .

The door flew open, interrupting Paula's thoughts. Her granddaughter ran toward her, shouting, "Gran, Gran, come and play with me."

Paula rose, moved forward, caught the child in her arms, hugged her closely. Over Adele's shining silver-gilt hair, she focused on Tessa, who stood near the door. "Is he all right with this one, do you think?" she asked. "Does she present any problems?"

"None whatsoever," Tessa answered with the utmost confidence. "We discussed the whole subject at length. He's very happy about her. Very happy indeed."

Paula nodded. Tessa might have her chance at happiness after all, provided Paula could put Mark Longden in his place.

24

The conference room of the law firm of Crawford, Creighton, Phipps, Crawford and Jolliet had not changed over the years. Paula had been coming here for most of her adult life, whenever it had been necessary to seek legal advice from John Crawford, senior partner of the firm and the family solicitor. And on this Monday afternoon there was something reassuring about the familiar room with its dark-paneled walls, mahogany conference table surrounded by twenty-four chairs, and handsome bronze chandeliers.

One of the secretaries had shown Paula into the room a moment ago, and she walked across to the window, looked down into the street, knowing Tessa was due to arrive at any moment. But there was no sign of her yet.

Moving away from the window, she strolled over to the large painting of John, stood thinking what a distinguished-looking man he was. He was semiretired these days, but readily available when his singular wisdom was required, or when some detail of the vast Harte family affairs was needed. He had a prodigious memory and a unique knowledge of the Hartes and their business empire stretching back to Emma's days.

In many ways John was like a member of the family, and he still had a meeting once a month with her mother, since he was a trustee of the Emma Harte Foundation, which Daisy ran. This organization regularly doled out large amounts of money to a variety of deserving charities carefully chosen by Daisy and John.

"Good afternoon, Paula," Christopher Jolliet, John's nephew, exclaimed, hurrying into the room. "I'm sorry to keep you waiting, I was just finishing a phone call with Uncle John when you arrived. He sends his love, by the way."

Paula smiled, nodded, and clasped Christopher's hand as he drew to a standstill and kissed her cheek. "Hello, Christopher." Indicating the wall, she added, "I was just admiring his portrait. And you didn't keep me waiting, I was early."

Quickly he took in her smart black suit and white silk blouse, the elegance of her overall appearance. But there was a severity about her, a grimness in her, and he knew better than anyone that she meant business. She was about to demolish a man, and he really couldn't blame her. Mark Longden had asked for what he was going to get. "It's nice to see you, but I must admit I'm sorry it's on such a miserable occasion," Christopher went on as he led her to the table. "You're looking well, Paula. New York must have agreed with you."

"It did. We were all rather busy, but I do love that city, and it was such a nice change."

"When does Shane get back?"

"He's leaving Tuesday—tomorrow. He has a meeting in the morning at the World Trade Center, and then he'll be taking the night flight to London, arriving on

Wednesday morning. He had to stay on in New York because of business, and then this meeting came up. It's about building a new O'Neill hotel in Manhattan. Usually his sister deals with the American business, as you know, but Merry's on vacation with her family somewhere in the Canadian Rockies."

"Shane's made such a success of the hotel chain, it's understandable why Grandfather Bryan is so proud of him."

Paula laughed. "His father adores him, as you know, adores all of us for that matter. He's a terrific old man."

"It would be nice if we could have dinner when Shane gets back," Christopher said, pulling out a chair for Paula, then sitting down next to her. He put the sheaf of manila folders he was holding down on the table, leaned back in the chair, and asked her, "Is there anything else we need to discuss before the others arrive?"

Paula shook her head. "I don't think so. You clarified various points over the weekend when we spoke on the phone. I'm fine with it. In fact, I've gone over everything so many times in my head, I know it all by heart."

"I'm sure you do." Christopher rose when the door opened, and one of the secretaries brought Tessa into the conference room.

"Hello, Christopher," she said and went to take his hand.

"Good afternoon, Tessa," he answered, smiling at her, kissing her cheek.

"Hello, Mummy," Tessa murmured and went to embrace her before sitting down. "I hope I'm not late."

"No, you're on time. As you can see, we're waiting for the other side," Paula replied, staring hard at her daughter.

"I look awful, don't I?" Tessa asserted and then began to giggle. "You told me to make myself look plain and drab, a victim, and I did."

Christopher burst out laughing. "I'm afraid your beauty does come shining through, Tessa my dear, despite your obvious efforts to the contrary. And I have a feeling it always will, whatever lengths you go to in order to obscure it."

"I've always hated you in brown. Where on earth did you find that frumpy brown linen dress?" Paula demanded, her dark brows coming together in a frown.

"I have a whole department store at my disposal," Tessa exclaimed. "And that's when I spotted it. I know brown is not *my* color, but it does have the desired effect, doesn't it? I think it sort of drains the color out of my face and kills my hair."

"Well, yes, I suppose it does, but after today throw it away, and get rid of the ponytail as well. That's not your style, my darling."

"I will, but Mummy, you did tell me I should look like the victim of the abusive husband." Tessa paused, looked from her mother to Christopher and back to her mother, and shrugged. "I was just following your instructions, Mums."

"I know that, and it's all right, Tess, you did well." Paula told Christopher, "Tessa's been away with her brother. He took her for a rest, and she came back looking so well rested and pretty I thought it might be better for her to play that down. I *know* Mark Longden, and he's going to walk in here and say to his lawyers, 'Look how well my wife is, I never abused her.' He'll deny everything if he gets a chance."

"I know that, Paula. But I saw Tessa's bruises, and the photographs. Unfortunately, I suppose it would be impossible for her to completely extinguish her inner flame."

Paula stared at him, thinking he was sounding quite poetic all of a sudden. But then men did rather go for Tessa; they always had, perhaps because there was such an ethereal quality to her, and it wasn't entirely dimmed today, he was correct about that.

At this moment the door opened and Geoffrey Creighton, one of Christopher's junior partners, came bustling in, also carrying a pile of manila folders. After greeting everyone, he took a seat on the other side of Tessa and told them: "Longden's solicitors are just arriving downstairs. But no sign of Longden yet."

"It's typical. He's been late for as long as I've known him," Tessa muttered.

"I'd like to go over a couple of points with you, Tessa," Christopher said, opening one of the folders. "Let's endeavor to get it out of the way before we're surrounded."

Mark Longden was the last to arrive.

From the moment he walked into the conference room, Tessa was on her guard, not knowing what to expect. His appearance was more or less the same, rather collegiate and youthful at first glance. But she noticed new lines around his mouth, and there was a strange bleakness in his eyes. She couldn't help wondering why his depravity didn't show more on his face. As he moved across the room, she saw that he was agitated underneath the surface. He was endeavoring to control this, but she spotted all the telltale signs at once.

She could not help comparing him with Jean-Claude Deléon, even though she knew comparisons were odious. Jean-Claude was calm, purposeful, self-confident without being overbearing. Mark, who was spoiled, undisciplined, and self-indulgent, showed how weak he was in everything he did. And he was avaricious beyond all reason.

When Mark smiled at her, Tessa was startled. Her face remained stony and unforgiving.

Mark turned away at once, the smile still lingering,

and then a smug look flashed across his face. He sat down with his solicitors and began to speak to them.

After a few minutes, Christopher cleared his throat and looked at Mark and his representatives, Jonas Ladlow and Herbert Jennings.

He began: "Gentlemen, as you know we are meeting today to work out the financial settlement between the two parties present, Tessa and Mark Longden, who are about to seek the dissolution of their marriage in the divorce courts. However, this—"

"I've made notes about what I want," Mark interjected. "Notes based on everything Tessa said to me several weeks ago, and what I want—".

"Please let me finish, Mr. Longden," Christopher said curtly, throwing Mark's solicitors a baleful look.

Mark gestured his annoyance, but Jonas put a restraining hand on his arm, leaned closer, whispered a few words.

Christopher went on, "I was about to explain that Mrs. O'Neill is now going to take over. She wants her daughter and Mr. Longden to understand the kind of settlement she is prepared to make to Mr. Longden. However, there are several provisos—"

"No provisos!" Mark cried in a nasty voice.

"Mark, *please*," Herbert said. "You must allow Mr. Jolliet to say what he has to say without these interruptions."

Mark threw him a dirty look but sat back in his chair sulking.

Jonas now spoke, addressing Christopher and Paula. "We are ready to hear the provisos, Mr. Jolliet, and then perhaps we can discuss them."

"*Proviso one.* After Mrs. O'Neill has presented her proposed settlement, and providing Mr. Longden accepts it, the contract between them must be signed today."

"That is rather fast," Jonas exclaimed, frowning. "I'm quite sure my colleague and I will have to study the contract at length."

"I don't think you will, but do let me continue," Christopher responded politely. "If Mr. Longden accepts the settlement and signs it, there is another condition. The *second proviso* is that certain aspects of the contract must go into operation as soon as possible."

"What aspects?" Jonas asked.

"Mrs. O'Neill will . . . explain them to you," Christopher murmured, looking unexpectedly enigmatic.

"Perhaps I should take over, Christopher," Paula suggested, glancing at her solicitor knowingly.

He nodded. "Of course. Do proceed, Paula."

"I am prepared to make a financial settlement on you today, Mark, as long as the contract is signed today, as Mr. Jolliet just mentioned. It must be signed in this office, witnessed by your solicitors and mine. Do you understand, Mark? Gentlemen?"

The three of them nodded, but Jonas asked, "Are you saying that your offer will be withdrawn if the contract is not signed this afternoon?"

"I'm saying exactly that, Mr. Ladlow."

"What are you offering me?" Mark asked, much to the irritation of his solicitors.

"Ten million pounds sterling," Paula said evenly, "a very generous sum in my opinion, and under the circumstances."

Mark smiled. "Where's the pen? I accept. I'll sign at once."

His solicitors exchanged swift glances, and Jonas said rapidly, "We need to know all of the provisos and see the contract."

"Of course you need to see it, so that you can familiarize yourselves with the provisos, Mr. Ladlow," Paula said with a small smile. "I doubt you need to study it, however, since it is couched in extremely simple terms and is very short. Let me just add this. If Mark does not accept my offer and does not sign the contract, he will have to take his chances in a court of law. And, under the circumstances, I doubt very much that the judge will award him anything."

Tessa leaned into her mother and exclaimed, "Don't do this, Mummy. It's far too much money. Withdraw the offer, let's go to court, leave him to the mercy of the judge, as you just said."

Tessa's words brought a look of concern to the lawyer's face. Jonas said, "What are the *other* provisos, Mrs. O'Neill?" He was fully aware of Paula O'Neill's reputation as a businesswoman and a tough negotiator. He was certain the ten million came with strings.

"I would prefer to discuss the terms of the payout first," Paula replied. "This is what I am offering you, Mark. One million pounds thirty days after the signature of the contract. One million pounds when the divorce is granted by the judge, and one million pounds per year for the coming five years, starting in 2002. That will make seven million pounds paid out over six years, bringing us to 2007. The final payment of three million pounds will be paid to you three years after that, in 2010."

No one spoke for a few moments.

The lawyers appeared perplexed.

Mark looked pleased.

Tessa was angry, and it showed on her face.

Jonas Ladlow and Herbert Jennings excused themselves from the table. They went and stood near the window. Jonas whispered, "There's a catch, Herb. Somewhere there's a catch."

"I agree, Jonas. She's far too smart to hand out ten million pounds just like that. It *is* over a nine-year period starting now, I realize that. Nonetheless, it's a lot of money."

"Under the circumstances, yes, because he's no angel."

"Say that again. But look, let's see what else she has to say."

The two solicitors came back to the table, and Jonas asked, "What are the other provisos exactly, Mrs. O'Neill?"

"If Mark signs the contract today, he will also be agreeing to move to Australia."

"That's fine by me," Mark announced. "I'm happy to sign. Oh, and what about my Hampstead house? Do I get that? Tessa promised it to me, you know."

"It's *not* your house, Mark. Nor is it Tessa's, actually. I gave it to you both when you married, but I never actually *gifted* it to Tessa. I retained the deeds. So actually it's mine, and I don't propose to give it to *you*. Or to Tessa for that matter. We are talking here about a ten-million-pound *cash* settlement. The Hampstead house doesn't come into play."

Mark opened his mouth, but Jonas cut across him, saying swiftly, "So if Mark signs the contract today, the payout will begin thirty days from today, with two million paid altogether. And after the divorce he must leave for Australia, to live there? Am I understanding you correctly, Mrs. O'Neill?"

"You are indeed, Mr. Ladlow. Mark will be able to leave for Sydney once the judge grants the divorce. That is when he receives the second payment of one million. He will remain in Sydney for the next five years without returning to England, or going anywhere else, actually."

"*What?*" Mark cried vehemently. "I can't leave there for five years? You're *exiling* me!"

"Call it what you will," Paula answered coldly. "But you will agree to stay there for five years, to build your architectural firm into a viable entity. After five years you can return to England for a visit of one month."

"One month!" he shrieked. "No way will I agree to these terms, Paula."

"Very well, I understand. But don't forget, there's ten million pounds at stake. Don't make any foolish or hasty decisions, Mark. Think about it."

"What happens when the five-year period is up?" Jonas asked quietly, staring at Paula. He couldn't help admiring her, although he kept his face neutral. She was a shrewd adversary, and she obviously understood Mark Longden very well.

Paula was silent for a moment, then responded softly, "After the five-year period ends, Mark can return to England once every two years, and after the final payment of three million pounds, in 2010, he is free to come and go as he wishes."

"Yes, and by that time Adele will be twelve years old!" Mark shouted. "I will have missed all of her childhood."

"That is true, but you should have thought of Adele from the start, Mark, then perhaps you would still have a marriage with Tessa. You are the author of your own life. You've written this script and played the part." Paula shrugged lightly and added, "Very sadly."

The two solicitors and Mark rose and walked over to the window, where they stood discussing the settlement for ten minutes. When they returned to the table, Jonas Ladlow took charge.

Clearing his throat, he looked directly at Paula and said, "Mark has decided that he prefers to pass on the settlement. He'll take his chances in the courts. We hope it will be a fair judge, one who will understand a father's right to have access to his child, if not, indeed, shared custody."

"Very well, Mr. Ladlow, I do understand. It is Mark's choice." Turning to Christopher, Paula said, "May I please have the folder which was sent to you two weeks ago? Oh, and the other one from the previous month please. From July."

Christopher handed them to her silently.

Paula opened the top one, glanced inside, then looked across at Jonas and Herbert. "Spousal abuse. Drug addiction. Alcoholism. *Kidnapping*. All the details are here."

"I didn't kidnap Adele!" Mark shouted, growing red in the face.

"Be quiet!" Paula stared at him furiously. "You beat my daughter, pushed her down a flight of stairs. What you did could have killed her or done permanent damage. You raped her. *Often*. You abducted Adele. Without telling her mother, you took Adele for a whole day. You've used her money recklessly. The list is endless, Mark." She took a deep breath. "So go ahead. Take your chances in a court of law. However, let me tell you this. With the dossier I have on you here"—she paused, patted the folder—"you'll be lucky if you don't get a jail sentence."

Jonas Ladlow and Herbert Jennings stared open-mouthed at Paula. Mark, who was seated between them, leaned back in his chair. He was suddenly gray faced.

"May I see those documents in the folders?" Jonas asked quietly, although he was almost fearful to open them. It struck him it would be like opening Pandora's box, letting hundreds of secrets fly out. Secrets he didn't particularly want to know about.

Paula nodded. "There is one other thing I must say before I pass these over to you, Mr. Ladlow."

"Yes, Mrs. O'Neill?" He gazed at her questioningly.

"Although I cannot prove it at this time, I want you to

be aware that I suspect your client of plotting with my cousin Jonathan Ainsley to do bodily harm to various members of my immediate family. I haven't taken my concerns and the information I have to Scotland Yard. But there is a strong possibility that I shall be doing that soon. You see, I know for a fact that Mark Longden and Jonathan Ainsley were in Paris together the weekend before last. I also know that Jonathan Ainsley wishes to harm Tessa and her brother, Lorne, and my daughter Linnet as well."

Jonas Ladlow sat immobilized, staring at her, as did Herbert Jennings. Both were wondering why they had ever taken Mark Longden on as a client.

As for Mark, he was speechless, too. But under his breath he was cursing Jonathan Ainsley.

Paula smiled faintly at Jonas and finished. "I don't think your client would want to be named in a charge of conspiracy to commit murder, would he?"

After a moment's consultation with his colleague, Herbert began to speak, looking over at Christopher, Geoffrey, and Paula. "Could we see the contract please? And may we use a private room for a short time, to confer with our client?"

"It will be my pleasure, gentlemen," Christopher answered.

When the three men had gone out of the conference room with Geoffrey Creighton, Tessa took hold of Paula's arm and asked in an urgent whisper, "Is it true, Mummy? Was Mark in Paris last weekend? And does Jonathan want to harm us?"

"The answer is *yes* to both questions. But you were not in any danger, darling. Jack Figg knew of Jonathan's presence in Paris, and Mark's also. He was having them tailed. He'd told Linnet, and she alerted Lorne. You and Lorne were protected, believe me."

"Did Linnet phone Lorne on Friday morning, do you think?"

"She did, yes, following Jack's instructions. Once she'd told him you were there, he thought it better Lorne was alerted. Your brother didn't tell you because he didn't want to alarm you."

"I see. Perhaps that's why his friend invited us for the weekend?"

Paula shook her head. "I don't think so. It's a coincidence, but one that turned out to be convenient."

"Is Adele at risk, Mummy?" Tessa asked, concern ringing her face.

"I don't think she is, darling, but just to be sure Jack is hiring a bodyguard. However, the man will function as your driver so as not to create undue alarm."

"I understand." Tessa sat back, staring off into space, and after a few moments she turned to her mother and said in a voice that was hardly audible, "I don't think you should have offered Mark all the money. He doesn't deserve to get anything, not after what he did to me."

"I agree with you," Paula replied. "But I like to be in control of certain situations, and if Mark signs the contract, accepts all the provisos, it's money well spent. Because he will be in my control. Absolutely in my control."

Tessa nodded, biting her lip. "I understand that, but even so it's an awful lot of money to give him."

"Here's a point you ought to consider, Tess," Paula told her. "I own the Hampstead house, and I paid about a million and a half for it. I was planning to have it done up for Lorne, but he never wanted it. So it was rented out, as you know. That's all of ten years ago now. I spoke to Emily about it, and she's going to have it sold through the real estate division of Harte Enterprises. She thinks it will fetch about three and a half, maybe even four million pounds. I'll be making a good profit. And if I invest the money from the sale of the house, it will go toward the ten million pounds I'm planning to give Mark."

"I see what you mean, and thanks, Mother, for looking after me and Adele in this way. Do you think he'll accept your offer?"

"I have no doubt about it." Paula began to laugh, and turning, she looked at Christopher. "What do you think?"

"I think you not only demolished him but put the fear of God into him, about the Ainsley business, I mean. I'm sure he feels decidedly lucky to be getting ten million pounds and a trip to Australia. Far away from any Scotland Yard detectives. Wouldn't you, under the circumstances?"

"I certainly would," Paula murmured.

And Tessa said, "So would I."

At this moment Geoffrey returned, followed by one of the firm's secretaries, carrying a tray loaded with all the necessary items for afternoon tea. "Only biscuits, no nursery sandwiches," he explained. "But they *are* Cadbury's chocolate fingers."

Tessa laughed for the first time that day. "My daughter's favorites," she explained to Geoffrey, who was staring at her in surprise.

Paula poured tea for them all. About twenty minutes later Mark and his solicitors returned to the conference room.

After sitting down, Herbert handed the two manila folders to Paula. "These make interesting reading, very interesting indeed. I'm assuming you would call Mr.

Jack Figg and his operatives as witnesses if this divorce case took the normal route?" He glanced away from Paula, focused on Christopher.

"Of course," Paula replied.

"We would have no alternative," Christopher said.

"Mark has taken our advice, Mrs. O'Neill, Mr. Jolliet, and he is ready and willing to sign the contract now," Herbert told them.

"The contract is perfectly clear," Jonas said to the room at large. "It was as you said, Mr. Jolliet. Precise and to the point, not to mention short."

"It's the way I like to work." Paula smiled at him. "Short and sweet. And this *is* a sweet deal. The sweetest."

The two solicitors nodded.

Mark signed all the copies of the contract first, then Tessa, and finally Paula. The copies were then witnessed by the legal representatives of both parties to the divorce.

As she put her pen back in her handbag, Paula thought: Got you, you bastard. Now you're under my control. You're no longer Jonathan Ainsley's creature. You're mine.

25

Evan Hughes was a very special woman. Gideon was well aware of that. She was also the first woman he had ever been serious about, had wanted to marry. But unexpectedly in the last few weeks, things had been strained between them, and he was having second thoughts.

He sighed. It was not like him to be indecisive, yet that was his state of mind at the moment. The problem was her recent behavior with her parents, perhaps most important her attitude toward her father. It seemed ridiculous to Gideon that she was so intimidated by Owen Hughes. Her father was a nice enough man but rather dull. An ordinary man, really. With extraordinary good looks. And that was about it. He liked Owen well enough; however, it was Evan's mother he was really taken with. Marietta was warm, loving, amusing, very intelligent, and she seemed perfectly healthy. He had seen no signs of the manic-depressive in her, quite to the contrary. He wondered what all *that* was about . . . the terrible worry Evan had about her mother's health, the way she trembled at the thought that she herself might have inherited her mother's illness.

Obviously Marietta had been a depressive when Evan was growing up, she wouldn't have invented a thing like that about her mother. But wasn't there something odd about this miraculous recovery? Oh well, he muttered to himself, there are all kinds of new medicines available today. That must be the reason for Marietta's radiant health. Because radiant she was.

Deep down he was still annoyed with Evan for not telling her parents she was engaged to him, not wearing her ring the day they had all gone to lunch at the Dorchester. He was hurt about that, and disappointed that she was so . . . *cowardly*. She was also weak-kneed about telling her father the truth about his parentage. Originally it hadn't really mattered to Gideon, but somehow, now, it did. He wanted Owen Hughes to know who his biological father was, to understand that *he* was a Harte and therefore Evan was, too.

Pity she's not acting like a Harte, he thought. In a sense that was at the root of his discontent. He wished he could get over it. Wasn't he being mean-spirited and juvenile? After all, if he—

Four phones rang at once. The mobile in his trousers pocket, and three of the four lines on the landline unit sitting on his desk. The shrilling brought him bolt upright in his desk chair, and he pulled out his cellular first. "Gideon Harte."

"Terrorists have attacked New York. The World Trade Center. Turn on your TV," his brother Toby yelled.

"Jesus Christ! Hold on. My other lines are ringing." Gideon grabbed the receiver of the landline, jabbed the first button. "Harte here."

"It's Andy, do you—"

"I know. I'll get back to you." He cut the reporter off, jabbed the second button. "Harte here."

"It's me, Gideon," his father said, sounding extremely strange. "The World Trade—"

"I know, Dad. Just hold on, let me get my other line." As he finished speaking, Gideon punched the hold button, jabbed the third line. "Gideon Harte."

"It's Joel. I'm pulling everybody in for an early editorial meeting for tomorrow's *Gazette*. Okay?"

"Okay. I'll get back to you in a minute." Gideon now punched the second line again. "I've got Toby on my mobile, Dad."

"All right, talk to him. I'm coming up to your office. Be there in four minutes."

"Okay." He hung up. Then, grabbing his cellular, he said, "Are you still there, Tobe?"

"Just about, I've got to get over to the newsroom. Can't talk now. Turn on CNN. Call me at the network if you need me."

"Thanks, Tobe." Gideon ran across the room, switching off the mobile and pushing it into his pocket as he looked for the remote control. Usually it was on his desk, but now he couldn't find the damn thing anywhere. He spotted it on the shelf above the television set, grabbed it, and punched buttons until CNN breaking news flashed across the screen.

Horror washed over him as he saw one of the twin towers crumbling before his eyes. He glanced at the clock on the shelf above the set and saw that it was two twenty-five, nine twenty-five on Tuesday morning in New York.

Gideon stood there in shock. He was mesmerized by the images on the screen. Flames rising sky high. Billowing smoke. Dust. Falling rubble.

His breath caught in his throat as he focused on people jumping out of windows, falling to their deaths. Oh God! People running in the streets. Sirens blaring. Crashing sounds. He closed his eyes for a moment, hardly able to take it all in.

The phone forced him to turn away. Seizing the receiver, he said hoarsely, "Yes?"

"Gideon? It's Andy again. I'm taking the editorial meeting for the *Post*. Tony Wharley had to leave early today. Doctor's appointment."

"Go ahead. I'm waiting for my father. I'll leave it to you."

Striding back to the television, Gideon watched the ongoing mayhem, myriad thoughts racing through his head. Wasn't this an act of war? *Who* was responsible for this catastrophe?

A positive attitude about life and enormous optimism were Winston Harte's stock-in-trade. His glass was always half full, never half empty, anything was possible, maybe he *would* conquer the world one day, and tomorrow could only be better. That was the way he had thought since his earliest days.

Optimism had seen him through some bad patches over the years. But this afternoon, for the first time in his life, his optimism had fled. Winston felt totally empty inside. He was downhearted, and extremely depressed, an emotion entirely unfamiliar to him, which he found hard to deal with.

As the elevator came to a stop, he stepped out onto the editorial floor of the *London Evening Post;* he walked over to the bank of plate-glass windows that allowed passersby to look into the newsroom from the corridor. He stood there for a moment or two, as he usually did.

The sight of any newsroom, most especially his own,

gave him a thrill, but the thrill was not there today. He was chilled to the bone, an aching sadness in his gut. Yet he knew he had to shake off these feelings. He was chairman, the boss; the staff would inevitably turn to him for guidance; he must be there for them today, and in the ensuing days.

He took a deep breath, pushing his shoulders back, reminding himself he was a newspaperman through and through. And for a few minutes he stood watching the activity in the newsroom . . . endeavoring to relish it, to feel proud of his team.

Winston Harte's love of journalism was inherited from his grandfather and namesake, the first Winston in the family, who had run this newspaper company for Emma; it had also come from his great-uncle Frank, Emma's younger brother, a renowned journalist in his day, a war correspondent and political columnist. Printer's ink was in Winston's blood, just as it was in Gideon's.

Winston's gaze was now fastened on the television set straight ahead of him. . . . The appalling images of New York were still unfolding. His heart tightened at the sight of the devastation and the panic.

Turning away, more sorrowful than ever, Winston headed down the corridor to Gideon's office. When he reached the door, he braced himself and walked in.

His son stood in front of the television set and, unable to tear his eyes away, cried, "Come and look, Dad! It's John Bussey of *The Wall Street Journal.* Reporting everything he's seeing from his office on the ninth floor. It's opposite the World Trade Center. Oh my God, the tower's coming down! *Oh my God!* This is *catastrophic!*"

Winston joined his son, but only for a moment. He

now found it difficult to look at the TV screen and abruptly went and sat down, shaking inside.

Swinging around, Gideon said, "We'll only be able to get a brief mention in the stop press. The late afternoon edition is already rolling, but—" He stopped speaking, startled by the look of anguish and despair spreading across his father's face.

"Dad, you look awful! *So white.* Aren't you feeling well?" Gideon asked, hurrying over, putting a hand on his father's shoulder. They were very close, and Gideon was aware he had always been his father's favorite, although Winston had never actually *shown* favoritism.

Winston looked up at his son, opened his mouth to speak, but no words came out. He simply put his hand on Gideon's resting on his shoulder.

Gideon noted the beads of sweat on his father's forehead, the chalkiness of his skin. He was now so unusually white the freckles, normally quite faint, seemed to stand out on the bridge of his nose and across his cheekbones. And then with a small shock Gideon became aware of the pain in his father's light green eyes, the unexpected glitter of tears.

Gideon knew his father was too much of a newspaperman to show his emotions about the events unfolding in New York, however much he was empathetic with the people caught up in them. In a flash Gideon understood that there was something else troubling his father, that it was serious. And very personal.

Trying to keep his voice even, Gideon asked, "Are you ill, Dad?"

Winston endeavored to steady himself, and slowly, in a voice that was gruff and thick with tears, he answered. "He's in there. In that lot. He'll never get out alive."

"Who, Dad? Who're you talking about?"

"Shane," Winston said. "He had a meeting at the World Trade Center this morning. That's why he didn't come back with us." He shook his head, and a sob broke free. Bringing one hand to his mouth, as though he wanted to push the sobs back inside himself, he went on shaking his head, finally mumbled, "He's probably dead already."

Horror-struck, Gideon bent over his father, holding him close to his chest. After a moment or two, he said in a low, very loving voice, "Dad, please don't jump to conclusions. You can't be sure Shane didn't get out. At this moment we don't know anything except what we're seeing on television. I know this is a stupid question, but you have tried to reach him, haven't you?"

"I have, and of course I can't get through on his cell. In fact, I can't get through to New York at all. Not to anyone."

Releasing his father, Gideon straightened and asked quietly, "Dad, what about Paula?"

"I phoned her as soon as I saw what was happening on TV. She was in a meeting. So I asked Emily to go over to the store, to be there for her."

"Yes, Mum's the best person to be with her at a time like this."

"Our mothers were close friends, you know," Winston volunteered, out of the blue. "They used to take us out in our prams together when we were babies. That's how long I've known him. Sixty years."

"I know. All your life."

"We've never had a disagreement. Never in all these years. He's my best friend, the brother I never had . . ." Winston stopped, unable to say another word.

"Let's try and be positive!" Gideon exclaimed. "Maybe the office Shane went to for the meeting was on a lower floor. Perhaps he was able to walk down the stairs, get out. And listen, Dad, if you couldn't get through, maybe he couldn't either. It's more than likely that's why you haven't heard from him."

"I pray to God that's so."

The ringing phone forced Gideon to hurry to his desk. "Gideon Harte here."

"It's Paula," she said in a faint voice. "Is your father there, Gideon?"

"Yes, Paula, he is, and——"

"Give me the phone!" Winston exclaimed before Gideon could say anything else. He jumped up, went to the desk, took the receiver from his son.

Gideon moved away to give them privacy. But even if he had wanted to eavesdrop it wouldn't have been possible. After saying her name softly, his father had lapsed into silence, become the listener.

Moving closer to the television set, Gideon seated himself in a chair, continued to watch the ongoing disaster. His heart ached when he thought of Shane O'Neill. How would any of them cope if he had been killed? He closed his eyes, envisioning his uncle Shane, and silently he said: Please, God, let Shane be alive. He repeated this prayer over and over again as he waited for his father to get off the phone.

Tessa stood staring at the portrait of Emma Harte which hung in an alcove in the main corridor of the management floor. Whenever she stopped to look at her great-grandmother, she thought she was getting a glimpse of the woman Linnet would become when *she* was middle-aged, as Emma was here.

Her sister truly resembled their great-grandmother. It was actually more than that: Linnet looked more like Emma Harte than anyone else in the family: the same clear, pink-and-white complexion, the large, sparkling

green eyes, the bright red-gold hair coming to a dramatic widow's peak. There were those in the family
who said it wasn't only her looks Linnet had inherited
from her famous predecessor but Emma's brains as
well. And perhaps that was true. Maybe Linnet was the
right one to run the department store chain, even though
she thought of herself as the heiress, the Dauphine. Did
she want to be the boss lady? The queen of the hill? She
wasn't sure how to answer that anymore.

What did she want?

She had a ready answer. *Jean-Claude Deléon.* All of
him. For always.

Well, that might mean giving up her career ambi-
tions. Could she do it?

Why not? She didn't want to sleep in a cold, lonely
bed every night, all by herself. As Emma had done after
Paul's death in 1939. They all knew the story of that
great love, of his tragic accident and death. Actually, his
suicide.

"You were a beautiful woman, Grandy," Tessa whispered. "And you were right about everyone having his
price. Mark Longden definitely had his price. But you'd
say good riddance to bad rubbish, wouldn't you?"

She couldn't change a thing now, but she still wished
her mother had not given Mark such a big settlement.
Her mother had told her again on the way home from
the solicitor's office that the money from the sale of the
house would be invested, and that it would all balance
out in the end; she supposed it would. What an avaricious rat Mark was. He had protested about being ban-
ished, exiled as he called it, but in the end he had signed
the contract. He preferred to take the money and run
rather than sweat it out in London so that he could visit
Adele.

Her mother had been smart, brilliant actually. She

had judged him accurately, had bought Mark off. By the time he could return to England, Adele would be twelve, going on thirteen.

Tessa shivered involuntarily, remembering that he had been in Paris when she was. How awful it would have been if she had run into him when she was with Jean-Claude.

Turning once again, she walked toward the door which led to the business offices of the store. But before she reached it, the door flew open, and Linnet came rushing out. She was wearing pale blue and looked like a young Emma. "Mummy wants you to come. *Now,* Tessa," Linnet exclaimed.

Frowning, Tessa said, "What's the matter? You seem upset."

"Where have you been, Tess?"

"In my storage room, going through inventory. For over an hour and a half. Why?"

"You don't know, do you?"

"Know what?"

"Terrorists have attacked New York . . . they've flown planes into the World Trade Center—"

"Oh God, no! Linnet, how awful!"

"Come on. Mummy's so upset. She needs us."

Shane, Tessa thought. Her father was still in New York. Had something happened to him? She was unable to move, now seeing her sister clearly: the drawn face, the mouth stern, tight. Her dreadful paleness. The startled look in her green eyes, like that of a deer frightened by headlights.

"Is Dad all right? He hasn't been hurt, has he?" Tessa demanded.

Linnet stared back at her. "We don't know anything. But we haven't been able to reach him. Or anyone else for that matter. I personally think all the phone lines are down in Manhattan." Linnet grabbed her arm. "Come on, please, Tess. Let's go to our mother. She really does need us."

Tessa allowed her younger sister to drag her through the door. And she thought: It's taken me all these years to understand he truly *is* my father. It was Shane who brought me up, loved me all my life. Helped to make me who I am. Not Jim Fairley. Jim was killed when I was just a toddler. Now she prayed that Shane had not been killed in a terrorist attack; her mother wouldn't be able to survive that. None of them would.

26

Linnet had seen this look on her mother's face only once before, years ago when her brother Patrick, Paula's first child by Shane, had died. *Devastation*. That was it, pure and simple. She's shell-shocked, Linnet thought as she followed Tessa into her mother's office. She thinks Dad is dead.

The mere idea brought a lump to Linnet's throat, and she blinked back the tears which had instantly sprung into her eyes. I don't believe it. And I won't. I would have known. Like Shane, Linnet thought of herself as a true Celt, and that meant she was more sensitive, spiritual, and intuitive than most other people. She and her father had a special bond, and if he were dead she would have known. *The moment he died.*

He's not dead. I know he isn't, she thought again; she also knew she must be strong for her mother. That was an imperative.

Linnet hovered near her mother's desk, not far from the sofa where Paula sat with Emily Harte. These two were first cousins, had grown up together, and Linnet sometimes thought they seemed like sisters, so close were they.

Her sister Tessa sat on the other side of Paula, and much to Linnet's amazement Tessa was sounding the way she had a short while before.

"Mummy, I don't believe Dad is dead, I honestly don't. You said he had an appointment around nine o'clock. If that's the case, then Dad would have been arriving at the building just as the first plane was plowing into it. Look, you can see the time frame there on the TV," Tessa pointed out. "He wouldn't have gone into a burning building, now would he?"

Passing a hand over her strained face, Paula endeavored to stay calm. Bleakly she stared at Tessa and finally nodded. Gulping air, she said in a low voice, "You're right, Tess. And your sister said the same thing. I just wish I could speak to him . . . be certain he's all right."

Emily said, "Darling, he's probably trying to get through right this moment. Winston told me when he called a few minutes ago that nobody can get through to New York. It could be a dreadful overload, or it could be some sort of breakdown."

"Have you tried to fax Daddy at his office?" Tessa asked, then grimaced. "Of course you have, I guess you've thought of everything."

"More or less," Linnet volunteered, sitting down in a nearby chair. "And Uncle Winston has tried to get through to our newspaper offices on Forty-second Street, and he can't. I saw another time line on TV about ten minutes ago, and by nine twenty-one all of the bridges and tunnels leading into Manhattan had been closed down. The city's isolated from the rest of the world right now, and who knows what's happened to the telephone systems."

"We just have to hope against hope he's safe," Emily murmured. "Look, maybe he never got to his appointment. If he realized something peculiar was going on, he might have just turned around, gone back to the apartment or his office."

Tessa exclaimed, "He might not have even been able to turn around, or get to a side street. If there was a traffic problem. All sorts of things could have intervened, you know, Mummy."

Paula took Tessa's hand in hers. "I know you're right, but I am going to be on edge until I hear his voice."

"Or get a sign," Linnet suggested. Noting the odd look in her mother's eyes, she decided to play it very safe and added, in a businesslike voice, "Such as a fax."

This comment startled Paula, and she said more energetically, "We didn't try to fax *him*, Emily, maybe we should. Right now."

"That's a great idea!" Linnet cried, rushing to Paula's desk. She grabbed a piece of store stationery and wrote, "Dearest Shane. We know you had an appointment at the World Trade Center this morning. Please let us know you are safe. Love, Paula, Tessa, Linnet, and Emily." Putting her pen down, she read it aloud to the others.

"Send it immediately," Emily exclaimed.

"Yes, do that," her mother added.

Paula had retreated to the dressing room which opened off her office some time ago, wanting to pull herself together. She loved her daughters and Emily, knew how well intentioned they were, but at this moment she needed space . . . peace and quiet.

It was unbearable even to consider that Shane might have been killed at the World Trade Center this morning, but there was that possibility. She shrank away from it yet again, curling up on the small love seat, pressing her face into the cushion. Had he been in the wrong place at the wrong time?

Avalanche . . . the decades fell away. She remembered that awful day when her father and her first husband had been killed in an avalanche at Chamonix. *They* had definitely been in the wrong place at the wrong time. Everyone had called it an act of God, or an act of Mother Nature. The catastrophic event that had taken place this morning in New York was an act of Terrorism . . . man-made.

She began to shake uncontrollably, feeling suddenly icy cold. And frightened. She could not contemplate life without Shane. They had grown up together, been best friends. And then they had gone their separate ways, in a certain sense, and she had eventually married Jim, the last of the Fairleys. But it was Shane she truly loved, with all her heart, and she had soon realized her mistake as her marriage to Jim had begun to fall apart. Their separation had been very bitter. And then, so unexpectedly, he had been killed. She had never wanted that, only wanted a divorce . . .

Of course Shane could be alive. The girls and Emily were right. He might well have arrived late for his appointment, seen the disaster happening from the street, and retreated. And even if he had been early for the appointment, he may have escaped; all of the things they had suggested *were* feasible. Think positive, she told herself sitting up, straightening her clothes. And think with your usual clarity.

After a moment or two Paula rose, went to the washbasin, cleaned her smudged eye makeup, put on fresh lipstick, and brushed her hair. Then she went back into her office, knowing that she must now take charge, hold everything together.

Three pairs of eyes swiveled to look at her as she walked into the room, and she saw the anxiety and worry on the faces of her loved ones. It was impossible for her to smile at them, but she knew she must reassure them, so she said in a steady voice, "I think we'd better start making phone calls to New York again." Focusing on Linnet, she asked, "Did that fax go through?"

"No, it didn't. Look, fax machines are linked to phones, so . . ." Linnet shrugged, lifted her hands. "Once that problem clears up, the fax will automatically pass, Mummy."

"I know. Please order some tea, Linnet dear. Emily, would you give Winston a call, see if he knows anything we don't. And, Tessa, perhaps you can try to get through to the New York apartment."

"Yes, of course," Tessa answered, walked over to the windows, took her mobile phone from her pocket, and began to dial. Linnet hurried out to ask Jonelle, one of her mother's secretaries, to order tea. And Emily phoned her husband at the newspaper offices.

Paula sat down at her desk, wondering what their next options were. Not many. *Damnation,* she muttered under her breath. If only the phone system in Manhattan would spring back to life. Without phones and faxes, they were indeed isolated.

As if reading her mind, Tessa said in a low voice, "No luck, Mums. Nothing happens, the number doesn't ring through."

Paula nodded, then looked at the clock. To her surprise, it was almost four. Eleven in the morning in New York.

Emily said, "I've just spoken to Winston, and he has the same problem we do. Not even e-mails are going through."

"Because everything is linked to the phone systems," Linnet exclaimed and went and sat on the sofa, her eyes glued to the television set once again.

After a short while, Jonelle brought in a tray of tea, and they sat drinking it, saying very little to one another, all of them thrust down into their worrying thoughts and watching television.

For the next hour the phones in Paula's office rang constantly, as various people checked in. Winston, Gideon, and Toby called Emily to find out if Paula had heard anything from Shane; Julian called Linnet several times, and Lorne phoned his mother from Paris. When Grandfather Bryan came on the line later, Paula lied and said Shane had been nowhere near the World Trade Center.

At one moment Linnet said to the room at large, "The airports are closed as well. So Manhattan is truly isolated now. Dad won't be able to get home for days."

Paula stared intently at her daughter. "You're convinced your father is all right, aren't you?"

"Yes, I am. We'll hear from him, you'll see. I just know it in my bones."

Grandfather Bryan called again, and so did India and Evan from the Leeds store. Shane's personal assistant, Edgar Madsen, rang up four times within thirty minutes on various pretexts. Paula knew that Edgar was as frantic as they all were, and kept calling her because hearing her voice reassured him. She almost told him to come over to the store, then changed her mind. It was far better he remain at Shane's office in Mayfair in case Shane managed to get through.

From time to time she glanced at her watch. She was relieved that Desmond had returned to boarding school on Sunday, and that Emsie was also back at school in

Harrogate, and so involved with her horses she was oblivious to most other things. Although they knew their father had remained in New York, neither of them had any idea that he had stayed behind to attend a meeting at the World Trade Center today.

As she leaned back in her chair, took a sip of the fresh tea Jonelle had just brought in, Paula's violet eyes swept the room. Emily was near the windows again, talking on her mobile, either to her own office or to Winston.

Tessa had joined Linnet on the sofa, and they were totally focused on the tragic events playing out in Lower Manhattan. Paula found she was mesmerized herself for a good fifteen minutes, until there was a lull in the coverage and earlier film was played again.

Linnet, who was holding the remote control, began to change stations in rapid succession, going from CNN to Sky News to the BBC, then zapping onto ITV. She zapped one more time and finally hit ITIN, their own Independent Television International Network. Part of Harte Media International, it was run by Winston and Toby, and had an affiliation with CNBC in New York. She watched closely.

Her mother now started to walk over to the TV set to join Linnet and Tessa when one of the phones on her desk shrilled. As she reached to pick it up, she saw it was her private line, and her heart missed a beat. "Paula O'Neill," she said in a low voice.

"It's me, darling."

"*Shane!* Oh Shane, darling! Thank God you're all right! I've been frantic. We've all been out of our minds with worry—"

She broke off, no longer able to hold herself together, and burst into tears. Her whole body was shaking. She sat down heavily in the chair, relief flooding her.

"I know, you must've been worried. Don't cry, I'm all right. I couldn't get through, sweetheart. Not to you, Dad, the office in London, or Winston. I couldn't even get through to my office here in New York or the apartment. The phones are overloaded, probably even down in some areas."

"Shane darling, I'm here with Linnet and Tessa. Emily's here as well. They're blowing kisses to you, and they'll come to the phone in a moment. But first tell me, what happened? How did you manage to get out of the World Trade Center? It must be a miracle."

"I never made it to the meeting, Paula," Shane said, his voice sober. "Thomas Mercado, the chap I was having the meeting with, called me at home at eight this morning, asked me to come to his office at nine-thirty instead of nine. He had to take his son to school. By nine-twenty I was stuck in downtown traffic. I never got to the World Trade Center. But I saw it all happening, Paula, it was horrendous. I can hardly describe it. I realized after about ten minutes that there was nothing else to do but try to get back uptown. But we were in a gridlock. I finally had to abandon the car. The driver came with me. I stood on the street trying to phone you and Winston with no success. And I called everybody's mobiles as well."

"You're so lucky, Shane," Paula whispered, suddenly choked, her eyes filling with tears once more.

"I'm the luckiest man alive, darling," he replied. "I saw the South Tower collapse around ten o'clock and then the North Tower at about ten-thirty. A fireman nearby shouted at me, told me to run like hell. And I did. With my driver and everyone else, I ran through the streets of Lower Manhattan. The roar was like nothing I'd ever heard in my life. I'll never forget it."

"Oh, Shane, we're so lucky, you and I . . ." She was

quiet for a moment, thanked God silently. And then she said, in a shaky voice, "Here's Linnet."

Linnet, Tessa, and Emily all spoke to Shane, and finally Paula came back to the phone. "I suppose you're stuck there, Shane?"

"I am, I'm afraid. All of the airports are closed. But I think they'll open up by the end of the week."

"I am awful, darling. I've never even asked you where you actually are."

"At the apartment. As I said, I've been dialing numbers for several hours, and I couldn't believe it when I finally got through to you. Now I'll try to phone my father. But please call him in ten minutes to tell him I'm all right. Reaching you might have been a fluke."

"That it might. I love you, Shane."

"And I love you."

27

From the moment she met Robin Ainsley, Evan had felt at ease with him. She realized this was because he had treated her in such a warm and friendly way. And he had continued to be natural, outgoing, and open with her, spoke to her as if she were his only confidante. Perhaps she was. Certainly he unburdened himself to her from time to time, and she had understood for months how important she was in his life. She was his granddaughter, and he treated her as such, and she treated him as her grandfather, having adjusted her thinking. He *was* her biological grandfather and she loved him, but it did not make her love Richard Hughes any less. *He* had been her grandfather as well, for her entire life until he died.

Now, as she sat on the terrace at Lackland Priory, waiting for Robin to come back outside, she experienced a little rush of sadness that her parents had decided to go back to the States earlier than planned. She had hoped to inveigle them to come to Yorkshire, to stay at Pennistone Royal with Paula, and to meet Robin when they were here. But that idea would not play anymore.

The terrorist attacks on New York and Washington four days ago had made them realize how much they wanted to be at home, "to help in any way we can," her mother had explained yesterday. And Evan understood their patriotism, felt the same way they did. But she had responsibilities here, crucial matters to deal with in the next few weeks.

They'll meet Robin another time, she thought. They'll have to come back for my wedding, won't they? If it ever happens, she then added glumly. Gideon had been difficult lately; they had not seen each other all week, and so they had not been able to settle the differences between them. She had been busy with the remodeling of the Leeds store, and he had had his hands full in London with the breaking news on the terrorist attacks.

He had chosen to stay in London for the weekend, and although she understood why, she was disappointed not to be with him. But the newspapers came first, she had long known that. All of the Hartes put business first.

Lifting the silver coffeepot, Evan poured herself another cup, added milk and a sweetener, sat sipping it, enjoying the lovely September day. It was unusually warm, a pretty day with a blue sky and bright sunshine. A very clear day. *Crystalline*. No mists creeping down from the moors this morning.

She heard Robin's step and glanced over her shoulder, smiling at him.

He smiled in return and came and sat down next to her. "I'm sorry I was so long, but my sister Edwina needed to discuss a bit of business with me, and she doesn't take no for an answer." He chuckled, then added, "She's in her nineties, as you know, but nobody would ever guess it."

"So I've heard," Evan replied. "India and Tessa talk about her as if she's a bright young thing."

Robin laughed again. "*She* thinks she is, I can tell you that."

"Robin, there's something *I* want to tell you," Evan said, leaning closer, looking at him squarely. "I'm afraid I won't be able to bring my parents up to Yorkshire as I'd planned. They're going back to America sometime next week. They feel they must, because of the terrorist attacks."

Disappointment instantly flickered in his eyes, but he nodded and told her, "I do understand. I think I'd feel the way they do if this country were attacked like that. An act of war was perpetrated on the United States on Tuesday. Your mother and father have the genuine need to be at home; it's only natural." He gave her a loving smile. "But they'll come back to England, I'm sure. And anyway hadn't we once decided that it might be better if your father didn't know who I am?"

She nodded. "We did, but I'm ambivalent about it now, and I know Gideon feels Dad ought to know the truth, and my mother, too, now that Gideon and I are engaged. After all, the entire family knows. It's bound to leak out, isn't it?"

"More than likely, but I can meet Owen another time. Don't fret yourself about it, Evan."

"Thank you for being so understanding, always so kind to me, Robin."

"I love you, my dear, and you are my only grandchild." After refilling his cup with coffee and adding sugar, he continued carefully, "Evan, I have something to explain to you, but it must remain just between us."

"I understand. You know I would never betray a confidence."

"Of course I do. But what I am about to tell you *must*

remain a secret, because I would not want Jonathan ever to find out about it. Do you understand?"

"Yes," Evan said quietly, feeling suddenly cold as she always did when she heard that name.

Reaching into the pocket of his old tweed jacket, Robin took out a small white card and handed it to her. "I have created a trust for you. All of the details are on the card. It's been handled in such a way that it can never be traced to me. But just to be certain, please don't discuss it with anyone, not even Gideon. All right?"

"I give you my promise," she answered and went on quickly, "But this wasn't necessary. I've told you before, I don't want anything from you, Robin. Only your affection."

"I know, I know," he said, sounding slightly impatient. "However, I have a lot of investments and interests my son knows nothing about, and which cannot be traced back to me. I have transferred part of them to you."

"But Robin—"

He shook a finger at her, looking stern. "No buts, Evan. I don't want to hear another word about this. Put the card in your handbag, study it properly later, digest it, and then file it away somewhere safe."

She did as he told her, then, putting her bag on the flagstones again, she reached over and took hold of his hand. "Thank you, Robin, you're very generous," she said softly, genuinely touched by his gesture.

"It's my pleasure, my dear. Now, tell me, how's Paula? I know she's been upset about Shane getting caught up in the terrorist attacks in New York. Daisy told me."

"She's feeling much better, I heard. She was exhausted on Wednesday, all that tension and anxiety got to her, Linnet told me. She and I had breakfast together this morning, before I drove over here, and Linnet sends her love, by the way. Anyway, JFK is open again, and Shane's coming back to London tomorrow morning. On Concorde, and the company plane will be waiting to fly him to the airport at Yeadon." Evan gave him a shy smile and finished, "It must be wonderful to have their kind of marriage. Linnet says they're still in love after all these years."

Robin looked at her keenly as he murmured, "Indeed it must. But you sound wistful, Evan. Are things not going right with you and Gideon?"

"Yes, everything's fine . . ." Evan bit her lip and then went on. "It's just that . . . well, I think he's still miffed because I hadn't told my parents we'd gotten engaged."

Robin sighed and shook his head. "Men are such fools at times. *I know.* I'm a man, and I've been a fool myself many times in my life. I wish Gideon would just move on from this situation. You're engaged, everyone knows it, including your parents. Now you and he should be planning your marriage, setting a date, not quarreling."

"We're not really quarreling," Evan explained. "He's just . . . snippy with me. And remote sometimes, distant. And quiet."

"Is he in Yorkshire this weekend?"

"No. He felt he had to stay in London with his father and Toby. He said there'd be a lot of breaking news."

"Oh yes, he's a true Harte, Gideon is, totally dedicated to his work, and that's not a bad thing, I suppose. He's a newspaperman through and through, of course, like Winston and my uncles."

The two of them sat talking for a short while longer, and then Evan said, "I'm sorry about not being able to have lunch with you today, Robin, but Linnet and I are in the throes of planning her wedding, and I promised I'd work with her this afternoon."

He smiled, and they both stood up. Robin took her arm, and they walked around the terrace to the area at the back of the house where she had parked her car. "I hope we can have lunch next weekend instead. When are you off to London?"

"On Tuesday morning. To be with my parents for a couple of days before they go home. I'm coming back to work with India early on Friday, and I'll be at the Leeds store on Saturday. How about lunch next Sunday?"

"That's splendid!" he exclaimed, instantly looking more cheerful.

When they came to her car, he hugged her and kissed her cheek. "Perhaps Gideon can be induced to join us for lunch?"

"Absolutely. I'll make sure he comes." Opening the car door, she got in, rolled down the window. "Thank you," she murmured. "See you next weekend."

"It's a date, my dear."

Evan turned on the ignition and immediately frowned when the car did not start. She tried again with no success, and Robin looked in the window and said, "Do you think you've flooded it?"

Evan shook her head. "No. It was flat."

"It's more than likely the battery. This is one of Paula's old cars, isn't it? One of her ancient run-arounds she calls them."

"Yes, she always lets me use it. But I think it needs to go in for an overhaul."

"I tend to agree. Well, there's no problem. You can borrow my Rover. It's a perfectly good car."

"But won't you need it?" Evan asked, getting out of Paula's slightly dilapidated Jaguar.

"I have my favorite jalopy in the garage."

"Oh yes, your beautiful old Bentley Continental Drophead Coupe. Circa 1960."

"Ah, so you do remember what I told you." He laughed, looking pleased.

"I do. And you told me it has a fluid flywheel and that's why it has that special gearshift. I remember everything you tell me, Robin."

"But it's not often girls commit to memory things about cars," he shot back, laughing again as he led her toward the garage.

Within seconds she had driven the Rover out onto the gravel driveway. "This is great, Robin!" she exclaimed, leaning out of the window. "Thanks so much. I'll return it tomorrow. Linnet or India will come in another car to take me back."

"There's no problem at all," he called, waving as she slid forward toward the iron gates. "'Bye, my dear."

Evan liked the solid feel of the Rover, and she found it easy to drive. It rolled along smoothly as she headed out of the tall gates of Lackland Priory and turned left on the road which led to the small hamlet of Lackland; beyond Lackland was the main road to Pennistone Royal.

She sat back, deciding she really liked these old models. There was something different about them. Maybe it was the sense of luxury, of times long gone. She knew Paula felt the same way. Paula had told her that everyone in the family hung on to their old models. "Maybe out of a sense of thrift," she had said and added, with a dry laugh, "But I doubt that." Even India drove an ancient Aston Martin that every male in the family coveted. And Gideon had raved about Robin's forty-year-old Bentley Continental.

When she came to the rim of the hill, Evan put her foot on the brake gently. The hill was steep, and she felt the instant pull of gravity as she began to roll down, pressed her foot harder on the brake.

Nothing happened. The brakes didn't work! The car went hurtling down the hill; there was no way she could stop it.

Halfway to the bottom she saw the horse and cart come rumbling out of a side lane. Evan hit the horn hard. The man sitting on the cart looked up the hill, saw her coming, but seemed unable to move. Evan understood that she had to swerve to avoid hitting the horse and cart, possibly even killing the man and the animal at the speed she was going. She pulled the wheel around with all of her strength, gritting her teeth and veering off to the right. She saw the drystone wall too late. As it loomed up in front of her, she knew that she would hurtle into it head-on.

Had somebody tampered with the brakes? she suddenly wondered. It was the last thing she thought.

Billy Ramsbotham sat on the cart staring at the smashed-up car for only a split second, then he flicked the reins, made a clicking noise with his tongue, and went off down the rest of the hill hell for leather to get help.

But before he got there he saw Frazy Gilliger coming toward him on his bicycle and flagged him down.

"What's up, Billy? You're going lickety-split! Summat wrong?" Frazy asked, noting the old man's agitation.

"Aye, there is. Up yonder, near bottom of t'hill, there's a lass in a smashed-up car. It b'aint hard ter see it's a Rover. Aye, it looks like Mr. Ainsley's Rover she's gone and bunged up. And she's in a right bad way, she is, poor lass."

"Oh my God, it must be Miss Evan!" Frazy cried, and without another word to Billy he began pedaling up the hill toward Lackland Priory as hard as he could.

He was panting as he cycled through the gates and around the back of the house. He leapt off the bicycle, threw it down haphazardly, and burst into the kitchen.

Bolton, the butler, was talking to Mrs. Pickering, the cook, and he swung around, looking startled. "Good heavens, Frazy, what's wrong?"

"It's Miss Evan. She's crashed the Rover. I saw it out of t'corner of me eye, but I didn't stop ter look. I knew I had ter get here as quick as I could. Billy Ramsbotham saw her hit yon drystone wall. He's sure she's in a right bad way. Best phone for t'ambulance, Percy."

"Oh my God, yes!" He turned to the cook. "Can you make the phone call, Maude? I'd best go and speak to Mr. Ainsley. And ring the hospital in Ripon, not Harrogate. It's closer, and they've got an ambulance and paramedics. They'll be able to treat her. If not, they'll move her to Harrogate."

"I will do that right away, Percy," Mrs. Pickering said and hurried to the phone.

Bolton headed for the library. Within seconds he was relating Frazy's story to Robin Ainsley.

Robin was standing near the window, and he reached out, held on to the back of the wing chair as he listened to the butler. His heart was thudding hard in his chest, and he thought his legs might buckle.

"Is she alive?" he finally managed to ask.

"I don't know, sir. I'm going to nip down there right now. Cook is calling Ripon hospital for an ambulance."

"I'll come with you, Bolton," Robin said.

"Very well, sir." Bolton rushed off, followed by Robin, who thought his world had just been torn asunder. To lose this girl now, when he had just found her, was inconceivable. And for her to lose her life would be a tragedy. He prayed she was not dead, prayed she was not badly hurt. Evan had everything to live for, a whole future ahead of her, a life with Gideon, a career at Harte's, children . . .

As he followed his butler into the backyard, Robin asked himself if someone had tampered with the car, the car he used more regularly than the Bentley. He knew Evan was an excellent driver. So what had gone wrong?

It suddenly struck him that if the car had been tampered with, whoever had done it had been gunning for him, not her. He dreaded conjuring up the name that lingered at the back of his mind. No, he thought, he wouldn't do that, surely not. Why would he try to kill me?

It took Bolton only a couple of minutes to drive to the scene of the accident. He insisted Robin remain in the Bentley.

"Let me go, Mr. Ainsley," he said gently. "*Please,* sir."

"All right then," Robin reluctantly agreed.

Bolton hurried over to the mangled Rover and peered in through the open window. He saw at once that Evan lay across the steering wheel at a strange angle, but her seat belt was on, and this brought him a little comfort. He couldn't tell if she was dead or alive, and then he heard her moaning and his heart lifted. Turning, he ran back to give this news to Robin.

"Miss Evan's alive, sir!" he exclaimed. "I heard her moaning. I daren't touch her, Mr. Ainsley. We'll just have to wait for the ambulance men to arrive. They have the proper experience."

"Thank God she's not dead," Robin responded, a great weight lifting. "And you're right, I know it's best not to move an injured person, damage can be done so easily by those who aren't trained medics."

Robin sat back against the car seat and began to breathe more normally. He closed his eyes and offered up a silent prayer to the God he had long ago ceased to believe in, understanding, suddenly, how comforting prayer is in a crisis. Believing in an omnipotent higher power somehow offered hope. He prayed for Evan's recovery.

Bolton had gone back to the crash site. He didn't hear any more sounds from Evan, and his belief that she was still alive began to waver. Then, suddenly, he heard sirens. A few minutes later the ambulance was speeding toward him.

Once their vehicle was parked, two ambulance men and a paramedic took over. Evan was lifted carefully out of the car, put on a stretcher, and taken to the ambulance.

"Who is she?" the driver now asked Bolton.

"Evan Hughes, Mr. Robin Ainsley's granddaughter," he explained.

"Of Lackland Priory?"

"Yes, that's correct. Is she alive?"

The driver nodded. "But we've got to get her to the hospital. At once. We can't tell what condition she's in."

"Thank God she's not left us. We'll follow you to Ripon."

"See you there," the driver replied.

It was Bolton who drove the Bentley to the hospital; once he had parked the car, he accompanied Robin into the waiting room. They sat together, not saying anything, waiting for news. After a few minutes had passed, Robin realized he must let Linnet know what had happened to Evan, since she had been expected back to lunch.

"Do you have the mobile phone, Bolton?" he asked.

"I do, sir, yes. Here it is."

Robin dialed Pennistone Royal, and Linnet herself answered. After telling her what had transpired, he added swiftly, "Evan is alive, Linnet. However, we don't know the extent of her injuries."

"Oh my God! I'm coming right over, Uncle Robin."

"No, no, it's not necessary. You can't do anything, and I'll stay in touch with you, I promise."

"I don't want you to be alone," Linnet told him firmly. "I'm coming, so don't try to stop me. I'll let Mummy know, she's at the Harrogate store. See you in about half an hour."

"All right then," he acquiesced, knowing it was futile to argue with her. If anyone was like his mother, it was Linnet. Once she'd made up her mind to do something, there was no stopping her.

Half an hour after this conversation, Dr. Gibson came out, and much to his relief, Robin noted a smile playing on the doctor's face.

"Good morning, Mr. Ainsley," the doctor said. "I've examined Miss Hughes, and she's going to be all right. She's suffering from shock, of course, and she has a broken rib, a broken ankle, and a lot of bruising to her arms and legs. But as far as I can ascertain, there are no internal injuries. And I know you'll be relieved to hear she hasn't lost the baby. She's a very lucky young woman; her injuries could have been much worse. She could have so easily miscarried."

Somehow, Robin managed to keep his face neutral.

He was an old man now, and hardly anything shocked him. But he had to admit that he was surprised to hear Evan was pregnant. He had judged her to be practical and cautious, and he wondered how she had allowed this to happen before her marriage to Gideon. Then it struck him that she might have done it on purpose. To bring the situation with Gideon to a head? He wasn't sure. All he knew was that he loved this young woman and he was delighted that she was pregnant, that she was carrying his great-grandchild.

The doctor opened the door, showed Robin into a small private room, and disappeared. Evan was lying propped up on a gurney, wearing a white hospital gown. She looked pale and was still coming out of shock. There was a large bruise on her cheek, and he realized she was in pain when she tried to move her body and winced.

As Robin walked over to her, she muttered in a faltering, strained voice, "I'm sorry about the car."

"That doesn't matter, Evan dear. All that matters is that you are alive." Leaning over her, he kissed her forehead, then took her hand in his. "Are you able to tell me what happened? Or is that too much of an effort?"

"The brakes failed . . . on the hill. No control of the car." She took a breath and added weakly, "The horse and cart appeared. I swerved to avoid them."

Robin was silent for a moment; then he gave her a questioning look. "Do you think the brakes simply failed because the car is old? Or because they'd been tampered with?"

"I don't know. . . ."

He shook his head, tightening his mouth, and said in a low voice, "The Rover is kept in good condition. I'll have my garage check the brakes, but the police might want to do that themselves."

Evan sighed, looked at him, but remained silent, not wanting to mention the name hovering in the back of her mind.

"I telephoned Linnet," Robin went on, "she's coming." Pulling a chair over to the side of the gurney, he explained, "They're going to throw me out of here in a moment, they've got to put a cast on your leg. It must be painful."

She nodded, feeling suddenly weak.

He said quietly, "Evan, the baby's perfectly all right. Dr. Gibson told me."

Taken aback, she stared at him, and color rose to fill her cheeks with a bright pink blush. She finally said in a low voice, "Please don't tell anyone."

"Of course I won't. How does Gideon feel about the baby?"

"He doesn't know."

"Why haven't you told him?"

"Don't want it to influence him . . . about our future."

"I understand. Whether you two marry or not is your business, my dear, but I just want you to know that I will be there for you and my great-grandchild no matter what."

Evan's eyes brightened, and she gave him a faint smile. "Thank you."

There was a sudden knocking on the door, and Robin called "Come in."

A moment later Linnet was hurrying over to the gurney, exclaiming, "I've been scared to death all the way over here, Evan! Whatever happened?" She came to a standstill and took Evan's hand, staring at her in concern.

"The brakes failed," Robin explained. "It was nice of you to come, Linnet. Thank you."

Linnet smiled at Robin and turned back to Evan. Pushing back thoughts of Jonathan Ainsley and his vendetta against them all, she said, "Are your injuries very bad?"

"Broken rib, broken ankle," Evan whispered. "Getting a cast."

"Thank God it's nothing worse," Linnet said.

Russell "Dusty" Rhodes stepped out of the elevator onto the fifth floor of Harte's department store in Leeds. He glanced around, understanding immediately why India's secretary had told him to be careful. He had to walk around the roped-off area to get to India.

He could see her in the middle of the floor, dressed in beige cotton trousers and blouse, clipboard in hand, tortoiseshell glasses pushed up on top of her bright blond hair. Normally casually chic in the latest styles, she was much more workmanlike this afternoon. But he understood how practical her understated outfit was, and she was nothing if not practical. There were piles of rubble everywhere; obviously a minor demolition job was in progress.

India was talking to two workmen, looking concerned, and for a split second he hesitated. He had not seen her for over a week. They'd parted on a sour note, and he was certain she would not take his phone call, so he had come here instead.

After a moment he decided to brave it, so he stepped over a pile of planks, avoided a wheelbarrow and buckets of plaster, and moved in her direction.

It was one of the workmen who spotted him first. "Hey, Dusty, how're yer?" the man asked, his smile wide, his light green eyes suddenly sparkling. "Long time no see, mate."

Before Dusty could answer, India swung around to face him, surprise flickering on her face, but only momentarily. She was good at hiding her feelings and instantly became poker-faced again.

"Hello, India," he said.

"Dusty," she answered, inclining her head.

Looking past her, he addressed the workman. "It's Jackie Pickles, isn't it?"

The man grinned. "Yer've got that right, Dusty. So yer remember our old school, do yer?"

Nodding, Dusty laughed. "I do indeed. Christ Church C of E, in Theaker Lane, Upper Armley."

"Lotta water under t'bridge since then," Jackie said. And glancing at the man next to him, he added, "I bet yer don't remember Harry Thwaites, do yer, Dusty?"

"I certainly do. Hello, Harry. Last time I saw you was at West Leeds High School, right?"

Harry smiled. "Long time ago, Dusty. I'm a married man now. With a couple of kids."

India, who had been paying great attention to this little exchange, now said, "You wanted to talk to me, Dusty, didn't you?"

"Yes." But again looking past her, he said to Jackie, "What's the problem you've encountered here? Those steel girders, I'll bet."

"Correct. Lady India's sketches for this area don't show them, because we didn't know they were there. We found 'em when we knocked a wall down."

"Show me the sketches, India, please," Dusty said, glancing at her. "I studied architecture."

Handing him the sketches, she said, "Yes, I know. I'd like the girders to be removed."

Dusty stared at the sketches, walked over to the floor-to-ceiling beams, looked around the area, and then said, "I'll bet my bottom dollar these steel pillars are supporting the ceiling, which is also the floor above."

Harry said, "That's what we thought . . . they can't be removed."

Gazing at India, Dusty explained, "Take these out, the floor above will be weakened. You'll have to incorporate them into your new scheme somehow."

The two workmen were beaming at him.

India looked annoyed with him, and then a resigned expression settled on her face. "Okay then, that's it."

Turning to the two workmen, she said, "Please excuse me for a few minutes. Maybe you want to take your tea break?"

"Thanks, Lady India," they said in unison as they gave Dusty another grin and moved away.

"You are sure I can't move the beams?"

"Well, you can move them," Dusty replied, "but I wouldn't. It'll be a disaster."

"I understand," she replied and glanced up at him, adding, "This is a surprise. Why did you come looking for me?"

Running into the two men he had gone to school with, having the discussion with them about the beams, had somehow broken the ice, and Dusty felt quite relaxed as he answered, "First to apologize and second to try to explain . . . about Melinda and Atlanta."

"Let's go to my office, we can talk there."

"Thanks, India."

They rode up to the seventh floor in silence.

When they came to her office, India opened the door and said in a very brisk tone, "Well, let's talk. But I haven't got long."

"This won't take long." Dusty closed the door behind him, knowing she was not going to be very forgiving.

India went and stood behind her desk. His arrival had thrown her off balance, but the chitchat between her carpenters and Dusty had given her time to recover her equilibrium. Much to her surprise, she discovered she was now calm inside. And she had to admit that she had missed him, had longed to go to him. She was still in love with him, and he haunted her days.

Dusty looked well, she decided, but there were dark rings under his eyes. She suddenly understood that he had more than likely buried himself in his painting to counterbalance his unhappiness about her and her defection.

Hovering in front of her desk, Dusty exclaimed, "Look, I admit I was pretty bloody stupid. I should have told you about my child when I explained who Melinda was. I was embarrassed, though, and in a blue funk. Also, I'm not used to discussing my private life with anyone."

"I know that," India said. She sat down, motioning for him to be seated also.

He took the chair on the other side of her desk and continued. "I never confide in anyone. I'm a loner, independent, you know that. I've never, ever made a commitment to anyone, I mean to a woman, and I vowed long ago never to get married. To be honest, until you walked out on me that day, I didn't understand how I really felt about you."

She gave him a long, hard stare and snapped, "At least you're honest. What you're saying, Dusty, is that I was just another woman passing through your life, that you saw no reason to share your past with me. Correct?"

"In a way, I suppose. But not quite. . . . You see, I did know I was hooked on you, although perhaps I didn't understand how much. I respected you, India, and I looked up to you. I realized all those things that afternoon, but I was also confused, self-conscious, and I didn't know how to explain that she and I had a child."

"I would have understood, and that's why I was so upset. You underestimated me. You didn't give me the benefit of the doubt."

"I know, and I'm sorry for that. I'm an idiot."

"Well, it was nice of you to come and apologize." She stood up. "I've got to get back to—"

"India, there's something else I need to tell you," he said, cutting her off. "I have always supported Melinda, her mother, and Atlanta. And I pay Melinda's medical bills."

She nodded, began to edge around the desk, anxious to return to work.

"I just wanted you to know this."

"Why didn't you two get married?" India asked, suddenly wanting to know more.

"I wasn't in love with her. Actually, we broke up before she knew she was pregnant."

"I see."

Dusty walked toward the door, realizing there was no point continuing the discussion. He felt depleted, worn out. He had told her the truth about Melinda, and there was nothing else to say. She was not in the mood to hear his declarations of love.

India said, "When did she get hooked on drugs?"

"Just after Atlanta was born. Thank God for that at least. The child was never at risk." He opened the door, turned around, gave her a faint smile. "Well, that's it, I guess—" His throat felt constricted, and he realized he was on the verge of tears. How stupid he was.

India felt herself growing panicky as Dusty walked out. *She couldn't let him go.* Now was her chance to make everything right between them. Moving around the desk, she exclaimed, "Dusty, wait! Please don't leave!"

He swung around, his eyes widening when he saw the look on her face. It was one of absolute love.

He came back into the office, closed the door, walked toward her, saying, "What is it, India?"

"I love you," she said. "I've always loved you. And I just wanted you to know that before you left."

"Do you want me to stay?"

"Oh yes. *Yes.*"

He moved closer, put his arms around her, held her tightly. "I love you, too. I want to spend the rest of my life with you, if you'll have me."

She looked up at him, her silvery eyes glazed with tears. "Is this a proposal of marriage, by any chance?"

"It is. I love you. I want you to be my wife."

"And I want you to be my husband," she whispered, and standing on tiptoe, she kissed him on the mouth.

28

❧

As it so often did in Yorkshire, the weather underwent a sudden change. After a warm and sunny weekend, it rained on Monday, and Tuesday dawned cool and overcast, the leaden sky threatening rain again. As she always did when the weather turned inclement and hinted at autumn, Margaret had gone around lighting fires in the downstairs rooms which were used the most—the Stone Hall, the breakfast room, and the library. The fires took the chill out of the air and were a lovely antidote to the gray skies, the housekeeper thought.

Evan happened to agree with her, and after a light lunch, which Margaret had served her in the breakfast room, she said, "I think there's nothing nicer than a fire, Margaret, even on a summer's day. My grandmother often used to have them going in our Connecticut house, even when the weather was sunny and warm. She just loved fires."

"My mother does, too," Margaret remarked and continued, "Her name is Hilda, and she worked for Mrs.

Harte for years as her housekeeper. Emma Harte, that is, and she told me Mrs. Harte used to stoke the fires herself. Anyway, the rooms in this great big house are always chilly, what with their wood floors, high ceilings, and all. They need to be warmed up long before winter comes, at least I think so."

"It's true. And a fire's so cozy and welcoming, Margaret."

"It is indeed. Now, would you like some more coffee, Miss Evan?"

"No, thank you, and thanks for a lovely lunch."

"It's my pleasure, miss. And what time can we expect your parents to arrive?"

"My father insisted on driving up from London, and he said they'd be here in time for tea. So I suppose they'll arrive at—*teatime*." Evan started to laugh. "Four o'clock, right?"

"That's correct."

Pushing back the chair, Evan struggled to her feet with Margaret's help, and she made her way across the Stone Hall to the library. She had been discharged from the hospital yesterday afternoon, but only after promising the doctor she would call him if she had any unusual pains which might suggest problems with the baby. It had taken her only a couple of hours to get used to the cast on her right leg, but her broken rib was painful, especially when she tried to sit up. Yet, all in all, she knew she had been lucky. She might easily have been killed. An involuntary shiver ran through her as she thought of the brakes failing the way they had, and she couldn't help wondering if Jonathan Ainsley had been behind that. But having resisted mentioning his name to Robin, she now decided to forget the vicious Jonathan.

A few weeks ago she had discovered Emma's photograph albums, wonderful, giant-size books which her great-grandmother had assiduously filled with pictures taken over the years. Joe, the estate manager and Margaret's husband, had taken them all out for her this morning, and she'd started perusing them again, tremendously interested in seeing her ancestors, mostly in black and white but sometimes in color as well.

Fascinated by the earliest photographs, she opened the first album once more. It was of Victorian style, handsomely bound in crushed red velvet, enhanced with ornate silver corners and a silver clasp, and filled with notations in Emma's neat but flowing script.

The man who fascinated her the most was Emma's older brother, Winston. There was a picture of him in his Royal Navy uniform, taken when he was only seventeen, during the First World War. He was Gideon's great-grandfather, and she saw the man she loved reflected in this ancient snapshot. Gideon had inherited the Harte good looks from Winston the first, it wasn't hard to spot that. A photograph next to it had been removed, but beside the gap Emma had written: "My father, Big Jack Harte." Evan couldn't help wondering who had taken the picture out of the album, and why. Further along there was another snapshot with the notation "My father," and it was Emma's writing.

Evan sat staring at it, and she suddenly realized who the man in the picture reminded her of . . . Toby, Gideon's brother. And why not? Toby was also descended from Big Jack's son Winston. Next to this Brownie snapshot of Big Jack was a faded picture of Elizabeth Harte, Big Jack's wife and Emma's mother. Goodness, Robin's twin sister, Elizabeth, looks just like her, Evan whispered to herself. *And so do I.* Robin was right when he said I was a true Harte.

Carefully, she turned the pages, intrigued by pictures of Paul McGill in his army uniform; Robin and Elizabeth when they were small, with their father, Arthur Ainsley; Kit, Emma's son by Joe Lowther, her first husband, with Edwina, who was all dressed up in elegant clothes that smacked of the Roaring Twenties.

In the second album were pictures of Kit, Robin, and Elizabeth during the Second World War. How glamorous her great-aunt Elizabeth looked, with her flowing black hair and dressed in her Red Cross uniform. And here was her great-grandmother standing outside the House of Commons with an elegantly dressed couple. Emma had written: "My dear friend Jane Stuart Ogden and her husband, Bill.

The third album held photographs of Daisy, Emma's daughter by Paul McGill. And there was a snap of Paul and Emma together, another with their only child, Daisy. And next to that there was a picture of Paula and Philip with their mother, Daisy, and their father, David Amory.

Evan sat back, amazed at the hundreds of photographs, which dated back to the beginning of the twentieth century. The albums, twenty-one in all, covered almost a hundred years. If I were a writer, I could create a history of this family from these photographs, she thought. What a wonderful family saga.

And now *she* was carrying another Harte, the next generation. Evan sat back, placed her hands on her stomach, thinking of her baby. It had not been planned, it was an accident, but she was glad she was pregnant. Again she shivered at the thought that she and the baby could so easily be in the morgue.

Evan closed her eyes, drifting with her thoughts of the baby and the change in her life that she or he would bring. She hoped she would be married to Gideon. He was the love of her life, and she knew what she had to do now to make things right between them.

• • •

Robin stood in the doorway of the library appreciating how lovely Evan looked this afternoon. So much better than yesterday, not so pale and wan, and the periwinkle blouse she was wearing was the perfect color for her. She was a good person, he had known that from their first encounter—ethical, sincere, and straight as a die—and he knew she would come through this current minor crisis with flying colors. She was practical and down to earth, and he believed she would be able to settle the differences she had with Gideon.

Tapping on the open door, he walked in, exclaiming, "There you are, Evan! I hope I'm not disturbing you."

She looked up at once, her face breaking into smiles. "Robin, you're early!"

"Yes, I am, but I wanted a few moments alone with you before your parents arrive." He walked over to the table where she was seated, his eyes focused on the piles of photograph albums. With a chuckle he said, "Boning up on the family, are you?"

"Of course. And it's fascinating!"

Leaning over her, Robin kissed her cheek, sat down, and went on, "I want to tell you again how thrilled I am about the baby, Evan. And although I said it was Gideon's business and yours the other day, I was just wondering whether you plan to tell him."

"Yes, I will tell him, but I have to choose the right time." Leaning toward him, she gave him a radiant smile. "I'm going to call the baby Robin whether it's a girl or a boy. I hope that pleases you."

He beamed. "Of course it does, my dear. Now what do you have in mind for this afternoon? When you said I should come to tea with your parents, I must admit I was somewhat startled. What are you actually planning?"

She laughed. "I'm not too sure, to be honest. But I

thought I'd get you all together and . . . let the chips fall where they may."

"I see. And when do they plan to return to New York now?"

"I'm not sure. When I called them after the crash, they were sort of hysterical until I convinced them I was actually all in one piece. My mother insisted on coming up to see me. So they've postponed their trip home for the moment. Anyway, I do plan to go back to work at the Leeds store later this week."

"Don't rush it, Evan. I'm sure Paula's not quite the slave driver we sometimes all imagine." He laughed. "I suppose I'm the only person who knows you're pregnant?"

"Oh yes, and please keep it a secret, won't you?"

"I will. You did tell Gideon about the car crash though, didn't you?"

"Yes, and he was concerned. He said he'll get here to see me as soon as he can. But there's such a lot going on because of the terrorist attacks in America, and he does like to be at the center of the action at the papers."

"I know. He's very dedicated." Clearing his throat, reaching for her hand, Robin said slowly, "I don't want you to be upset or fearful, Evan, when I tell you that the police phoned me this morning. They did a thorough examination of the car and looked at the brakes. The pipes had been cut."

She was not surprised to hear this. "You mean someone tampered with them?"

"I do," Robin answered. "The brakes were gone when you started down the hill. But the police say they have no way to find the culprit. No fingerprints, you see."

She felt chilled to the bone. Not only she and the baby but the old man on the cart and his horse might have been killed. She said softly, "Nobody knew I would use the car. . . ." Her voice trailed off, and she stared at him, her large, gray-blue eyes filling with concern for him.

"No, they didn't. I think I was the intended victim, my dear, which is why I don't want you to worry too much about yourself."

"But I'll worry about you!" she cried. "How could I not?"

"Please don't, I shall be fine. And certainly more on my toes than before. I promise."

"Has . . . has *he* been here?"

"You mean Jonathan, of course. No, he hasn't, but you know as well as I do that doesn't mean a thing. He can get lots of people to do his dirty work for him, and I'm sure he's willing to pay well for such *favors,* shall we call them."

Evan remained silent, sat back in the chair staring at Robin, thinking what a lovely, dignified old man he was. Her heart went out to him. How terrible to think that your own son had tried to do you harm. She leaned forward again, squeezed his hand, then glanced up as she heard a noise.

"I got here as soon as I could," Gideon exclaimed, appearing in the doorway, looking anxious, his eyes riveted on her.

"Gideon! I didn't expect you until later in the week."

Rushing over to her, he wrapped his arms around her and held her close but gently. "I can't bear to think you might have been killed, darling." Drawing away from her, he looked into her face. "How's the rib? I didn't hurt you just now, did I?"

"No, I'm fine. I *was* lucky, Gid, just a broken rib and a broken ankle, a lot of bruises. It could have been so much worse."

"I realize that, darling." Turning to Robin, Gideon shook his outstretched hand and said in a quiet voice echoing with gratitude, "Thanks for looking after her for me, Uncle Robin. I really appreciate it."

Robin merely smiled and nodded, pleased his great-nephew had arrived.

Evan said, "Sit down. Gideon, there's something I want to tell you." The moment he had walked in so unexpectedly she had made a snap decision to tell him about her condition.

Staring at her questioningly, he took a chair next to Robin at the other side of the card table. He said, "You sound odd. . . . Is there something wrong?"

"No. At least I don't think so. . . . I'm pregnant. . . . I'm carrying our child, Gid."

Gideon, flabbergasted, jumped up and went to stand over her, his hands on her shoulders. "We're having a baby. This is wonderful news, Evan! Just wonderful!"

Looking up at him, she saw the genuine pleasure on his face, and those light green eyes, often so cold, critical, and appraising, were filled with joy. There was no doubting his feelings, and relief flooded through her.

"Why didn't you tell me before?" he suddenly demanded.

"I didn't want it to influence you—about *us,* our *future.*"

"I understand. But you didn't think I'd be upset, did you?"

"I don't know what I thought . . . except that I was happy I had your child inside me, growing . . . part of you, Gid."

He smiled at her, sudden laughter rising in his sparkling eyes. Then he tilted her face to his, bent down, and kissed her forehead. "I'm *thrilled,* Evan. Thrilled

and happy, and I feel . . . so blessed to have you, sweetheart." He glanced at Robin and raised a brow. "What do
you say?"

"I'm as happy and as thrilled as you, Gideon. It's
wonderful news, and I know your parents are going to
be just as excited as I am."

"That's right. They'll be over the moon, in fact."
Standing behind Evan, his hands resting on her shoulders again, Gideon gave Robin a very direct look and
asked in a low voice, "What about the brakes in the
Rover? Evan told me they failed."

A long sigh escaped Robin, and Gideon saw the
worry suddenly flickering in his blue eyes. "Don't tell
me they'd been tampered with?" Gideon said.

There was a silence, and Robin finally nodded. "Yes.
The police just told me this morning that the brake pipes
had been severed."

Gideon shook his head. "*Unbelievable.* Let's not go
into the whys and wherefores right now, Uncle Robin,
but you must be very careful. You were the target here."

"Oh yes, I realize that. I just told Evan I was going to
be very, very wary in future. But let us move on, Gideon
my boy. Evan's parents are due to arrive any moment.
For tea."

Startled yet again, Gideon exclaimed, "Well, well,
well, that's going to put the cat amongst the pigeons!"

There had been a change in her, Evan was well aware of
that. It was a subtle change, but it was important. It had
occurred because of the car crash, and if something
good could come out of something bad, then it was this
change.

The day after the crash she had come to understand
how vulnerable she was, and she accepted that life as
such was not in her control. Life was life. It happened.

You never knew what was going to come at you. Or how you would defend yourself. The only thing she was certain of was herself. And unexpectedly, she knew exactly *who* she was. Not her mother, not her father, not her grandmother Glynnis. *She was herself.* She *knew* herself. And with this sudden knowledge came the understanding that no one could lead her life for her.

It was her life. And how she lived it was up to her. She knew deep in her bones that she must take charge of herself, no longer be influenced by her father, her image of him, or by the past. The past was always there, lived inside of you, and it helped to make you who you were. But it had to be placed in perspective. The past could not dominate the future.

So Evan had made her mind up to be open with her parents, her father in particular. In the same way, she had made up her mind to be absolutely honest with Gideon. The moment he arrived she had told him about their baby. She hadn't expected him this afternoon, but she had taken it in her stride, taken a deep breath and plunged, in a way reveling in the truth. What a wonderful relief it was to be truthful.

Pushing herself up before either man could help her, she steadied herself against the table, then walked across the room, carefully maneuvering her leg in the cast. It was good to be upright. Her rib cage hurt much less when she was standing. Sitting down wasn't too bad either. But when she lay down to sleep she felt discomfort, even a little pain. Despite this, she kept telling herself how fortunate she had been on Saturday.

Laughingly, Linnet had said yesterday that she had a guardian angel, and perhaps she did. All she knew was that her baby was safe inside her, and she herself was strong and vital and would soon be back to normal.

She was thrilled that Gideon was thrilled. His response to the news had been genuine, and there was no question in her mind that they would now be able to work things out. Especially after today.

"Are you all right, sweetheart?" Gideon called across the room.

"I'm fine and dandy," she shot back, smiling at him. "I just needed to stretch. My rib cage gets a bit . . . uppity."

He laughed with her and turned back to Robin, who had been talking about the attacks on New York and Washington. As a former Member of Parliament, he still had a lot of important connections and access to information.

Evan, standing near the window, watched them talking for a moment or two longer, smiling to herself. Gideon would be a father in seven months and Robin a great-grandfather. Her child was going to be well blessed. She wondered if she were carrying a girl or a boy.

At this moment she heard a car in the driveway, and walking back to the card table she said, "I think Mom and Dad are just arriving, I heard a car pulling up."

"Did they drive?" Gideon asked, sounding surprised.

"Oh yes, Dad insisted. He said he knew the way. The night we had dinner, when they first arrived in London, he told me he'd been to Yorkshire as a child."

Robin looked as if he was about to say something, then changed his mind. He walked over to the window, stood next to Evan, and putting his arm around her, he said, "Let me second-guess you, my dear. You invited me because you're going to tell him who I am."

"Do you think I'll have to, Robin?"

"What do you mean?"

"You two look very much alike. Don't you agree, Gid?"

"Afraid so." Her fiancé laughed and joined them; laughing again, he added, "And we look like a church welcoming committee, the way we're standing here so serious, somber even."

"I'm just more comfortable standing at the moment," Evan explained, leaning against Robin.

Margaret appeared in the doorway and said, "Oh hello, Gideon, I didn't know you were here."

"I just crept in like a little church mouse, Margaret," he answered, his manner jovial, "like I've done all of my life."

"Aye, that you have," she shot back, and then, looking across at Evan, she continued, "Your parents have arrived, Miss Evan. I've shown them to their room. They'll be down in a moment or two, they're just freshening up. I told them where the library is. I'm going to bring the tea tray in straightaway. They must be parched. Not to mention famished."

"Thank you," Evan replied as Margaret disappeared.

"I'd better move those few things off the coffee table," Gideon muttered, hurrying over to the fireplace. He removed an ashtray, a bowl of flowers, and a book, then pulled two chairs closer to the sofa. "There, that's fine, we can now seat five. In a circle."

Margaret returned with a large wooden tray laden with the tea things. After placing it on the coffee table, she told them, "Back in three shakes of a lamb's tail with the nursery sandwiches, scones, and one of my cream sponge cakes."

"My mouth's watering already," Gideon told her. "And your jam-and-cream sponge is the best in the world."

"You've always been a flatterer, Mr. Gideon," she muttered and left the library again. A few moments later the housekeeper came back with a second tray of food, which she placed on the desk. "Do you want me to stay and pour, Miss Evan? Or can you manage?"

"I think we'll be all right, Margaret. Thanks anyway."

"I'm a dab hand at pouring tea and passing cake," Gideon reassured Margaret, who nodded and was off again.

Gideon said, "I'm glad I'm here to witness this, Evan. How're you going to do it?"

"I'm not sure . . . play it by ear, I guess."

"It's up to you, my dear," Robin ventured. "Don't do it for *me* . . ."

"I want to do it for myself, my child, Gideon, and *you*, Robin. The truth matters to us all, don't you think? Especially with my child on the way."

"Indeed it does," he responded, looking at Gideon. "I'm sure you agree?"

"I certainly do. Are you going to tell them about the baby, Evan?"

"Maybe."

"In which case, let me just say this . . . I am expecting you to marry me, and as soon as possible. Please say yes."

"Yes!"

"Yippee! We're finally getting married!"

Robin smiled to himself. They were going to be all right, these two. Very happy together, if he knew anything about human nature. They were well suited.

Suddenly Owen and Marietta were hovering on the threshold of the library, staring into the cavernous room.

"Mom! Dad! Come in, come in," Evan cried, hobbling forward, her face full of smiles. "It's wonderful to see you both."

Her mother rushed into the room but embraced her gingerly. "I know all about broken ribs," she whispered against her hair. "Oh, Evan, thank God you're all right. I've been so worried about you."

"I'm great, Mom, really fine."

A moment later her father was kissing her cheek, grabbing her hand. "We're so glad to see you, honey," he said, his bright blue eyes warm and loving as they searched her face. "You're sure you're all right? No internal injuries?"

"Don't be silly, Dad! The doctor wouldn't have let me come out of the hospital if that were the case."

Gideon was suddenly by their side, hugging her mother, shaking her father's hand. "It's good to see you both, Mr. and Mrs. Hughes. Welcome to Pennistone Royal."

"We're glad to be here," Marietta answered, giving him a wide smile. "We're only—" Marietta stopped speaking as she caught sight of Robin standing near the fireplace. She stared at him, then looked at Owen swiftly.

Not missing a thing, Evan saw her opportunity, took hold of her father's hand, and said, "I want you to meet someone, Dad. This is Robin Ainsley, Emma Harte's son."

Leading Owen over to Robin, she went on, "Grandfather, I want you to meet your son at long last. Dad, I hope this is not too much of a shock, but this is your biological father. . . . He and Glynnis were together during the war."

Robin put out his hand.

Owen took it, staring at Robin, recognizing himself in the older man. For a long moment he was unable to speak.

It was Robin who spoke the first words. Releasing Owen's hand, he said, "We met once before, so long ago I'm sure you've forgotten it. Here in this house with my mother, your grandmother, Emma Harte. Glynnis . . . your mother, brought you to see Emma, and I stopped by quite unexpectedly. Do you remember?"

"Vaguely," Owen replied quietly, still staring intently at Robin. "We'd come up to Yorkshire because Mom loved it so much. We came here to tea. Yes, I do remember. But I didn't know . . . you were my father. I thought Richard Hughes was my father."

"And he was, Owen, he was! He brought you up, loved you as his own. He *was* your father and a wonderful one," Robin told him in all sincerity. "You must believe that."

Owen simply nodded.

Marietta came forward, edging closer to Owen, and he said quickly, "This is my wife, Marietta."

"I'm pleased to meet you." Robin took her hand in his, smiled at her.

"My goodness, don't you look alike," Marietta exclaimed after a moment. "I always thought Owen resembled Richard. But he's the spitting image of you."

She had been remarkable. So remarkable, in fact, she had startled him. And brave . . . to be as honest as she had been *had* taken bravery. She had left nothing to chance, speculation, or innuendo, and it had worked. Perhaps because of her genuineness and simplicity. She had been so straightforward, had not dressed her words up, and that counted, too.

Now she lay on the bed next to him, propped up by pillows, dozing in the dim light of early evening. She had been so tired all of a sudden, he had helped her upstairs to her bedroom and stayed with her . . . because he didn't want her to be alone, and because he himself had felt so alone of late, so lonely without her. Their differences had created distance between them. But now, thank God, that distance had closed, and no matter what happened in their life together, he would not let anything come between them ever again.

Gideon propped himself up on his elbow and looked down at Evan's face. Calm in repose, and lovely. How could he have ever doubted her? Through his own stupidity, of course.

He had realized when he met her nine months ago that she was different from the other women he had known, that she was as straight as an arrow, a young woman with moral fiber and ethics, and great intelligence. It had been her ambivalence of late that had put him off. That, and her attitude about her father. But her adoration of Owen was only natural—he felt the same way about his father, didn't he?

He moved a strand of hair away from her face, and she opened her eyes and looked straight at him.

He stared back at her, a smile playing around his mouth, his clear green eyes filled with love.

"Penny for your thoughts, Gideon Harte."

"That's simple. I was thinking how much I love you." He placed his hand on her stomach gently. "And how much I love this child of ours growing inside you."

A surge of happiness brightened her face, and her blue-gray eyes seemed light-filled and translucent. "Me too."

"Oh, Evan, darling, I'm so sorry I was difficult these last few weeks. Forgive me?"

"There's nothing to forgive. I was being very ambivalent."

"But today you were courageous, telling your father about Robin."

She made a face. "Telling the truth can be hard. But in the end it's worth it. How awful it would be if my father found out about Robin before I'd told him. Imagine how he would feel—*betrayed*, I'm certain."

"He didn't bat an eyelash when you said *we* were pregnant and getting married in January. And you hoped he and your mother would come to the wedding, that it wouldn't be the same without them present. You were so matter-of-fact, even I was startled for a second."

"I knew I had to get it out, just tell them, and in the most down-to-earth way. I didn't want a lot of free-floating emotion getting in the way."

"He took it very well, Evan, I must say, and your mother was just over the moon about the baby. 'My first grandchild' she kept saying, and in the end your father was smiling, too. And he didn't pose one question, but I have one, darling."

"Yes, what is it?"

"Why January? Why can't we get married sooner?"

"In a way, I'd like to, Gid, but we can't upstage Linnet. We really can't, and even if we had a quickie wedding at a registry office, or eloped, it would still upstage her marriage to Julian, don't you think?"

"Yes, you're right. But you're going to look . . . very pregnant when we tie the knot."

Evan began to chuckle, nodding. "I am, yes, but I don't care, and anyway, I want a small wedding. Just your family and mine."

"Mine's quite large, and it's yours as well, come to think of it."

"True. There's another thing, Gid. People are a little trepidatious about traveling right now, wouldn't you agree?"

"I know what you're getting at . . . your sisters might not want to fly the Atlantic with terrorists in the news, and perhaps in the air."

"*Exactly.*"

"January it is then," Gideon agreed and glanced at his watch. "I think I'd better go downstairs and see what's happening. Are you coming?"

"Yes, I think I'd better, I'd like to know what's transpired between Robin and my father."

The three of them were sitting in front of the fire in the Stone Hall: her mother, her father, and her grandfather. She had called Robin "Grandfather" to make a dramatic point earlier, but now she wondered if he would mind if she called him that all the time. She would ask him later, when they were alone.

Three pairs of eyes gazed at them as Gideon helped Evan to the big armchair, but it was her mother who said, "That cast must be unwieldly to drag around."

"It sure is, Mom. And tiring." Looking from Robin to her father, she then said apologetically, "I was rather blunt earlier, Dad, but I thought it was the only way to tell you about Robin and Glynnis."

Owen hurried over to her, kissed the top of her head. "You did the right thing, Evan. It was only a question of time before I discovered the truth. Better coming from you, honey. Your mother and Robin agree. And I'm a grown man. I can handle the truth, however unexpected it is."

"I know that, Daddy."

Aware of the time, Gideon said, "I'm afraid I do have to leave, Evan."

"Oh, but it's such a long drive!" she exclaimed. "You're going to be tired."

"No, I won't be, because I'm taking a helicopter from Yeadon Airport. I'll be in London before you can blink, almost." Gideon kissed her on the cheek, telling her, "Don't get up, sweetheart. I'll call you later."

"All right, Gid," she answered, smiling up at him. Kissing her fingertips, she pressed them against his mouth. "I love you."

"And I love you."

He took his leave of the others and was gone, and Evan leaned back in the chair, enjoying the cushions, the warmth of the fire, the lambent light. It was very cozy here in spite of the vastness, and she was suddenly happy sitting with her parents and Robin . . . her family.

The three of them had cocktails and chatted amicably, and she sipped a glass of orange juice, thinking about the baby and Gideon and the future they had together. Her overwhelming joy seemed unreal for a while.

Later Margaret announced that supper was served in the breakfast room, and her father helped Evan up out of the chair; it was Robin who led them out of the Stone Hall, chatting to her mother about horses, of all things. She had never known her mother liked horses and horse racing. She wondered why not. But then there was so much she didn't know about her mother. And about her father. This afternoon it had come out that he had met Robin before, had been to this house. Why had he been so mysterious? Well, she knew the answer to that . . .

Evan was so tired after dinner she asked her mother to help her upstairs. Once she was undressed and in bed, Marietta sat down on the edge of the bed and took hold of her hand.

Clearing her throat, looking serious, she said, "I'm glad you told your father about Robin, and about the baby, Evan, but most especially about Robin. He needed to know."

Evan looked at her mother alertly and said slowly, "You say that in the strangest way, Mom, as if *you* knew already."

There was the merest hesitation before Marietta answered, "I did, actually, although I didn't tell your father."

Evan's eyes opened wider, and she drew closer to her mother. "Who told you? Why do I ask that? It must have been Gran, who else?"

"That's right. Your grandmother told me, but not in so many words."

"I'm not following you."

"I realize that. Give me a moment, I'll be right back." Marietta was heading for the door, and she went out without another word.

Evan had barely had time to ponder her mother's sudden confidences when Marietta came back to the bedroom, closing the door behind her quietly. She was carrying a brown paper parcel, and returning to the bedside, she put it in Evan's lap.

Evan glanced up at Marietta and asked, "What's this?"

"Letters from Emma Harte to Glynnis, written over the years. Glynnis kept them all, and one of the last things your grandmother asked me to do was retrieve them from her apartment. She told me I had to give them to you, and *only* to you. She made me promise, and of course I did."

"You read them, though." It came out sounding like a statement rather than a question, and Evan's brows lifted.

"Most of them, yes. The package wasn't sealed like this. I wrapped them up. I knew, deep within myself, that she wouldn't mind. . . . We had a special relationship, and your grandmother loved me, trusted me."

"I've always known that, Mom. So you read the letters and discovered that Dad was Robin's son."

Marietta sighed. "Yes . . . and other things. But she did insist I give them to you, and so here they are."

Evan leaned back against the pillows. "She wanted me to know everything, didn't she? But why?"

"I have always believed that the truth sets you free . . . and I think that was her reason. She wanted you to know the truth about her, about her life long ago and your father's heritage." Bending toward Evan, her mother kissed her on the cheek. "They're yours now, honey . . . to read whenever you feel like it. But remember, they're not for anyone else's eyes."

"I understand, Mom, and thank you for bringing them to me. But are you sure Dad doesn't know anything about them, that he hasn't peeked while you've been here?"

"Oh no, I've kept them in my bank deposit box," Marietta reassured her.

Evan couldn't help laughing. "Mom, you constantly surprise me!"

Once she was alone, Evan couldn't resist looking inside the parcel even though she was tired. After untying the string, she found a large cardboard box filled with letters. She pulled one out at random, and for the next two hours she read the letters from Emma to her grandmother . . . until she could hardly keep her eyes open. What she read startled and amazed her, sometimes made the tears well up.

Eventually she had no choice but to turn out the light and go to sleep. But it was not a restful sleep; her dreams were filled with Emma and Glynnis and everything that happened over fifty years ago. . . .

Part Two

~

EMMA AND GLYNNIS

Summer 1950

Love is a breach in the walls, a broken gate,
Where that comes in that shall not go
    again;
Love sells the proud heart's citadel to Fate.

—"LOVE," RUPERT BROOKE, 1913

29

～

A rush of warm memories flooded Emma when she saw the postmark on the letter. WALES. Instantly she knew who it was from, because she also recognized the handwriting. She opened it eagerly and read it swiftly.

> *May 27, 1950*
>
> *Dear Mrs. Harte,*
>   *I'm here in the Rhondda visiting my family in the Valleys. It's been wonderful seeing everyone, and now I'm planning to come up to London for a visit. I do hope you'll have time to have lunch with me, or a cup of tea. I will be staying at the Hyde Park Hotel, and I expect to be there toward the end of next week.*
>   *Love from Glynnis.*

Emma slipped the letter back into its envelope, reached for a piece of her personal stationery, and wrote back.

June 1, 1950

Dearest Glynnis,

   What a lovely surprise to hear from you. I'm thrilled to know you're on our shores, and it will be so nice to see you after all these years. Actually, I can't wait. Please phone me as soon as you arrive in London, and we'll arrange to have lunch.

                With much affection,
                E.H.

After folding the letter in half, Emma put it in an envelope, addressed it, and added a postage stamp. She propped the envelope against the lamp, stared at it for a moment, another smile spreading across her face. To see Glynnis again would be such a treat. She'd missed her former secretary . . . missed her beauty, her glamour, her charm and grace, her pretty, lilting Welsh voice. Emma couldn't help wondering how Glynnis looked these days. She hadn't sent any photographs lately.

Pushing back her chair, Emma rose, walked across to the large window which faced the moorland. It was such a glorious day, sunny and warm, and the sky was as blue as speedwells.

If the weather was anything to go by, they would be in for a lovely summer. She hoped so. It had been quite rainy last year, and she'd felt as though she was living in the middle of a rain forest.

Emma was planning to spend as much time in Yorkshire as she could this year, although she was aware she also had to go to the Villa Faviola in the South of France.

Even though the war had been over for five years, the villa needed much work. Wartime neglect and its occupation by Nazi officers had created a great deal of damage. Some of it she had attended to last year, but a number of areas still required her attention.

Perhaps she could go over in August or September; Blackie had promised to make the trip with her, and she knew that she needed the benefit of his expertise and skill. She often teased him, said he was still a bricklayer at heart, as he had been when she met him over forty-five years ago. He always laughed with her, enjoyed her teasing, and like her he remembered, with much nostalgia, their early days together; in those days they were both impoverished and wondering how to improve their lot in life.

Glancing at her watch, Emma saw that it was only eleven o'clock. There was time for a walk on the moors after all. Turning her back on the magnificent view, she walked across the upstairs parlor, sat down at her Georgian desk once more, and finished going through her correspondence. After she had phoned the Leeds store and rung her secretary in London, she hurried into her bedroom and changed her shoes.

A short while later she was hurrying downstairs and heading for the kitchen.

Hilda glanced around with a start when the door flew open and exclaimed, "Oh goodness me! You did make me jump, Mrs. H. Gave me a right start, that you did."

"I'm sorry, Hilda. I just wanted to tell you I'm going for a walk. I need a bit of fresh air. I thought I'd have lunch around one-thirty. Is that all right with you?"

"It is, madame. I'd planned on making you some lu-vely plaice and chips, with fresh summer peas, and cauliflower from the garden, steamed that way you like it, and a right grand parsley sauce. Do you fancy that, Mrs. Harte?"

"It sounds delicious, Hilda. And when I come back we can plan tomorrow's dinner if you like. Mr. O'Neill's coming, as he always does on Fridays, and I think you should consider making a few of his favorites. Miss Daisy's going to be here with Mr. Amory and little Paula."

Hilda's face became one huge happy smile. "Oooh, madame, she's a right bonny snippet, that she is. We all luv her, Mrs. H."

"Yes, there's no doubt she's the most adorable child, Hilda. But she knows it, you know."

Hilda laughed and turned back to her pots and pans, thinking about tomorrow's dinner.

As she walked toward her beloved moors, which she had claimed as her own when she was only a child of ten, Emma took in the cool, solitary beauty of this land. There were those who thought it bleak and unwelcoming, but she found it consoling and restful, and it was from the implacability of this land that she drew her strength and determination. She never felt lonely up here, and she was always at peace amongst these rolling hills, for it was from here that she came.

She climbed steadily to the top, noticing how parched and dried out patches of grass looked, but then it was always dun-colored at this time of year. By late August the heather would be blooming, and even though it was only the plain ling, it covered the hills like mantles of purple, was a sea of undulating color under the late-summer breeze.

Finally, she came to her favorite spot at the top and sat down on the big stone wedged into the niche created by two giant boulders. Above her soared great monoliths which she had always marveled at. Dropped here by nature millions of years ago, they resembled massive sculptures carved by some mighty omnipotent hand. And in front of her stretched the breathtaking panorama she knew so well, the encircling moors and below them the verdant valley where the flowing river was a sliver of silver in the bright June sunlight.

Emma suddenly caught the scent of the moorland flora. It carried her back to her childhood, and she closed her eyes, for a moment thinking of her mother, who had also loved these moors. Most especially the Top of the World. One day she would go there again . . . where she had gone so many times with her mother, and with Edwin Fairley. So long ago, when she had been a very young girl, unexperienced and far too trusting. She heard the faint buzzing of the bees as they danced in the air above the yellow gorse and tiny moorland flowers, and when she glanced up she saw the linnets and larks wheeling and turning against the sun. It was a gorgeous day, soft, enfolding.

Closing her eyes, she drifted, thinking of Paul as she always did here on the moors. But then she thought of him every day at some moment or other. He was in her heart forever. How much she missed him, missed his irreverent humor, his love and understanding, his charm, his devilishness. There never had been a man like him, and there never would be. She missed him so much . . . more, sometimes, than she could bear.

Yet she was so lucky in her life. She had her devoted brothers, Winston and Frank, and her beloved friend Blackie O'Neill. And her children and grandchildren, even another grandchild now, her darling Paula. Named for Paul McGill, she was *his* granddaughter, and so like him in looks. Dark, exotic, with those wonderful blue-violet eyes.

Emma's mind suddenly went to her son Robin, and she felt a little flash of dismay when she considered his old romance with Glynnis. She must be very careful not to let him know Glynnis was in London. He might want to see her.

But then there was no problem, Emma reassured herself; Glynnis had told her long ago that she never wanted to see Robin Ainsley again. Because he had treated her so badly, had broken her heart. Well, broken hearts did mend; but Glynnis obviously had no interest in Robin. She had married her G.I. Joe, Richard Hughes, and he was bringing up Robin's child as his own. What more could a woman want than a good man, a loving husband who accepted her as she was and adored her in the process? Glynnis was lucky, too.

"You've never looked better, Blackie," Emma said, staring him fully in the face. "You're quite . . . splendid. Yes, that's exactly the right word to describe you. Or perhaps *magnificent*. And incidentally, that's a beautiful suit you're wearing."

He threw back his head and laughed uproariously. After he recovered from his mirth, he peered at her and said, "Flattery will get you everywhere, mavourneen, and if I didn't know you better, after all these long years, I'd be saying you were after something."

"Don't be silly. Of course I'm not."

"That's what I just said, Emma, my sweet. But just so you know, you can have anything that I have. Anything at all. You know how much I love you, Emm."

"And I love you, too, Blackie. Goodness, all these years we've been friends. All of my life, actually."

"Aye, and what a funny little snippet of a lass you were, all skin and bone, but so beautiful, even then, me darlin'. Like a precious flower growing among the weeds of Fairley Hall." He let out a sigh. "Aye, that was long ago now, almost fifty years." He eyed her carefully.

"And I might say you're looking pretty nifty yourself, Emma Harte. All dolled up for a party, eh?"

She smiled at him indulgently. "No, not a party. However, when you said you wanted to come early, I thought I'd better be dressed and ready for the rest of the day."

"You look as elegant as you always do, Emma. Now I understand from Winston that congratulations are in order."

She stared at him blandly, and her green eyes narrowed.

"I was told by your brother that the Yorkshire Consolidated Newspaper Company has taken control of the *Yorkshire Morning Gazette*. It's yours now, Emma. You've finally bested Edwin Fairley. You've won, me darlin'."

"You always knew I would, didn't you, Blackie O'Neill?" she answered, and there was an undercurrent of defiance in her tone. She sat up straighter in the chair.

"I did. It seems to me you had set your mind to getting that paper, come hell or high water. So tell me . . ."

"I've been very patient, and I had a weak adversary. My newspapers are the most successful in the north, and they've eaten up a lot of the *Gazette*'s circulation, as well as the circulation of a few other newspapers. To be honest, Blackie, the *Gazette*'s been losing money since the end of the war, and anyway, I ran it into the ground."

"Deliberately?" Blackie took a puff on his cigar, sat studying her thoughtfully.

"But of course. And without compunction. Edwin Fairley's never been a good businessman. He's a much better lawyer. And he should have stuck to the law, in my considered opinion."

"Winston told me Edwin sold off a lot of his shares. That was obviously a foolish move. He weakened his position, didn't he?"

Emma nodded. "He's not been dealing from strength for a long time. But he stayed on as chairman, and that was *really* a mistake."

"Why?"

"Because his situation was very tenuous, and the other shareholders were upset with him, but he paid no mind to them. He thought he was in the right. He didn't understand, and they weren't loyal to *him,* they were only concerned about their own bank balances. I made them a huge offer, volunteered to put new management in, but it was the money that did it. Naturally. *Money talks,* Blackie. You taught me that when I was still a bairn."

He smiled at her, rose, and walked over to the balustrade of the terrace, looking down the long stretch of lawn. Suddenly he turned and nodded, saying swiftly, "Winston said Edwin finally sold his shares to Harte Enterprises."

"He did. He had no alternative."

"Winston calls it a coup for you, and I agree with him. But I'm surprised you didn't go to that board meeting."

"Why would I go? Winston was representing me."

"To witness Edwin's defeat, Emm."

Those beautiful green eyes turned flinty and cold. Emma drew herself up in the chair, her head held proudly, and said in a voice that was glacial, "Forty-five years ago I told Edwin Fairley I never wanted to see him again as long as I lived, and I haven't. You surely can't think that I want to set eyes on him now. Not you, Blackie. My one true friend."

"I don't suppose you would," he murmured, memories rushing at him. Once he'd been ready to horsewhip Edwin Fairley because of his treatment of Emma. And for a long time, many years in fact, he had regretted that he hadn't done so. Edwin had deserved it.

Emma said, "But all that's water under the bridge. However, Winston said Edwin seemed to look gratified at the meeting. I thought that was a strange thing to say, and I told him that more than likely it was *relief* he saw on Edwin's face."

"I can't imagine he'd be gratified, Emma. The *Gazette*'s been in the Fairley family for three generations. Now he's lost it to you."

She began to laugh. "*Relief,* Blackie, I've lifted a burden from Edwin's shoulders. For a second time."

"True, mavourneen," Blackie replied softly, his face bland. And then he thought that perhaps Edwin had indeed been relieved, but not for any reason Emma could conjure up.

"Grandy, Grandy, Grandy! Here I am!" Paula cried, the five-year-old child running along the terrace on her fat little legs, her summer frock billowing around her, her face full of smiles.

Emma jumped up, rushed forward to meet her granddaughter, exclaiming, "Not so fast, darling, I don't want you to fall!" Bending down, Emma caught hold of Paula and hugged her. "You mustn't run so fast, lovey."

The child looked at her solemnly; then she struggled free and ran to Blackie at the end of the terrace. "Uncle Blackie, hello, hello!"

Smiling in delight, Blackie bent over her, smoothing her dark curls gently with the palm of his hand. "And aren't you just the most beautiful girl, mavourneen," he said softly, his black eyes full of love for this child.

"Shane, I want Shane, Uncle Blackie. *Where's Shane?*" she demanded.

"He's at school, me darlin'."

"Can he come and play tomorrow?"

"I'm sure he can, Paula."

She clapped her hands. "Oh good."

As she came toward them, Blackie looked up, and his breath caught in his throat. From even this short distance she looked as she had when she was a girl, her red-gold hair shimmering in the sunlight. And she was as beautiful to him now as she had been then . . . so many years ago when he had met his little starveling girl on those mist-filled moors and followed her to that wretched house, Fairley Hall. An involuntary shiver ran through him.

When Emma came to a stop, she looked up into his face and said with a frown, "You look so sorrowful, Blackie. Is something wrong?"

"No, not anymore, mavourneen. Not anymore." He gave her a bright smile, leaned over the child, and kissed Emma's cheek. "But I just want you to know you're still my young colleen of the moors. And you will be till the day I die."

30

The moment Glynnis walked into the office Emma felt as though she had never left. In an instant, a decade fell away, and Emma was back in the war years. Memories came at her in full flood, bringing a lump to her throat.

She hurried across the floor of her office, and the two women embraced affectionately. Standing away from her former secretary, Emma looked into her face and smiled. "Glynnis, you've hardly changed!" she exclaimed. "You look just the same, perhaps a tiny bit thinner, but as lovely as you always were."

"I'm a few years older now, Mrs. Harte, but thank you. And you never get a day older, I must say."

Emma chuckled as the two of them walked to the seating arrangement at one end of her office in the London store. "I'll let you in on a secret," Emma confided as they sat down opposite each other. "I was sixty-one this past April, not that I feel it, mind you. Actually, I still feel like a young woman inside."

"And that's how you look," Glynnis answered, meaning it.

"I did want to take you to lunch, Glynnis dear, but you said you preferred to have tea, and you mentioned a problem when we spoke on the phone. Is there something the matter?"

"Oh no, Mrs. Harte. It's just that . . . well, you see, I brought Owen with me to England. My parents haven't seen him since he was a baby, and he's with me now, in London. He does like his lunch, it's his favorite meal. That's the only reason I suggested tea."

Emma shook her head, suddenly laughing. "He could have come to lunch with us, you know. And let's not forget, he's *my* grandson, too. I'm so glad he's here. I haven't seen him since he was a toddler."

"He's a nice boy, I'm proud of him." Glynnis hesitated, then went on in a lowered voice, "He looks like Robin."

"Does he really?" Emma responded, her vivid green eyes lighting up with interest. Leaning forward, she asked, "And where is Owen now?"

"With my cousin Gwyneth. She's taken him to the zoo. She's married now and lives in Hampstead, but it's only a small flat, so I decided it was better for us to go to a hotel. That's why we're at the Hyde Park."

"I understand. And she's well, is she? Your cousin, I mean."

"Oh yes. No children yet, but she's very happily married . . ." Glynnis let her sentence trail off.

There was a little silence.

Emma sat back on the sofa, scrutinizing Glynnis Hughes intently, her mind full of questions. She couldn't help wondering if Glynnis was happy in her marriage to Richard Hughes, if it had worked, still was working. Although Glynnis continued to write to her on a regular basis, she never said much about Richard or referred to her domestic life.

Becoming aware of Emma's scrutiny, Glynnis cleared her throat. "You're staring at me, Mrs. Harte. Now it's my turn to ask if something's wrong."

"Not at all, Glynnis, I was just wondering if *your* marriage had worked out all right. You never really reveal anything in your letters. At least about Richard. But I always thought he was such a nice young man."

"He is, and it's fine. I mean everything's good. The marriage is sound, and he does love Owen so very much. Richard's treated him like his own child since the day he was born, but then you know that. And he's never asked me who the father was. He's a good man, and kind."

"Then my judgment of him was correct. I never doubted him, Glynnis, and I'm glad you have him. By the way, why didn't he come with you?"

"To tell you the truth, he didn't want to come. You see, in the past year his business has grown by leaps and bounds. He's doing really well with his antiques shop in Manhattan; he's even done some interior design for a couple of clients who collect English Georgian furniture. He's an expert in that field. Anyway, he has a couple of big jobs at the moment, and nothing ever interferes with *his* business." A smile suddenly played around Glynnis's mouth. "He's like you in that way, Mrs. Harte. I'm sure that's why I understand him so well, because I worked for you."

They both laughed in a conspiratorial way, and then there was a sudden knock on the door and it opened. Alice, Emma's secretary, popped her head around it and asked, "Shall I bring the tea in now, Mrs. Harte?"

"Yes, thank you, Alice." Looking across at Glynnis, Emma asked, "What are your plans for the weekend?"

Her guest gave a little shrug. "I don't really have any. I thought I'd take Owen to Hampton Court, do a few jaunts like that. I want him to know his other country . . . my country."

"How about showing him Yorkshire?" Emma suggested, an auburn brow lifting. Seeing the surprise crossing Glynnis's face, she continued, "I think you ought to bring Owen to Yorkshire, to stay at Pennistone Royal with me. For the weekend. I'm leaving tonight, and if you travel up tomorrow you can spend Friday night, Saturday, and Sunday. I'm sure he'd enjoy it, my dear."

"Oh, Mrs. Harte, that would be lovely, but are you sure?" Glynnis's blue eyes sparkled.

"Absolutely positive, and I would love to get to know Owen. In a way, I feel as if I do already, because your letters are very enlightening, but having the boy around me in the flesh, so to speak, would be . . . well, it would make me very happy."

"There's just one thing." Glynnis paused, her face changing. She gave Emma a worried look. "*He* won't be around, will he? **I wou**ldn't want to run into him."

"No, no. He **always** calls if he's going to pop in to see me, but usually **he** stays in London these days. He's made a success of being a Member of Parliament."

Glynnis merely nodded, not trusting herself to say his name or ask any questions.

Alice came in with the tea tray and put it on the coffee table between them; then, smiling at Emma, she hurried out.

After pouring the tea and passing a cup to Glynnis, Emma said, "Tomkins is driving me to Yorkshire later, but I'll arrange a car and driver for you, Glynnis. For tomorrow morning."

"No, no, I don't want you to do that, Mrs. Harte! It's

kind of you, but we can come on the train to Harrogate. Really, that'll be—"

"I think you'd better come by car," Emma cut in. "The trains can be slow, and therefore often late. However, if you prefer to drive yourself, you can borrow my Riley, that's no problem at all."

"If you're sure, Mrs. Harte," Glynnis began, nodding. "I think I'd like that, and certainly it's a chance for Owen to see the English countryside."

"So it's settled then." Emma said, beaming at her former secretary. "I'm looking forward to our weekend. The three of us will have fun."

"We've now become the biggest newspaper proprietors in the north," Emma said, gazing at Winston across the desk. "But I want to expand further, I want to own . . . a *national*."

Winston looked back at her, as usual taking everything in his stride. Long ago he had ceased to be surprised by Emma. She was a wonder to him, a wonder to them all, and she had expanded her business empire enormously since the end of the war. He knew she had done it by using a combination of determination, sheer nerve, and hard work. She was a genuine tycoon now.

"You're not saying anything, Winston."

"I was just thinking . . . thinking that there're no newspapers for sale at the moment, our Emm, as far as *I* know, anyway. National *dailies* I'm talking about."

"I know that. And I've been thinking, too. . . . Perhaps we ought to start one of our own. From scratch."

"Good God, Emma, that'll cost a fortune!"

"And buying one wouldn't? Come on, you know I'd have to pay through the nose if I attempted to buy an existing newspaper. It might even be cheaper, starting one."

"Well, let's not rush in. Remember what Henry Rossiter always says. Fools—"

"Rush in where angels fear to tread," Emma interrupted him. "But I've done that all my life. So I guess I'm a fool," she quipped, laughing, her eyes full of spirit.

"Nobody could call you that. Many other things, but not a fool," Winston declared.

"Let's at least think about it, Winston," she said, her tone a shade lighter. "Also, when I saw Blackie last Friday I asked him about the land we looked at last week, that bombed out building site. He thinks we should buy it, since it *is* a commercial property and it could become very valuable."

Winston nodded. "To tell you the truth, it is already, Emma. Very valuable, in fact, and I was going to suggest we put in a bid for it on Monday."

"Yes, do it, Winston. Blackie said we can't go wrong."

Emma stood up, walked over to the big window in the upstairs parlor, glancing out. The weather was sunny and warm, as it had been for the past week. Her gardens were beginning to look truly beautiful, and she made a mental note to tell Mr. Ramsbotham, the head gardener, how pleased she was. She would also give a word of praise to Wiggs, his nephew, who would take over from him one day. They had done a wonderful job with the parterres.

Finally swinging around to face Winston again, she said, "You'll never guess who I had tea with in London yesterday."

"I'm sure I won't, you know so many people. So why don't you tell me?"

"Glynnis . . . the lovely Glynnis Jenkins from Wales."

"Good Lord, is she here from New York?" He grinned. "Well, of course she is, that's a daft question. How long is she staying? I'd like to see her again."

"Several weeks I think, and I invited her up to York-shire for a couple of days, with her little boy, Owen."

"How old is he now?" Winston asked.

"He's six, and quite a smart little lad from what she's said. Anyway, she was thrilled to be invited, and she's arriving today. I was always very fond of Glynnis."

"Weren't we all?" Winston murmured succinctly and looked off into the distance.

"What do you mean?" she asked, detecting a strange note in her brother's voice.

"I didn't mean anything actually, except that she was always tremendously popular, and she was such a lovely person, I think we were all a little bit infatuated with her. Not only the men but you, too, our Emma, and some of the other women at Harte's. Glynnis had the knack of making everyone love her, and she was very beautiful."

"She still is," Emma remarked. "A little thinner, but there's an aura of glamour to her that will never fade, I don't suppose. It comes from inside, glamour, although not everyone understands that. It's nothing to do with the length of one's hair or the color of one's eyes."

Hovering near the fireplace, Emma continued after a moment, "I thought you and Charlotte might like to come to lunch tomorrow, or on Sunday. Or perhaps supper tomorrow evening. If you're free, that is. It's up to you. I can ask Blackie, too, he's always at a loose end."

"We'd enjoy that. Charlotte likes Glynnis, she always thought she was the best secretary I'd ever had. I'll ask her when we can come over for a meal. Anyway, I thought Blackie always came on Fridays for supper."

"He does, but he can come on Saturday as well, can't he?"

Winston chuckled. "You and Blackie might as well tie the knot, you're always together."

Emma stared at him in surprise.

"Don't look like that, lass. Blackie adores you, he always has. You just went off and married other men, that's what *you* did."

"I love Blackie, I always have, for as long as I've known him, and he's my best friend. But I don't want to get married again."

"Not even to that handsome American major?" Winston teased, his eyes full of mischief.

Emma gave him a long, blank stare and asked haughtily, "Which American major?"

"Don't pretend you don't know who I mean . . . the one you met at our brother's house," Winston shot back.

"Oh *him*. . . . I thought you were referring to *my* American major, my nice pilot who I used to entertain here during the war."

"I never knew about that," Winston replied, looking at her in astonishment.

"Well, I don't have to tell you everything, you know."

"Who was he?"

"He still is, Winston, he didn't get killed or die. His name's James Thompson, and he's been to see me several times since the end of the war. He's a good friend."

"How did you meet him?"

"He was stationed at Topcliffe, and I used to give Fourth of July parties. I had them over often . . . James and the whole crew."

"I see." Winston looked at her carefully and wondered, suddenly, about Emma. He'd never known her to be secretive, but certainly she had been about this major. Was she involved with him in a romantic way? "Don't you ever feel lonely, our Emm?" he blurted out before he could stop himself.

"How could I ever feel lonely, Winston dear, with your lot running in and out and looking over my shoulder? And Blackie, too. I'm always surrounded."

Emma knew exactly what Glynnis had meant when she said Owen looked like Robin. The six-year-old boy was a small replica of her favorite son; he had the same dark hair, and those vivid blue eyes that were one of Robin's best features. Even the shape of the child's face was the same, and when he grew up he would be tall and slender, as was Robin.

As he came to a standstill in front of her, the boy gave her a tentative smile and put out his hand. "I'm Owen Hughes," he said, being scrupulously polite.

Emma gave him a wide smile and took his small hand in hers. "My name's Emma Harte, and welcome to Pennistone Royal."

"Thank you, and I'm pleased to meet you."

"We actually know each other, Owen, we met long ago. But I'm afraid you won't remember. You were just a little baby and then later a toddler."

He frowned and looked up at Glynnis, his intelligent eyes full of questions.

Bending over him, Glynnis explained, "It's true, Owen. Mrs. Harte did know you when you were a baby, but we left England when you were quite small, and we haven't seen Mrs. Harte since then."

"And more's the pity," Emma murmured, moving across the terrace, sitting down. "I've missed watching you grow up, Owen, and I'm sorry about that. You're quite a tall boy for six, aren't you?"

"Like my father," he explained solemnly. "Dad's tall. And dark and handsome, Mom says. And it's true."

Emma chuckled, and even Glynnis smiled and said, "It's so nice of you to have us for the weekend. I've always loved this house. Very tranquil, and it's such a treat to be here."

"I'm glad you could come, and it is indeed quiet, but I get a great deal of joy out of it, Glynnis. Now, Owen, come and sit next to me on this little seat. We can have a chat until Hilda brings the tea. Do you like strawberries and cream?"

He nodded, his eyes focused entirely on her, and he decided he liked her. His mother had told him she had once worked for Mrs. Harte.

"Good. Because that's what we're going to have. There's nothing like strawberries and cream on a warm June day in Yorkshire. Now tell me about your journey."

"Mom drove here, and I saw a lot of sheep and cows in the fields. Do you have any cows?"

"Certainly," Emma replied. "And later you can go with Tommy, the farm lad, he'll take you to see them. Do you like animals?"

"Yes, but I don't want to be a farmer. I'm going to be the president of the United States."

"Are you now, Owen? Well, that's a truly wonderful ambition!"

"Dad says anybody can be president if they're clever, and work hard. And if they're good. I can work, and Dad says I'm clever." Owen nodded his head, looked across at Glynnis, and asked, "I am good, aren't I, Mom?"

"You're the best boy in the whole world, and—" Glynnis felt all of the strength drain out of her as she stared at the man walking along the terrace toward them. Her chest tightened. It was Robin Ainsley. The last person in the world she wanted to see. She was gripped by an internal shaking, and her mouth was dry.

Robin lost all of his color when he saw Glynnis, and then the child. *His child.* Oh my God, he thought, wondering why he had come to see his mother today of all days. He should have phoned first, he usually did. There was no way he could retreat now. But he *was* frightened . . . of her, and of himself most of all. He had never stopped loving her or dreaming about holding her and making love to her. Theirs had been such an all-consuming passion: Together they had soared. . . .

And, oh, how desirable she looked this afternoon. She was wearing a blue silk frock, the exact color of the sky, the exact color of her eyes. And her face was ravishing. She was around thirty now, just as he was, and these few additional years truly became her. Her hair was worn in the same soft pageboy he remembered, and it was luxuriant, a deep chestnut color touched with natural streaks of gold. God, how he wanted her again. But he couldn't have her. He had renounced her, and he knew how much he had hurt her. She could never want him, not ever again. And she was forbidden to him anyway, he understood that. But he could dream, couldn't he?

As Robin came to a stop, he looked across at his mother. Emma's face was inscrutable. He hurried over and kissed her on the cheek. "Hello, Ma."

"Hello, Robin, darling," she murmured and then hissed against his ear, "Why didn't you phone?" Drawing herself up, Emma added in a normal voice, "You remember Glynnis, don't you?"

"Yes," he managed and had no option but to walk across to the only woman he had ever truly loved. His legs felt unexpectedly weak. "Hello, Glynnis," he said and was relieved he sounded so normal. Robin offered her his hand.

"Robin," she answered in a low, throaty voice and reluctantly took his outstretched hand.

He discovered her hand was icy, and he wanted to hold on to it, to warm it, but he could not. He let it go.

Turning around, he looked down at her little boy, *his* little boy, and said, "I'm Robin. . . . *Hello.*"

"I'm Owen, and I'm pleased to meet you." He was very solemn.

"Mind if I join you all, old chap?" Robin asked, smiling warmly.

"Oh no. That's all right. Isn't it, Mom?"

All Glynnis could do was nod.

Emma explained, "Robin is my son, Owen, just as you are your mother's son."

And mine, Robin thought, as he sat down in one of the wrought-iron garden chairs. He had an overwhelming need to hug this boy. This was their love child. His and Glynnis's.

Suddenly Emma said, "Oh, Robin, would you please go and ask Hilda to bring another cup and saucer for you?"

Robin excused himself and went through the French doors into the library.

Glynnis looked across at Emma, unable to speak, especially in Owen's presence.

At once Emma recognized the look in her eyes. It was one of pure terror. Leaning closer to Owen, Emma said to him, "Do me a little favor, run after Robin. He's gone to the kitchen. Just through those doors and across the big Stone Hall. Ask him to please bring me a glass of water."

"Will I find the kitchen?" Owen asked, a bit tremulously, staring at her.

"You're a clever boy, of course you will," she reassured him.

Once they were alone, Emma explained in a quick, low voice, "This is an accident, Glynnis, truly it is. Robin always telephones me if he's coming, to make sure I'm here. For some reason he didn't today."

Glynnis could not speak. Tears filled her eyes. All she could do was nod. She had never stopped loving him. *Robin.* The name she could barely say . . . except when she was alone and wept into her pillow. *Robin Ainsley.* The only man she had ever loved . . . would ever love. Oh, to have him hold her in his arms once more, what she would give for that. Nothing else. Just that. To be in his arms for a few brief moments.

As if from a distance she heard Emma saying, "You mustn't see him, Glynnis. You mustn't see him alone."

31

It was seven years since he had seen her. Seven long years. But he knew he was already entrapped again . . . longing to be with her, to hold her in his arms, if only for a moment. He would settle for that, or less . . . a few minutes talking to her, just holding her hand.

He had been married for six years, had a small child, a son. His name was Jonathan. But little Jonny was very much his mother's child, a lot more like Valerie in appearance than like him. A handsome, fair-haired boy, but there was not much Harte in him, at least so it seemed to Robin.

It was the other son, *her* child, Owen, who was so obviously out of his loins. The boy was his spitting image, even down to his hands. He had noticed the boy's long, tapering fingers on Friday afternoon. Had his mother seen the likeness? Perhaps. And did it matter? Of course not. He had been quite certain for some years that his mother had known of his love affair with Glynnis. She was shrewd and smart, and understood the human heart.

Furthermore, she and Glynnis were close. Perhaps Glynnis had even confided in his mother, but *he* would never know that because Emma would never betray a confidence.

As he drove at a steady speed along the main Harrogate Road on Saturday night, heading from Leeds to Pennistone Royal, he thought of his mother's reaction yesterday. She had been perturbed by his unexpected arrival. Yet she had hidden her irritation behind her now famous inscrutable mask. She was good at that, disguising her real feelings.

A smile struck his face as he thought of Emma. They locked horns at times and could often quarrel. But he really loved his mother, respected her, and he knew he was her favorite son. Still, he didn't think she would approve of what he was about to do. Neither did he. Put simply, he couldn't help himself. He had to speak to Glynnis in person.

Now he asked himself if she would listen. Or would he get the door slammed in his face? He wasn't sure. All he knew was that he had to see her.

As Robin drove up to the back of Pennistone Royal, he saw that the house was dark except for a couple of upstairs rooms: his mother's and Glynnis's. Earlier that day his mother had told him that she was dining alone with Glynnis, that Winston and Charlotte were coming for lunch on Sunday. He had thought of cajoling an invitation out of her for the lunch but decided not to put her on the spot. It wasn't fair.

Parking near a copse of trees, Robin got out of the Humber and closed the car door gently. Then he walked quickly toward the service entrance of the house.

He glanced up. It was a beautiful June night, the sky a blue so deep it was almost black and filled with an abundance of shining stars. There was a gorgeous full moon, perfectly spherical and brilliant, and it lighted his way.

Fumbling in his jacket pocket, Robin pulled out the key to the kitchen door, which he had owned since he was a teenager, and let himself in, being careful to lock the door behind him. Moving quietly across the floor, he pushed open the door which led to the back service corridor.

Within seconds he was climbing a steep staircase. Bypassing the first floor, his mother's entire domain, he went on and finally opened the door to the bedroom floor. He stepped into the corridor and made his way to the Blue Room, knowing *she* was the occupant of that suite.

Owen had told him yesterday, when he had taken the child to see the cows. He had confided proudly he was in the Gold Room, all alone. The boy had also explained that they were staying at the Hyde Park Hotel in London. It had taken only a little prompting from him, and Owen had innocently revealed quite a lot. What pleased Robin was that the child appeared to like him.

The corridor was dimly lit by the moon shining in through the tall window at the far end. Robin tiptoed down the carpeted hallway until he came to the door with the brass plaque engraved *Blue Room*. After tapping lightly, he stood waiting.

Several seconds passed before the door was opened a crack.

When Glynnis saw him, her eyes widened in astonishment. He brought a finger to his lips, making a shushing sound. Pushing against the door, he slipped into the room before she could stop him.

Glynnis stepped back swiftly, glaring at him.

Robin closed the door, leaned against it, and said in a whisper, "I have to talk to you."

She backed away and moved across the sitting room floor quickly, stood leaning against the desk in front of the window. Then realizing, all of a sudden, that she was dressed only in a flimsy silk nightgown, she flew into the bedroom.

He remained leaning nonchalantly against the door, although he didn't feel at all nonchalant. He was also instructing himself not to follow her. Aware from their days together of her modesty, he was certain she had simply gone to get a robe. And a moment later she reappeared, wearing a blue silk kimono over the nightdress.

Robin locked the door and walked toward her.

"Why have you locked the door?" she hissed, her blue eyes angry, her face strained, even fearful.

"For no other reason than our son, Owen. If he wakes up he might come looking for you. This way, he won't be able to open the door. And I can go into the bedroom until you've taken him back to his own room. Do you follow my reasoning?"

Glynnis said nothing.

Robin said, "He shouldn't see me in here, especially late at night."

"Nobody should."

"I know."

"What actually *do* you want?" she demanded, her eyes growing icier by the minute. But he noticed that she was trembling uncontrollably.

"To talk to you, Glynnis."

"I've nothing to say to *you*."

"But I do, to you. I realize this is not the time and place. I came to ask you to meet me when you come back to town."

"I won't!" she snapped.

"In case you change your mind . . ." He searched around in his pocket, took out an envelope. "In here there's an address and a latchkey. I want you to have them."

"Why?"

"I want you to meet me there next week. Just to talk. I need to talk to you."

"I told you I don't want to listen to *you* about anything."

"The address—it's for Edwina's mews house in Belgravia. Her bolt-hole when she comes over from Ireland. There's a phone number as well. Please, Glynnis, come and meet me. On Wednesday." He offered her the envelope, but she crossed her arms tightly and pursed her lips, her eyes suddenly flinty as she stepped to one side.

Placing the envelope on the desk, Robin continued, "I just want to tell you why things happened the way they did. That's it, really."

"Oh, Robin, please," she muttered, "you must go. *Now.*"

Without moving, he gave her a small smile. "The boy is so handsome, Glynnis, and bright, and very well mannered."

She was silent.

Suddenly, he made a move toward her. Before she could utter a word of protest, or run, his arms were around her, and he was pressing her against his tall, lean body. "Oh, Glynnis, Glynnis," he whispered hoarsely and then kissed the hollow of her neck, her cheeks, and finally his mouth found hers.

Against her will, she kissed him back and clung to him, murmured his name, and she felt him harden against her thigh. He wanted her. She wanted him. For a moment she nearly gave in, almost pulled him into the bedroom.

But she did not. With enormous resolve she pushed him away, but gently, and a sob caught in her throat.

"Oh, darling, please," he begged, his eyes riveted on hers; they were twin reflections of his own, not only in their color but in the overwhelming desire raging there.

"No, Robin, no."

"Yes, Glynnis, yes."

Shaking her head, walking to the door on trembling legs, she turned and looked at him intently. "Please, you must go."

"There's the phone number for Edwina's mews," he reminded her. "Please call me between twelve and twelve-thirty if you're not coming."

She was silent.

When he stopped at the door, he added softly, "You must let me know if you're not coming. *Promise?*"

All she had the strength to do was nod.

After he left she lay on the bed, thinking what a narrow escape she had had. She had almost succumbed to his charms, and where would she have been then? Not only hating herself for running back to him the moment he beckoned, but guilt ridden for sleeping with him. Richard was a good man, he had been good to Owen, and she knew he loved her with great devotion. She loved him back, in her own way, and she had endeavored to be a good wife, was as devoted as he. And she had been a good mother to Owen, perhaps that most of all.

Robin, oh, Robin . . . How I love you . . . how I want you. Close in my arms . . . She began to cry, and she wept until she thought there were no tears left.

The weekend passed without further incident. Robin didn't drop in to see his mother again, and Glynnis was shocked when she realized she was disappointed.

After chastising herself quietly, and reminding herself that she was a grown woman, not a silly teenager,

Glynnis managed to shake that feeling off. And she made a supreme effort to be her normal, cheerful self.

She had always got on well with Emma; they were extremely compatible, both being positive by nature. Glynnis was able to chat to her about anything in the world, and Emma responded in kind. So they talked about many things over breakfast on Sunday morning and when they took Owen for a walk before lunch. He ran ahead of them to the pond, shouting that he was going to feed the ducks, and they both smiled indulgently. Owen was in his element, that was obvious. All morning he ran and jumped, laughed and chatted to them both, and Glynnis was gratified to see the look of approval in Emma's eyes.

At one moment her former employer turned to her and exclaimed, "He's such a lovely little boy, Glynnis, you've done a good job with him. I hope you'll bring him to England next year and spend a little time with me as well as going to see your family in Wales."

"I hope I can come, Mrs. Harte. I know my mother's anxious I bring Owen to the Rhondda next year . . . we'll see."

Emma sighed and said in a wistful tone, "I do miss you, Glynnis. You were my friend, you know, not only my secretary, during the war. I've always been so very fond of you, and now . . . Well, he *is* my grandson. If things had worked out differently, you would have been my daughter-in-law."

Glynnis merely nodded and looked off into the distance; after a moment, she said, "I know what you mean, but I've believed in destiny all of my life. It was *Fate* . . . that's why things are the way they are. Most of the time matters are out of our hands. They're in the hands of . . . Fate."

She forced a smile and then went on swiftly, "Mrs.

Harte, there's something else I need to talk to you about . . . *the money.* You really don't have to send the allowance every month. It's far too much, and Richard can support us. I don't *need* the money."

"Oh goodness, Glynnis, I know Richard is doing well! And I certainly never meant the money to *undermine* him in any way. However, I do want to send it to you. Remember, you refused Robin's help during the war, and this is my way of . . . well, ensuring Owen's future, in a certain sense. Save the money; put it away in the bank and let it earn interest. When he's ready for college, you'll have quite a little nest egg for the boy. I am going to continue sending it, my dear, it's the least I can do. And that's that."

Once again Glynnis endeavored to protest, but without success. She knew from experience that once Emma's mind was made up she wouldn't budge. Eventually she nodded and thanked her former boss in her most gracious way. It was all she could do.

Winston and Charlotte came for lunch several hours later, and it was a lovely reunion. It soon became apparent that Emma's brother was impressed with Owen, and if he noticed a family resemblance he didn't let on. Winston had a reputation for being the family diplomat.

All too soon the lunch was over, Winston and Charlotte left, and Glynnis went upstairs to pack. They were leaving for London early the following morning. As she folded Owen's clothes and laid them in his suitcase, she found herself sighing with relief that the day had passed so calmly. All had been tranquil, without event.

Suddenly, Owen's voice piped up. "Mom, why didn't Robin come back to see me? When he took me to visit the cows, he said he'd see me later." Putting his book down on the table, the child ran over to where she was packing and tugged at her sleeve.

Glynnis looked down at him and forced a smile. "He's a busy man, darling. Maybe he just got caught up in work."

"Oh. I see." The child's disappointment was apparent, and he muttered, "I liked him a lot. He was so nice to me."

When Glynnis made no response, Owen went on, "He's a politician, Mom. He's going to take me to the House of Commons."

"Oh, I don't know about that—" she began.

"He is!" Owen cried passionately, interrupting her. "He *promised*. And I *know* he'll keep his promise."

Seeing that her little boy was really upset, she hugged him to her and said soothingly, "I know he'll keep his promise, Owen. Actually, I'm sure of it."

32

Glynnis had never meant to go. All her instincts had told her to stay away from him, but in the end she had given in to her tumultuous emotions.

On Wednesday morning she had awakened with tension in her body, a dull, nagging ache in the pit of her stomach, and unable to control herself, she had phoned her cousin Gwyneth before taking Owen down for breakfast.

Plunging in before she could change her mind, she told Gwyneth that she could "borrow" Owen for the day. This made her cousin exceedingly happy; childless, she longed to have a baby, and loving Owen the way she did she took great pleasure from taking him sightseeing. "He's wanted to go to the Tower of London for ages," Gwyneth explained enthusiastically. "I'll come and collect him at eleven, is that all right?"

Glynnis told her it was, relieved that Gwyneth was free, and that she hadn't suggested later in the afternoon for the jaunt to the Tower.

But Glynnis became furious with herself when, after breakfast, she did her hair and makeup so carefully, sprayed herself with scent, and chose her clothes with such precision, picking out the blue-silk dress with the flared skirt because years ago he had said he loved her in blue.

When Owen had left with Gwyneth, excited to be going on this unexpected treat, she had begun to dress. After pulling on sheer silk stockings and a blue garter belt, she put on blue satin cami-knickers trimmed with blue lace, and finally stepped into a pair of high-heeled shoes. They showed off her legs to great advantage, and Robin had often told her that she had the loveliest legs in the world. Finally, she slipped into the dress and gazed at herself in the mirror, quite pleased by her appearance.

But a second later she felt wretched, and disgusted. Because she was going to *him*. It wasn't right. She knew that only too well. But she also knew she couldn't stop herself.

Now, getting out of the cab in Belgrave Square, she hesitated. It would be best not to go, she told herself firmly. She did not trust Robin. Nor did she trust herself, and being alone with him could only spell trouble. Even Emma had warned her of *that*.

Walking slowly around the square, she found herself growing more nervous than ever. She glanced at her watch and sucked in her breath. It was already twelve-fifteen. When he had come to her room at Pennistone Royal, he had asked her to phone by twelve-thirty. Frantically, her eyes sought out a phone box. There wasn't one in sight.

She stood perfectly still for a moment, panic rushing through her. *What to do? What to do?* And then, taking a deep breath, she crossed the square purposefully, hurried to the mews in one of the side streets just off the square.

Several seconds later Glynnis was ringing the bell of Edwina's house.

He opened the door immediately. Although he didn't smile or betray any emotion on his face, she saw the flash of happiness in his blue eyes the moment he saw her.

He was unable to speak.

So was she.

Silently, he opened the door a little wider; she stepped inside, hurried into a large, rather charming living room. As she moved past him, she was careful not to brush against him. Being in his presence was bad enough; if she touched him she would fall apart.

After closing the door, Robin walked into the middle of the room, stood staring at her. They were just a few feet apart.

Swallowing hard, he said at last, "I was waiting for you to phone."

She simply stared back, her legs shaking.

"Why did you come—just like this?" he asked softly.

"I couldn't help myself," she said, her voice sounding hoarse to her.

He gazed at her intently, wanting to hold her yet feeling nervous. And he was afraid to say the wrong thing, or to approach her, for fear she might bolt.

Glynnis gazed back, mesmerized by him. She thought she was going to burst into tears and stifled the sob rising in her throat.

As he continued to look at her, Robin noted the look of longing on her face. It reflected how he was feeling, and unable to hold back any longer, he took a step forward and so did she. They moved at the same moment, fell into each other's arms as if in desperation.

He held her against him tightly, whispering her name over and over again, smoothing his hand down her back. He was filled with the most extraordinary relief to be holding her like this at long last. After all these years, there was a sudden absence of pain.

Glynnis held on to him tightly. She thought that if he let go of her she would fall.

"Glynnis, darling, you're shaking. Don't be afraid . . . afraid of me. I won't do anything . . . anything you don't want me to do. I just need to hold you like this," Robin reassured her.

She moved slightly so that she could look up into his face.

Blue eyes locked with blue eyes.

She parted her lips as if to express a thought, but no words came out. After a moment, she whispered, "I'm not afraid . . . just nervous."

"So am I." Robin bent his head, kissed her fully on the mouth, and Glynnis kissed him back, felt as though she were slowly dissolving into him.

Without letting go of each other, they stumbled toward the sofa near the fireplace, fell onto it, lay entwined in each other's arms. Pushing himself up, Robin studied her face, hardly daring to believe she was here with him like this. He began to kiss her forehead, her cheeks, the hollow of her neck. Moving a strand of dark hair away from her face, he said gently, "I just need to be near you. . . . All these years I've ached for you, Glynnis. If you don't want to—"

Glynnis brought a finger to his lips. "I *do* want to . . . make love," she responded, her voice low. "I want *you*, Robin. . . . It's been so long since we've been together. Seven years."

He touched her face, let his hand trail down across her breast, and then slowly he began to unbutton her dress. But in a moment she stopped him and said quietly, "Take your jacket off, Robin, please."

Standing up, he did so, threw it on a chair, went to the door, slid the bolt, then closed the draperies. As he came back to her, he pulled off his tie, began to unbutton his shirt.

She rose from the sofa, stood in front of him, let her dress fall in a pool at her feet as he took off his shirt. Robin came toward her, wrapping his arms around her once again. And he led her to the sofa, made her stretch out on it; then he lay down next to her.

And very slowly he began to make love to her, touching her neck, her breasts, sliding his hand inside the satin underwear. He touched her breast lightly with his fingertips, bent his head to kiss the nipple. Then he looked up, stared into her eyes. There was enormous intensity in his voice as he said, "I love you, Glynnis, I've never stopped loving you. . . . Tell me you feel the same."

"You know I do, oh, you do know that, Robin. There's only ever been you. Only you can make me feel this way."

"It's the same for me," he said, a catch in his voice. "I belong to you, Glynnis. For always. I will be yours as long as I live. And you will always be mine, no matter what you think."

"Robin, oh, Robin," she whispered.

"Take this off, darling," he said suddenly, touching her underwear. Then he unfastened her garters and slowly rolled down her stockings one at a time. Once she was completely naked on the sofa, he finished undressing and rejoined her.

Lost in each other, they stroked and explored; after seven years apart they craved each other desperately, longed to be joined together.

Within moments Robin was bending over her, kissing her breasts and her thighs. And as his tongue slid down her stomach, went directly to the core of her, she let out a long sigh of pleasure. Slowly, he began to kiss her where no other man had.

In a moment she was shuddering with pleasure and crying his name, telling him how much she wanted him, and swiftly he positioned himself over her, slid inside her, took her to him exultantly, repeating her name over and over as he pushed his hands under her buttocks and brought her closer to him. She felt the heat flowing through her; she matched his passion and his ardor, and it was as if they had never been parted. They finally crested on a wave of love and emotion, and Robin called her name as he possessed her completely.

They lay together on the sofa for a long time, holding each other as if they were genuinely afraid to let go.

After a short while Robin said, "I *did* want to talk to you. I wasn't setting out to seduce you."

"I know that. And you didn't seduce me. It was a great example of the most splendid cooperation, wasn't it?"

"No better description! But just listen a moment, Glynnis, please. Look, I'm sorry I abandoned you when I did. But you and I had broken up when you came to tell me you were pregnant. And I—"

"Robin, this is not at all necessary," she cut in. "I *do* know all this. You'd become involved with Valerie by the time I appeared again to inform you that you were about to be a father. I truly understand your position, especially now. Also, I *was* difficult in those days, so volatile, anxiety ridden, and—"

"You were young, and so was I. It was wartime, and I was in the air in a Spitfire most of the time, dropping bombs on Germany and risking my life. I was as volatile as you were in my own way. We were all under massive strain. It was war, for God's sake."

"That's quite true, yes," Glynnis agreed. "I'm much calmer now. After all, I'm thirty, like you, a mature woman, a mother, a wife . . ."

There was a slight hesitation before Robin asked quietly, in a subdued voice, "Is it happy . . . your marriage?"

"In its own way, yes. You see, it does work, Robin. Richard loves me, and he adores Owen. He takes care of us very well, he's a good man."

"Do you love him?" He hated himself for asking this question, but he had to know how she felt. He could hardly bear to think of her with Richard Hughes. Or any other man, for that matter. What a terrible fool he'd been, letting her go.

She took a while to answer. Eventually she said, "Yes, I do. In a different way than . . . *us*. Let me put it this way, I do love Richard, but I'm not *in love* with him." She swiveled her eyes, looked straight at Robin. "And your marriage?"

"I suspect it's pretty much like yours," he replied. "It works, Glynnis. There's stability there, and Valerie's very practical, somewhat placid. Doesn't rock boats. And she's a good mother to Jonathan. Furthermore, she lets me have my life."

Glynnis stiffened next to him. "What life? What do you mean?"

He recognized that flash of jealousy he had been so familiar with in the past. "Oh God, *no*, Glynnis! Not other women. There are no women . . . just you. My one true love." He looked down at her. "Valerie never interferes, gives me enormous freedom to pursue my politics."

"I'm glad she does. Because that's what you always wanted. To be a politician, a Member of Parliament. I think you might even want to be Prime Minister one day."

"I want you, Glynnis," he shot back.

"Oh, Robin, darling, *don't*. We're both settled, married."

"I know." He sighed. "I want you always in my arms. It's such a relief to be with you. I can say anything I want to you, anything at all, and I can be myself. No pretense. I don't feel that with anyone else."

"I feel the same. I know whatever I say, you won't be shocked."

There was a pause.

"Are you hungry?" he suddenly asked.

"No. You?"

He shook his head. "Where's . . . *our* son?"

"My cousin Gwyneth took him to the Tower of London. He's been longing to go, and fortunately she was free to take him . . . so I could come to you."

"I'm glad you did . . . come to me," he murmured. "I can hardly bear the thought that you have to leave, go back to the States."

There was no response.

Robin said, "I want to see Owen again. Can I, darling?"

"I don't think you should, Robin. But only because he's such a little chatterbox. He might say something to Richard, mention your name. He's sort of fallen for you."

This brought a smile to his face. He said, "But Richard knows you know me. We all knew each other when we used to go to my mother's canteen for the troops. I know the boy's my look-alike, but Richard might not put two and two together."

"He just might."

Robin smiled at her. "Yes, you're right. It's best to be careful. I want to see you tomorrow. And the day after, and the day after that. Every day whilst you're here."

Glynnis looked stunned. "Robin, I don't know—there's Owen."

"Try to arrange it, my darling. Please. How long do we have today?"

He sounded desperate, and she glanced at him. "Until six. I must get back by six-thirty. Gwyneth and her husband are coming to dinner tonight. She'll go back to the hotel around five to wait for me, she has my room key."

"Talking of keys, please keep that latchkey for this house. It'll make me feel better, knowing you have it."

"If you're sure . . . I mean, what—"

"Oh, I'm sure all right," he exclaimed. "Come to me. Let me hold you the way I used to." Robin wrapped his body around hers. "This is what I've missed all these years, being entwined with the only woman I've ever loved."

She smiled against his arm. "I love you so much."

"And I you, Glynnis." He touched her mouth with his fingertips, kissed her, closing his eyes as he did. A moment later he was fondling her breasts. Their lovemaking started all over again, and so it went for most of the afternoon.

It was one of those lovely, balmy evenings in the middle of June. The sky was a soft, pale blue, with puffy white clouds scudding along the horizon. Although the sun had set some time ago, the evening sky had a wonderful shimmering clarity, and the Thames reflected that light.

Robin Ainsley took in all this as he stood on the terrace of the House of Commons, staring down the river toward Big Ben. He frequently came here in the summer for tea with a colleague or special guests. But he loved it most at this time of day in the summer months. There was a feeling of tranquillity here. It was a view that he treasured, the ancient river going down to the sea. Seen from this great seat of power, it seemed so special.

Robin leaned against the balustrade, his mind awash with diverse thoughts: *Glynnis*. The woman he loved and wanted to keep forever in his life. Their son: *Owen*. A most blessed little boy, so much like him, even more so than his other son, Jonathan.

More than anything else Robin wanted to spend time with Owen, a miniature replica of himself, but he could not. Glynnis would not permit it. There was nothing he could do. He knew he had relinquished any rights he had to the boy before he was even born.

In his mind's eye he saw them both . . .

Glynnis, lithesome, beautiful, the epitome of glamour, but without any vanity, soft and gentle. There was not one ounce of hardness in her. A warm and loving woman who loved him as much as he loved her. How easy it was to picture her in the blue dress, walking toward him, holding Owen's hand, the boy in his short gray pants and white summer shirt, both of them smiling, so happy to see him.

Oh God, what was he going to do about her? How could he ever let her go?

And then there was *Valerie*: his wife. So devoted to him; a calm, caring woman who loved him but was not in love with him, just as he was not in love with her. Yet she would be devastated if he left her and their small son, because her life revolved around him and his political career.

Robin was riddled with guilt about Valerie. Yet, oddly enough, not at all about his involvement with Glynnis. What Valerie didn't know couldn't hurt her, that was what he believed. His guilt sprang from the plans he was formulating in his head. Plans for a divorce. But then there was Richard Hughes. Would Glynnis agree to divorce Richard in order to come to him? He didn't know the answer to that; he was on the horns of a dilemma.

Who could he talk to? No one. Not his siblings, not even Edwina, to whom he was especially close. His mother? She would listen attentively and be sympathetic, but inevitably Emma would disapprove. Although she had lived with Paul McGill for sixteen years until his death, and he a married man, Paul had been separated from his wife long before he had met Emma. And there had been no divorce from Constance McGill because she was Roman Catholic. She had always refused to give Paul his freedom.

Robin knew Emma so well, and he could hear her telling him that it was not possible to build one's happiness on the unhappiness of another. That would be her attitude, and he knew it was right.

Suddenly tears welled, and Robin brushed his eyes, glanced around, relieved to see that the terrace was empty but for himself. Quite suddenly, anger rushed through him. Here he was, a man of thirty, weeping about a woman! Here on the terrace of the House of Commons, the place of his dreams, the place that was his whole life. How ridiculous he was being. Grow up, he chastised himself, anger still flaring inside. You let her go in 1943. You should have married her then.

Big Ben struck six, and he turned away, hurried to his office.

In an hour he would go to Edwina's mews cottage and wait for Glynnis. She had taken Owen to Wales for the past weekend and was leaving him there so he could spend a few days with his grandparents . . . before they left for the States.

His heart lifted. She would come to him soon, straight from the railway station. They had the whole evening ahead of them.

• • •

Robin was in the kitchen making himself a drink when he heard the door close, and he hurried out. Glynnis stood in the doorway, her suitcase at her feet, a wide smile on her lovely face.

"Darling," he exclaimed. "You got here sooner than I expected."

"I took an earlier train," she replied, her smile widening. "I just had to get back to you, Robin."

"I'm irresistible, I'm fully aware of that." He laughed.

"And so *modest*," she quipped, walking into his arms, holding on to him tightly, filled with such happiness she thought she would burst.

After a moment locked in their embrace, they stood apart, linked arms, and went into the kitchen. Robin fixed her a gin and tonic, and they returned to the living room, sat down on the sofa.

"Cheers, my sweet," he murmured, clinking his glass against hers.

"Cheers," she answered and took a sip of her drink.

"Tell me about your weekend in the Rhondda." Robin's eyes were fixed on her face. "Did Owen enjoy himself?"

Glynnis laughed, her bright blue eyes sparkling. "Yes, with his cousins, my brothers' children. As I told you, Dylan has two sons and Emlyn, a girl. They're a bit rambunctious, I'm afraid, but a good time was had by all, to quote Tiny Tim."

Robin smiled, touched her arm lightly, lovingly. "That makes me happy, knowing he's having a good time. And what did my darling girl do?" he asked.

"Nothing much. Visited family, helped my mother with her chores, did the shopping for her, and thought about you. *Constantly*."

"Likewise. You're rarely out of my thoughts."

She nodded. "Did you go to Yorkshire?"

"Yes, I went to Leeds. It's important to get back to my constituency whenever I can." Putting his glass of Scotch on the coffee table, he turned to her, took her drink, stood it next to his. Then he leaned closer, put his arms around her, kissed her passionately. She responded with equal passion, and after a moment, when they pulled away, he touched her face gently. He said in a low voice, "Let's go upstairs. I want you so much."

"I know, and I want you, Robin." She gave him a very direct look, finished, "But I want to talk to you for a moment first."

Her sudden seriousness brought him up short. "This sounds like bad news."

"Not bad news, Robin. Just a little bit of reality." Taking his hand in hers, she said slowly, "I know that you know how much I love you, more than anyone else in the world except for our child. I've always loved you, and marrying Richard didn't change that. You *do* know this, don't you?"

"Of course I do, and for the last few weeks I've been telling you the same thing." His face changed, became sad. "I made the worst mistake of my life when I let you go . . . and now I want you back. For always."

"*Listen to me.* Because I *do* love you with all my heart, I'm not going to let you ruin your political career because of me."

"Getting a divorce is not going to ruin it. This is 1950, don't forget that."

"I know what year it is, and perhaps you're right. But what if there's a scandal? What if I get dragged into it . . . by Valerie? I think she'd fight you if you attempted to divorce her, and I'm a woman, so I know women; we can fight dirty if there's a lot at stake. And what's at stake for her is you, your lifestyle, and your money."

"How could you be brought into it?" he protested, fearful of where this conversation was leading. He was determined to keep her. No matter the cost.

Glynnis was silent for a moment, then she said softly, speaking with great care, "I know what being a Member of Parliament means to you. I've always known. And actually you married Valerie because you thought she would make a better political wife than I would, a better wife for an ambitious politician like you."

"I won't deny that entirely," Robin answered quickly. "But it's not *all* true. Let's not forget that we *agreed* to split up. We were both crazy, not only crazy in love but crazy kids. We were too volatile together, Glynnis. Please don't deny that."

"I don't. We would have been a disaster together in those days."

"And now we're older. We've matured. We were stupid kids then, living through a world war. It could work now."

Ignoring his last comment, she said, "I know all this, we keep repeating it. Please let's not quarrel about what happened when we were in our early twenties. That's long gone, and—"

"I can't stand not being with you. I can't face that, Glynnis. I simply cannot." An ineffable sorrow struck his handsome face, and his blue eyes turned bleak.

"Neither can I. But I will not permit you to ruin your career for me. You're a young, very go-ahead MP. . . . Your constituents love you, you're highly successful. And there's even serious talk that you could be Prime Minister one day. You have an important life ahead. I won't let you change it, Robin. I will not have that on my conscience."

"Glynnis, honestly—"

She interrupted him. "I have an idea, a plan . . ."

"Tell me."

He listened, let her say everything that was on her mind, and when she had finished, he shook his head. "I don't know. . . . I don't know if it could work. . . . Anyway, that's not what I want, darling, not what I want at all."

"Neither do I. It's a compromise. But I haven't been able to think of anything better. Not yet."

He did not answer her.

She stood up, offered him her hand. "Come upstairs, Robin, let's make love. Let's seal our bargain with a kiss."

It seemed to Glynnis not only that their lovemaking was more passionate than usual but that it had a certain frenzy about it. And she knew this was because she was leaving at the end of the week.

She clung to him tightly, her hands moving down his back, up into his thick dark hair, and to the nape of his neck as she murmured his name, her voice urgent with her need for him. She moved with him rhythmically, her legs high around him, her head thrown back in pleasure, and when he convulsed unexpectedly, coming to a climax, so did she.

She held him in her arms until the light in the room dimmed and all went black.

∽

Much later, as they lay together, their need for each other slaked for the present, Glynnis flung one arm over his body and lay her head on his chest. His hand moved into her hair, but they said nothing, just lay together, lost in their myriad thoughts.

She contemplated their conversation of a short while before. She was aware she had averted disaster, had at least delayed the idea of him leaving his wife.

Sudden tears slid down her cheeks, fell onto his

chest, and he sat up at once, filled with alarm.

"Darling, what is it? What's wrong?" Worry ringed his face.

"Nothing," she said, smiling at him through her tears.

"Why are you crying then?"

"I'm missing you already," she whispered.

"But it's just au revoir."

She was silent.

"You *are* coming back to me, aren't you?" Robin asked in a low, concerned voice. "Promise me, Glynnis."

"I promise," she answered, wondering if she would have to break her pledge.

Part Three

~

ANGELS SINGING

Winter 2001

The world in solemn stillness lay
To hear the angels sing.

—"It Came Upon the Midnight Clear,"
EDMUND HAMILTON SEARS, 1849

33

It was Saturday, December first, and in a short while Linnet O'Neill would go to the church in the village of Pennistone Royal on the arm of her father, Shane. There she would marry her childhood sweetheart, Julian Kallinski. And with their nuptials the three clans—the Hartes, the O'Neills, and the Kallinskis—would finally be united in marriage.

At this moment, Linnet stood in the middle of her bedroom at Pennistone Royal, wearing her wedding gown. She thought it was the most wonderful creation, made of cream-colored, heavy duchesse satin, cream-colored guipure lace, and thousands of tiny pearls and crystal beads.

Evan had designed the gown, and it was she who stood staring at Linnet. Her head was to one side, and she was studying the gown intently, taking in every detail, looking for tiny flaws she might have missed earlier in the week, when the dress had arrived from the seamstresses. But she could find nothing amiss, and after a few more seconds of scrutiny she announced: "There's not a thing wrong! It's just perfection on you, Linnet, even though I do say so myself. You look like a dream in it."

Linnet's sister Emsie, who was also in the bedroom, exclaimed, "Evan's right, Linny. I've never seen you look like this. Not ever. Julian's going to fall in love with you all over again."

"He'd better," Linnet said with a chuckle. "Thank you both for your compliments. And, Evan, thanks for designing my gown. And the bridesmaids' dresses, and for everything else you've created for the wedding. I don't know what we'd have done without you."

"You're welcome, it's been my pleasure," Evan replied. Moving across the floor, she took hold of Linnet's hand and carefully led her to the *cheval* mirror in the corner near the window. "There! Just look at yourself."

Linnet stepped in front of the mirror and caught her breath. She'd never seen herself looking so . . . *fantastic*. It was the gown, of course. Evan had adapted the Tudor style to suit her, and how well it worked. Although Linnet was of medium height, the gown made her look taller, and very elegant. Yet there was a youthfulness to it because of the cut.

The dress had a square neckline that cleverly came right to the middle of her shoulders, so that they were shown to advantage. The sleeves started narrow but became very wide bells, almost like kimono sleeves, while the skirt was also bell-shaped and fell into a longish train at the back. The tight bodice gave her a very narrow waist.

The front of the skirt was cut away to reveal a panel made of guipure lace, and the same lace lined the insides of the bell-shaped sleeves. The final touch was the embroidery. The front panel was covered in pearls and crystal beads, as was the guipure lace lining the sleeves. Bands of tiny crystals and pearls outlined the square neckline and the outer edges of the sleeves, and the billowing skirt of cream duchesse satin had scatterings of tiny crystal beads all over it.

A single short strand of South Sea pearls encircled her long neck, and there were pearl clusters on her ears. The set was a gift from her parents. The only other piece of jewelry Linnet wore was her engagement ring.

Staring at herself, she shook her head. "Evan, it's just the most gorgeous dress . . ." Her voice trailed off, words failed her.

"On you, yes, Linnet. I told you I was going to turn you into a young Tudor queen for your wedding, and I have."

Emsie, twirling around, asked, "How do I look then?"

Linnet smiled indulgently and was glad she was able to say, in all sincerity, "Beautiful, Emsie, *beautiful.*" Usually Emsie looked somewhat bedraggled, was careless about her clothes. But this afternoon she looked lovely in the silvery gray-blue watered-taffeta gown all of the attendants were going to wear.

Touching her red-gold hair, Linnet now asked Evan, "Are you sure my hair's all right, going back like this? Will the headdress sit well?"

"It will, trust me," Evan replied. "But don't put it on just yet, I'll do that. *And don't sit down.*"

Linnet laughed. "Gosh no, I mustn't get all rumpled." Glancing across at the eighteen-year-old Emsie, she sternly cautioned, "You'd better not sit down either, my girl."

There was a sudden loud knock on the door. "Who is it?" Linnet called.

"Linnet, dear, it's Uncle Robin."

"Oh, don't come in, I don't want you to see me!"

"I'm looking for Evan. I got a message from her."

"I'm here, Robin. I'm coming." Hurrying toward the door, Evan said to Linnet, as an afterthought, "You didn't forget, did you? Something *old,* something *new,* something *borrowed,* something *blue.*"

Linnet nodded. "I've got all that. . . . Emsie remembered, actually."

"Good for you," Evan remarked, glancing at the younger girl, and went gliding out into the corridor, looking exquisite in her silvery-gray taffeta.

Robin Ainsley was waiting near her bedroom door, and she hurried along the corridor, smiling affectionately.

"Hello, Robin, thanks for coming. How did you know I was now ensconced in the Blue Room?"

Bending toward her, he gave her a kiss on the cheek. "Hello, darling girl," he said and added, "Margaret told me you were moved earlier this week in order to accommodate your parents. But the Blue Room's much nicer than the Yellow Suite, don't you think?" His eyes roamed over her, and he said in a loving voice, "Oh, Evan, how truly lovely you are today, and the dress is superb. I do think you've done yourself proud with the design."

"Thank you." She gave him a knowing glance and asked, "I don't look too pregnant, do I?"

"Not really." His mouth began to twitch with silent laughter, and he added, "Only to those of us who know your condition."

"Oh God, how awful!'

"Don't say that, it's my great-grandchild you're carrying. However, quite seriously, my dear, your version of the Tudor style helps greatly. Actually, it is rather deceptive. Yes, very deceptive indeed."

"I hoped that would be the case," she answered and couldn't help laughing herself when she remarked, "What a bride I'm going to make in January. I'll be very big then. Anyway, don't let's stand out here in the corridor. Come on in."

Evan opened the door of the Blue Room, and Robin followed her into the sitting room. She hurried over to a chest of drawers, took something out of the top drawer, and holding it tightly in her palm, came back to Robin, who waited in the middle of the floor.

Evan stood only a few feet away, staring up at him.

"That's a rather appraising look you're giving me," he exclaimed, suddenly frowning. "Is there something on your mind, Evan?"

"My glance was one of admiration, not appraisal, and I was thinking how handsome you look in your morning suit, Robin." She nodded to herself. "You know something else, you've looked so much better lately, especially since Dad's arrival in Yorkshire in September. Don't *you* think you look better?"

"Yes, I do, and I feel very fit these days."

"Certainly you seem less frail," she added quietly.

"Now, Evan, earlier you left a message that you needed to speak to me about something before the wedding. About something very important," he said, and his eyes went to the clock on the mantelpiece as he explained, "I'll have to be going quite soon, you know. Your parents and I must arrive at the church well before the bridal party because of the special seating for the family, and all that security Jack Figg's put in place."

Evan nodded. "This won't take too long, but won't you sit down, Robin? *I can't*, because of my dress, I don't want to crush it. But there's no reason for you to stand."

"I'm perfectly all right, my dear," he reassured her.

Leaning against the desk in front of the window, Evan said slowly, "I've got something interesting to tell you."

"About what? Or should I say whom?"

"I've unraveled the mystery of Glynnis. Or perhaps I should say I've solved the puzzle. . . . I now know *exactly* why Glynnis sent me to London."

"You do?" Robin Ainsley sounded taken aback, and a silver brow shot up quizzically. His eyes focused on her keenly as he continued, "I would like to hear what's on your mind, Evan dear."

"Okay, here goes," she responded. "Last year, when Gran told me to go to London to find Emma Harte, saying that Emma was the key to my future, she had only one motive really."

"And what was that?" he asked.

"Actually, I'll get to it in a second. Let's first examine Glynnis's method. When she told me to go to London to look for Emma, she was absolutely certain I would do so. You might wonder why, so let me explain. *I had always done everything she told me.* She knew she was the biggest influence on my life. Then again, she was well aware that I was bored with my job in New York, that I wanted a change. A chance *to fly,* she called it. In other words, she didn't doubt that I would go, especially since she had left me money. However, when she sent me here Glynnis *knew* Emma Harte was dead." Evan paused, stared hard at Robin, waited for a reaction.

His face revealed nothing; his expression was inscrutable, just like his mother's had frequently been. There was a lot of Emma in Robin.

Taking a deep breath, Evan continued, "Consider this. . . . There was no way Glynnis could have foreseen that I would end up getting a job at Harte's that first day. Or that I would meet Gideon in the corridor and we would fall in love. Am I right?"

"Yes, you are."

"Basically, Glynnis had no *guarantee* that any of those things would happen. *None at all*. So her method of getting me to the Hartes, which was important to her, was somewhat flawed and also convoluted, wouldn't you say?"

"I suppose it was," Robin agreed, looking baffled. Then he asked, "So what are you getting at?"

"Glynnis, our very clever Glynnis Hughes, apparently wanted to heave *me* into the orbit of the Harte family, as we both know, and before she died she told my mother I would be *irresistible* to them. And by the way, that's something I only recently found out. Still, there wasn't any guarantee I would ever meet a Harte, was there, Robin?"

"No. In fact, the way you're putting it now, it was quite unlikely. You could have gone to the store, discovered my mother was dead, and gone away. But you fell in love with the store, at least so you told me." He paused, nodded. "And so you decided your grandmother had been wandering in her mind that day, dismissed her words about Emma as unimportant, and got yourself a job. All very admirable on your part, but Glynnis didn't know this would happen. Of course you're correct about that, Evan."

"But she knew that, too, and our very smart Glynnis covered her flanks, so to speak."

"How?" he asked, his eyes narrowing.

"When my grandmother was in the hospital in New York, November a year ago, she told my mother to go to her apartment and remove a suitcase of letters. They were letters from your mother. Emma had consistently written to Glynnis over the years, and Glynnis kept the letters . . . just as Emma had kept hers."

"I see." Robin walked over to the window and sat down in the wing chair, his eyes thoughtful.

"Glynnis told Mom to give the letters to me, and she impressed upon Mom that I should read them all. She was very insistent about that apparently, and just as insistent that my mother not show them to my father, or even tell him about them."

"Really," Robin muttered. Throwing her a very direct look, he asked, "And did Marietta give you the letters?"

"She did, Robin, but only recently. She says her reason for holding on to them was that she wished to give them to me in person, and to relate face-to-face what Gran had told her when she was in the hospital. But, in fact, Mom kept them for nearly a year. She says that was because I started working at Harte's in Knightsbridge and got involved with Gideon. She decided the letters could wait. After all, I'd done what Glynnis had planned, had hoped would happen . . . I'd fallen right into the middle of the Harte family and, let's face it, in a very big way."

"Yes, that's true. But when did your mother actually give you Emma's letters to Glynnis?"

"This past September, after the car crash. She brought them with her when she came up to see me, before she and Dad went back to New York. I read most of them while I was recovering."

"I see. And I suppose my mother's letters were revealing?"

"Oh yes. And I realized something crucial as I read the letters. If I hadn't met any of you, and if Paula hadn't found out the truth about Glynnis's past, I would still have discovered that you were my father's biological father. *Because of those letters.* That's why Glynnis wanted me to have them. She protected her flanks, as I said earlier. She wanted me to know the truth about my heritage no matter what."

"I think you're correct," Robin admitted, leaning back against the cushions, letting out a small sigh. Somehow he knew that there was much more coming, and he steeled himself.

"That's why she wanted me to go to London . . . to find my heritage."

"But we've always known that, haven't we?" he answered. "Or rather, assumed it. However, you are right about your grandmother's method." Robin shook his head. "Wouldn't it have been easier simply to tell your father and you the truth when she became so ill? After all, Richard Hughes was dead. What harm could be done? None, really, to my way of thinking."

"Glynnis was not from my generation, or my mother's . . . she came from the old school. She was *afraid* to tell us, most especially Dad. That's what I believe, anyway. She didn't want to disillusion him, to be diminished in his eyes. She was proud, and she loved Dad very much. I guess she was scared—in the way I even was—about revealing the truth to Dad."

"I understand what you're saying, I do, Evan. And you're right. Your grandmother and I grew up in a different world. A very strictured world, in which illegitimate children were frowned on."

"And so Glynnis *set me up*. And left it to Fate with a capital *F*. Gran was always talking about Fate and Destiny, she believed in those things. Yet she left it to Fate only *partially* . . . because she made sure I would get my hands on those letters from Emma Harte."

Robin closed his eyes, his silver head resting against the back of the wing chair. In repose she saw his age more fully. He was, after all, eighty years old. Her heart went out to him. But after a moment, clearing her throat, Evan said softly, *"Robin."*

He opened his eyes and promptly sat up. "I wasn't asleep," he said with a slight laugh. "I was just pondering your words."

She nodded, took a step closer to the chair. "I worked it all out, you know." There was a pause, and then Evan finished, "She was sending me to you, Robin."

Not a word left his mouth, but his blue eyes turned flinty, and the look he gave her was shrewd.

"Glynnis was so worried about you when she was ill, she needed *me,* and possibly my father, too, to come to *you.* But it was mostly me she wanted in London with you."

"Why do you say all this?" Robin asked, his voice rising slightly.

"Because it's true! Glynnis wanted you to have the grandchild you'd never had, and she didn't want you to be alone. When she was gone, I mean."

Robin let out a long sigh. "Continue," he said in a low voice.

"You never gave each other up, did you?"

There was a silence. The only sound was the clock ticking.

"No," he admitted at last. "No, we didn't." His voice was resigned.

"You and Glynnis got back together when you were both thirty!" Evan exclaimed. "And you were together for almost *fifty* years, weren't you?"

"Yes," Robin answered softly. "We were, thank God."

"In your own way you were like a married couple," Evan went on. "Glynnis came to London at least several times a year, using any excuse she could think of, and you came to New York and Connecticut. You spent all of your vacations with Glynnis, never with your wife. You came to New York when the House of Commons was in recess. You were so in love with her you would have done anything to get her. Divorced Valerie, given up your political career, anything to be with my grandmother *always*." Evan gazed at him, her eyes warm, and spoke again.

"But Glynnis loved you so much, Robin, she wouldn't permit you to do that, to ruin yourself in politics. It *was* different in those days, and there could have been a scandal about her. So you . . . *compromised*. That's what she called it . . . *The Compromise*. You stayed in your marriages so as not to hurt Richard or Valerie. But you loved only each other, and you spent as much time together as you could."

After a few minutes, Robin murmured, "This is too much—"

"Robin, Robin, *don't*! It's me, your grandchild. I'm not angry or upset, and you mustn't be upset either."

Drawing closer to him, Evan put her hand on his shoulder and looked down into his upturned face. "Glynnis did something else. She left me *your* letters to *her*. Hundreds and hundreds of letters. She kept them. In fact, she kept everything . . . your Christmas cards, birthday cards, the cards which came with your many gifts to her—" Evan broke off, suddenly noticing how stricken he looked.

Bending over him, she murmured gently, "Please don't think I'm criticizing you, or Glynnis. Because I'm not. I'm happy that you had each other, that you gave each other so much joy. She loved you with all of her heart, and she was loyal to you all of her life." Evan's eyes were suddenly very moist, and she brushed them with her hand.

When she looked at Robin, she saw that tears were rolling down his face and his mouth trembled. He said in a slightly quavering voice, "It's been so hard without her. I wanted to die, too . . . until you came to me."

"I know, I know," she soothed, her hand still on his shoulder. "I really do understand . . . very few people have a love like yours."

"Have you read my letters to Glynnis?" he asked, his eyes fastened intently on hers.

"Yes, but Mom only gave them to me the other day, when she arrived here from New York for Linnet's wedding. There's a huge suitcase in that cupboard over there, and it's *full* of your letters."

"Did I write so many?" he asked and unexpectedly smiled at Evan.

She smiled back. "Oh yes, you did! But I read only some of the recent ones. You saw her a few days before she died, didn't you?"

He nodded. "How do you know?"

"I found the letter you sent to her in early November last year. You were coming to her. You wanted to bring her back to England. After all, you were both widowed, you could actually be together, could be married—"

"We *were* married," he cut in, "but without the benefit of a piece of paper. I consider Glynnis the only wife I ever had."

"I understand," Evan replied softly. "But she was suddenly and unexpectedly so ill, wasn't she? And she couldn't travel. . . . The last time you saw her was in the hospital in Manhattan."

Robin could not speak. His grief was a palpable thing. He took out a handkerchief, wiped his eyes, blew his nose, and tried hard to bring his swimming senses under control.

When he had recovered himself sufficiently, Evan opened her hand, showed him her palm. "This is for you, Grandfather."

She rarely ever called him that, and his eyes widened as he stared up at her.

"It was in a small envelope with your writing on it, Robin. You wrote out an address and a phone number."

The sight of the latchkey brought a sparkle to his eyes, and the tiredness seemed to slip off his face.

"It's for Edwina's house," Evan remarked.

"No. Ours. Glynnis's and mine. A lovely old mews in London. I used to borrow it from Edwina, and one day she finally agreed to sell it to me."

"And you bought it?"

"Yes. For Glynnis. But the deeds have always remained in Edwina's name, for certain reasons. If she dies before me, it comes to you through her son, Anthony, India's father. If I die first, it's the same process. The house will be yours, Evan."

Evan stood looking at him, unable to say anything.

He said, with a little smile, "That's where I still live when I go up to London. It's full of memories . . . of Glynnis . . . of our years together." The tears came again, and he searched for his handkerchief. "Do forgive a foolish old man, my dear."

"There's nothing to forgive," Evan reassured him and began to laugh. "Look at me, I'm crying, too, and ruining all my makeup. And it's Linnet's wedding in an hour."

"I'm very aware of that, and I must go and find your father."

"Your son, Robin, your son by Glynnis."

Nodding, he gave her the benefit of a huge smile. "We loved each other so much, and we pulled it off, you know. All those years we pulled it off, Evan, and we never hurt anybody."

I wonder about that, Evan thought, then pushed the thought away.

He handed her the latchkey. "It was Glynnis's. I gave it to her. And now it's yours, Evan. Take it."

She did, then walked with him to the door. "I'll drive over next week with the suitcase," she told him. "But I wonder . . . could I keep some of the photographs? The two of you were so gorgeous when you were young, you looked like movie stars."

"*Glynnis.* Not I," he protested.

"Yes, you too. Anyway, I'll bring your letters over to Lackland Priory."

"*No.* Glynnis wanted you to have them, and you should." Robin stared into her blue-gray eyes and added, "If you wish, I will give you Glynnis's letters to me. She wrote to me every week from 1950 until this past year." He paused, and the look he gave her was odd, even worried, before he added softly, "But I think they might be a little . . . *private,* shall we say."

Evan burst out laughing. "I'll bet! Because some of yours certainly are! *Red hot.*" Her eyes were sparkling as she went on. "And why not? Yours was quite a love story, incredible really, Robin."

Now she came into his outstretched arms, and he held her close to him, thinking how like his Glynnis she was sometimes. "Glynnis was so worried about dying on me, leaving me on my own. We weren't together all the time, but what we had over all those years was something really quite . . . *magnificent.* Magnificent."

34

⚮

The lovely little stone church in the village of Pennistone Royal dated back over nine hundred years to the time of the first Norman kings of England. Its square Norman tower was original, but the glorious stained-glass windows had been put in only two hundred years ago.

For the entire time she had lived at Pennistone Royal, Emma Harte had paid for all the restoration work the church required, and Paula was now following in her footsteps. In consequence, the church was beautifully kept, both inside and out.

On this Saturday afternoon, the first day of December, the weather was cold. But there was no wind, and the sky was ice blue and cloudless. The orb of the sun was pale, but it *was* shining, and the day was pristine, with that clarity of light so peculiar to these northern climes.

Robin alighted from one of the first cars to arrive at the church, and he helped Marietta out. She looked extremely smart in a dark red silk skirt to her ankles and a trim, fitted jacket embroidered with jet beads. Once Owen joined them, they walked up to the church.

The entire village had turned out for Linnet's marriage to Julian. Bundled up in warm clothes, they stood around in groups; hands waved enthusiastically, familiar faces broke into smiles as Robin was recognized.

He had grown up in Pennistone Royal and was very popular. He waved back, smiled graciously, and escorted Marietta and Owen along the church path.

Continuing to glance around, he spotted a number of faces he did not know. Men in dark suits with earpieces and small microphones in their lapels. He knew at once they were Jack Figg's operatives. *Security.*

As they drew closer to the porch, Robin noticed Jack hovering on the steps, dressed in a gray top hat and morning suit. He was a guest at the wedding, since he was like a member of the family, but he was also head of security again. Now he was scanning the crowds intently.

Jack's face broke into smiles when he saw Robin. The two men shook hands warmly, and Jack greeted Marietta and Owen, whom he had met the night before at the dinner given by Paula and Shane.

Robin drew much closer to Jack and said in a low voice, "I see you've got good security in place."

Jack's brow lifted, and he muttered, "I've got more men here than there are barnacles clinging to the hull of a ship. But Paula wanted it, and I aim to please, old chap."

"Jonathan wouldn't dare attempt anything," Robin said, the specter of his other son rising up. He clamped down on it.

"I agree, but Paula's fearful of him, and especially today. It's better to go overboard," Jack explained, "than to have too few men on hand. But they'll be invisible for the most part, especially in church and at the reception.

Don't worry, nothing's going to happen," he finished in a reassuring voice, then added, "I'll join you inside shortly."

Jack stepped away from the porch, headed toward the graveyard. As he did so there was a tiny crackle of noise in his earpiece, and Chris Light's voice came in: "Jack, there's a white van coming down the hill from Lackland village. It's got to be the yobbos we were warned about."

"Right, Chris. Move in. *Now*. Block the road with our cars and bring in the cavalry. And block the other roads leading into Pennistone village. I don't want any slipups. Keep them out of the village, and alert the police. Now. If they won't leave, we'll have them arrested."

"You've got it, Jack," Chris exclaimed.

Standing alone in the middle of the graveyard, Jack Figg thanked God that Mark Longden had a streak of humanity in him. If Longden had not had the good sense to alert him about Jonathan Ainsley's wild talk in Paris in September, they might have had a tragedy on their hands today. A church burning to the ground and killing everyone inside. Because of Longden's phone call in October, they had been able to find out the *real* plan, through an operative who had infiltrated the gangs. And so today Jack was fully prepared. For anything. And anybody. Security was in place everywhere.

Mark Longden *thought* he had prevented a wedding from being ruined. Unbeknownst to him, his phone call had saved all their lives. Including Adele's.

Lorne Fairley and Desmond O'Neill, Linnet's brothers, were two of the ushers who greeted Robin, Marietta, and Owen when they entered the church. They showed them to the correct pew on the bride's family's side of the aisle, and after a few words the two young men departed to take care of other guests.

"It's breathtaking," Marietta whispered as she glanced around the church. "Just extraordinary."

"It's Evan's floral design," Robin whispered back. "She's very talented, don't you think?"

"I'll say she is," Owen murmured, a proud look crossing his face.

There were great banks of white orchids everywhere, and in various areas small leafless trees stood in smart white tubs. The trees had been painted white, and from their branches hung nosegays of delicate white flowers held in small silver-lace ruffs, following through the Elizabethan theme. And throughout the church were huge vases of white tulips, carnations, and jonquils, as well as hundreds of white candles, from tall, slender tapers to votives in little glass pots. Like every other person in the church, Robin was struck by the beauty of the flowers set amidst the flickering candlelight.

Suddenly a burst of sunlight flooded in through the stained-glass windows, and he thought they looked like shimmering jewels set high in the ancient stone walls. This little church, which he had known since he was a boy, was the most beautiful setting for a wedding, and he silently vowed that his only grandchild, Evan, would be married to Gideon here next month. It would be a wedding equally beautiful. She deserved no less.

More of his family began to arrive and went into the pew in front of him. Edwina, his favorite, was regal as always in an outfit of purple, a color she seemed perpetually to choose for special events. She glanced at him, smiled, then winked and nodded at her escort. It was Russell Rhodes, the artist, looking handsome, if a little pugnacious, in his morning suit.

Robin was delighted that he was present this afternoon; he had warmed to Dusty last night when he met him for the first time. Evan had confided that India had made up with him and all was well between them. Dusty had obviously been welcomed into the family with open arms; he was seated next to India's mother, Sally, who was looking elegant in deep blue and sapphires. Anthony Standish, India's father, turned around, smiled at Robin, nodded to Owen and Marietta, then said something to Edwina, his mother.

Robin saw Sir Ronald Kallinski, Julian's grandfather, coming up the aisle, accompanied by his son Michael, and Michael's ex-wife, Valentine, Julian's parents.

A moment or two later, Robin's twin sister, Elizabeth, walked in on the arm of her husband of many years, Marc Deboyne. Although she was the same age as Robin, she looked much younger than eighty, and he noticed how chic she was in a tailored midnight blue silk dress and coat.

She whispered her greetings to Robin as she hurried to her pew, followed by her daughter Emily, granddaughter Natalie, and Winston. Emily was in a plum-colored floor-length suit, Natalie in amethyst silk, and both of them gave him a small wave when they spotted him.

Within fifteen minutes the church had begun to fill up, and as he saw Paula walking up the aisle to the front pew, accompanied by her mother, Daisy, and Grandfather Bryan O'Neill, he knew the bride could not be far behind.

Robin had always admired Paula's ability to be a businesswoman, a wife and mother, and somehow manage to look like a world-class model at the same time. Fifty-six years old, she seemed more like forty, and she was elegance personified in a dark fir-green velvet sleeveless coat, which came to her ankles and was worn over a matching dress with lace sleeves. His mother's famous emeralds blazed on Paula's ears, and she wore Blackie's emerald bow pinned on the shoulder of the coat.

Daisy, his youngest sister, was dressed in gold lace, and her face broke into a smile when she glanced at Robin before walking to the first pew with her daughter.

"So many people, so many friends," Marietta whispered to Robin. "Heavens to Betsy, it's some crowd! Well, at least Evan's wedding will be much smaller, I guess."

Robin chuckled quietly, shook his head. "There aren't that many friends here. What I mean is not too many outsiders. Almost everyone here is called Harte, O'Neill, or Kallinski. It'll be the same group at Evan's marriage to Gideon, I can assure you." As he spoke he looked around, saw so many Hartes he hadn't set eyes on for years. Wasn't that Amanda with her twin, Francesca? And surely that was Sarah Lowther Pascal with her Yves, her French husband, and their daughter, Chloe. Goodness me, what a family, he thought. My mother and her brothers spawned quite a troop.

There was a sudden flurry of activity, and peering ahead Robin realized that the choirboys were filing in; ten minutes later he saw Julian arriving with his best man, Gideon. The two of them stood near the altar, the bridegroom waiting for his bride.

Robin thought that both young men looked composed, ready for anything. And next month Gideon would be standing in the same spot, waiting at the altar for Evan to arrive on the arm of Owen. His son. His granddaughter.

And then, before Robin could blink, the organist began to play the wedding march from Wagner's *Lohengrin,* and it rang out gloriously, rising to the rafters.

Everyone turned around. Here she came, the bride. In her cream satin and lace gown, Linnet looked beautiful and regal as she slowly walked up the aisle, holding on to the arm of her father, Shane.

"Her gown's magnificent," Marietta whispered to Robin, and he nodded in agreement. There was no other word to describe it.

On her burnished red hair, Linnet wore a simple diamond tiara to hold her delicate tulle veil in place, and Robin recognized the tiara as his mother's. His eyes were riveted to her face . . . she resembled Emma so much, looked the way she must have when she was the same age.

Behind the bride followed her attendants in their billowing taffeta gowns. Linnet's sisters, Tessa and Emsie; then came India and Evan; and finally, all alone and walking as sedately as she could manage, came little Adele. She was a miniature version of the older bridesmaids and her mother, Tessa, the matron of honor.

Robin smiled, and he felt everyone else smile when they saw this most beautiful blond child carrying her nosegay of flowers in the silver ruff so carefully. Her pretty face was solemn, her steps dainty, as the occasion merited. A Fairley, he thought. She looks like a Fairley; no doubt about where *she* sprang from.

For Robin Ainsley the ceremony passed as if he were in a dream, memories of long ago crowding his mind, thoughts of his wonderful Glynnis uppermost. How he missed her, yet they had had so much, more than most. His thoughts turned to Evan. How clever she was, the way she had fathomed out everything for herself, although she'd had a great deal of help from Glynnis. He smiled to himself. Glynnis had wanted him to have Owen and Evan in the end, when she was gone. She had always felt guilty about keeping him away from his son. But Robin knew this was because she had not wanted to ruin the relationship Owen had with Richard Hughes. She had been right, as she usually was.

Yet he knew there was another reason. Glynnis had needed their grandchild to know who she was, what her heritage was, and that was why she had made sure Evan would receive all those letters. Letters that told their own story. And that was all right, too. Whatever Glynnis did had always been all right with him.

Robin's head came up suddenly as the music intruded on his thoughts. His heart squeezed and squeezed as the choirboys began to sing "O Perfect Love," such a favorite of Glynnis's and an anthem he loved himself. He thought the choirboys had wondrous voices, and drawing closer to Marietta he said softly, "They sound like angels singing, don't you think? So pure."

She touched his arm, nodded, loving this man for his sensitivity and kindness, and his enormous generosity of spirit. No wonder her mother-in-law had been so much in love with him all those years.

The bride and groom came walking down the aisle arm in arm, smiling and joyous, stepping out to the strains of Mendelssohn's "Wedding March" from *A Midsummer Night's Dream.*

Slowly all the guests left the church, following the loving couple, and when Robin stepped outside, he couldn't help smiling at the scene. Snowflakes and flower petals blowing in the breeze. A radiant Linnet clinging to Julian's arm. The two of them laughing as they were driven off. Sitting in the wedding car beribboned in white silk bows. Old boots and cans tied to the back fender, rattling loudly, making everyone chuckle at the incongruity.

The three of them stood in a corner of the big library. Tessa, India, and Evan. All around them swirled the guests, who were drinking champagne, eating canapés, and having a wonderful time. A small trio played background music, and guests waved and smiled at them, but although they waved back, the three young women remained aloof, waiting for their beaus to join them.

Tessa said, "Come on, tell us about it, Evan. What was the big secret you discovered about Robin and your granny?"

"She was never a *granny*." Evan laughed and took a glass of orange juice from a passing waiter. "But let's wait until our men get here."

"I've got something to tell you in the meantime," India murmured softly. "But we must keep it a secret between the three of us. I don't want Linnet to know, because she'll make a big noise about it tonight, and that wouldn't be right."

"So tell us quickly, whilst she and Julian are having their photographs taken," Tessa instructed, taking a swallow of champagne.

India smiled. "Dusty and I are going to get engaged next week, while my parents are still here from Ireland. They think he's fabulous, and he's all turned around about them. So there's no problem."

"Congratulations," Evan said. "I know you don't want to steal any of Linnet's thunder today, that's so nice of you."

India gave a little shrug. "I never thought we would get it together, but he's been so abject and apologetic about the Melinda mess. Edwina told me to stop squawking, grow up, and marry him."

Tessa grinned. "She's such a card! Congratulations, India darling."

Evan looked over at Tessa intently and announced, "I like your Jean-Claude. He's fascinating, and Gideon was very taken with him last night. So tell us quickly, before they arrive, is he going to become a member of the family, too?"

Tessa blushed. "I hope so. Actually, he's proposed. But I have to get the divorce first. When Great-Aunt Edwina met him earlier this week, she actually told me, in front of him no less, to grab him fast before another woman did. Can you believe that?"

"She's incorrigible, that granny of mine," India exclaimed and began to laugh.

Tessa also laughed. "*She's* no granny either! Oh look, our chaps are heading this way." Tessa moved her head slightly, began to wave.

Gideon, Dusty, Jean-Claude, and Lorne strolled over, each nursing a glass of champagne. It was Lorne who said, "Why are the three beauties huddled in the corner? Are you in hiding? Gosh, the three of you should be circulating, shouldn't you?"

"Oh, phooey," Tessa answered. "Anyway, we were waiting for you to get here. Evan discovered something about her grandmother and Uncle Robin, and—"

"But we all know that story!" Lorne interrupted. "It's been circulating in the family ever since Ma found out about their love affair during the war."

"Oh, but there's something else, isn't there, Evan?" India said.

Evan nodded. "Yes, there is. I'll try to make this short. My mother brought me a package of letters from Emma Harte to my grandmother, and also letters from Robin to Glynnis, and you'll never guess—"

"Oh, do tell us, darling," Gideon interrupted. "It sounds very romantic."

"I will, if you'll stop interrupting me," Evan responded. Leaning against the window frame, she told them about Glynnis and Robin and the years they had spent together.

Everyone had listened attentively, but Jean-Claude was the first to make a remark. "But what a *magnificent* love story. Unbelievable!" Tessa put her arm through his and responded, "Yes, it is, and certainly a story a Frenchman like you would appreciate."

They all laughed, and then Gideon, frowning, asked Evan, "How the hell did they manage it? I mean, manage not to get caught?"

"They were careful," Evan told him, "and they lived in different countries part of the year. I guess that helped. And they made it work."

"I bet they had an accomplice," Dusty pointed out softly. "They had to have had help at some time or another. Nobody can do that, not without a third person to give them cover."

"Emma!" Gideon said, looking at Evan, his eyes fixed on hers. "Did *Emma* know? Was *she* their accomplice?"

"I wouldn't exactly call her that, Gid. But our great-grandmother did learn they'd started their affair again. After it had been going on for a couple of years, in fact. Since she knew she was unable to stop it, I guess she decided to help them."

"I'll be damned," Lorne said, astonishment crossing his face.

Gideon also looked surprised. "How old were they when they started up again?"

"They were both thirty. And they hadn't seen each other for seven years. Imagine that. But they were hot stuff," she said, shaking her head, laughing.

"How long were they together?" Jean-Claude asked.

"Fifty years, just about," Evan told them all.

"Mon dieu!" Jean-Claude looked at Tessa and added,

"That was some love affair. I'd like to meet that gentlemen again. Come, Tessa, let us seek out your Great-Uncle Robin. He must be . . . rather unique."

"Oh, he is! He sure is," Gideon called after them.

"It's so sad she died," India said, "especially since they were both widowed ultimately. They could have been married."

Dusty said, "Isn't that your mother, isn't she beckoning to us?"

India followed his gaze. "Oh yes, I suppose Grandmother wants us to join her. She's fallen for you, Dusty."

"And I'm crazy about her," he replied, leading India across the library.

Lorne bent over, gave Evan a kiss on her cheek. "It's an extraordinary story, it truly is . . . magnificent, as Jean-Claude said. I wish I could find someone to love like that. Oh well, I'll go and look around, maybe one of Linnet's girlfriends might strike my fancy."

Evan and Gideon laughed, and Evan linked her arm through Gideon's as they watched the handsome young actor saunter off. Then Gideon stared down at her and asked softly, "Do *you* guarantee *me* fifty years, Evan?"

Gazing up into his face, that face she had come to love so much in the past year, she nodded. "I guarantee you *forever,* Gideon Harte. I promise I'll be with you all the days of my life."

PROLOGUE

London: 2002

The man stood in the doorway of the shop, huddled in a corner, sheltering from the icy wind. It was freezing on this bitter January morning, and he felt tempted to hurry off to the nearby Hyde Park Hotel for a cooked English breakfast.

Yet he was unable to tear himself away from this doorway, where he had always had a perfect view of the building opposite, one which he had for so long coveted as his own.

Leaning forward, he focused his eyes on the grand and impressive edifice across the road. It had been standing there for over eighty years, but it was unscathed, untouched by the passage of time and impregnable. He thought of it as a bastion of prestige, privilege and wealth, the center of that enormous, world-wide business empire created by his grandmother.

And it should have been his.

Tragically, he believed he had been cheated. It had fallen into the hands of Paula O'Neill, who now thought of it as her own, when in reality it *was* his by rights. But it wasn't; that idea sprang from his irrationality and jealousy.

In the mid-1980s he had almost wrested the flagship Knightsbridge emporium and the provincial Harte stores away from Paula, when she had made a series of mistakes in a deal related to the stores. So flawed was her judgment she had played right into his waiting hands.

Unfortunately, just as he reached out, had the stores almost in his grasp, he had been betrayed. As a consequence of this unwarranted and unexpected betrayal, Paula O'Neill had managed to outwit him. Curiously, losing had been the spur; he had created his own empire and was today a billionaire.

She had been his nemesis for years, but it was from this precise moment in time that he had become her sworn enemy, had vowed to wreak his revenge on her. And soon he would do that, and he would finally triumph over her.

Abruptly, the man stepped forward, moving out of the doorway, his attention riveted on two young women who had hurried out of the store and were studying the windows fronting onto Knightsbridge.

One of them was a redhead, and he knew her at once. She was Linnet O'Neill, Paula's daughter; however, she was now a Kallinski, after marrying the Kallinski heir last month. His thoughts settled on the little church in Pennistone village where they had been married. How easily it would have burned to the ground, killing everyone in it, and his problems with the Hartes would have been solved forever more.

For a moment the man was baffled, unable to pinpoint the other woman's identity. She was bundled up in a loden cape and long scarf, and her face was obscured. But then she turned, and he instantly recognized the distinctive chiselled profile.

His chest tightened, and a virulent anger surged through him as he gazed at Evan Hughes. She was his new nemesis, the American woman who had insinuated herself into the family and was about to become a Harte. He muttered an expletive . . . she was already a Harte, thanks in no small measure to his father's long-ago lust. And now she threatened everybody by her very existence, especially himself. She, too, was now a target along with Paula and her redheaded brat.

A smug and knowing smile slid onto his handsome face; he stared hard at the two women, and for a very long moment, before setting out in the direction of the hotel for breakfast.

That self-satisfied smile remained intact as he turned up the collar of his expensive and impeccably-tailored vicuna coat and increased his pace.

As he walked, he considered a plan he had recently formulated . . . one so devilishly clever it might have been devised by Prince Machiavelli himself. How ingenious it was and it would surely help to bring about the fall of the house of Harte. He was convinced of this outcome.

Jonathan Ainsley laughed out loud. They were going to get their just rewards. He would see to that.

Part One

∾

QUARTET

"Envy slays itself by its own arrows."

MEDIEVAL SAYING: ANONYMOUS

I

Flurries of silvery snowflakes were blowing in the wind, sticking to the plate-glass windows of Harte's and on the faces of the two pretty young women gazing so intently into those windows.

Evan Hughes brought a gloved hand to her cheek and wiped the dampness away. Then she drew closer to Linnet O'Neill, shivering and hunching into her dark-green loden cape, feeling the sharp bite of the intense cold.

Instantly, Linnet glanced at Evan, and exclaimed, "I'm so thoughtless, dragging you outside to look at our windows on a day like this! You're freezing. Come on, let's go inside. We've seen enough, actually."

Linnet took hold of Evan's arm and hurried her toward one of the double doors leading into Harte's.

"I'm all right, honestly," Evan protested as she was propelled across the floor of the cosmetics department, adding irately, "I'm not a cream puff, you know, I'm not going to melt away."

"You've got guts of steel, I'm very well aware of

that!" Linnet shot back. "It just became frightfully cold all of a sudden, and if you catch a cold, or get sick, Gideon will have my guts for garters."

Evan burst out laughing, as usual amused by Linnet's penchant for quaint, rather odd sayings; she was frequently startled by the other girl's bluntness, as well as her pithiness, which could be quite stringent at times. Evan considered her recently discovered cousin to be a most unique person. She had never met anyone quite like her, and in this past year of working together, they had become close, the very best of friends.

Moving through the eye-catching, glamorous displays of cosmetics and perfumes, Evan felt her icy limbs beginning to thaw in the warmth of the store, and she loosened her scarf, opened her cape. Smoothing her hand over her huge, bulging stomach, she confided, "I feel like an enormous beached whale, Linny. I can't wait to give birth."

Linnet's expression was sympathetic. "I know. But just imagine, Evan, you're about to have twins. TWINS! You've certainly given Tessa, India, and me pause for thought. We have a tendency to forget that twins run in this family, that they're quite the norm. Grandy had twins, and so did Mummy the first time around, when she was married to Jim Fairley. It's only just struck *us* that we also might be candidates, have the same fate as you." Linnet smiled engagingly. "What do *you* think?"

"We share a lot of the same genes, I guess, so you're probably right."

"Julian's hoping so, and actually so am I. It makes life easier, having twins. Two children born together saves so much bother in the long run . . . an instant family and less time off work."

"Very well put," Evan responded softly, laughter filling her eyes. She couldn't help thinking that Linnet's inborn pragmatism inevitably came to the fore, but she admired her for being so down to earth.

By now the two women had arrived at a bank of elevators, and they stepped into one as soon as its doors slid open. Falling silent, they rode up to the management offices and hurried down the long corridor.

When they reached the alcove in the center, where the famous portrait of Emma Harte hung, the two of them automatically came to a standstill, looked at each other, smiled, and then briskly saluted their great-grandmother and moved on. It had become something of a ritual with them of late, whether they were together or alone. It signified their pride in being her progeny and of working in the renowned store she had founded.

A few minutes later, settled comfortably in Evan's office, Linnet said, "So, give me your opinion about the windows."

"I have to agree with you, they are a bit outdated. Oh, they're beautiful, Linnet, of course. So well dressed. And they do evoke the kind of image we want for Harte's, but they could bc a bit . . . *fresher*."

"Not enough pizazz, perhaps?" Linnet suggested.

"Not pizazz, that's not quite right for Harte's, is it?"

"I suppose not," Linnet agreed, sitting back in the chair, her eyes focused on Evan, whose opinion she valued.

Evan bit her lip, then shook her head. "I think the word I'm looking for is . . . *glamorous*. I'm talking about the fashion windows *per se*, Linnet, and they ought to be just a tad more eye-catching and inviting. Listen, they should say something to the customer . . . they should say *come in, try me on, buy me*."

Linnet nodded, her face lighting up. "That's true. And you've just put your finger on it."

Evan said, "You've only recently come back from New York, and you've seen the store windows there, and I believe you're now finding our windows somewhat flat." Evan raised a brow and her pellucid gray eyes rested on Linnet thoughtfully. When Linnet made no response, she asked, "Am I not correct?"

"I think you are . . . but I'm not sure Mummy would agree."

"Have you discussed the windows with Paula?" Evan probed, sounding anxious.

"No, I haven't had a chance, and she and Dad are staying in Yorkshire this week, recovering from Christmas, the New Year, and all of their entertaining. Anyway, they're taking a week off from work, and they just want to stay put, potter around at Pennistone Royal. They enjoy being at home with each other, doing what they've always done since they were kids growing up together." Linnet shook her head. "Anyway, I'm not going to say a word until she's back here at work. Actually, Evan, there are some other things I want to discuss with her, certain changes I believe we should make at the store."

Evan sat up straighter but said nothing, merely raised a brow quizzically, her eyes full of questions.

"You look surprised," Linnet exclaimed, eyeing her carefully.

"I am. What kind of changes do you have in mind?"

"I'll get to those in a minute, just let me say this first. As you well know, the fashion retrospective was a big success last summer. We gained lots of new customers, and we did terrifically well, but eventually sales dipped. What we need to do is keep our customers coming in, and we need to garner those important new ones as well. I truly believe we're in a new age of retailing. We have to make shopping a unique experience, and offer other services."

"Obviously you've studied this carefully, and come up with some fresh ideas," Evan ventured cautiously, wondering if Paula would permit any changes at the Knightsbridge store.

"I have," Linnet asserted. "For example, Harte's ought to have a day spa, a really beautiful spa offering every kind of treatment."

"That would be great!" Evan was swift to agree, and then thought to ask, "But where would you put it?"

Linnet grinned, and explained, "I think one of those boring departments such as *mattresses* would have to go. But seriously, we could carve out space, I know this store inside out and we *could* do it."

"I guess it doesn't have to be a huge spa, just a unique one."

"That's it exactly. Evan, listen, don't you think we ought to have more places to eat? Snack bars, for instance. Especially on the ground floor near the food halls. We could feature shellfish, pizza, hot dogs, deli sandwiches, and pastas. The kind of fast food that's actually tasty. I'm sure they'd be successful, and they would appeal to people who work in Knightsbridge and the areas nearby, as well as our customers."

"That's a great suggestion," Evan agreed, "and the bars *would* be popular. I can feel my mouth watering just at the thought. What I wouldn't give for a plate of oysters right now."

"And ice cream on top, I've no doubt," Linnet said, grinning at her. "Isn't that your favorite lunch these days?"

Evan shook her head. "Not quite, although I have had a few peculiar longings for some very strange food combinations."

Linnet leaned forward, her expression intense. "I'd appreciate any ideas *you* might have, Evan, you're always so creative, and I do think we really *have* to re-vamp the store. A little bit anyway."

Evan nodded. "I agree . . ." She paused, hesitating, and then confided, "I did have an idea a while back. A floor devoted to brides. Called . . . BRIDE. Naturally we would feature bridal gowns, bridesmaids dresses, page boy suits, and all those things. But we could also sell bridal shoes, jewelry, gifts for the bridesmaids, and even bridal lingerie. And there's another thing, in the States wedding planners are very popular, and we could offer that kind of service as well. People would welcome it."

"Evan, I love it! What a brilliant idea. And what about the Evan Hughes Bridal Collection? You know you'd love to design bridal gowns. How about it?"

Evan considered Linnet's words. "I think I'd enjoy that. I guess I've been itching to design again." Evan's enthusiasm was apparent. "Actually, the store has had inquiries about your wedding gown. There were lots of photographs in the newspapers, and women seemed taken with it."

"I don't blame them, you created something out of this world. So, let's sell it to them," Linnet replied in a rush, and at the same pace she continued, "Also, I think your idea for an entire floor for brides is inspirational. I'd really appreciate it if you could give me something on paper. As soon as possible."

"I've got a lot of stuff on my computer already. I'll print it out for you before I go to Yorkshire."

"Thanks, and when are you going to Pennistone Royal?"

"In three days. Gideon and I are driving up on Saturday. I'm glad. I'm already a bit panicky to tell you the truth, I feel as if I'm about to give birth at any moment." She said this lightly, laughing as she spoke, but she was genuinely concerned that this actually might happen.

So was Linnet. Evan and Gideon had delayed getting married until January, because her big, splashy wedding to Julian had been long-planned for this past December. They hadn't wanted to compete. Pushing aside her worries Linnet now also laughed and endeavored to reassure Evan. "You'll be fine, darling. Julian and I will be there for the weekend, so I can help with any last-minute details for the wedding."

"That's lovely, thanks for offering, but there's not much to do. It's only the family, after all."

"Your parents are coming over though, aren't they?"

"Oh yes, and my sisters. My mother's already here, she arrived several days ago, and the others will be flying in next week. Robin's being wonderful, very kind, and he's invited my parents and sisters to stay at Lackland Priory."

"Well, that's nice of him, of course, but don't forget you've given him a new lease on life, Evan. Mummy says he's never looked better."

Linnet now pushed herself to her feet and picked up her coat. "I'd better go, I've loads of paperwork to catch up with. Thanks for listening, and for your input. It was just what I needed." She paused at the door, blew a kiss. "I'll see you later." Smiling, she was gone.

Evan gazed at the door, her face already clouding over.

She was fully aware that Linnet's nonchalance was assumed, that in point of fact she was concerned, worried what her mother's reaction would be to her ideas for the Knightsbridge store. Although they were not particularly radical, Evan knew they would fall flat. As a newcomer, she saw Paula O'Neill from an entirely different viewpoint than her daughters and India Standish, Paula's niece. Evan was aware that their boss was a woman who had become a trifle set in her ways. She was also determined to keep Harte's in its traditional mode, to keep its image intact. What Linnet wanted to do wouldn't destroy Harte's image. On the other hand, Paula would be upset. She was Emma Harte's granddaughter and heiress, and she never deviated from the rules set down by Emma. Having run Harte's in exactly the same way for well over thirty years, since before Emma's death, she wasn't likely to make any changes now.

There'll be trouble between them, Evan suddenly thought with a sense of foreboding. Real trouble.

JUST REWARDS

#1 *New York Times* bestselling author

BARBARA TAYLOR BRADFORD

❧

*The astonishing final episode of the Harte family saga
from the blockbuster* New York Times *bestselling author…*

The Harte women find themselves in the midst of weddings, in the hold of intrigue, and at the crossroads of the old ways and the new. Linnet O'Neill, great-granddaughter of Emma Harte, finds herself following in the footsteps of the original woman of substance as she battles to modernize the family business. Tessa Fairley, Linnet's sister, is ready to start a new life after an acrimonious divorce. India Standish, in the midst of planning her glamorous summer wedding in Ireland, is thrown off balance when her fiancé's daughter comes to live with them. And Evan Hughes, their American cousin, unwittingly brings an enemy into their midst—an enemy who conspires with Jonathan Ainsley, the deadly foe of the Hartes.

Just Rewards is the dramatic conclusion of the extraordinary tale of Emma Harte's great-granddaughters.

❧

"Bradford's characters are so real,
readers clamor to know them better."

—USA Today Weekend Magazine

ISBN: 0-312-30706-3

COMING SOON IN HARDCOVER FROM ST. MARTIN'S PRESS

Visit www.barbarataylorbradford.com

JR 06/05

Enter a glittering world of wealth, power,
and fame with the novels of
Barbara Taylor Bradford

Author of the #1 *New York Times* bestseller

A Woman of Substance

"An extravagant, absorbing novel of love, courage,
ambition, war, death, and passion."

—*The New York Times*

"It is easy to want every item Bradford catalogues,
easy to imagine wearing it, eating and drinking it,
driving it, smelling like it."

—*Los Angeles Times*

AVAILABLE FROM ST. MARTIN'S PRESS

Visit www.barbarataylorbradford.com

BTB 06/c